D0865415

Royal Temptation

January 2023
Becoming His Queen

February 2023
Her Secret Crown

March 2023
Playing for Keeps

April 2023
A Convenient Crown

May 2023
A Passionate Seduction

June 2023
His Secret Heir

Royal Temptation:
Her Secret Crown

CATHERINE MANN

KIM LAWRENCE

MAISEY YATES

MILLS & BOON

First Published in Great Britain 2023
by Mills & Boon, an imprint of HarperCollins*Publishers* Ltd,
1 London Bridge Street, London, SE1 9GF

www.harpercollins.co.uk

HarperCollins*Publishers*
Macken House, 39/40 Mayor Street Upper,
Dublin 1, D01 C9W8, Ireland

ROYAL TEMPTATION: HER SECRET CROWN © 2023 Harlequin
Enterprises ULC.

The Tycoon Takes a Wife © 2010 Catherine Mann
A Ring to Secure His Crown © 2017 Kim Lawrence
Crowned for My Royal Baby © 2020 Maisey Yates

ISBN: 978-0-263-31863-0

THE TYCOON
TAKES A WIFE

CATHERINE MANN

To my intrepid traveller and oldest daughter, Haley. Congrats on taking the world by storm! You'll always be our princess.

Prologue

Madrid, Spain: One Year Ago

He wanted to drape her in jewels.

Jonah Landis skimmed his fingers along the bare arm of the woman sleeping next to him and imagined which of the family heirlooms would look best with her dark hair. Rubies? Emeralds? Or perhaps even a string of fat freshwater pearls. His knuckles grazed from her shoulder to her collarbone, his five-o'clock shadow having left a light rasp along her creamy flesh.

He usually didn't dip into the family treasure trove. He preferred to live off the money he'd made with his own investments. But for Eloisa, he would make an exception.

Early morning light streaked through the wrought-iron window grilles in the seventeenth-century manor home he'd rented for the summer. A gentle breeze rustled the linen draping over the bed. At first he hadn't even realized she was American, she'd looked so at home walking among the Spanish castle ruins. And exotic. And hot as hell. While she'd picked her way through the scaffolding making notes, he'd lost track of his conversation with fellow investors.

Most labeled him the impulsive one in his family, not that he cared much what others thought of him. Sure he took risks on a regular basis in his work realm and private life, but he always had a plan. And it had always paid off.

So far.

Last night, for the first time, he hadn't planned a damn thing. He'd simply jumped right in with both feet with this coolly intriguing woman. He wasn't sure how the decision would pan out in the long run, but he knew they were going to have one helluva summer.

The rest? They could take a day at a time.

"Uhmmm," she sighed, rolling to her side and draping her arm over his hip. "Did I oversleep?"

Her eyes were still closed but their dark, rich color had cloaked the hauteur of an Ottoman empress. He'd lost plenty of time wondering about the woman behind them during historical reconstruction meetings.

He checked the digital clock resting on a carved walnut end table. "It's only six. We still have a couple of hours before breakfast."

Eloisa burrowed her head deeper in the feather pillow, her black hair fanning a tempting contrast across white cotton. "Am still so sleepy."

She should be. They'd stayed up most of the night having sex…catnapping…showering…and ending up tangled together all over again. It didn't help that they'd had a few drinks.

He'd limited himself to a couple, but those two seemed to hit her harder than him. He stroked back her long black hair, so smooth it glided through his fingers now as it had when she'd been over him, under him.

He throbbed from wanting her all over again when he should be down for the count for a while yet. She needed the rest more.

Jonah eased from the bed, fresh morning air from outside whispering over his skin. "I'll call down and have someone from the kitchen send breakfast up here. If you have any preferences, speak now."

She flipped to her back, eyes still closed as she stretched, her perfectly rounded breasts on amazing display as the comforter slipped to her waist. "Hmmm, anything is fine with me." Her words were slurred with sleep. "I'm having the most wonderful dream—"

Eloisa paused, scrunching her forehead. She peeked through barely open inky lashes. "Jonah?"

"Yeah, that would be me." He stepped into his silk boxers and reached for the phone.

Her gaze darted around his room quickly, orienting. She grasped the comforter and yanked it up, bringing her hand closer to her face. Suddenly she went stock-still and frowned.

"What's the matter?"

She couldn't possibly be shy after last night. It wasn't as if they'd kept the lights off.

"Uh, Jonah?" Her voice squeaked up a notch.

He sank to the edge of the bed and waited, already thinking through at least five different ways he could distract her throughout the summer.

She extended her arm, splaying her fingers wide. Sunshine through the window glinted off the simple gold wedding band he'd placed there last night. Eloisa blinked fast, her eyes going wide with horror.

"Oh my God," she gasped, thumbing the shiny new ring around and around. "What have we done?"

One

"Congratulations to the bride to be, my little princess!"

The toast from the father of the bride drifted from the deck of the paddleboat, carried by the muggy Pensacola breeze to Eloisa Taylor back on the dock. Eloisa sat dipping her aching feet in the Florida Gulf waters, tired to the roots of her ponytail from helping plan her half sister's engagement party. Her stepfather had gone all out for Audrey, far more than a tax collector in a cubicle could afford, but nothing was too good for his "little princess." Still he'd had to settle for a Monday night booking to make the gala affordable.

The echo of clinking glasses mingled with the lap of waves against her feet. Dinner was done, the crowd so well fed no one would miss her. She was good at that, helping people and keeping a low profile.

Putting together this engagement party had been bittersweet, forcing her to think about her own vows. Uncelebrated. Unknown even to her family. Thank God for the quickie divorce that had extracted her from her impulsive midnight marriage almost as fast as she'd entered it.

Usually she managed to smother those recollections, but how could she not think about it now with Audrey's happily-ever-after tossed in her face 24/7? Not to mention the cryptic voice message she'd received this morning with *his* voice. Jonah. Even a year after hearing it last, she still recognized the sexy bass.

Eloisa. It's me. We have to talk.

She swept her wind-whipped ponytail from her face, shivering from the phantom feel of *his* hand stroking her face. A year ago, she'd indulged herself in checking out the heritage of her real father. A summer indulgence had led her to one totally wrong man with a high-profile life that threatened her carefully protected world. Threatened secrets she held close and deep.

Eloisa blinked back the memories of Jonah, too many given how little time she'd spent with him. They were history now since she'd divorced him. Not that their twenty-four-hour marriage counted in her mind. She should ignore the call and block his number. Or at least wait until after her sister's "I do" was in the past before contacting him again.

A fish plopped in the distance, sailboat lines clinking against masts. The rhythmic, familiar sounds soothed her. She soaked up the other sounds of home, greedily gathering every bit of comfort she could find. Emerald-green waters reflected a pregnant moon. Wind rustled through palm trees.

An engine growled softly in the distance.

So much for a late-night solitary moment. She shook dry one foot, then the other and glanced over her shoulder. A limo rolled closer. Late arriving guests? Really late since after-dinner dancing was well underway.

Reaching for her sandals she watched the long black stretch of machine inching beside the waterway. The shape of the sleek vehicle wasn't your average wedding limo. The distinctive grille glinted in the moonlight, advertising the approach of an exclusive Rolls-Royce. Tinted windows sealed off the passengers from view, but left her feeling like a butterfly pinned to the board of a science project. The private area should be safe. Yet, was anywhere totally secure, especially in the dark?

Goose bumps stung along her skin and her mouth went dry. She yanked on her shoes, chiding herself for being silly. But still, Audrey's fiancé was reputed to have some shady connections. Her stepdad could only see power and dollar signs, apparently unconcerned with the crooked path that money took.

Not that any of those questionable contacts had cause to hurt her. All the same, she should return to the floating party barge.

Eloisa jumped to her feet.

The limo sped up.

She swallowed hard, wishing she'd taken a self-defense class along the way to earning her library studies degree.

Okay, no need to go all paranoid. She forced her hands to stay loose and started walking. Only about thirty yards ahead, and she would alert the crew member at the gangway. Then she could lose herself in the crowd of dancers under the strings of white lights. The engine grew louder behind her. Eloisa strode longer, faster.

Each breath felt heavier, the salt in the air stinging her over-sensitive pores. Her low heel caught between planks on the boardwalk. She lurched forward just as the car stopped in front of her.

A back door swung wide—not even waiting for the chauffeur—and blocked her getaway. She couldn't continue ahead, only sideways into the car or into the water. Or she could back up, which would take her farther from the boat. Frantically she searched for help. Would any of those seventy-five potential witnesses in party finery whooping it up to an old Kool and the Gang song notice or hear her?

One black-clad leg swung out of the limo, the rest of the man still hidden. However that Ferragamo python loafer was enough to send her heart skittering. She'd only met one man who favored those, and she hated how she still remembered the look and brand.

She backed away, one plank at a time, assessing the man as he angled out. She hoped, prayed for some sign to let her off the hook. Gray hair? A beer belly? Anything non-Jonah.

But no such luck. The hard-muscled guy wore all black, a dark suit jacket, the top button of his shirt undone and tie loose. He wore his brown hair almost shoulder length and swept back from his face to reveal a strong, square jaw.

A jaw far more familiar than any shoes. Nerves danced in her stomach far faster than even the partiers gyrating to the live band on the boat.

He pivoted on his heel, facing her full on, the moonlight glinting off the chestnut hints in his wavy hair. Sunglasses shielded his eyes from her. Shades at night? For a low profile or ego?

Regardless, she knew. Her ex-husband wasn't content with just calling and leaving a message. No, not Jonah. The powerful international scion she'd divorced a year ago had returned.

Jonah Landis whipped off his sunglasses, glanced at his watch and grinned. "Sorry I'm late. Have we missed the party?"

To hell with any party. Jonah Landis wanted to find out why Eloisa hadn't told him the entire truth when she'd demanded a divorce a year ago. He also wanted to know why his passionate lover had so dispassionately cut him off.

The stunned look on Eloisa's face as she stopped cold on the dock would have been priceless if he wasn't so damn mad over the secret she'd kept from him, a secret that he'd only just found out was gumming up the works on their divorce decree.

Of course when he'd met her in Madrid a year ago, he'd been distracted by the instantaneous, mind-blowing chemistry between them. And looking at her now, seeing her quiet elegance, he figured he could cut himself some slack on missing details that could have clued him in—like how much she'd fit into her Spanish surroundings.

The woman was a walking distraction.

Wind molded her tan silk dress around her body. The dimly lit night played tricks with his vision until she looked nearly naked, clothed only in shifting shadows.

Had she known that when she chose the dress? Likely not. Eloisa seemed oblivious to her allure, which only served to enhance her appeal.

Her sleek dark hair was slicked back in a severe ponytail that gave her already exotic brown eyes a tug. Without so much as lip gloss, she relegated most models to the shadows.

Once he had her name on the dotted line of divorce papers—official ones this time—he would have nothing to do with her ever again. That had been the plan anyway. He didn't need round two of her hot-cold treatment. So he'd misread the signs, hadn't realized she was drunk during the "I do" part. That didn't mean she had to slap his face and fall off the planet. He was over Eloisa.

Or so he'd thought. Then he'd seen her and felt that impact all over again, that kick-in-the-gut effect he'd thought must have been exaggerated by his memory.

He tamped back the attraction and focused on seeing this through. He needed her signature and for some reason he refused to leave it up to lawyers. Maybe it had something to do with closure.

Eloisa inched her heel from between the planks and set both feet as firmly as her delicate jaw. "What are you doing here?"

"I came to accompany you to your sister's engagement party." He hooked an elbow on the open limo door, the chauffeur waiting up front as he'd been instructed earlier. "Can't have my wife going stag."

"Shhh!" Lurching toward him, she patted the air in front of his face, stopping just shy of touching his mouth. "I am not your wife."

He clasped her hand, thumb rubbing over her bare

ring finger. "Damn, I must have hallucinated that whole wedding ceremony in Madrid."

Eloisa yanked her hand away and rubbed her palm against her leg. "You're arguing semantics."

"If you would prefer to skip the party, we could grab a bite to eat and talk about those semantics." He watched the glide of her hand up and down her thigh, remembering well the creamy, soft texture under his mouth as he'd tasted his way up.

She stared at him silently until he met her eyes again. "You're kidding, right?"

"Climb into the car and see."

She glanced back at the boat, then at him again, her long ponytail fanning to rest along her shoulder. "I'm not so sure that's a good idea."

"Afraid I'll kidnap you?"

"Don't be ridiculous." She laughed nervously as if she'd considered just that.

"Then what's holding you back? Unless you want to continue this conversation right here." He nodded toward the boat full of partyers. "I thought you wanted me to be quiet."

She looked back over her shoulder again, and while it appeared no one noticed them, who knew how long that would hold? Not that he gave a damn what anyone thought, unlike his enigmatic wife. He'd learned a long time ago he had two choices in this world. Let others rule his life or take charge.

The second option won hands down.

He cocked an eyebrow and waited.

"Fine," she bit out between gritted teeth.

She eyed him angrily as she angled past and slid into

the car without even brushing against him. Eloisa settled into the leather seat.

Jonah tucked himself inside next her, closed the door and tapped the glass window between them and the chauffeur, signaling him to drive. Just drive. He would issue a destination later.

"Where are we going?" she asked as the limo eased into motion, the tinted windows closing them in their own private capsule.

"Where do you want to go? I have a penthouse suite farther down on Pensacola Beach."

"Of course you do." Her gaze flicked around the small space, lingering briefly on his computer workstation to her left before moving on to the minibar and the plasma screen TV.

"I see you haven't changed." He'd forgotten how prickly she could be about money. Still, it had been refreshing. He'd had plenty of women chase him because of the Landis portfolio and political influence.

He'd never had a female dump him because of it. Of course back then he hadn't known she had access to money and influence beyond even his family's reach. Mighty damn impressive.

And confusing since she hadn't bothered to share that even after they married.

He put a damper on the surge of anger, a dangerous emotion given the edge of desire searing his insides. To prove to himself he could stay in control, he slid two fingers down the length of a sleekly straight lock of her black hair.

Eloisa jerked her head away. "Stop that." She adjusted the air-conditioning vent nervously until the blast of air ruffled her ponytail. "Enough playing, although you certainly seem to be an expert at recreation. I just want to know why you're here, now."

With all he knew about her, she still understood so little about him. "What's wrong with wanting to see my wife?"

"Ex-wife. We got drunk and ended up married." She shrugged casually, too much so. "It happens to lots of folks, from pop stars to everyday Joes and Josephines. Just check out the marriage logs in Las Vegas. We made a mistake, but we took steps to fix it the morning after."

"Do you consider all of it a mistake? Even the part between 'I do' and waking up with a hangover?" He couldn't resist reminding her.

A whisper of attraction smoked through her dark eyes. "I don't remember."

"You're blushing," he noted with more than a little satisfaction, grateful for the soft glow of a muted overhead light. So he was smug. Sue him. "You remember the good parts all right."

"Sex is irrelevant." She sniffed primly.

"Sex? I was talking about the food." He turned the tables, enjoying the cat-and-mouse game between them. "The *mariscada en salsa verde* was amazing." And just that fast, he could all but taste the shellfish casserole in green sauce, the supper she'd shared with him before they had after-dinner drinks. Got hitched. Got naked.

He could see the same memory reflected in her eyes just before her mouth pursed tight.

"You're a jackass, Jonah."

"But I'm all yours." For now at least.

"Not anymore. Remember the morning-after 'fix'? You're my *ex*-jackass."

If only it were that simple to put this woman in his past. God knows, he'd tried hard enough over the past year to forget about Eloisa Taylor Landis.

Or rather Eloisa *Medina* Landis?

He'd stumbled upon the glitch in a church registry, a "minor" technicality she'd forgotten to mention, but one that had snarled up their paperwork in Spain. The sense of shock and yeah, even some bitter betrayal rocked through him again.

No question, he needed to put this woman in his past, but this time he would be the one to walk away.

"Now there you're wrong, Eloisa. That fix got broken along the way." He picked up a lock of her hair again, keeping his hand off her shoulder.

Lightly he tugged, making his presence felt. A spark of awareness flickered through her eyes, flaming an answering heat inside him. He looked at the simple gold chain around her neck and remembered the jewels he'd once pictured there while she'd slept. Then she woke up and made it clear there would be no summer together. She couldn't get out of his life fast enough.

Her breath hitched. He reminded himself of his reason for coming here, to end things and leave.

Now he wondered if it might be all the more satisfying to have one last time with Eloisa, to ensure she remembered all they could have had if only she'd been as upfront with him as he'd been with her.

He glided his knuckles up her ponytail to her cheek, gently urging her to face him more fully. "The paperwork never made it through. Something to do with you lying about your name."

Her eyes darted away. "I never lied about my name—" She sat up straighter, her gaze slamming back into his. "What do you mean the paperwork didn't go through?"

She seemed to be genuinely surprised, but he'd learned not to trust her. Still he would play this game out in order to achieve his ultimate goal—a final night in her bed before leaving her forever.

"The divorce wasn't finalized. You, my dear, are still Mrs. Jonah Landis."

Two

He had to be joking.

Eloisa dug her fingers into the leather seats, seriously considering making use of that bottle of bourbon in the limo's minibar. Except indulging in a few too many umbrella drinks had landed her in this mess in the first place.

She'd taken pains to cover her tracks. Her mother had warned her how important it was to be careful. Keep a low profile. Stay above reproach. And never, ever invite scrutiny.

Eloisa looked out the window to see where they were headed. They passed nail salons and T-shirt shops along the beachfront, nightlife in full swing on open-decked restaurant bars. The chauffeur truly seemed like he was simply driving around, not headed anywhere specific—such as Jonah's hotel.

She simply couldn't pay the price for being impulsive again. "We signed the divorce paperwork."

His blue eyes narrowed. "Apparently there's some—thing you neglected to tell me, a secret you've kept mighty close to the vest."

Eloisa bit her lip to hold back impulsive words while she gathered her thoughts and reminded herself to be grateful he hadn't stumbled upon her more recent secret. Her empty stomach gripped with nerves. She tried to draw in calming breaths, but had to face a truth learned long ago. Only when working at the library could she relax.

Best she could tell, there weren't any books conveniently tucked away in this superbly stocked luxury ride. Although the backseat area was packed with enough technology to provide a command central for a small army. Apparently Jonah preferred to have the world at his fingertips. Odd, but she didn't have time for distractions right now.

"What secret?" she asked out of a long-honed habit of denial. To date, no one had pressed the point so the strategy hadn't let her down yet. "I have no idea what you're talking about."

His jaw went tight with irritation. "That's the way you want to play this? Fine." He leaned in closer until she couldn't miss the musky scent of him mixed with his still-familiar aftershave. "You forgot to mention your father."

Her chest went tighter than her hands twisting in the skirt of her dress. "My dad's a tax collector in Pensacola, Florida. Speaking of which, why aren't you home in Hilton Head, South Carolina?"

He gripped her wrists to stop her nervous fidgeting. "Not your stepdad, your biological father."

Apparently, Jonah wasn't easily diverted tonight.

"I told you before about my biological father." A shiver passed over her at even the mention of the man who'd wrecked her mother's life, the man she lied about on a regular basis. "My mother was a single parent when I was born. My real father was a bum who wanted no part in my life." True enough.

Her dad—no more than a sperm donor as far as she was concerned—had broken her mother's heart then left her to raise their child alone. Her stepfather might not have been Prince Charming—wasn't that damn ironic?—but at least he'd been there for her and her mother.

"A bum? A royal bum." Jonah stretched a leg out in front of him, polished snakeskin loafer gleaming in the overhead lamp. "Interesting dichotomy."

She squeezed her eyes shut and wished it was that easy to shut out the repercussions of what he'd somehow discovered. Her mother had been emphatic about personal safety. Her biological father still had enemies back in San Rinaldo. She'd been foolish to tempt fate by going to Spain in hopes of unobtrusively learning about half her heritage on the small island country nearby. Damn it all, fear was a good thing when it kept a person safe.

She steadied her breath, if not her galloping heart rate. "Would you please not say that?"

"Say what?"

"The whole *royal* thing." While her stepfather frequently called Audrey his "little princess," he—and the rest of the world—didn't know that Eloisa was actually the one with royal blood singing through her veins, thanks to her biological father.

Nobody knew, except Eloisa, her deceased mother and a lawyer who conducted any communication with the deposed king. Eloisa's so-called real father. A man still hunted to this day by the rebel faction that had taken over his small island kingdom of San Rinaldo off the coast of Spain.

How had Jonah found out?

He tipped her chin with one knuckle as his driver slowed for jaywalking teens. "You may have been able to fool the world for a lot of years, but I've figured out your secret. You're the illegitimate daughter of deposed King Enrique Medina."

She stiffened defensively, then forced herself to relax nonchalantly. "That's ridiculous." Albeit true. If he could figure it out, how much longer until her secret was revealed to others? She needed to know, hopefully find some way to plug that leak and persuade him he was wrong.

Then she would decide what to do if his claim was actually true, a notion that could have her hyperventilating if she thought about it too long. "What makes you think something so outlandish?"

"I discovered the truth when I went back to Europe recently. My brother and his wife decided to renew their wedding vows and while I was in the area, I stopped by the chapel where we got married."

A bolt of surprise shot through her and she couldn't help but think back to that night. She'd been emotionally flattened by her mother's death and had only just returned to finish her studies in Europe. She'd shared some drinks with the guy she'd secretly had a crush on and the next thing she'd known, they were hunting for a preacher or a justice of the peace with the lights still on.

Visiting the place where they'd exchanged vows sounded sentimental. Like that day meant more to him than a drunken mistake.

She couldn't stop herself from asking, "You went back there?"

"I was in the neighborhood," he repeated, his jaw going tight, the first sign that the whole debacle may have upset him as much as it had her.

He'd let her go so easily, agreeing they'd made an impulsive mistake rather than asking her to crawl back in bed with him and discuss it later. A huge part of her had wanted him to sweep away rational concerns. But no. He'd let her leave, just as her father never claimed her mother.

Or her.

She tore her eyes away from the tempting curve of his mouth, a mouth that had brought such intense pleasure when he'd explored every patch of her skin later that night after their "I do." Except they'd exchanged vows in Spanish, which had seemed romantic at the time. Between her hiccups. "Everyone knows King Enrique doesn't live in San Rinaldo anymore. Nobody knows where he and his sons fled after they left. There are only rumors."

"Rumors that he's in Argentina." Jonah lounged back in the seat, seemingly lazy and relaxed, except for the coiled muscles she could see bunched under his black jacket.

She knew well he came by those muscles honestly. Her first memory of him was burned in her brain, the day she'd joined the restoration team on a graduate internship to assist with research. Jonah had been studying blueprints with another man on the construction site. She'd mistakenly thought Jonah worked on the crew, from his casual clothes and mud-stained boots. The guy was actually a couple of credits away from his PhD. He wasn't just an architect, he was a bit of an artist in his own right.

That had enticed her.

Only later, too late for her own good, had she discovered who he was. A Landis, a member of a financial and political dynasty.

Eloisa looked away from his too-perceptive eyes and swept her hem back over her knees. "I wouldn't know anything about that."

Lying came so easily after this long.

"It also appears that neither you nor your mother has been to Argentina, but that's not my point." His eyes drilled into her until she looked back at him. "I don't give a damn where your royal papa lives. I'm only concerned with the fact that you lied to me, which gummed up the works for our divorce."

"Okay, then." She met his gaze defiantly. "If what you say is true, maybe it means the marriage is void, too, so we don't need a divorce."

He shook his head. "No such luck. I checked. Believe me. We are totally and completely husband and wife."

Jonah slid his fingers down the length of her hair until his hand cupped her hip. His hand rested warm and familiar and tempting against her until she could swear she felt his calluses through her dress. She struggled not to squirm—or sway closer.

She clasped his wrist and set his hand back on his

knee. "File abandonment charges. Or I will. I don't care as long as this is taken care of quickly and quietly. No one here knows about my, uh, impetuosity."

"Don't you want to discuss who gets the china and who gets the monogrammed towels?"

Argh! She tapped on the window. "Driver? Driver?" She kept rapping until the window parted. "Take me back now, please."

The chauffeur glanced at Jonah who nodded curtly.

His autocratic demeanor made her want to scream out her frustration but she wouldn't cause a scene. Why did this man alone have the power to make her blood boil? She was a master of calm. Everyone said so, from the stodgiest of library board members to her sixth grade track coach who never had managed to coax her to full speed.

She waited until the window closed before turning to him again. "You can have every last bit of the nothing I own if you'll please just stop this madness now. Arguing isn't going to solve anything. I'll have my lawyer look into the divorce issue."

That was as close as she would come to admitting he'd stumbled on the truth. She certainly couldn't outright confirm it without seeing what proof he had and hopefully have time to take it to her attorney. Too many lives were at stake. There were still people out there tied to the group that tried to assassinate Enrique Medina, had in fact succeeded in killing his wife, the mother of his three legitimate heirs.

Enrique had been a widower when he met her mother in Florida, and still they hadn't gotten married. Her mom vowed she hadn't wanted any part of the royal lifestyle, but her jaw had always quivered when she said it. Right now Eloisa sympathized with her mother more than she could have ever imagined. Relationships were damn complicated—and painful.

Thank goodness the limo approached the paddleboat again because she didn't know how much more of this she could take tonight. The car stopped smoothly alongside the dock.

"Jonah, if that's all you have to say, I need to return to the party. My attorney will be in touch with you first thing next week."

Eloisa reached for the door.

His hand fell to rest on top of hers, his body pressing intimately against her as he stretched past.

"Hold on a minute. Do you really think I'm letting you out of my sight again that easily? Last time I did that, you ditched before lunch. I'm not wasting another year looking for you if you decide to bolt."

"I didn't run. I came home to Pensacola." She tried to inch free but he clasped her hands in his. "This is where you can find me."

Where he could have found her anytime over the past twelve months if he'd cared at all. In the first few weeks she'd waited, hoped, then the panic set in as she'd wrestled with contacting him.

Now, they had no reason to talk.

"I'm here now." His thumb stroked the inside of her wrist. "And we're going to fix this mess face-to-face rather than trusting the system again."

"No!" Already her skin tingled with awareness so much more intense than when he'd cupped her hip—and she'd been mighty aware.

Damn her traitorous body.

"Yes," he said, reaching past and throwing open the door.

He was letting her go after all? But hadn't he just said they were going to confront things face-to-face?

However, who was she to waste time questioning the reason he'd changed his mind? She rushed out of the limousine and turned at the last second to say goodbye to Jonah. Why was her gut clenching at the notion of never seeing him again?

She pivoted on her heel only to slam into his chest. Apparently he'd stepped out of the vehicle as well. Distant voices from her sister's party drifted on the wind, something she could barely register since his sun-bronzed face lowered toward hers.

Before she could breathe, much less protest, his mouth covered hers. His eyes stayed open, which she realized must mean hers were open, too. Just like a year ago, she stared at his eyes, the kind of blue poets wrote about. His wild and fresh nature scent was the same sort evoked by a literary walk through Thoreau's *Walden*.

And just that fast, her lashes fluttered closed. She savored the taste of him on her lips, her tongue again. Her hands slid up to splay on his chest, hard muscles rippling under her fingers.

Then unease niggled at the back of her brain, a sense of unrest. Something was off about this kiss. She remembered what it was like to be kissed by Jonah, and as nerve tingling as it felt to be pressed against him, to inhale the scent of him, this wasn't right.

She tried to gather her thoughts enough to think rationally rather than just languish in sensation. His broad hand moved along her waist, lightly, rhythmically.

Totally in control.

Where everyone could see.

He was putting on a display for the partyers on the boat, damn him. Indignation, anger and a hint of hurt smoked through her veins, chasing away desire. She started to pull back then reconsidered. The damage was already done. Everyone at the party had seen them kiss. They would assume the worst. She might as well take advantage of the opportunity to surprise Jonah for a change. And yes, even to extract a little revenge for how he'd staged this whole encounter tonight to knock her off balance rather than simply notifying her through their attorneys.

Eloisa slid her arms around his waist, not that anyone could see behind him. But what she was about to do wasn't for public viewing anyway.

It was all for Jonah.

Eloisa grabbed his butt.

Jonah blinked in surprise, her hand damn near searing through his pants. He started to pull away…then sensation steamrolled over him. This kiss wasn't going the way he'd planned. He certainly hadn't expected her to take control of the game he'd started.

Now that she had? Time to turn the tables again.

Gasps of surprise drifting on the wind from the boat, he cupped her neck and stroked his tongue along the seam of her lips, just once, but enough, if the hitch in her breathing was anything to judge by. Her body turned fluid as she pressed closer to him. Her hands skimmed up along his spine to his shoulders. Then she speared her fingers through his hair, sending his pulse spiking and placing his self-control on shaky ground.

Without question, he wanted to take this encounter

further, but not here. Not in public. And he knew if they moved to the limo, reason would pull her away again. So with more than a little regret, he ended the kiss. He'd made his point anyway.

Jonah eased away from her, still keeping his hands looped behind her back in case she decided to bolt—or slap him. "We'll finish this later, princess, when we don't have an audience."

When he could take this to the natural finish his body demanded. And when she was totally consenting rather than merely acting on impulse. The kiss may have started as a staged way to make her family aware of their connection, but halfway in, he'd realized his instincts were dead-on.

He couldn't walk away without one last time in her bed.

Her lips pursed tight as if holding back a retort, but her hands shook as she slid them from behind him to rest on his chest. He watched over her shoulder as a small group left the boat and started toward them on the boardwalk. A trio led the pack. Thanks to photos from an investigator, Jonah IDed the three right away. Her stepfather, Harry Taylor. Her half sister, Audrey Taylor. And Audrey's fiancé, Joey.

Eloisa leaned closer and whispered through tight teeth. "You are so going to pay for doing this."

"Shhh." He dropped a quick kiss on her forehead, liking the taste of his revenge so far. His appetite for it—for her—only increased the longer he spent by her side. "We don't want them to hear us fighting, do we, dear?"

Jonah slipped his arm around her shoulders and

tucked her by his side, her soft curves pressed enticingly against him.

She stiffened. "You can't be planning to tell them... uh..."

"About your father?"

Her brown eyes flashed with warring anger and fear. "About your theories. About you and me."

"My lips are sealed, princess."

"Stop calling me that," she said through gritted teeth as the footsteps thunked louder and closer.

"You and I both know it's true. There's no more denying it. The only question is, how far will you go to keep me quiet?"

She gasped. "You can't mean—"

"Too late to talk, Eloisa dear." He squeezed her lightly as the group closed in, her family leading. "Trust me or not."

The older man in the lead fanned a hand over his wind-blown blond hair, whisper thin along the top. His daughter—the bride to be—was an even paler version of her father. Even her hair seemed bleached white by the sun, yet she didn't sport even a hint of a tan. Her fiancé hovered behind, fists shoved in his pockets. He shuffled from foot to foot as if impatient to be anywhere but here. A small crowd gathered behind them while others watched from the deck railing.

Jonah extended his hand to Eloisa's stepfather. "Sorry I'm late, sir. I'm Eloisa's date for tonight's shindig. I'm Jonah Landis."

She wouldn't be able to dismiss him as easily this time.

Harry Taylor's eyes widened. "Landis? As in the Landises from Hilton Head, South Carolina?"

"Yes, sir, that would be my family."

"Uh, Harry Taylor, here. Eloisa's father."

The guy all but had dollar signs flashing in his pupils like some cartoon character.

Jonah stifled the irritation for Eloisa's sake. He appreciated the advantages his family's money had brought him, but he preferred to make his own way in the world.

Meanwhile, though, Jonah knew how to deal with money suck-ups like this. He'd been on guard against them since the sandbox. Even kids figured out fast whose dad had the biggest portfolio.

A photographer stepped from the back of the pack, lifting the lens to his eyes. Eloisa tucked behind his shoulder as flashes spiked through the night.

Smiling widely, Harry shuffled aside to clear the way for the photographer to get a better angle. The old guy all but offered to hold the photographer's camera bag.

Audrey elbowed her yawning fiancé, hooking arms with him and stepping closer. "When did you and Eloisa meet, Mr. Landis? I'm sure our guest—the editor of the local events section of our illustrious paper—will want plenty of deets for her column."

"Call me Jonah." He could feel Eloisa's heart beat faster against him.

He could claim her easily here, but then their separation would be out in the open as well. He intended to be much closer to her. "I met Eloisa during her study-abroad program last year. I found her impossible to forget and here I am."

Every word of that was true.

Eloisa's sigh of relief shuddered against him.

Audrey loosened her death grip on her fiancé's arm

long enough to sidle beside her sister for the next round of pictures. "Aren't you full of surprises?"

"Not by choice." Eloisa smiled tightly. "Besides, this is your night. I wouldn't want to do anything to detract from that."

Her stepsister winked, eying Jonah up and down. "Hey, if he were my date, I'd be lapping up all the media attention."

What the hell kind of family was this?

Jonah pulled Eloisa closer to his side, sending a clear "back-off" signal to Audrey. She simply smiled in return, tossing her hair over her shoulders playfully. Her fiancé seemed oblivious, poor bastard.

Eloisa buried her face against Jonah's shoulder and he started to reassure her—until he realized she wasn't upset or even seeking him out. She was just hiding from the clicking camera.

The photographer snap, snap, snapped away, the flashes damn near blinding in the dark night.

Audrey reached for her sister. "Come on. Just smile for the camera. You've been hiding out here all night and I could use some fun and interesting pictures to add to my wedding album."

Eloisa thumbed off the band from her ponytail. Her hair slid free in a silken sheet that flowed over her shoulders and down her back. She'd never seemed vain to him, but then most women he knew primped for the camera. Even his three sisters-in-law were known to slick on lipstick before a news conference.

Except as he watched her more closely he realized she used the hair as a curtain. The guy might be getting his photos—to deny them would have caused a scene with

Audrey—but there wasn't going to be a clear image of Eloisa's face.

Realization trickled through of a larger problem between them than even he had anticipated. He knew she wanted to keep her royal heritage a secret. That was obvious enough and he respected her right to live as she pleased. But until this moment he hadn't understood just how far she would go to protect her anonymity. A damned inconvenient problem.

Because as a Landis, he could always count on being stuck in the spotlight. Just by being with her, he'd cast her into the media's unrelenting glare.

He'd wanted revenge, but didn't need to unveil her secret to repay her for her betrayal. He had other, far more enticing ways of excising her from his mind.

Three

Eloisa wished that photographer would tone down the flash on his camera. Much more of his nonstop shutter bugging and she would have a headache. As if this evening wasn't already migraine material enough.

Thank God the party had finally all but ended, only a few stragglers hanging on and sidling into the photo ops. Jonah—the cause of her impending headache—stood off to the side with her stepfather. Determined to keep her cool, Eloisa stacked tiny crystal cake plates left haphazardly on the dessert table. Her sister watched from her perch, lounging against the end of the table.

Audrey balanced a plate with a wedge of the raspberry chocolate cake on one hand, swiping her finger through the frosting and licking it clean. "You should let the catering staff take care of that. It's what they're paid to do."

"I don't mind, really. Besides, the cleaning staff charges by the hour." She also needed a way to burn off her nervous energy from Jonah's staged kiss.

"That doesn't mean you need to work yourself to the bone. Go home."

She wasn't ready to be alone with Jonah. Not yet. Not with her feelings still so close to the surface. But judging from the stubborn set of his jaw as he stood under a string of white lights, he wasn't leaving her life anywhere anytime soon.

"I'm staying here with you." Eloisa sidestepped a band member carrying two guitar cases. "No arguments."

"At least have some cake. It's so amazing I almost don't care that I'll have to get my wedding gown resized." Audrey swiped up another gob of frosting, her blue eyes trekking over to Jonah, then sliding back. "You're just full of surprises, aren't you, sister dear?"

"So you said earlier." Eloisa placed the forks in a glass so all the plates stacked evenly and handed over the lot to a passing catering employee.

How rare that someone accused her of being full of surprises. She'd always been the steady one, tasked to smooth things over when her more-sensitive baby sister burst into tears.

"But it's true. What's the scoop with this Landis boyfriend?" Audrey gestured with her plate toward Jonah who looked at ease in his suit jacket, even in Florida's full-out May heat.

Eloisa had found his constant unconcern fascinating before. Now it was more than a little irritating, especially when she couldn't stop thinking about the feel of plunging her fingers into his thick hair when they'd kissed.

She forced her hands to stay steady as she clasped them in front of her, leaning against the table beside Audrey, her half sister topping her by five inches. Her willowy sister looked more like her blond father.

But they both had their mother's long fingers. What would it have been like to turn to her mother right now? And how much it must hurt Audrey not having their mother around to help plan the biggest day of her life.

Certainly their mother's shocking death from an allergic reaction to medication had stunned them all. Eloisa had been numb throughout the entire funeral, staying in the fugue state all the way back to Spain, to her study program.

And into Jonah's bed.

Waking up the morning after with that ring on her finger... She'd felt the first crack in the dam walling up her grief. She'd barely made it out of Jonah's rented manor home before the tears flowed.

Which brought her back to the dilemma of Jonah.

What was the scoop? Why had he shown up now when he could have sent a lawyer? It wasn't like he wanted to see her or he could have contacted her anytime in the past year. "His arrival tonight came as a total shocker to me."

Audrey set aside her plate, plucked a pink stargazer lily from the beach-themed centerpiece and skimmed it under her nose. "You never mentioned meeting him before."

She hadn't mentioned even the working relationship because she'd been afraid they would hear in her voice what she could barely admit to herself then, much less now. "Like I said earlier, this is your time, your wedding. I wouldn't want to do anything to distract from that."

Audrey bumped her waif-thin shoulder against Eloisa's. "Could you please drop the altruistic gig for just a few minutes while we squeal over this like real sisters? He's a Landis, for crying out loud. You're rubbing elbows with American royalty."

"Who wouldn't squeal over that?" She couldn't resist the tongue-in-cheek retort.

"You, apparently." Audrey twirled the lily stem between her fingers. "Heaven knows I would be calling a press conference."

Eloisa laughed, then laughed some more, so much better than crying, and let all the tension from the evening flow out of her. Audrey had her faults, but she never pretended to be anything other than who she was.

Which made Eloisa feel like a hypocrite since she hid from herself every damn day.

Her laughter faded. "Forget all about this evening and Jonah Landis. I meant it when I said these next couple of weeks are totally about you. This is the wedding you've been planning since you were a kid. Remember how we used to practice in the garden?"

"You were always the best maid of honor." She tucked the stargazer lily behind Eloisa's ear. "I wasn't always a nice bride."

"You were three years younger. You got frustrated when you couldn't keep up."

"I still do sometimes." Her smile faltered just a bit.

"Remember the time we picked all the roses off the bushes?" Eloisa steadied the lily behind her ear, the fragrance reminding her of their childhood raid on their mother's carefully tended yard. "You took the rap."

Audrey rolled her eyes and attacked her cake again

with her pointer finger. "No huge sacrifice. It's not like I ever got in trouble. I cried better than you did. You were always into being stoic."

"I'm not the weepy sort." Not in public anyway.

"Tears can be worth their weight in gold. I may be the youngest, but you should take my advice on this one." Audrey fixed her stare on her father, her fiancé and Jonah. "When it comes to men, you have to use whatever tools you have."

"Thanks for the advice." Not that she could see herself taking it even in a million years. "Now can we get back to focusing on your wedding? We have a lot to accomplish in the next couple of weeks."

She tried to stem her reservations about Audrey marrying a guy with questionable connections. Her little sister had ignored all the warnings, even threatening to elope if Eloisa didn't keep her opinions to herself.

Audrey pulled another flower from the centerpiece for herself. "And about Jonah Landis?"

Eloisa shrugged, suddenly hungry for the cake after all. "He's my date." She forked up a bite from the lone remaining slice on a plate the caterers hadn't yet cleared. "It's as simple as that."

"Guess you don't need a ride home tonight." Audrey needled with the same practiced teasing she'd used on her since the days of Eloisa's first boyfriend—the librarian's son who occasionally snitched the keys to the reference room so she could read the Oxford English Dictionary in total privacy after hours.

"I have my car here."

"One of Joey's brothers can drive it over for you." Audrey arched up on her toes. "Hey, Landis? My sister is ready to go. How about you get your chauffeur to pull up that Rolls Royce limo of yours. Eloisa's been on her feet all day."

Jonah's gaze slammed into hers, narrow and predatory. She'd seen that look before, right before she'd shimmied out of her dress and fallen into bed with him.

Shoveling a bite of cake into her mouth, Eloisa tried to tell herself it would be enough to stave off the deeper hunger gnawing through her tonight.

Eloisa shifted uneasily in the limo seat.

Climbing back into Jonah's car had seemed easier than discussing driving arrangements in front of the gossip rag reporter. Now that she was alone with Jonah, however, she questioned her decision. The drive to her town house felt hours away rather than a couple of miles.

Searching for something, *anything* to talk about other than each other, Eloisa touched the miniprinter and laptop computer beside her. She started to make a joke about checking Facebook from the road, but paused when her finger snagged on a printed-out page.

She looked closer before she could think to stop herself. It seemed like some kind of small blueprint—

Jonah pulled the paper from the printer and into a briefcase. "Why were you so camera shy at the party earlier?"

"I prefer to keep a low profile. Not everyone is hungry for a spot on the front page." Ouch. That sounded pretty crabby coming out, but Jonah had a way of agitating her every nerve.

"Do you avoid the press because of your father? You can't expect to stay under the radar forever."

Did he realize how intimately their thighs pressed

against one another? Eloisa slid her hand from the printer and scooted an inch of space between them. "My mother and I managed over the years. Do you intend to change that?"

She bit her lip, unable to stop from holding her breath after finally voicing the question that had chewed at her all night long. Her mother may have managed but it didn't escape Eloisa's notice that she'd screwed up mere days after the funeral. She waited through Jonah's assessing silence so long that dots began to spark in front of her eyes.

"Breathe," he commanded, holding her gaze until she exhaled then nodding curtly. "Of course I'll keep your secret. If anyone finds out, it won't be from me."

Sighing with relief she flopped back in her seat and fanned her face, relaxing for the first time since she'd heard his engine growl around the corner. That was one secret taken care of, and she had no reason to believe he could have found out her other. "You really could have saved me a lot of angst tonight if you'd told me that from the start."

"What kind of guy do you think I am?"

A rich one judging by his clothes, his lifestyle and famous surname? Yet all of those were superficial elements. She scoured her mind for things she'd learned about him a year ago…and most of it focused on attraction. She wasn't so sure she liked what that said about her. "I'm not really sure how well I know you."

"Then you'll have the next two weeks to figure me out."

"Two weeks?" Her muscles kinked all over again. "I thought you wanted a divorce."

"I do." He secured the lily behind her ear, his knuckles

caressing her neck for a second too long to be accidental. "But first, I want the honeymoon we never had."

She gasped in surprise, followed by anger...then suspicion. "You're just trying to shock me."

"How do you know I'm not serious?" His blue eyes burned with unmistakable, unsettling—irresistible?—desire.

She'd barely survived their last encounter with her heart intact. No way in hell was she dipping her toes into those fiery waters again. "You can't really believe I'll just crawl into bed with you."

"Why not?" He angled closer to her, so close she would only have to lean just a little to rest her cheek against his amazing hair. "It isn't like we haven't already slept together."

Not that they'd slept much. "That night was a mistake." One with heartbreaking consequences. "A mistake I do not intend to repeat, so get back on your side of the car."

"Fine then." He eased away, leather creaking at his every lazy, slow movement. "Whether or not we have sex will be your call."

"Thank you." She laced her fingers together on her lap to keep from hauling him over again. Why hadn't she eaten more cake?

"Just give me two weeks."

"What the hell?" The words slipped out of her mouth, startling her as much as it appeared she'd surprised him. "I can't deal with you right now." There. She'd actually been honest with him about how she felt. "My sister needs me."

And then she had to muck it up with a half truth to hide how much he tempted her.

"Doesn't she have a wedding planner or something?"

"Not everyone has unlimited funds."

"Your father doesn't send support?"

"That's none of your business, and regardless, it wouldn't have been Audrey's anyhow."

"Ah, but if you had a king's ransom tucked away, I am certain you would have shared it with sister dear. Am I wrong?"

His words stung and she hated how that hinted at his power over her. "I'm not a pushover."

Although Jonah was right, damn him, that if she did have money, she would have written her sister a big fat check to cover wedding expenses.

Regardless, she didn't want Enrique Medina's money. Her mother had insisted she didn't want it either, but she'd married another man for what appeared to be financial security. What a confusing tangle.

She knew one thing for sure. "I'm not a minor. I make my own way in the world. Besides, he's not a part of my life and I am not for sale."

She wouldn't allow herself to be dependent on any man. Even months after the fact, it scared her to her teeth to think of how close she'd come to mirroring her mother's past—alone, unloved.

And pregnant.

Four

Jonah told the driver to wait, then pivoted toward Eloisa as she raced toward her town house. Hopefully he would be sending the driver on his way soon, because quite frankly, he didn't trust Eloisa not to bolt the second he left.

Not that it was any great hardship to be with her. God, he could watch her walk all night long, the gentle sway of her hips and the swish of her ponytail illuminated by the street lamp.

He didn't expect to get any further than talking tonight. He needed to take his time with her now in a way he hadn't back in Spain.

Problem was? He could only afford to take these next two weeks off, then he needed to get back to work on his next restoration project. Working on architectural designs around the world fed his wanderer's spirit.

Next stop? Peru in two weeks.

And if he hadn't finished business with Eloisa by then? Could he just walk away?

He refused to consider failure. They would go to bed together again. And they would exorcise the mess from last year.

Hands stuffed in his pockets, he followed Eloisa along the walkway. Waves rolled and roared in the distance, the shore three streets away. She lived in a stucco town house, the fourth in the row. New, they'd been built to resemble older, turn-of-the-century construction. Each unit was painted a different beachy color—peach, blue, green and yellow.

She marched toward the yellow home, calling back over her shoulder. "Thank you for seeing me safely to my front stoop, but you're free to leave now."

"Not so fast, my dear wife." He stopped alongside Eloisa at her lime-green door. Keys dangled from between her fingers but he didn't take them from her. He wanted her to ask him inside of her own free will, no coercion. But that didn't exclude persuasion.

She faced him with a sigh. "You managed a whole year without speaking to me. I'm sure you'll do just fine without me for another night."

"Eloisa, just because I didn't contact you doesn't mean I stopped thinking about you." That was sure as hell the truth. "We left a lot unsaid. Is it so wrong for me to want these next couple of weeks to clear the air before we say goodbye?"

Eloisa studied her clunky key chain, a conglomeration of whistles, a lanyard from some children's festival and a metal touristy-looking token. "Why a couple of weeks?"

Damn. It wouldn't be that persuasive to say that was all the time he had available to pencil her into his work schedule. His brother Sebastian's marriage had fallen apart because of his insane hours at his law practice.

"That's how long my attorney says it will take to get the ball rolling." He'd asked for Sebastian's help this time, as he should have done a year ago. "You can't blame me for wondering if you will disappear again."

Sure the morning after their spur of the moment wedding, they'd both agreed it was a mistake. Okay, they'd both agreed after she'd slapped him. Then she'd gasped in horror and yanked on her clothes as she'd stumbled toward the door. He'd expected once she cooled down, they would at least talk about things, maybe take a step back—a few steps back.

Except once she'd left his place in Spain, she'd ignored any further communication other than mailing the paperwork his way. So actually, the crummy paperwork was her fault.

And his. He couldn't deny it. He shouldn't have been so damn proud he didn't show his lawyer brother Sebastian.

Jonah tugged the dangling keys from her loose grip, sifting the bulk in his hands. The touristy token caught his attention. He looked closer and found…an ironwork reproduction of the house he'd worked on restoring the previous summer. Interesting. Encouraging. "Nice key chain."

"I keep it as a reminder of the risks of impulsiveness." She tugged her keys back, gripping them so tightly her fingers turned bloodlessly white.

"Risks?" Anger kicked around in his gut. She was the one who'd walked out, after all. Not him. "Seems like you walked away mighty damn easily. If it wasn't for this inconvenient legal snafu—" not to mention her lies "—you would have gotten away scot-free."

"Scot-free?" Her face went pale in the moonlight. "You can't possibly think this didn't affect me. You have no idea how deeply I've wrestled with what we did, the mistake we made."

Confusion dulled the edge of his anger. She'd left. She'd never called. Why the hell had she been hiding out if their time together stayed with her this heavily?

"Well, Eloisa? What do you say we make every effort possible to put this to rest once and for all? For the next couple of weeks, you can just call me roomie."

She gasped. "You can't really expect to bunk at my place?"

"Of course not." Jonah focused on the little piece of memorabilia on her key chain, a sign that she'd remembered and even cared. He let her relax for a second before retorting, "I could phone the chauffeur and we could be taken to my beachside suite."

Shaking her head, she slid the key into the lock. "You're outrageous."

He clapped a hand over his chest with a half smile. "That hurt. I prefer to think I'm being considerate to my wife's needs."

"I'm just dying to hear how you reached that conclusion." Shaking her head, she pushed her front door open and stepped inside without giving him the boot.

He took that as an invitation and followed. Victory pulsing inside him, he checked out the space she called home for clues about her. The more he knew the better his chances. He wouldn't make the same mistake again of letting her keep him in the dark.

The living area was airy and open with high ceilings in keeping with the historic-reproduction feel. Her tastes ran to uncluttered, clean lines with a beach theme— white walls, wood floors and rattan furniture with cushions in a muted blue, tan and chocolate. And of course books—in end tables, shelves, curio cabinets. She'd always carried books in her purse in Spain, reading during breaks.

Her reed roll-up shades covered the windows from outdoor eyes. Only the French doors gave a glimpse to a garden patio with an Adirondack chair and ferns. Did she lounge there and read? Soak up the sun?

What he wouldn't give to take her to his penthouse suite with a rooftop pool and deck where they both could do away with restrictive bathing suits.

He slid his jacket off and hooked it on the coatrack made from a canoe paddle. "Nice place."

"I'm sure it's not near the luxury level you're used to, but I like it."

"It's lovely and you know it. Don't paint me as a bad guy here just to make it easier to dismiss me."

She glanced back over her shoulder, her purse sliding from her shoulder onto the island counter separating the kitchen from the living space. She tossed her keys beside the bag, the cluster jangling to rest. "Fair enough."

He'd spent more than a few nights in tents or trailers during the early, intense stages of a restoration project, but he didn't intend to make excuses to her. "Would you like more luxury in your life?"

His brothers showered their wives with pampering extras and while his sisters-in-law vowed they didn't need them, he'd noticed they always used those spa gifts.

He thumbed a thick silver binder with an engagement photo of Audrey Taylor and her fiancé. "You said earlier you're swamped with wedding plans." He tapped the three-ring binder. "If we stay at my suite, you won't have to cook or clean. You can indulge in the spa. A massage would take care of your stress at the end of the day. You and your sister and all the bridesmaids could avail yourselves of the salon the day of the wedding, my gift to the bride, of course."

She slid out of her gold strappy heels and lined them up side by side on the floor mat by the patio door. "You can't buy me off any more than my father could."

He took his cue from her and toed off his python loafers, nudging them near the coatrack. How much further could they take this undressing together? "I was brought up to believe it's not what a gift costs, it's whether or not the gift is thoughtful. Needed."

"That's nice." She relaxed a hip against a barstool.

"Then pack your bag and let's go to my penthouse."

She stiffened again. "I'm not leaving."

"Then I guess I'm bunking on your sofa." He stifled a wince at spending the night on the couch at least six inches too short.

"You can't tell me you actually wanted me to stay together?" Her eyes went wider with shock. "Every woman on that site in Madrid knew what a playboy you are."

"Were. I'm a married man now." He still had his ring and hers in a jeweler's box in his suite. He wasn't sure why he'd brought them.

She shook her head slowly with a weary sigh. "I'm too tired for this tonight, Jonah. Go back to your hotel. We'll talk tomorrow when we've both had a good night's sleep."

"Honestly? I don't trust you."

"Excuse me?" she gasped in outrage.

Then something else shadowed through her eyes. Guilt?

"You didn't tell me about your father, a pretty major part of your past. You may have done a damn fine job hiding the truth over the years. But when my divorce attorney compared the information you filed on our marriage license at the church registry with your passport information, he found a red flag in the slightly different way you listed your name and your parents. He dug deeper and found your birth certificate. The original one, not the one reissued when Harry Taylor adopted you." The shock he'd felt upon discovering the whole mess roared back to life inside him. "With a little help from a private detective, the rest of the pieces fell into place about your real father. I'm surprised you got away with it for this long."

"You had no right to send private detectives snooping into my private business."

Her words stoked his barely banked anger. "I'm your husband. I think that gives me a little latitude here. For God's sake, Eloisa, what if I'd gotten married again, thinking we were divorced?"

"Are you seeing someone else?" Wow, she sure had

that prim librarian gig down pat. She could have stared down an armed gang.

"Hell no, I'm not seeing anyone else." He couldn't keep himself from comparing other women to her and they all came up short. "Bottom line? Like I said, I don't trust you. You ran once before. I intend to stick close until we have this settled."

She pointed to the binder. "I have my sister's wedding. I'm not going anywhere."

"There are a lot of ways to lock a person out of your life." He'd seen his brother Sebastian and his wife put a massive chasm between each other while living in the same town.

"You can't really expect to stay here, in my town house."

He would have preferred they stay in his suite where he could have wooed her with all the resort offered, but sleeping under the same roof would suffice.

Jonah picked up her keys from the island and held them up so the Spanish charm caught the light. "We both have a lot of unresolved business to settle in two weeks. We should make the most of every minute."

She stared at the keys in his hand for so long he wondered if she was halfway hypnotized.

Finally, Eloisa pressed her fingers to her forehead. "Fine. I'm too tired to argue with you. You can stay, but—" she held up a finger, the stern glint in her eyes relaying loud and clear she was done compromising for the night "—you'll be sleeping on the sofa."

All the same he couldn't resist teasing her, suddenly needing to see if her smile was as blinding as he remembered. "No welcome-home nookie?"

She frowned. "Don't push your luck."

"A guy can still hope." He turned on a lamp, his gaze dropping to the glass paperweight sealing off a dried rose and seashell. He scooped it up, tossed it, caught it, tossed, caught…

"Could you put that down, please?" she snapped with an edge to her voice he hadn't heard since the morning she'd left.

He looked back at the paperweight in his hand. Was it something sentimental? A gift from another guy perhaps? He didn't like the swift kick of jealousy, but damn it all, she was his wife, for now at least. "Should I be worried about a boyfriend showing up to kick my ass?"

"Let's talk about you instead. What have you been up to over the past year, thinking you were a bachelor?"

"Jealous?" God knows he was because she hadn't answered his question. Except if there had been another guy, surely he would have been at the party with her tonight.

His conclusion wasn't proof positive, but he took comfort in it all the same.

She snatched the paperweight from his hand. "I am tired, *not* jealous."

Did he want her to be? No. He wanted honesty. So he settled for the same from himself. "I've spent the past twelve months pining for my ex-wife."

As much as he'd meant to be a sarcastic joke, it hadn't come out of his mouth the way he'd planned.

Confusion flickered through her dark eyes. "The way you say that, I can almost believe you. Of course I know better."

"I thought you said we barely knew each other. We only spent a month together. And we spent most of the time in bed." He sat on the sofa, stretching his arm along the back. "Let's talk now."

"You first." She perched on the edge of the chair beside the sofa.

"You already know plenty about me. My family's in the news and what you don't see there you can find on Wikipedia." He watched her chest rise and fall faster with nerves, lending further credence to his sense she disliked anything high profile.

"None of that information tells me anything reliable about who you are." She counted on her fingers. "I remember you were always on time for work. You never talked on your cell phone when you spoke with the foreman on the site. I liked that you gave people your full attention. I remember you downplayed the Landis connection so well I didn't even know you were related until three weeks into the job." She folded her fingers down again. "But Jonah, that's not enough reason to get married. Even with the divorce, we have a history now. We should know more about each other than our work habits."

"I know you like two sugars in your coffee," he offered with a half smile.

This didn't seem the right time to mention he knew her heart beat faster when he blew along the inside curve of her neck. The sex part would have to wait.

Talking appeared to be the only way to get closer to her, so he would talk. "You want to know more about me? Okay. My brother Kyle got married recently."

"You mentioned that already when you talked about their vows renewal."

"They went to Portugal, which is how I ended up in Spain again." Nostalgia had pulled him over there, the hope that if he revisited the places he'd been with Eloisa he could close the door on that chapter of his life. "The press doesn't know the reason they renewed their vows so soon after saying them in the first place. They got married to safeguard custody of my niece, my brother Kyle's daughter. Her biological mom dumped her on Phoebe, then disappeared." Anger chewed his gut all over again when he thought of how close his niece Nina had come to landing in foster care. "The whole mess really rocked our family. Thank God little Nina is safe."

"You love your niece?" she asked, her face inscrutable.

"Gotta confess, I'm a sucker for kids. I take pride in being the favorite uncle. Want to see pictures of the rug rats?"

"You carry family pictures?" she squeaked incredulously.

"Got a whole album on my iPhone." He unclipped the device from his belt and tapped the screen until pictures filled the display. He leaned closer to her. "My brother Sebastian and his wife remarried after divorcing each other. They have a son."

He brought up an image of his toddler nephew taking his first steps. Then clicked to an infant girl. "That's Sebastian and Marianna's daughter. They adopted her then her birth mother changed her mind."

He swallowed down a lump in his throat and kept his eyes averted until he could speak again. "Here's my brother Matthew—"

"The senator from South Carolina."

"Yes. This is him with his wife and their daughter at the beach." He shuffled to the next photo. "And this is a family portrait taken in Portugal. There's Mom with her husband, the General, his three kids with their spouses and children."

"Your family is huge."

Her family wasn't so small either, when taking into account her biological father and his three sons, but mentioning that didn't seem prudent. "Christmas can be rather noisy when we all get together at the family compound in Hilton Head."

"It's amazing you can gather everyone for any event with all the high-profile commitments."

"We make time for what's important." Would she see and understand that his family was about things more important than a press release or bank balance?

She leaned back in her chair, crossing her arms defensively. "Your brothers are happily married, which means your mother is probably riding your back to produce a happily-ever-after of your own with a wife and make chubby-cheeked cherubs, so you dig up me."

Not even close to what he'd intended. He placed his phone on the end table by the glass paperweight. "That's one helluva scenario to draw from a simple update on my brothers."

"You're not denying it."

He was losing ground here and he wasn't even sure why. "My mother may be a strong-willed politician in her own right, but I'm also very much her son, strong will and all. No one coerces me into anything."

"Unless that influence comes from the bottom of a bottle."

"I wasn't drunk the night we got married." He'd only had two of the local beers. "That was you."

"Are you saying you actually wanted to be married to me?"

"I thought so at the time."

Her mouth fell open, her eyes wide with horror. "You were in love with me?"

"The magnitude of your horror is positively ego deflating."

She shoved up to her feet. "You're playing with me." She walked across the room and opened a closet full of linens. "I don't appreciate your making fun of me."

The way she so easily dismissed what had happened between them a year ago really pissed him off. Okay, so their wedding had been an impulsive mistake. His brothers had been getting married. He'd had this idea that what he felt around Eloisa resembled what his brothers described about finding "the one." He may have been wrong about that. She may have had a couple of drinks, but she'd been clear about how much she wanted him, too, how much she'd needed him.

Need wasn't love. But they had felt something for each other, something strong and undeniable.

"I would never mock you." Frustration sliced through him with a razor-sharp edge. "There are far more interesting things I would like to do with you tonight. Let's back up to the part about sex."

She laughed. "At no time were we talking about sex."

"You mentioned making cherubs." Yeah, they were engaging in good old-fashioned bantering but damn, he found it arousing and a fine way to take the edge off his anger. "I'm sorry if your mother never got around to giving you the talk, but sex makes babies."

Her face closed up again. "You're not half as funny as you think you are."

"I'm halfway funny? Cool."

She dumped an armful of linens into his lap. "Make up your own bed on the sofa. I'm done here."

He watched her grab her purse before pounding up the steps to her bedroom, and he couldn't even rejoice over the fact she'd let him stay. Her door clicked shut behind her, the sound of a lock snicking a second later.

Somewhere along the line he'd misstepped. And he didn't have a clue what he'd done wrong now any more than before.

Upstairs in her room, Eloisa sunk to the edge of her bed, sliding down to the floor. She clutched her knees, tears making fast tracks down her face.

Seeing Jonah touch that glass paperweight had almost driven her to her knees earlier. After she'd lost the baby four months into her pregnancy, she'd had a private memorial service all her own for her child. She'd taken a tiny nosegay of white rosebuds to the beach and let waves carry them away as she'd prayed.

She'd kept one rose for herself. The bloom had dried far faster than her tears. Then she'd had the bud encased in glass along with a couple of tiny shells and some sand from that stretch of shoreline.

Jonah obviously loved children, evident not just from his words but from the way his eyes had gone soft over that family photo album. Each beautiful baby's face had torn a fresh hole in heart, tormenting her with what her child—hers and Jonah's—might have looked like.

The doctors had told her it was just one of those things. There was no reason why she couldn't have more children, but she couldn't see any way clear to having forever with any man, much less starting a family.

Between fears about threats from her father's enemies to even deeper fears about living out her mother's legacy… Eloisa swiped her eyes with her forearm.

God, she was mess.

What would Jonah say if he learned she'd kept the pregnancy a secret from him?

She still didn't understand why she'd delayed contacting him about the baby. She'd told herself she would let him know before their child was born. When she'd miscarried and her emotions had been such a turmoil of grief, contacting him seemed an overwhelming hurdle.

Every day that passed, it seemed easier to stay quiet. Telling him now wouldn't serve any purpose.

Her cell phone chimed from inside her purse, startling her midsob. She definitely didn't feel like speaking to anyone this late. Thank goodness the chimes indicated a text message.

She fished out her phone. Her sister's name scrolled across the screen. Eloisa thumbed View.

R U home? Worried about u.

Eloisa clutched the phone. She'd never shared her burdens with anyone before. The secrets were too big, too deep. Unburdening herself would be selfish. She stifled back the crazy notion of what it might feel like to spill her guts to her sibling.

Eloisa typed out, *Am home and ok. No worries.*

She sent the message and pushed to her feet. She needed to splash water on her eyes and go to sleep. Would that be possible with Jonah downstairs on the sofa?

Her phone chimed in her hand. Audrey again.

What about tycoon hunk? Is he there?

She set the cell on the bathroom counter next to the sink. Her fingers hovered over the keypad. What should she tell her sister?

He was most definitely bothering her by his mere presence so much more than she could have even expected. But if she wanted time to figure out what to do about him, her father, her biology, she needed to play along with his bizarre game a while longer.

Beyond that? What did she want?

Eloisa looked at herself in a mirror framed with seashells and sand dollars. She picked at a strand of hair that had slipped loose from her severe ponytail, her face devoid of makeup. But her cheeks were flushed in a way they'd never been before—except for that too-short month in Spain.

The truth settled inside her with a resounding thud. She couldn't be the sort of person who would walk into that living room, whip the covers off Jonah and say to hell with the consequences, she was making the most of her marital status. She'd gone that route before and it only led to their current mess.

A tempting alternative tickled at her brain. What if she did sleep with him again, but the next time was more about fun, with no ring? She'd let things get too serious before. That had obviously been a mistake on so many levels.

Could she forget the past and have an affair with her ex-husband?

Five

Eloisa made it through the night without a trip downstairs, although it had been rough going when she'd woken up at around four.

But finally the morning sun streaked through her reed roll-up blinds. She could leave her room without feeling she'd caved. Since it was only six-thirty, she might just get to watch him sleep, something she'd missed out on during their one night together.

She pulled on a white terry-cloth robe, securing it tight before leaving her bedroom. Halfway down the stairs she realized the sofa was empty. Well, empty other than the thin quilt straggling off the side. The pillow still bore the deep imprint of a head. Eloisa padded barefoot down the rest of the steps, her toes sinking into the carpet runner along the wood.

Where was Jonah? The spare bathroom downstairs

was silent, the door cracked open, steam still lightly fogging the mirror and a pale blue towel hung on the rack. Had he left as abruptly as he'd shown up, even after joking about wanting a final night together? Just the thought of being with him again sent a tingle along her skin, a tingle doused by the possibility he'd already left.

Her bare feet picked up speed along the hardwood floor, but the kitchen was empty, too.

"Uh-huh…" His voice drifted inside.

She spun around. The French doors were open an inch. She sagged back against the island counter and stared through to the patio. Jonah lounged in her Adirondack chair, cell phone pressed to his ear. Curiosity held her still and quiet when she probably should have done something to announce her presence, like slam a couple of cabinets open and closed.

His jean-clad legs stretched out long and so damn sexy, showcased by the morning sun. There was something hot and intimate about his bare feet and while she couldn't see his chest, his arms appeared bare as well.

Memories of making love in Spain flamed hotter in her mind after simmering below the surface all night long. She may have had a couple of drinks and lost some inhibitions, but she remembered the sex. Good sex. Amazing sex. She'd been so hungry for him as she'd torn away his shirt, popping buttons in her frenzy. His chest had captured her attention all by itself. She'd known he was muscular. The ripples under his shirt had been impossible to miss, but she hadn't been prepared for the intense definition, the unmistakable strength and power far more elemental than any money or prestige.

She'd always considered herself the cerebral sort, attracted to academic types. So it had totally knocked her off balance when she'd gone weak-kneed over a peek at Jonah's pecs.

"Right," he said to whoever was on the other end of the line. He thrust a hand through his still-damp hair, slicking it back. "I realize that cuts a week off our timeline. Go ahead and send me the new specs. I'll get back to you with an answer by the end of business today." He listened and nodded. "I can be reached at this number. Meanwhile, I'll be on the lookout for your fax."

He disconnected and didn't show signs of dialing again, apparently done with chitchatting for the moment. Any second now, he might stand and notice her. Eloisa looked around for some excuse to appear busy rather than to be eavesdropping. She snatched the empty coffeepot from the coffeemaker.

Jonah stood, stretching his arms overhead.

Her mouth went dry. His chest was everything she remembered and more. She'd forgotten about the deep tan. The honey-warm glow of his skin made her want to taste him all over.

She visually traced the cut of his six-pack lower, lower still down to…oh my…he'd left the top button of his jeans open.

No boxers.

Just a hint of a tan line.

Eloisa grabbed the counter for balance.

She tore her gaze off his bare stomach and brought it to his face. He was looking straight back at her as she stood in the kitchen, stock-still, holding on to the counter with one hand. Her other held a coffeepot dangling uselessly from between her fingers.

"Sorry, uh, Jonah," she babbled, startling into action and shoving the coffeepot under the faucet as he sauntered inside. "I didn't mean to interrupt your call."

"It's okay. We'd already wrapped up business." He tucked the phone half into his pocket, studying her as intently as she'd studied him. "Are you making coffee or tea?"

The intensity of his gaze made her edgy. Was her robe gaping? Her hair a mess?

She glanced at the pot…. Damn. She'd forgotten to turn on the faucet.

"Coffee." Eloisa turned her back to him and focused on making extra-strong java. Hopefully by the time the last drop dripped she would have scavenged some self-control and dignity. "Were you talking to your lawyer about moving forward on the divorce?"

"That was a work call." The heat of his voice and breath caressed her shoulder and she hadn't even heard him approach. He moved quietly for such a big man.

"You have a job?" she asked absently, setting the glass pot on the counter rather than risk dropping it. When had her fingers gone numb?

He flicked her ponytail forward over her shoulder. "I think I'm insulted you have to ask."

Ducking away, she opened the cabinet and foraged for her favorite hazelnut-cream-flavored beans. "Weren't you working on your grad studies like the others when we met?" She glanced back at him. "I assumed…"

He cocked an eyebrow. "You assumed that I was a perpetual student content to live off Mom and Pop's nickel? You sure painted quite a picture of me with very little info."

She finished pouring coffee beans into the coffeemaker, closed the lid and hit Start. The sound of the grinder grated along her already ragged nerves. "You made assumptions about me, too."

"Such as?" He leaned against the counter, dipping his head into her line of sight.

"I gave off the appearance of being someone different during those weeks in Madrid." She crossed her arms over her chest, keeping her robe closed and her hands off his chest. "That time of my life was very out of character for me."

"How so?"

"I'm a homebody, not a world traveler. I like my books and my Adirondack chair with a mug of coffee. That sort of exotic adventure was a onetime good deal. I lucked into a scholarship program that granted me the extra credits I needed. Bottom line, I'm a bookish librarian, not a party girl who gets drunk and impulsively marries some hot guy."

"You think I'm hot, huh?" His blue eyes twinkled as brightly as the rising sun glimmering through the sliding patio doors.

"You already know I find you physically attractive." She conjured her best "librarian" voice that put even the rowdiest of hoodlums in place. "But there are more important issues to address here."

"Of course." He selected an apple from her wicker fruit bowl on the counter. "I have a theory."

"What would that be?" They were nearly naked. He had an apple.

Where was the snake? Because she certainly was tempted.

He gestured with the fruit in his hand. "I think you *are* the sort of woman who travels the world and impulsively takes risks, even knowing sometimes those risks may not work out. Deep down you want to take more of those risks because you also know that sometimes things do work out."

"You seem to have decided a lot about me."

Without answering he crunched a big bite off the side. Why couldn't he have chosen one of the more innocent oranges or plums?

She watched his mouth work. She'd done that before, in Spain during a late-day picnic with the whole crew. Back then she'd only indulged in what-if fantasies about Jonah, never for a second thinking she would one day act on them.

And here she was daydreaming about the feel of his mouth moving along her skin...

Except his mouth was moving because he was talking and she didn't have a clue what he'd said.

"Pardon me?" She rearranged the plums until the fruit was balanced again.

He set aside his half-eaten apple. "Our time together was intense. You can learn a lot about a person in time-compressed moments."

What was he driving at? "But you agreed with me the morning after that we'd made a mistake."

"Did I?"

She stared back into his serious blue eyes and tried to understand him, understand this whole bizarre reunion. But he wasn't giving away anything in his expression. She wasn't so sure she could say the same for herself.

Eloisa touched his hand lightly. "Don't play mind games with me. I know what I heard. And it's not like you came after me."

"I'm here now."

What if he'd come after her right away? She would have told him about the baby. She wouldn't have been able to stay silent if face-to-face with him. How much different things might have been.

Or maybe not. Her mother certainly hadn't experienced a fairy-tale ending when she'd gotten pregnant.

Eloisa shook off the haze of what-ifs. "You've shown up for your one night of sex. Followed by a divorce."

"Who says we can't change our minds?" Before she could answer, he pitched his apple into the corner trash can. "I have to check on that fax."

Blinking fast, she watched him walk out the door shirtless, her head still spinning from his abrupt departure. The front door closed, but she could still see him through the skinny windows on either side of the door. The limo loomed conspicuously in the parking lot, idling alongside the curb. Jonah ducked his head and climbed inside and she remembered that mobile office/command center.

And she realized he'd never answered her question about his phone call or what he did with his life now. While Jonah seemed to have figured out so much about her, she had precious little other than Wikipedia information on him.

If she really wanted to move forward with her life, the time had come to quit drooling over the guy's body and start seriously looking at the man underneath.

* * *

He'd seen the desire in her eyes underneath her veneer of calm.

Jonah tugged on a black polo shirt while he waited for Eloisa to finish her shower upstairs. No amount of work in his fax machine could distract him from thoughts of her under the spray. In some ways he thought he remembered every nuance of her body. That night was burned in his memory.

Would his fascination with her ease if he had more time with her? He certainly hoped so because he didn't want another year like the one he'd just endured.

The sound of water faded, then ended. Silence echoed for what felt like forever before he heard the rustle of her upstairs in her bedroom. Getting dressed.

He'd never considered himself a masochist, but listening to her was serious torture. Jonah pivoted away from her door and opened cabinet after cabinet in search of a coffee mug. As he started drinking his second cup, he heard her door click and swing open.

Jonah poured some java for her, spooning two sugars in the way he remembered she preferred. And why he recalled that detail, he didn't know. He turned to face her.

He stopped short. Reality definitely beat the hell out of memories—and she wasn't even naked.

Eloisa stepped into the kitchen barefoot, wearing a simple blue sundress. The flowing lines clung subtly to her curves, and her skin glowed warm and pink from the shower. Her black hair was wet and pulled back in her signature ponytail, exposing her neck. He'd seen her arousal earlier when he'd hung up the phone and he could probably persuade her now....

But he didn't want to win in some all-out seduction. He wanted *her* to come to *him*.

Eloisa took the cup from his hand carefully, so carefully their fingers didn't even brush. "Did you get your paperwork?"

"Yes, I did." His next job didn't begin for another thirteen days. Most times, he would have headed out early. He was about to tell her about the nineteenth-century Peruvian hacienda he'd been hired to renovate and expand into a resort.

Then remembered she'd only asked because she thought he was contacting his attorney about the divorce.

She blew air across the top of the cup, watching him through upswept lashes. "I don't have much for breakfast, just some granola bars or toast and whatever's in the fruit basket. You're welcome to what's here."

If only she meant that the way he wanted her to. "I can feed myself."

"Good then." She nodded. "Tell me more about your job."

Hey, wait. "But I don't have one, remember? I'm just a lazy playboy."

She lowered her cup, genuine contrition lighting eyes as dark as her coffee. "I was wrong to make that assumption. I genuinely want to hear now."

He wasn't so sure he wanted to be in the hot seat, and definitely didn't know what had brought her to this about-face from pushing him away to shooting the breeze together. "Don't you have to get to work or help your sister with wedding plans?"

"Audrey's busy today, and I have a half hour before I have to leave for the library."

"I'll let the chauffeur know."

"No need." Turning away, she cradled her mug in both hands and walked to the sofa, her hips swaying gently, loose folds of the dress swishing a hypnotic *follow me*. "My sister's fiancé took care of returning my car. She already texted me that it's out in the parking lot."

"Then you're all set." He watched her place her coffee on the end table.

She pulled his blanket from the sofa and began to fold. "Tell me about your job."

He set his mug beside hers and reached for the end of the quilt trailing the ground. "What do you want to know?"

"Why do you hang around historic sites rather than slick new buildings?" She came closer, nearly chest to chest, and met his hands.

His eyes held hers and he considered kissing her right then and there, but he was determined for her to close that last gap. He knelt to sweep up the ends of the blanket and stood again. "I'm a history buff, always have been even when I was a kid, and my family traveled overseas a good bit."

Finishing the final fold, she clasped the quilt to her chest and sat on the sofa. "Tell me more."

She hadn't taken the chair this time and he wasn't missing the chance to get a little closer.

Jonah swept aside a couple of froufrou decorative pillows and sat beside her, keeping space between them. For now. "I'm an architect. I specialize in historic landmarks."

"That's why you were in Spain last year." She sagged back, her face relaxing into a smile for the first time since he'd seen her last night. "But you were also a student, right?"

He shifted uncomfortably. Couldn't he just give her a résumé? "I finished my dissertation."

"You completed your PhD? I'm impressed."

He winced. He hadn't shared that with her to wow her. He preferred not to talk about himself at all. "I enjoy the subject matter." He shrugged offhandedly. "I had the luxury of not worrying about school loans."

"But you were also in Spain in a more official capacity?"

"Yes, I was." What did she hope to accomplish by grilling him?

"Why did you keep it a secret?"

Was this a trap? "I didn't keep anything a secret."

He just didn't feel the need to relay everything to everyone.

"You're playing with words." She leaned closer, her shower-fresh scent, the tropical perfume of her shampoo, teasing him. "You can't blame me for making assumptions when you won't share. Well, tell me now. What else were you doing there?"

To hell with figuring out motives or playing games. He had her here. Talking to him. Not running. If he had to scavenge chitchat to make headway with her, then fine. Might as well dish up some information about his past. "When I turned eighteen, I decided I didn't want to live off my family. While I was in college, I started flipping houses."

"You worked construction in college?" She set aside the quilt and reached for her coffee.

Good. He had her relaxing bit by bit. "Is there something wrong with that?"

She paused midsip. "Of course not. I just... Okay, I made assumptions about your college years."

"I didn't have time for the frat-boy scene, princess." He'd worked his ass off, and considered the time well spent as it gave him real-world experience once he'd graduated. "So I flipped houses, made investments then took things to another level by underwriting renovations of historic manor homes and castles. I made more investments." He shrugged. "And here I am."

"What about your family's influence in world politics? What about your inheritance?"

Some of the women in his life had been sorely disappointed to hear about his lack of interest in being a part of the political world his family inhabited. "What about it?"

"Do you just leave the money sitting around?"

"Hell, no. I invest it. I expect to leave more for my kids."

"You want children?" She averted her eyes, setting her mug down.

"Damn straight, I do. A half dozen or so."

She pushed to her feet abruptly, backing away, nearly stumbling over her bare feet. Eloisa grabbed the chair for balance. "I need to finish getting ready for work."

What the hell had caused her quick turnaround? He'd been sure he was making headway and suddenly she was checking her watch, shoving on her shoes and scooping up her purse.

Maybe he'd hit a snag there by pushing too hard, too fast. But he wasn't one to admit defeat. It was all about building on the progress he'd made, one brick at a time. He watched her rush around the town house, gathering herself on her way out the door. And as she turned to wave goodbye, he realized.

She'd put on lip gloss.

He thought back to the evening before. She'd been stunning, silhouetted against the waterside, wind rippling her dress and lifting her hair. She had an unstated style and innate grace that proclaimed her timeless beauty regardless of what she wore.

And he was damn sure she hadn't worn makeup last night or a year ago. Yet for some reason, she'd slicked on gloss today. Sure, it was a minor detail, but he found himself curious about every detail surrounding the woman he'd married.

They'd made a decent start in getting to know each other better today. Although they'd mostly talked about his job. And now that he thought about it, he didn't know much about her career since she'd transitioned from being a student.

If he wanted to get closer to Eloisa, perhaps it was time to learn a little more about *her* workplace.

Six

Eloisa perched on the second-to-top step of the rolling ladder, replacing two copies of *The Scarlet Letter*. They'd been returned by a couple of high schoolers who'd lost their classroom edition and had to check it out from the library in a panic before the test. And while work usually calmed her, channeling peace through the quiet and rows of books… Today the familiar environment fell short of its normally calming effect.

She placed the blame squarely on her husband. Having Jonah show up in her life again so unexpectedly was unsettling on too many levels. No wonder she was having trouble finding her footing. She'd contacted her attorney and it appeared Jonah's claim was correct. The divorce hadn't gone through after all. Her lawyer had received the paperwork just this morning, although he vowed he had no idea how Jonah had learned of her Medina roots.

The lawyer had gone on to reassure her he would look into it further. In fact, he planned to go straight to the source and speak with her father and brothers directly. If they didn't have the information, they would need to be warned, as well.

She aligned the books and started back down the ladder. A hand clamped her calf. Gasping, she grabbed the railings to keep from pitching over backward. She looked down fast—

"Jonah," she whispered, her world righting and narrowing to just him, "you scared the hell out of me."

"Sorry about that. Wouldn't want you to fall." He kept his hand on her leg.

Eloisa continued down, his hand naturally sliding up for an inch, and another. Her heart triple-timed as she wondered how long he would keep up this game.

She descended another step.

His hand fell away. The heat of his palm remained.

Soft chitchat sounded from a couple of rows over, the air conditioner nearly as loud as the conversation. Otherwise, this section of the library was pretty much deserted this morning.

Eloisa gripped a shelf since the floor felt a little wobbly. "What are you doing here?"

"I came to take you out. Unless you have to do something with your sister's wedding plans, in which case, I'm here to supply lunch." He gripped the shelf just beside her, his body blocking the rest of the row from sight and creating a quiet—intimate—haven.

A lunch date? God, that sounded fun and wonderful

and more than a little impulsively romantic. *So* unwise if she wanted to keep her balance while finding out what made Jonah Landis tick. "I already bought a sandwich on my way in."

"Okay, then. Another time." He looked past her, then over his shoulder, a broad shoulder mouthwateringly encased in his black polo shirt. "Mind if I have a tour of the place before I leave?"

Her mouth went dry at the thought of more time with him. She eyed the water fountain. "It's a public library. As in open. To the public. Like you."

He traced down the binding of a misplaced Dickens book. "I was hoping for my own personal tour guide. I'm partial to sexy brunette librarians who wear their long hair slicked back in a ponytail. And if she had exotic brown eyes with—"

"I get the picture, you flirt." She held up her hand and stifled a laugh. "You want a tour?" She pulled *A Tale of Two Cities* from the shelf and tucked it under her arm. "Of a library?"

"I want a tour of *your* library. You saw my workplace in Spain." He propped a foot on the bottom step of the ladder. "Now I want to see yours."

Could he really be serious here? Could he perhaps, like her, need some additional insights in order to put the past behind him? The whole flirtation could just be his cover for a deeper confusion like she felt.

And she was probably overanalyzing. Didn't men say things were a lot simpler for them?

Regardless, what harm could there be in showing him around the library? She couldn't think of anywhere safer than here. Now where to start?

If she took him downstairs to the reception area, she

would face questions later from the rest of the staff. Better to go farther into the stacks.

She mentally clicked through other areas to avoid. A book-group discussion. A local artist in residence hanging her work. Eloisa discussed the facility's features by rote.

Jonah reached ahead to push open a doorway leading into a research area. "What made you decide on this career field?"

She looked around. Definitely secluded. She could talk without worrying about being overheard, but also she wouldn't have the same temptations of being alone in her town house with Jonah. "My mother spent a lot of time staying under the radar. I learned low-key at an early age. Novels were my…"

"Escape?" He gestured around the high-ceilinged space that smelled of books and air freshener.

"Entertainment." She shoved a chair under the computer desk. "Now they're my livelihood."

"What about after your mother married what's-his-name?" Jonah followed, palming her back as she rounded a corner.

"My mother still liked to keep things uncomplicated." How in the world had her mother ever fallen for a king? And a deposed king at that, with all sorts of drama surrounding his life? Enrique Medina seemed the antithesis of her stepfather, a man who might not be perfect, but at least had been a presence in her life. Loyalty spurred her to say, "His name is Harry Taylor."

"Yeah, what's-his-name."

Eloisa couldn't help grinning. Her stepfather wasn't a bad guy, if a bit pretentious and pompous…. And she knew in her heart he loved his biological daughter more than he loved her. It hurt a little to think about that, but not anywhere near as much as it used to. "While I appreciate your championing my cause, I truly can stand up for myself."

"Never doubted that for a second," Jonah answered without hesitation. "What's wrong with other folks— like me—throwing our weight in along with you?"

She simply shook her head. "I thought you wanted a tour."

"We can tour and talk."

Sometimes she wasn't sure if she could walk and chew bubblegum around this man. She plastered on a smile. "Sure we can. And here's my office."

Eloisa swept the door open wide and gestured for him to follow her into the tiny space packed full of novels, papers and framed posters from literature festivals around the world. She placed the Dickens classic on a rolling cart to be shelved later.

The door clicked as it closed. She turned to find the space suddenly seeming way smaller with Jonah taking up his fair share of the room that wasn't already occupied by her gunmetal-gray desk, shelves and an extra plastic chair for a guest.

Maybe her office just felt claustrophobic because there weren't windows or even a peephole in the door. Not because they were alone.

Totally alone.

He hadn't planned on getting her alone in the library.

Yet here they were. Just the two of them. In her tiny, isolated office.

Jonah pivoted away to find some distraction, something to talk about, and came nose to nose with a shelf of books. Art books and history books, all about Spain and Portugal. She wasn't as detached from her roots as she tried to make out.

Jonah thumbed the gold lettering along the spine of a collection of Spanish poetry. He recalled she spoke the language fluently. "Have you ever met your biological father in person?"

"Once." Her voice drifted over his shoulder, soft and a little husky. "I was about seven at the time."

"That's years after the last-known sighting of him." Jonah kept his back to her for the moment. Perhaps that would make it easier for her to share. So he continued to inventory her books.

"I don't know where we went. It felt like we took a long time, but all travel seems to take forever at that age."

He recalled well the family trips with his three brothers and his parents, everything from Disney to an Egyptian pharaoh's tomb. Their vacations would have been so different from that mother-daughter trip to see a man who barely acknowledged her existence. Sympathy kicked him in his gut. "Do you remember the mode of transportation?"

"Of course."

"Not that you're telling." He couldn't stop the grin at her spunk.

"I may not have a relationship with my father—" sounds rustled behind him, like the determined restoring of order as she moved things around on her desk "—but that doesn't mean I'm any less concerned about his safety, or the safety of my brothers."

"That's right. Medina has three sons." He clicked through what he knew about Medina from the research he'd been able to accomplish on his own—when he should have been working. But damn it all, this was important. "Did you meet them as well?"

"Two of them."

"That must have seemed strange to say the least."

"I have a half sister, remember? It's not like I don't understand being a part of a family unit." Her voice rose with every word, more than a little hurt leaking through. "I'm not some kind of freak."

He turned to face her again. Her desk was so damn neat and clean a surgeon could have performed an open-heart procedure right there. Germs wouldn't dare approach.

Jonah, however, had never been one to back down from a dare. "Your mother would have already been remarried by the time you were seven."

"And Audrey was a toddler." She clasped her hands in front of her defensively.

Her words sunk in and...holy hell. "Your mom went to see her old lover after she was married to another guy? Your stepfather must have been pissed."

"He never knew about the trip or any of the Medinas." She stood straight and tall, every bit of her royal heritage out there for him to see. She ruled. It didn't matter if she was sitting in a palace or standing in a dark, cramped, little office. She mesmerized him.

And she called to his every protective instinct at the same time. What kind of life must she have led to build defenses this thick?

"Your stepfather didn't know about any of it?" Jonah approached her carefully, wary of spooking her when she was finally opening up, but unable to stay away from her when he sensed that she could have used someone to confide in all these years. "How did she explain about your father?"

She shrugged one shoulder. "She told him the same thing she told everyone else. That my father was a fellow student, with no family, and he died in a car accident before I was born. It's not like Harry talked about my dad to anyone else. The subject just never came up for us."

Jonah skimmed his fingers over the furrows along her forehead. "Let's not discuss your stepfather. Tell me about that visit when you were seven."

Her forehead smoothed and her face relaxed into a brief flicker of a smile. "It was amazing, or rather it seemed that way to me through my childish, idealistic eyes. We all walked along the beach and collected shells. He—" she paused, clearing her throat "—uhm, my father, told me this story about a little squirrel that could travel wherever she wanted by scampering along the telephone lines. He even carried me on his shoulders when my legs got tired from walking and sang songs in Spanish."

"Those are good memories."

She deserved to have had many more of them, but he kept that opinion to himself. Better to wait and just let her talk, rather than risk her clamming up out of defensiveness.

"I know it's silly, but I still have one of the shells." She nudged a stack of already perfectly straight note slips. "I used to listen to it and imagine I could hear his voice mixed in with the sound of the ocean."

"Where is the shell now?"

"I, uh, tucked it away in one of my bookcases at home."

A home she'd decorated completely in a seashore theme. It couldn't be coincidence. He gripped her shoulders lightly. "Why don't you go see him again? You have the right to do so."

"I don't know where he is."

"But surely you have a way to get in touch with him." The soft give of her arms under his hands enticed him to pull her closer. He should take his hands off her, but he didn't. Still he wouldn't back off from delving deeper into this issue. "What about the lawyer?"

She avoided his eyes. "Let's discuss something else."

"So the lawyer is your point of contact even if the old guy never bothers to get in touch with you."

"Stop it, okay?"

She looked back at him again hard and fast. Her eyes were dark and defensive and held so much hurt he realized he would do anything, anything to make that pain go away. "Eloisa—"

"My biological father has asked to see me." She talked right over him, protesting a bit too emphatically. "More than once. I'm the one who stays away. It's just too complicated. He wrecked my mother's life and broke her heart." Her hands slid up to grip his shirt. "That's not something I can just forget about long enough to sit down for some fancy dinner with him once every five years when his conscience kicks in."

He churned over her words, searching for what she meant underneath it all. "I miss my father."

His dad had died in a car wreck when Jonah was only entering his teenage years.

"I told you I don't want to see him."

Jonah cupped her face, his thumb stroking along her aristocratic cheekbone. "I'm talking about how you miss your mother. It's tough losing a parent no matter how old you are."

Empathy softened her eyes for the first time since they'd stepped into her office. "When did your father pass away?"

"When I was in my early teens. A car crash. I used to be so jealous of my brothers because they had more time with him. Talk about ridiculous sibling rivalry." He'd always been different from them, more of a rebel. Little did they know how much it hurt when people said he would have been more focused if only his father had lived. But he refused to let what others said come between him and his family.

Family was everything.

"We almost lost our mother a few years ago when she was on a goodwill tour across Europe." The near miss had scared the hell out of him. After that, he'd knuckled down and gotten his life in order. His skin went cold from just thinking of what had almost happened to his mother. "An assassin tried to make a statement by shooting up one of her events."

"Ohmigod, I remember that." Her fists unfurled in his shirt and her hands smoothed out the wrinkles in soothing circles. "It must have been horrible for you. I seem to recall that some of her family was there…. You saw it all happen?"

"I'm not asking for sympathy." He clasped her wrists and stilled her hands. She might mean her touch to be comforting, but it was rapidly becoming a serious turn-on. "I'm only trying to say I understand how you feel. But, Eloisa, once you're in the spotlight, there's no way to step back out."

"I completely get your point," she said emphatically. "That's why I've kept a low profile."

He brought her hands together, their hands clasped as he tried to make her understand. "You were born into this. There's no low profile. Only delaying the inevitable. Better to embrace it on your own terms."

"That's not your call to make," she snapped, pulling her hands away.

God, it was like banging his head against bricks getting this stubborn woman to consider anything other than a paradigm constructed a helluva long time ago. "Are you so sure about your father's reasons for choosing to close himself away?"

Her spine starched straight again, ire sparking flecks of black in her eyes. "What are you hoping to accomplish here?"

He'd been hoping to learn more about her in an effort to seduce her and had ended up pissing her off. But he couldn't back down. "You don't have to play this their way anymore, Eloisa. Decide what you want rather than letting them haul you along."

Her hands fisted. "Why does this need to get so complicated, and what the hell does it have to do with you?"

Anger stirred in his gut. "I'm the guy who's still married to you because it's so complicated. Damn it, Eloisa, Can you understand my need to do something, fix this somehow?"

"Maybe there's nothing to fix. And even if there is, do you know what I really want?"

"Okay. Mea culpa." He thumped his chest. "You've got me there. I haven't got a clue what you want from me."

"Well, prepare to find out." She clasped his face in her hands, only giving him a second's warning.

Eloisa planted her mouth on his.

He blinked in shock—for all of three seconds before he hauled her against him and kissed her right back.

As her arms slid around his neck, he decided the time had come to take this as far as she would go.

Seven

Eloisa couldn't decide if she'd just made the best or worst decision of her life. Regardless, she knew she'd made the inevitable choice in kissing Jonah. They'd been leading up to this from the second he'd stepped out of his limousine last night.

She pressed her body closer to his, fully, for the first time in a year, her mouth opening to welcome him. Last night's staged kiss outside the party had been too brief. She'd somehow forgotten how well they fit, the way she tucked just inside his embrace, his head angling down. He was taller than she was, but somehow it worked just right for her arms to rest on his shoulders while she burrowed her hands into his hair.

And ohmigod, his hair.

Eloisa touched and roved and savored his head, the slight waves curving around her fingers as if coaxing her to stay. No persuasion needed, she was on fire with want after a year without this kind of sensual contact.

She'd reached for him in frustration, her desire slipping past when her defenses were weakened by irritation. But now that he was touching her, stroking her, coaxing her body against his, she forced all that ire away, just put the whole argument right out of her mind.

Still, part of her feared he'd sparked something deeper inside just by caring enough to ask the hard questions others avoided. He confronted things she liked to keep tucked away.

Either way, she didn't want to argue. She wanted that connection she remembered from a year ago, and she didn't want to fight it another second.

"You taste like apples."

"My lip gloss," she gasped.

"Ah," he said, smiling against her mouth. "You're wearing lip gloss today." He traced her lips with his tongue, then dipped deeper, sharing the hint of flavor with her.

His kiss growing bolder, fuller, he backed her against the desk and she welcomed the bolstering because she wasn't sure how much longer her legs would hold. Jonah stroked her back, her sides, the tops of her thighs, nowhere overtly intimate but intensely arousing all the same. His hot breath caressed her neck a second before his mouth skimmed her oversensitive flesh. Her spot. *He remembered.* The fact that he still knew what she liked turned her inside out as much as the touch of his lips to her skin.

She bit back a moan, her head falling to rest on his shoulder. "We need to slow this down. I'm at work."

He pressed a finger to her lips, still paying detailed attention to her neck. "Shhh. We're in a library. Haven't you ever made out in the library?"

"Never," she answered, one word all she could manage.

"Or caught people making out in the stacks?" His hands slid up and down her sides, each time grazing farther and farther over her ribs, just below her breasts.

"A time or two." She'd sent them on their way like a good, responsible adult, but right now she was feeling anything but responsible.

Jonah nudged his leg between hers, the thick press of his muscled thigh sending sparks of pleasure radiating upward. And clearly she wasn't the only one feeling the effects of their clench. There was no mistaking the rigid press of his arousal against her stomach. He wanted her. Here. Now.

And heaven help her, she wanted him too and to hell with the emotional fallout later. Hadn't she thought just this morning about how wonderful it would be to indulge with Jonah, no marriage, no strings? And other than a piece of paper, they weren't really married. Their lives wouldn't be tangled up beyond these next couple of weeks.

"Let's continue this at my house." She took the leap. "Or at your place even."

"Trust me. I wouldn't risk getting you in trouble." He kissed her quiet again.

They had their clothes on. She was off the clock for lunch. He was only kissing her.

Kissing her senseless.

But still. Who could object? When she'd stumbled

upon other couples necking in the library before, while it had been mildly embarrassing for the people caught, all had just laughed good-naturedly. And she was locked in her office on her lunch break.

Why not?

"Okay then, I trust you," she vowed against his mouth, meaning the words for now, this moment.

"That's what I want to hear." A smile kicked up into his cheek as he lowered his head to hers.

She threaded her fingers through his hair again. Thick and luxurious, wild and sexy. Like the man.

Jonah angled her closer. His palms spanning low on her back, he urged her into a gentle rock against him. His leg pressed more firmly. Pleasure tightened more insistently. She ached for release but held back, nervous and excited by the notion of losing control. They were just making out, for heaven's sake.

Memories of a similar embrace in his rented home in Spain steamed through her mind, of him pressing her just this way against the kitchen counter when they'd made a 3:00 a.m. forage for food. Naked. Both of them had been exhausted and starving from their workout in bed. The images of then tangled with the present until the clothed kiss became so much more in her mind.... She could almost smell the sangria and fruit juices they'd licked from each other's bodies.

It had been so long, too long, a whole damn year without this feeling, a growing sense of frenzy no man other than Jonah had been able to engender. What if he were the only man who could stoke her passion to this level? What would it be like to go through life never feeling this level of want and pleasure and pure sensuality again?

The warm sweep of his tongue, the familiar taste of him, stoked her need higher, hotter, tighter. She wriggled to get closer. The tension gathered low, right where he so perfectly teased. He pressed his leg more insistently against, rocking it rhythmically against her until she realized...

Gasped...

Couldn't stop...

He caught her moan with his mouth. She arched her back, flinging full-out into her release. Every muscle inside her pulled taut as if to hold on to the sensation as long as possible, clenching up each sparkling aftershock.

Slowly, the warm flush along her skin began to cool. She shivered and he gathered her against his chest. Thank God he didn't speak. She would have been mortified, but she could barely think, much less talk.

Jonah brushed his mouth along the top of her hair. "Enjoy the rest of the lunch break and your sandwich. I'll pick you up for supper."

Then he was gone. The door to her office closed behind him with a gentle swoosh while she sagged into her chair. Eloisa smoothed a shaky hand over her hair, to her lips, against her still-racing heart.

She didn't regret her decision, but had to admit, she'd been so very wrong. Things with Jonah could never be uncomplicated. She'd just had the best orgasm of her life.

And he'd only kissed her.

He'd only kissed her.

Parked in her town house lot five hours later, Jonah shut off the engine on his rental car—top-of-the-line

Range Rover, the same sort he always picked and owned because it worked best for him on work sites.

He'd spent the afternoon settling into Pensacola a little deeper, renting wheels. He'd stopped by his penthouse suite to complete paperwork and calls, also lining up two of his employees to oversee the early work trickling in unexpectedly.

Basically, he'd spent the afternoon figuring out ways to make his schedule more open to Eloisa. Damn, how his brothers would laugh at him if they were here to see, but he refused to lose this chance to settle things with Eloisa.

With the scent of her still all around him, he knew he wasn't giving up. He had to have her.

Jonah draped his wrist over the steering wheel and stared at her door. Their encounter in the library had gone just as he'd planned…and yet it hadn't turned out at all the way he'd imagined.

No way in hell could he have imagined being this rocked by seeing her come undone in his arms. This was moving so fast and if he wasn't careful, she would bolt again.

Good thing he'd made reservations at a restaurant. He wasn't sure he could withstand another evening alone with her in her place.

He reached for the car door and his cell phone chimed, stopping him short. He unclipped it from his waistband. His mother's number from her airplane phone scrolled across the screen.

It still blew him away that diplomats and politicians around the world feared his mother's steely nature. Ginger Landis was tough, sure, but she was also fair with a soft heart.

He thumbed the Talk button and turned on the speaker phone. "Hey Mom, what's up?"

Jonah cranked up the Range Rover again so the A/C would keep the car cool on the muggy May afternoon.

"Just checking in on your schedule." Computer keys clicked in the background. Ginger was undoubtedly working while talking, the phone tucked to her ear, holding back her signature grey-blond bob that always stayed as in control as she did. His mom took multitasking to a whole new level: ambassador, wife, mom to four children and three stepchildren and known as a superwoman to boot. "I'm finishing up a summit in Washington. I'll be back in South America before you arrive in Peru for your next project. I'm looking forward to living near my youngest son, even if it's for a short time."

"Me, too." The Landises all spent so much time on the road with their careers, family visits were valued all the more. And while he had his ambassador mother's ear. "Hey, do you have any inside-track info on the deposed king of San Rinaldo?"

She hesitated for a beat before answering. "Why would you ask that?"

"Rumor has it, he's in Argentina." And his mom just happened to be ambassador to a small neighboring country.

"That's the word around town."

He knew his mother would never break security rules, but if she could just point him in the right direction…. "Officially or unofficially?"

"Honestly, I don't know the answer either way," Ginger said, her voice even tighter. He thought of it as her office voice. "Jonah, I can say that there is a compound in Argentina built like a fortress. There's a lot of activity going on inside and very little coming out. Either he's living there, or he's done a good job of creating a red herring."

"Medina has the money to accomplish that."

She laughed lightly. "That, I most definitely can confirm. The old king built a fortune beyond the royal inheritance. The estate continues to multiply itself. We know he has three sons—Carlos, Duarte and Antonio."

And he had a daughter, a daughter no one knew about. Eloisa, so unforgettable and deserving of so much better than she'd gotten from the people who were supposed to care about her.

And what about how *he* had treated her? Damn it all, Eloisa deserved to have someone a hundred percent on her side. "Thanks, Mom. I would appreciate it if you could ask around—quietly, please—about the Medinas."

"Certainly, I'll see what I can find." Curiosity slipped ever so subtly into her voice. "Would you like to tell me why?"

Eloisa's secrets weren't his to share. But the time would certainly come when his family would have to learn he'd married her. The fact that he'd hidden it for the past year was going to piss them off enough. "Is that a requisite to your help?"

"Of course not," she said, backing off smoothly. "I'll let you know if I discover anything soon. Otherwise, I'll see you in a couple of weeks."

"Looking forward to it. And hey, Mom? Love you."

"I love you, too, Jonah," she said softly before disconnecting.

Perhaps talking to his mom had heightened his conscience or maybe he'd just woken up. But regardless, he needed to shower Eloisa with romance as well as sensual enticement. He couldn't be sure how this was going to turn out. But he wasn't walking away or letting her walk away until he was damn sure everything was out in the open and resolved.

Jonah rang the doorbell and waited…and waited. No answer. Eloisa had told him she would be home around this time, but wasn't answering her phone or cell. His instincts burned. Something was off.

She'd given him a key and he intended to use it.

He opened the front door and pushed inside fast. "Eloisa? Are you home?"

His heart slugged his rib cage harder with each step as he searched her empty town house. Then he thought about her patio. The curtains were closed over the French doors. She must be outside relaxing.

He opened the doors to the patio and sure enough the chair was full. But the person most definitely wasn't Eloisa, or even a female.

Jonah scrubbed a hand over his jaw to mask his surprise and figure out what to do about this intruder who looked completely at home. As if he belonged in that chair, at Eloisa's place.

Jealousy cranked into high gear as he summed up his opponent.

A large male sat in the Adirondack chair—dark haired, about six foot three inches. The guy appeared toned, but Jonah had a few pounds on him. He just needed to decide what move to make next.

At first the guy's eyes seemed closed, but when Jonah

studied him further, he could see the man watching ever so carefully through narrow slits.

This guy was ready to pounce.

Jonah blocked the exit. "What the hell are you doing on Eloisa's patio?"

His eyes opened slowly, a haughty smile not far behind. "I've come to visit my sister."

Eight

Well, that took care of the jealousy.

Jonah stared at the guy in front of him claiming to be Eloisa's brother. How could he trust this dude was on the up and up? But then perhaps he was someone who'd just ended up on the wrong patio. After all, the stranger had simply said he was visiting his sister, no name given.

"Who did you say you're looking for?" Jonah asked.

The man smoothed the front of his dark suit jacket—no tie on his white shirt open at the collar. "Where is Eloisa? My sister. Our family lawyer informed us she has concerns. I came right away."

First, he needed to determine if this man could be trusted. Sure, he looked like he could be Eloisa's brother, same dark hair and brown eyes. The aristocratic air was there, too, but his skin was more olive toned.

Because both of his parents were from the Spanish region?

Still, he needed to go on the assumption that this guy knew nothing about Eloisa, that he could be some reporter searching for information...or worse.

Jonah shut the door to the town house and stepped closer to the looming guy in a dark suit. "And your name is?"

He thrust out his hand, lean and ringless, no jewelry other than a pricey watch peeking from his cuff. "I am Duarte. Hello, Jonah Landis."

Jonah jolted. How did the man know him? Sure his family name was easily recognized, but it wasn't like his face was familiar to the average Joe—or in this case, Duarte. "How did you get in here?"

"I jumped the fence."

This guy in a suit hopped fences? Odd, and not the sort of behavior he expected from a prince.

Still the fence apparently posed a security problem he would be addressing shortly. "Do you make a habit of that? Jumping fences? Breaking and entering?"

Duarte—or whoever the hell he was—arched a single brow slowly. "I would have come through the door but she is not here."

"Eloisa doesn't have any brothers. Just a sister named Audrey."

Duarte simply smiled. "Eloisa can clear this up soon enough. And as you noticed, I already know who you are, and I know how you are connected to my sister." He frowned slightly. "I guess that makes us brothers."

Jonah braced his feet, shocked that Eloisa would have

revealed their marriage to anyone, but she said she didn't talk to her family, only communicated through a lawyer. How had this guy found out? And was he even who he claimed to be?

This joker wasn't getting past him. "How about you leave a calling card?"

"Good, good." He nodded curtly. "I like it that she has you to protect her."

That threw him off-balance for a second. The last thing he'd expected was acceptance, encouragement even.

Except he knew better than to be swayed by calculated words. "What did you say you're doing here?"

"I've come to see Eloisa for our father. And you're wise not to trust me. That's best for her."

While they may have found a point of agreement, that didn't mean Jonah intended to back off pushing for whatever he could get out of Duarte. "Where does your father live?"

"Ah, you're tricky, not ever saying the last name either, never giving anything away. Your questions and answers are as nebulous as my own." He gestured toward the French doors. "Let's go inside. Less chance of being overheard."

"I don't think so. Until I hear from Eloisa that you're welcome, we can stay right here."

Duarte glanced around at the small fenced-in patio, vines growing up the wood, a small fountain in the corner with a cement conch shell pouring water into a collection pool.

And only one chair.

Duarte nodded regally. "We will stand here, then, until she returns."

Jonah leaned on the doorframe with affected nonchalance, every muscle still on high alert as he watched the man for any signs of aggression or deception. "So step out on a limb and spill your guts for me."

The strange guy threw his head back and laughed. Finally, he shook his head and quieted. "I travel everywhere. But our father? He can no longer travel anywhere because of his health, and he wants to see his children. You don't have to confirm anything I say. I don't expect you to."

"Dude, I'm thinking it's time to call the cops and arrest you for trespassing."

"I could give you all sorts of identification, but you know that IDs can be purchased. Instead I will tell you a story about the last visit Eloisa made to see her biological family when she was seven—I was seventeen. We all went on a picnic, then walked down the beach. We collected shells. Then Eloisa rode on our father's shoulders while he told her a story about a princess squirrel who could travel anywhere she wanted, anytime."

Damn. This guy could really be...

"Then he sang her songs in Spanish. Does that answer your questions?"

"You've definitely captured my interest enough to delay calling the cops." He might not know everything about Eloisa, but he was certain she would blow a gasket if her family news was splashed all over a police blotter where any newspaper could snatch the scoop.

"I'm not worried."

"You're a cocky bastard."

"Thank you." He slid a finger along his shirt collar,

the first sign that he felt the heat or any tension. "I'm not only here because Eloisa called the lawyer. I am also here because our father is sick."

"Your dad, the guy who sings lullabies in Spanish? How sick is he?"

"I am not the kind to predict worst-case scenarios. Let's just say he's very ill. A visit is in order before the opportunity is lost forever."

How would Eloisa take hearing Enrique Medina could die…or was already dead and she'd missed seeing him? He'd encouraged her to make contact with the old king if for no other reason that to settle the past, and now the clock was ticking. If this man could help persuade her, all the better. And with Jonah by her side, nobody would stand a chance at hurting her ever again.

In fact, there should be some apologizing and amends for needing such a dire prod to make this offer.

"Even if I might think it's in her personal best interest to see him, why should Eloisa—or any woman—visit a family you say she hasn't seen since she was seven? If that's all true, perhaps they should have tried harder to contact Eloisa more often over the years." The silence stretched between them, birds chirping, cars roaring and honking in the distance, even the ocean echoed distantly. "What? No disagreement?"

"Why would I argue when you're absolutely right? That doesn't mean Eloisa could live with doing the wrong thing now."

Jonah checked his watch. Where the hell was Eloisa? She should have been home twenty minutes ago. "Your family is exempt from the rules but she's not? She's supposed to do the right thing regardless? That's bull."

"She is a part of our family."

"Says you. I'm still not sure what you're talking about."

"It's her choice to live this way rather than claim her birthright." He tipped his head to the side. "You didn't know that? She and her mother chose a long time ago not to accept anything from him. He slipped help how he could. Surprise prize winnings, bonuses at work, even a fellowship to travel to Europe."

Eloisa would spit nails if she found out the whole trip was a setup. But given her prickly ways about money, that would have been the only way to get her to accept anything. "Most women I know wouldn't like being manipulated that way."

"Then don't tell her."

"Why are you telling me?" That put him in a tough position, forcing him to keep secrets. He hated lies. Always had. His father had hammered that into his head from a young age. His dad had been in the military before he'd gone into politics. He'd prided himself on being a rarity—a guy who shot straight from the hip, no matter what.

He'd always said the measure of a man was how he acted when no one was looking.

"I am hoping you can hold some sway over her to see my father for what may very well be the last time. She needs persuading. She's a stubborn woman."

"Wait. Hold on for just a damn minute. You say you haven't seen her, but you know all about her personality?"

He shrugged. Did this dude ever relay any emotion? "I never said we haven't kept close watch over her."

She definitely wouldn't like that. Even if this guy

was on the up and up, another possibility still existed. He might be a stalker. Family could stalk. And dealing with that possibility took precedence. "It's time for you and me to leave."

"You and I?"

"I'm not letting you walk away until I am one hundred percent sure who you are. I have connections of my own."

"Fair enough. Just one question first." Duarte's dark eyes narrowed as if zeroing in for the kill. "Who did you think I was when you entered?"

The sound of a key rattling in the front door jarred the silence between them. Damn it all. He should have moved faster. The hinges creaked and Jonah put himself between this man and the path Eloisa would take.

Eloisa filled the open French doors, two grocery bags in her arms and her mouth open wide.

"Duarte?"

Shock nailed her feet to the floor.

Eloisa blinked fast twice, unable to believe her eyes. It couldn't possibly be one of the Medina brothers.... Did he even go by Medina?

But she'd seen a few pictures over the years and she would never forget the faces of her faraway brothers. That summer she'd visited, Duarte had told her of his dream to take a new last name, maybe his mother's maiden name, and move out of the compound, into the world. Duarte had been emphatic about making his own way in the world.

She'd understood that, even at seven, when he'd talked about his plans for "getting the hell off this island."

Island? Until just this moment she'd forgotten that part of talking with him.

From his slick suit, gold watch and some kind of signature cologne, it didn't seem he'd done too badly for himself. She was glad for him if he'd managed to fulfill those dreams of leading his own life.

Although he had managed to send all her evening plans up into smoke.

Eloisa juggled bags of groceries in her arms as her purse dangled from her elbow. She would have set them on the counter when she'd entered the apartment, but she'd heard two voices on the patio and rushed out there, food and all.

She'd traded a favor at work and clocked out early. She was always the one staying late for others who had surprise dates.

It was fun to be on the other side of that for a change. So much for fun.

Both men stepped forward to take a sack from her arms, the food she'd bought with such grand ideas for her evening. She'd taken great care in making her selections at the market. Deciding had been tougher than she expected because what could you serve a tycoon world traveler?

She'd opted for a simple regional classic that might actually have a chance at being heavy enough for a big guy like Jonah—shrimp and grits, with slaw and biscuits on the side. She'd splurged on a bottle of good wine. Well, what she considered good, which could very well be swill by his standards. Not that it mattered now since they had an extra guest.

Her hands shook with nerves and she nearly dropped

her purse. How silly to be this uptight about making dinner for a guy.

Dinner for her husband.

She felt the smile on her face before she ever realized she'd reacted. Seeing him made her happy. Wow. What an awesome—and scary—notion.

Especially with this huge distraction between them. Before she could do anything, she needed to find out why her brother had shown up here so unexpectedly.

The space between them might be short—the patio was microscopic, after all—but there might as well have been a mile between them. Hugging this distant man she'd only spoken to once seemed awkward, even if they shared the same DNA.

And now that she thought about, how strange for him to be here. A trickle of unease tickled inside her stomach. "Come into the town house, gentlemen. Let's get those groceries inside before the shrimp spoils in this heat."

Eloisa flashed a grateful smile to Jonah. She couldn't miss the tic in the corner of his eye, but wasn't sure what put it there.

"Duarte," she touched her brother's arm lightly, "welcome. You might as well stay for supper. Unless you've already made other plans?"

Once in the kitchenette, Jonah's somber gaze stopped her midramble. "Your brother said he needs to talk to you."

"Right, of course. We have a lot to catch up on, I'm sure." God, this felt so surreal, having her brother here after so many years.

She put away groceries on autopilot. Holding a wrapped and taped bag of shrimp in her hands, she pivoted toward the refrigerator and almost slammed smack into her brother. "Sorry, uhm, not much space."

"How did you recognize me?" Duarte asked simply, with no preamble.

She looked into dark eyes identical to her own, ones that had also stared back at her from her father's face during that memorable encounter years ago. "You look just like him."

"Our father?" Duarte blinked slowly, his eyes more enigmatic than their dad's. The old king's eyes had been mostly sad. "You were only seven years old."

"But Enrique was younger then." Although in her childish view he'd seem so very ancient. "And my mother kept a picture of him from when they, uh, knew each other. She let me hide it in my sock drawer sometimes. I mixed it in with fan clippings and posters so no one would ever guess. And it's obvious I'm right."

She couldn't bear this standoff positioning. Eloisa strode past to shove the bag of seafood into the refrigerator. She had to be in control of something, even if it was making sure the shrimp didn't spoil. "Why are you here? Now?" Eloisa froze as a horrible possibility avalanched over her, far more chilling than the blast from the fridge. She spun back around. "Is he dead?"

"He's alive," Duarte reassured her quickly, even though his somber face gave her pause. "I'm here because you contacted the lawyer. And we would have been in touch with you soon anyway. Our father is sick, most likely dying. He wants to see his children."

"How many of us are there?" Damn, where had that cruel response come from? From the deep recesses of her late-night childhood fears and tears, no doubt.

Jonah placed a comforting, steadying hand between

her shoulder blades, while nudging the refrigerator closed with his foot.

Duarte stuffed his hands in his pants pockets. "Just you, our two brothers and, of course, me."

"Pardon me if I'm not so sure." Eloisa breathed deeply to expand the tightness rapidly constricting her rib cage with tension. "I am sorry he's sick, but I don't think we have anything to say to one another. Not after so many years."

She expected an argument, smooth persuasive reasons why she was wrong. But Duarte simply shrugged.

"Okay then. I'll let him know the message was delivered and you declined. Since you don't have any questions, I've completed my task."

That was it? He was leaving?

Duarte slid a card onto the sofa end table, simple white vellum with a number printed in raised, black ink. He anchored it with a paperweight. "You can contact me when you decide to see him."

When?

Another decade or two?

Duarte had simply shown up, rocked her balance until she didn't know what she thought, and then he was gone again before she could gather her thoughts. He hadn't come to *see* her. He'd come to pass along information. God, she was such an idiot, still hiding hopes deep in her heart like those pictures of her biological family tucked under her socks.

She wanted to cry but her eyes were dry after all these years.

Jonah stepped around her, nearly nose to nose with her brother. "I'll walk you to the door."

"No need." Duarte nodded to Eloisa, starting toward

the front door. "I'll let our father know you will be visiting soon."

She stifled the urge to scream out her frustration. Who did these Medina men think they were to blast into a person's life once every decade or so and wreak total havoc? "You're assuming a lot."

He pivoted back toward her fluidly. "There are many times when my life has relied on my ability to read people."

Duarte Medina slipped out of the door as quietly and quickly as he'd arrived.

Jonah rubbed between her shoulder blades. "Are you all right?"

"I'm fine. Totally fine. Why wouldn't I be? It was just five minutes out of my life. No big deal. Now he's gone and everything's back to normal again." She pulled away and yanked open the refrigerator. "I'll start supper."

His hands landed on her shoulders, squeezing gently with a sympathy and comfort that swept away her defenses. She shattered inside from endless vows that she didn't care if her father never fought for her. And when her brothers struck out on their own, they never even bothered to contact her. Years of being everyone's support and nobody's princess crashed down on her until she hurt so bad inside she couldn't find any corner of her soul to hide and escape.

She had nowhere to go except straight into Jonah's arms.

Nine

Eloisa blocked out the ache in her heart left from her brother's shocking visit and focused on Jonah. Just Jonah, with her, both of them hopefully naked very, very soon.

She wrapped her arms around his neck and flattened herself to him. He stumbled back a step and nearly slammed into the kitchen counter.

"Whoa." He gripped her hips, steadying them both so they didn't knock off the remaining groceries or tumble to the tile floor. "Let's slow this down a minute and think things through. I know you're upset—"

"Damn straight, I'm upset. I'm angry and hurt and confused and want it all to go away. You can fix that for me, so let's get to it."

She plastered her lips to his, opened, demanded. The ever-ready attraction between them blazed to life on contact, thank goodness. She welcomed the blissful sensation expanding within her, pushing everything else to the far corners. Less pain.

Total pleasure.

Muscles in his chest and arms twitched and flexed under her searching fingers. "Eloisa, I hear you and I understand. And God knows, I'm more than glad to comply until you're not able to think or talk, but I also have to know you're not going to bolt out of here afterward before I even have time to pull on a pair of boxers."

Eloisa nuzzled along his ear, kissing, nipping, whispering soft gusts of air over his skin as she buried her face in his hair. "We're in my home. That makes leaving a lot tougher for me."

"But not impossible," he insisted even as his hand slid down to cup her bottom and lift her closer, more intimately against him until she could feel the fly on his jeans straining against the thickening length of him.

"We're here to resolve things," he said, "not make them more complicated between—" He clasped her hand already making fast work of his jeans snap. "Take a breather, for now, anyway."

She flipped her hands to link in his as she met his eyes square on. "Jonah, look around you. Think. What did I bring in when I got home from work? Dinner. Wine. I planned a romantic meal because after what we did—" she paused, suddenly breathless at just the mention, the memory "—after the way you made me feel, I've been thinking about finishing this every second since. I've been planning what I want to do to you, how to make you every bit as crazy as you make me."

"Eloisa," he groaned, loosening his hold on her hands

until she flattened her palm to his fly. "You already make me crazy just by walking through my mind, much less the room."

"Then it's time to do something about that."

She peeled his black polo shirt over his head. Was it only last night he pulled up at her sister's party? It seemed like a lifetime ago, as if the past year apart hadn't even happened.

But it had and oh God, she couldn't let herself think about that. Better to focus on now, with him. He was right. They did need time together to work through their feelings or she—he too?—would spend forever wondering, wanting.

Growling low, he tunneled his hands under her dress, bunching it up and away in a deft sweep that left her breathless and bare, other than her icy-blue lace bra and panties. "Do you have any idea how gorgeous you look right this second?" He reached behind her to pull the scarf from her ponytail, releasing her hair. "I've lost a lot of sleep this past year thinking about you like this."

"I hope you're going to lose even more tonight." Her hair teased along her skin until she was ready to scream for a more insistent touch.

Thank goodness he didn't need any further encouragement. He kissed her again, backing her as he moved forward, their legs tangling in the desperate dance toward the stairs, which stopped them short.

But not for long.

Jonah ducked his shoulder into her midsection and lifted her into a fireman carry. Eloisa squealed, but certainly wasn't about to tell him no because he was making fast tracks for her bedroom.

Once in her room, he flipped her over and onto the

antique bed with a smooth sweep, the wooden thrift store find she'd painstakingly whitewashed. She bounced once in the middle of the pouffy comforter. A pink tulip print hung over the headboard.

Her haven where no one entered.

Until Jonah.

He traced her collarbone. "When I watched you sleep before, I fantasized about what kind of jewels would look best nestled right here." He skimmed his mouth along after his fingers' path.

"And here." He nipped her ears.

"I didn't think I slept," she gasped as his mouth trekked lower, "for even a minute that night."

"I didn't need more than a minute to picture you in my world."

Her breath caught as his words sunk in. Her eyes met his, so deeply somber for a second, then he smiled and she lost the chance to decipher what she'd seen.

"Besides," he said, shuffling away the seriousness, "I have an active imagination." He traced her belly button with his tongue, flicking her simple silver ring between his teeth. "Most definitely a diamond here."

Jonah kissed her hip, his hand sliding down her leg and scattering thoughts as quickly as the rest of his clothes and their underwear. "And anklets. There are so many options for stones I would have specially set for you to wear right there for trips to the beach."

A ceiling fan clicked, gusting over her bare skin and ruffling airy sheers that hung from bamboo rods. She felt like those curtains, fluttering and writhing with every brush and breath of Jonah's along her body. She grasped at his back, his taut buttocks, his chest, touching and tasting frenetically in contrast to his smooth exploration.

How could she be this hungry for Jonah when by all rights, he had taken care of her needs just a few hours before in her office? That should have at least eased the edge, but instead seemed to have only made her ache for more. Then he slid up along her, over her, the solid weight of him anchoring her to the bed and the moment so perfectly.

She slid the arch of her foot along his leg, opening for him, wanting him, welcoming him inch by thick, delicious inch.

"Shhh..." he whispered in her ear although she couldn't for the life of her remember what she'd said or asked for. "Patience. We'll get there."

Unable to wait, she slid her hand between them and clasped him, caressed him, coaxed him until his hands shook, too. He reached to the floor, to his pants, his hand returning with a condom. He tore open the packet and sheathed himself before she had time to do more than be grateful one of them was thinking clearly enough to take care of birth control.

Finally, he was inside her again, the pressure of him familiar and new at the same time, but then Jonah had always been an unpredictable mass of contradictions that shuffled her perfectly ordered world.

Braced on his elbows, he stared down at her, holding her with his vivid blue eyes. His jaw, tight with restraint, told her he ached for this as much as she did. She'd been tipsy when they'd been together before, but this time she was stone-cold sober, aware of every moment and sensation. And it was even better. Her senses were heightened, sharp, *responsive.*

He moved over her while the bed rocked under her. He was so large and gentle, completely focused on her and…oh my, what a heady feeling that was after so long in shadows. She wanted to stay right here and bask in the sparks showering through her, but knew there was no way in hell this could last. Maybe next time… There had to be a next time.

Frantic to hold on to the feelings, to him, she clenched around him.

"Eloisa…" His eyes closed, his jaw clamping tighter as he said her name again and again, telling her exactly how often he'd thought of her, the other ways he dreamed of adorning her in jewels, erotic images and possibilities she'd never considered and now couldn't forget.

She tried to answer, but words… She had nothing except a moan of increasing need. Jonah's hands fisted in the pillow on either side of her head, his head dropping to rest on her brow.

His hair slid forward, covering most of his face. She cupped his cheeks, her fingers playing with the wavy strands and wondered if he'd ever considered letting it grow longer. Somehow it seemed more lord of manor, leader of the land, with its extra length. He was the epitome of fairy-tale fantasies she'd only barely dared acknowledge to herself.

More, she wanted more of him, of this, of the whole fantasy. She hooked her heels behind his back and arched upward, accepting him deeper. Her fingernails scored desperate furrows down his back as the intensity gripped her, begging for release. This couldn't last much longer. It was too intense. Too much of everything and already the ending built and tightened and tingled through her in ripples she couldn't hold back any longer.…

She didn't bother trying to hold back the shout of pleasure. Jonah thrust faster. She gripped his back harder. Sparks glinted behind her eyes much like the jewels he'd detailed earlier. With one last prolonged thrust, he buried himself inside her…and stayed, his face in her hair, his groan against her ear until his arms gave way and he rolled to his back, taking her, replete, alongside him.

His hand slid over her stomach, his finger tracing a circle around her belly button, his breathing ragged. "We're definitely going shopping for a diamond soon."

Her heartbeat tumbled over itself at the mention of diamonds…until she realized he meant navel rings, not engagement. Technically, they were already married anyway. But for how long?

Jonah continued to draw lazy circles with the backs of his fingers. A murmur of unease echoed inside her as she thought of their baby that had rested there, tragically too briefly. She should tell him, and she would, but how could she just toss it into the mix right now? More importantly, how could she trust he would stay? He'd made it clear he'd been angry with her for leaving. She couldn't help but wonder if he'd come looking for revenge.

Could he be that calculated? She had no way of knowing because as she'd told him before, they didn't know each other well enough to be certain of anything. Her best bet? Wait—a couple of days, perhaps?—to let the dust settle. To let her mind clear while she got her bearings. Then she would tell him about the baby they'd lost.

As the fan dried the perspiration on her body, she

wondered how long she could selfishly take from him before the truth put this tenuous connection to the test.

Reclining in Eloisa's antique bed, Jonah tested a lock of her hair between his fingers, so long and soft. He'd wanted to have her and walk away. He'd expected to put an end to their unfinished business by being with her one last time, and instead? He couldn't imagine how the hell he would let her go.

If they weren't married, he would have asked her to travel with him. Why not ask her anyway? Certainly they couldn't solve anything continents apart.

He knew her secret now, after all. Sure, being with him brought an added level of attention, but her heritage could too easily come out no matter what in an unexpected instant. Better to be prepared.

He was the man who could keep her safe.

Now he had to persuade her to go with him to Peru after her sister's wedding. And wouldn't waking up beside Eloisa daily be a pleasure? Not that he expected her to agree right away. She was stubborn, and she had a blind loyalty to her sister and stepfather that made him grind his teeth in frustration.

He needed to show her the way their lives could blend, that she deserved better from people. He cared about her in a way her self-absorbed family never had.

Jonah took in the every curve draped in a cotton sheet, a light purple. She looked damn good in that color. Natural purple diamonds were among the rarest. Like her. But he intended to shower her with jewels *and* his undivided attention.

He released the strand over her breast where it curled

to rest around the creamy swell. "I've missed you so damn much this year."

"We barely knew each other then." She rasped a fingernail lightly down his chest. "And things are happening so fast again now. Can't we just enjoy this moment?"

"Think how much we've learned in just a day of really talking. Let's talk some more." He splayed his hand over her rib cage, then upward to toy with a pert nipple. "I've missed being with you, seeing you, feeling you move underneath as you whisper how much you need me, need more of what I can give you."

She laughed, covering his mouth with her hand. "Okay, okay. I get the picture."

He nipped her finger, then drew it in to soothe away the sting with his tongue. "You can't tell me you never thought about those days together."

"Of course I thought about it." The sheets rustled as she sat up, hugging her knees to her chest. "You have a way of making an impression on a person that isn't easy to forget. Staying away was my only option for keeping my sanity."

"I make you crazy? Good." He swept her hair forward over her shoulder and traced down her neck to her spine, one vertebrae at a time. "Let's see if I can do it again."

"You know you do, on so many levels." Sighing, she rested her cheek on her knees as he made his way down her back.

"Then let's *talk* some more."

"I'm still finding my footing. I'm not exactly the tumultuous type, you know. Let's deal with the most basic level for starters."

"You've got a one-track mind right now." And while he sure as hell wasn't going to complain about that, he also noticed the way she wouldn't meet his gaze. Not a good sign.

She smiled, still not looking at him, instead inching the sheet ever so slowly off him. "What's so wrong with a married couple having sex? Lots of sex. In every room and vehicle at our disposal. We can talk the whole time. In fact, I've already got a pretty good idea of some things I'd like to say to you, too."

He clasped her wrist, stopping her, holding her until finally she met his gaze. "I'm being serious here, Eloisa. We shared something special just now. We'd be fools to just toss that away again. But for it to work, I need you to be honest with me this time."

Eloisa clutched a pillow to her stomach, the shadows and pain so intense in her eyes he wanted to scrap the whole conversation and just hold her. What in the world could have hurt her so deeply? He started to ask, but she pressed her fingertips to his mouth.

"Jonah, I hear what you're saying, and while I joke about all that married sex, honestly, in my mind—" she tapped her temple "—we're divorced. We have been for a long while. It's going to take time before I can reconcile all these changes. So much is happening so fast…I want to trust it…trust you."

"Then do it."

"That's easy for you to say. You're adventurous by nature." She eased her wrist free then clasped his hand. "Just this—" she raised their linked fingers "—is risky for me."

"I don't believe that, not after the woman I met a year ago." He paused, realizing, holy hell, she really was scared. There was a side to her he hadn't met in Spain. He honestly didn't know the woman he'd married. And if he intended to stand a chance with her now, he needed to push harder than he had before.

He had to understand her in order to keep her. He searched for the best place to start. "Are you upset about your brother showing up tonight? Hearing your father is ill had to be upsetting. Are you going to see him? Is that what's wrong?"

She looked down at the bedspread for so long he wondered if she would answer. Would she decide to cut him off at the knees? He wouldn't be pushed aside again without seeing this through.

"Eloisa?" He tipped her chin up with a knuckle. "I asked about your father."

"My father...right...uh, I haven't decided." Her grip eased on the hugged pillow. "I don't even know what to think about Duarte showing up here. It was so unexpected, I'll have to give this more thought."

"But you believed him when he said your father is ill." He sat up beside her, stroking her hair back from her face.

She didn't flinch away.

"My lawyer does keep me informed to a certain degree. I know what my brothers look like. They were already teenagers when I saw them before. Even if I don't know where everyone lives." She laughed dryly. "Actually I don't want to know. Being responsible for their safety would be too scary."

He didn't like the way they left her out here, unprotected. Then it hit him that he couldn't let her go. *He* couldn't leave her out here unprotected. There weren't many who could protect her at the level she needed.

But he was a Landis.

And even though there had been times he'd bucked the Landis conventions, right now he welcomed every bit of power the Landis influence could bring if it kept Eloisa from being hurt in any way—physically or emotionally—by her Medina ties.

The Landis influence and money could also bring her peace in other ways, pampering that by rights should have been hers from the start. "You need a distraction."

"You've done a mighty fine job of that tonight." Looping an arm over his shoulders, she leaned against him, kissing him with unmistakable promise.

His pulse jackhammered in his chest, throbbing through his veins thicker, lower, urging him to act now. He steadied his breathing and his resolve.

Stick to the plan. More time with her. Show her how well she could fit in his world, how easily she could leave her old one behind. "I'll up the ante. You took the afternoon off. Any chance you can call in sick for a couple of days?"

Interest lit in her eyes, followed by wariness. "I have to help Audrey."

"When's her next shindig?"

"Joey's family is throwing a party—" a tentative hope replaced the wariness on her face "—but it isn't until the weekend."

"So that's not a problem for you as long as you come back. Can she handle her own plans for two days?"

"I could take care of things by phone." Her words

tumbled over each other faster. "The bridesmaids' fittings are already done."

"That just leaves your job at the library. Can you get time off?"

"There are people who owe me favors." Her slow seductive smile turned him inside out. "It depends on what you have to offer."

"Trust me," he urged her, determined to make that happen on every level. "You won't be disappointed."

Ten

"Open your eyes."

Late afternoon nipping her arms with prickly heat, Eloisa pulled Jonah's hands from her face and gasped in awe. She stood on top of a building overlooking a massive canyon sprawled out in a craggy display of orange, brown and bronze rock. Wind tore at her clothes with an ends-of-the-earth force. She inched to the edge, grasped the scrolled iron railing and found she stood on top of a mammoth hacienda-style retreat, built on the edge of a cliff corner.

When they'd left Pensacola earlier this afternoon, Jonah had kept the windows closed on the airplane and the limo windows had been shaded. By their fourth hour traveling she was nearing the edge of her trust factor, but wow, had her patience ever paid off.

The property was deserted. Scaffolding remained

visible on one side of the expansive resort building, though no workers filled the platform levels of it today, their work apparently complete for the week. The historic hacienda appeared to have had a recent makeover, the scent of fresh paint mingling with the light fragrance of a potted crepe myrtle nearby.

She leaned farther over the rail. Terra-cotta pots were strategically placed around the patio with a variety of cacti—prickly pear, blooming hedgehog, spiking organ pipe, saguaro, even a towering Joshua tree. Below, in a stomach-lurching drop, away from the sculpted rooftop garden, cacti dotted the landscape in sparse and erratic abandon, no less beautiful. "This is magnificent. Where exactly are we?"

An eagle banked into a dive—*down, down, down*—so far it seemed impossible to continue, then it swooped upward again into the purple-blue sky. Warm sun counteracted the dry breeze pinning her cotton halter dress to her skin.

"Does it matter where we are?" He dismissed the luxurious digs around them and pointed outward. "Can't it be beautiful just because it is, rather than because it has a fancy pedigree attached?"

She snorted on a laugh. "Spoken like a savvy investor who can see the possibilities in previously unappreciated properties."

He clapped a palm over his chest. "I'm wounded you would think I'm so calculating."

"You're practical, and I admire that." In fact, the more she learned about him the more she realized how she'd stereotyped him from the start. "You're not at all the reckless playboy I mistook you for last year."

"Don't go romanticizing me. I simply found a

job that suits my wandering feet and desire to create luxurious digs."

She started to laugh, then stopped to look beyond his casual dismissal of her compliment. "I think it's more than that for you."

"Maybe. I'm a guy. I don't analyze like you women. I just know that I like transforming things others have overlooked." He smiled distractedly before his eyes cleared again. "We're in West Texas, by the way. I figured that was about as far as I could go without you freaking out over the secrecy or worrying about getting back for your sister's party."

"You guessed right." She accepted his conversational shift for now since he actually had shared more than she expected. "I'm glad I took the leap of faith and joined you."

Thank goodness Audrey hadn't been upset by the prospect of her leaving for a few days. In fact, Eloisa had been surprised at how readily her sister had encouraged her to go away. Only a week ago, Audrey had been hyperventilating over punch flavors, insisting she needed Eloisa and the caterer's input on everything. Brides were notoriously edgy. She could understand and be patient.

Yet suddenly Audrey seemed calm. Go figure.

Regardless, that seemed a universe away now. She'd packed so carefully for this trip, choosing her most silky underwear, remembering to pack cologne, and her favorite apple lip gloss he'd so intensely—deliciously— noted in the library. Just this morning she'd even spied him sniffing the tube at her dressing table.

Yes, she'd taken care in choosing what to bring along, cautiously pinning high hopes on this outing.

She wanted reassurance they had a chance at a future before she could open herself up to him totally. This compressed time together, away from distractions offered that opportunity.

She trailed her fingers along the curved railing. "So this place is your work? I'm very impressed."

She couldn't miss his artistry as she looked down at the structure built in such a way she couldn't distinguish the old from the new.

"The resort is set to open in another month once the decorators have finished their gig inside. Working this place landed me a contract in Peru to pull off something similar with a nineteenth-century structure. It'll need expansion as well as renovation." He shook his head. "Enough about work. We're here to relax, alone up here where no one can see us and no one will dare interrupt. Now it's time for the real reason I brought you."

Jonah turned her to the right along the corner for even more canyon panorama and, just to her side...

Rippling water slipped off the edge of the building, somehow disappearing. She pivoted to find a rooftop pool, but unlike any she'd ever seen before. It stretched off the end of the building and seemed to blend into the horizon.

"Jonah?"

"It's an infinity pool," he announced.

It was magnificent. "Infinity pool. That makes sense in theory—" given the way it blended into the canyon view "—but I don't understand how."

Her feet drew her closer to the clear waters swirling over the blue tiles, sunlight sparkling diamondlike dots along the surface. The romanticism reached to her heart already softened by a night spent in Jonah's arms.

Even now, she could feel her body reacting to just his presence, the knowledge that she could have him right now and indulge herself in everything he had to offer. And he did offer her so very much on so many levels.

Eloisa reached for his hand, listening to his explanation and letting herself dream. Maybe, just maybe her instincts had been right that all they needed was more time.

Jonah linked his fingers more firmly in hers. "The pool is architecturally designed with the edge smoothed out until it seems to extend forever, blending into the horizon. Some call it a negative edge. A side is built slightly lower with a catch basin that pumps water back into the pool."

"That sounds extremely complicated." She didn't have to be an architect to tell this required incredible talent and expertise. She imagined the least miscalculation during construction could crumble the cliff. Much like the delicate balance and attention to detail needed in building a relationship. "Tell me more."

"An infinity pool can be built on a rooftop or into the side of a mountain or right against a larger body of water." He stretched a hand toward the horizon. "The effect is the same. While you float and stare out, boundaries disappear."

"Possibilities are limitless." That sounded good in theory, but felt scary for a woman who found comfort and safety in the cool confines of her dimly lit library stacks. She would take it one deep breath at a time, because the thought of turning back scared her even more than standing here at the precipice.

His arm dropped to his side. "There's an infinity pool in Hong Kong on the roof of a hotel that's the most amazing thing I've ever seen." He squeezed her fingers. "Wanna go?"

"What? Now?" Startled by his abrupt offer, she backed away a step, instinctively craving the safety of even a few inches away from wide-open abandon. "We just got to Texas. I'm still soaking everything in."

"But you want to go."

Did she? Could she just drop everything at his whim and see the world?

"I think so, maybe," she said to the adventure. To him. This didn't seem the place for stark realities and secrets. It was the ultimate place to lose yourself. Here, she didn't have to worry about what it meant to be a Medina or a Landis. "For a short time perhaps, but—"

"Quit thinking about afterward. Enjoy the now, here at the edge of a canyon. Take a risk, librarian lady."

She bristled instinctively. "Who says there's anything wrong with being a librarian in Pensacola, Florida?"

He tugged her closer to him, his hand soothing along her waist. "I never said there was anything wrong with your profession. I'm just offering you the chance to *experience* the books. You can have it all."

Stark realities intruded all the same, memories of her mother, memories of her own, even glimpses of her father's pain-filled eyes. Consequences for stepping out of her safety zone could be huge. "They killed my father's wife, you know. They assassinated her while trying to get to him." She looked into his eyes for answers, for reassurance. "Doesn't your family worry about that kind of lurking threat? Your father may have died in a car wreck, but you had to be aware of danger at an early age."

God knows, she had worried for her mother. And in

the darkest, quietest times of night, she even worried for herself.

The wind lifted Jonah's hair and flapped the edges of his sports coat. "I hear you, and yes, my family has lived with the reality of possible kidnappings and bribes and threats because of political stands. It's not fair, but that's how things are even if we gave away the money and left the public scene tomorrow. No one would believe we didn't have something hidden somewhere. The influence remains and we have a responsibility to use it wisely." He cupped her face in his sun-warmed hands. "You can't live your life dictated by fears."

She pulled out of his arms. Leaning against, leaning *on* him would be too easy.

"Tell that to Enrique Medina." Her chest went tight. How much longer did her father have left? "He's spent nearly three decades hidden away from the world, living out his life."

"If I knew where he was, I would tell him face-to-face."

"I thought you would have learned that when you found me." Maybe she'd hoped he knew so she wouldn't have to make the choice to search. Jonah would know, blindfold her and take her there. And only now did she realize she'd hoped he would do just that today. Good Lord, she was a coward.

"Medina keeps his secrets well."

"I guess he does." As did his daughter. Guilt pinched over what she should explain to Jonah.

He drew her to his side again. "What do you think he wants to talk to you about?"

"I have absolutely no idea. Probably just to say goodbye, which I should probably go along with. It sounds simple enough. Except I have this sense that if I step into his world, I will have made an irrevocable change." She blinked back tears until they welled back up inside her soul. She tipped her head up to look at him. "Jonah, we should talk."

He thumbed under her eye, swiping away dampness that must have leaked anyway. "I think we've done enough talking for one day."

She wanted to agree, reminding herself of her resolve to wait until she was sure he would stay before risking the pain that would come from sharing all. Still, her conscience whispered. "Seriously, Jonah, I need to tell you—"

"Seriously, stop arguing. We can talk about whatever you want later." He slid his other arm around her and pulled her flush against him again, rekindling the desire that had been barely banked all afternoon. "Right now, I want to make love with you in this pool while we look out at infinity."

Infinity.

Forever.

They could have it all. She could have the time to tell him the things that needed explaining. The possibilities truly seemed as limitless of the edge of that pool reclaiming and holding everything in an endless cycle.

Jonah kissed her and she allowed herself to hope.

Jonah hauled Eloisa closer, sensing something shifting inside her, tension flowing from her in a tide as tangible as the infinity pool streaming away. He didn't know what exactly brought about the change, but he wasn't one to argue when it brought her warm and willing into his arms.

"Inside," she whispered, "to your suite."

"Here," he answered. "We're alone. No one can see us, of that I'm certain. I designed this patio with complete privacy in mind."

Over the past few months, he'd tortured himself with fantasies of bringing her up here and baring her body to the sun. "Do you trust me?"

"I can't think of anything more exciting than making love to you out here in the open." Her arms slid around his neck, her fingers in his hair. "I want to trust you."

He noticed wanting to trust wasn't the same as giving trust, but still a step in the right direction. And since he had her in his arms, ready to have sex outdoors? No way in hell did he intend to dwell on semantics.

Eloisa slid his sports coat from his shoulders, his shirt open at the collar, no tie to bother with removing. Backing him toward the double lounger beside the pool, she toyed with one button at a time, unveiling his chest until the shirt whipped behind him in the wind.

Smiling, Jonah shook his head no and danced her toward the pool instead. Her eyes widened momentarily before she grinned in return. Eloisa kicked off her sandals and trailed a toe in the water.

Her sigh of pleasure left him throbbing against his zipper damn near painfully. But soon…so soon…

He toyed with the tie behind her neck holding her halter dress in place. A simple tug set it free and falling away to reveal her breasts to the sun. He nudged the fabric down around and past her waist to pool at her feet. She kicked it away behind her, their clothes littering the stone tiles, lifting on the wind and catching on the furniture.

Eloisa glanced over her shoulder with a flicker of concern. He guided her face back toward him again. "To hell with the clothes. We brought suitcases. I'll buy you more."

"In that case…" She unbuckled his belt, slipped it free and flung it out into the canyon, with a *flick* and a *snap*.

Her uninhibited laughter rode the wind along with the rest of their clothes and his shoes until they stood bare in the open together. Her breasts brushed his chest as she took him in her hand and stroked until he worked to keep his feet steady under him.

He clasped her wrist and draped her arm back over his shoulder. Leaning, he scooped her up against his chest and started down the stone steps, the sun-warmed water churning around his legs, his hips, around his waist and higher until he slid her to her feet again. The light waves lapped around her shoulders and she leaned into him with buoyancy.

He slid his hand between her legs, the essence of her arousal mixing with the water, leaving her slick to his touch. He tucked two fingers into her warm silken grip, stroking inside, his thumb teasing outside. Sighing, she pressed closer to him just as she'd done in the library, so hot, so responsive. So damn perfect he almost came undone from just the feel of her on his hand.

She sprinkled frenetic kisses over his face, working her way to his ear. "I want you inside me, totally, I want it all here. Now," she demanded.

"More than willing to accommodate," he growled.

Jonah cupped her bottom and lifted. She wrapped her

slick wet legs around his waist, the core of her pressing closer to him, her damp heat against him. He throbbed from wanting to be inside her again. And again. How often would be enough?

She slid down on the length of him.

"Birth control," he groaned into her ear. Only now did he realize they'd forgotten and he wanted to kick himself off the damn cliff for being so reckless with her. He never, never forgot. He always protected.

Her arms clamped tighter around him. "I'm on the Pill."

"You didn't mention that when we were together before."

"My thoughts aren't always clear around you, especially when we're naked. Now can we stop with the talking and move on to the fun part? I want this—I want you. How convenient for us both that you happen to be my husband, after all."

But she hadn't known that for the past months when they'd both assumed their divorce had gone through. He didn't want to know why she'd used it in the year they were apart. He chose instead to focus on how glad to have that last concern taken away so he could...

Plunge inside her.

Her head flung back, her wet hair floating behind her. He dipped his head to take the pink pert tip of her breast in his mouth. He teased her with his tongue, gently with his teeth, using his mouth in all the ways he wanted to touch her but couldn't since he held her, guided her.

The cool jet of water from the side of the pool didn't so much as take an edge off the heat pumping through him. Water sluiced between them as they writhed against each other. Her hair floated behind her, long and dark. Beads of water clung to her face, her shoulders. He sipped from her skin, the taste of her overriding any chlorination.

He palmed her upright until her head rested on his shoulder. "I want you to see."

To look out at the endless view, the endless possibilities *he* could give her.

Eloisa gripped his arms, her nails furrowing into his skin. He welcomed the tender bite into his flesh, the tangible sign that she felt the same frenetic need.

Water lapped around them, encircling them in a vortex as he clasped her closer. He had to make this last. He refused to lose her. While they'd made progress today, still he sensed her reservations. Whatever was holding her back, he needed to reassure her she didn't have to be afraid, because he could take care of her.

He *would* take care of her, sensually, physically and any other way she needed.

The primal drive to make her his clawed through him, intensified by the open elements. He'd come here for her and found it tapped into something inside himself he hadn't anticipated. Something basic and undeniable. He thrust inside her as her hips rolled against him, her breath hitching against his neck, faster as her skin began to flush with…

Gasping, she flung her head back again, her back arching, her eyes closed tight. He watched and savored every moment of her sweet release across her face, echoed in the spasms of her moist clamp around him, drawn out until…hell, couldn't hold back.

He surged inside her. The sunset shot purple, pink and orange spiking through the horizon as sharp and deep as the pleasure blasting through him. She was his, damn it. No more barriers, boundaries, secrets.

He'd won her.

Eleven

Eloisa surrendered to the languid weightlessness of floating in the water and watching the stars overhead. How blessedly freeing to put the world and worries on hold for once. She wasn't a wife, a sister, a daughter.

Today, tonight, she was simply a woman and a lover.

After Jonah had brought her to such intense completion while she stared over the infinity pool edge, they'd held on to each other for…well…she didn't know how long. At some point she'd floated away and he'd begun swimming lazy laps. They were simply coexisting in the water without talking. Being together so perfectly, even in silence, surpassed anything she'd imagined gaining from this time away.

The near-silent sluice of his arms through the water announced his presence a second before he passed. She reached out, grazing him with her fingers. His head slid from the water and he stood beside her, not even panting.

He shook his head, swiping back his hair. "Are you ready to go in? There's a cold supper waiting in the refrigerator."

She looped an arm around his neck and let her feet sink. "It's getting late. I just don't want this day to end."

"We're not even close to finished."

Scooping an arm behind her legs, Jonah pulled her to his chest again, carrying her dripping wet into the shallow end, up the stone stairs just as he'd brought her in earlier. Rivulets of water slid along her skin, caressing, then cooling in the early evening air. Her breasts pulled tight and she couldn't miss the way his gaze lingered appreciatively.

This new ease with each other was as thrilling as his hands on her body, but also a little frightening. She pulled her focus in on the moment, on these stolen days she'd promised herself.

He cleared the last step and walked under the covered porch, elbowing open double doors to a penthouse suite. The hacienda décor reminded her of the Old World Spanish manor home Jonah had rented a year ago. Was this simply the style he was drawn to naturally, or had he somehow been as caught up in their time together as she had been?

Bold tapestries hung on the goldenrod-colored walls. She bypassed surveying all else for later. Right now, her focus stayed on the king-sized bed, definitely a reproduction of the carved walnut headboard from the room they'd shared in Madrid. Linen was draped from the boxed frame overhead, wafting in the wind from the open doors.

He set her on the thick layers of cream, tan and burnt sienna, piped in red. On her back, she inched up the bed, soaking up the amazing view of muscled, naked Jonah against the backdrop of the pool blending into the horizon. He ducked into the bathroom and came back with two fluffy towels. Jonah passed one to her and began toweling his wet hair with the other.

Eloisa knew her own sopping locks would take eons to dry out so she turbaned the soaked mass. He pitched aside his towel and gave his head a quick shaggy shake before settling beside her on the pile of feather pillows.

Tracing lazy circles on his bare chest, she stared out the open double doors, the fresh air swirling the scent of Jonah and a hint of chlorination she would forever find arousing. "I can't believe the awesome sense of privacy here."

"That's something I work to achieve with any of my projects—" his hand settled on her hip, curving to a perfect fit "—seclusion, even if there are multiple units in the resort."

"You learned the value of privacy growing up in the public eye."

"To a degree." He slid an arm behind his head, his eyes focused on the faraway. "My parents did their best to shield us, make sure we didn't feel wealthy or different."

"They sound wonderful. You're lucky to have had parents like that."

"I know." He shifted uncomfortably, then smiled as

if to lighten the mood. "And if I ever forget, my mother will most definitely remind me."

She nudged her toes against his foot. "You must have been an adventurous child, looking for new territories to explore."

"I may have given my folks a heart palpitation or two." He trapped her foot between his.

"Today, I most certainly benefited from your adventurous spirit. Thank you." She stretched upward to kiss him, not long or intense, just holding and enjoying the contact for the sake of simply kissing, even if it wouldn't go further. Yet. She tucked back against his chest. "I never even dreamed of making love on a beach, much less something like this. The fear that someone could stumble upon us, rob us, even worse…"

She shivered and wished she could have attributed it to the wind kicking in faster as night set.

Jonah unfolded a downy throw blanket draped along the end of the bed, pulling it up to their waists. "You have to know I would never put you at risk."

Eloisa snuggled closer. "Not intentionally, no."

"Not ever." He stroked her shoulders. "You're tensing up again. Stop it."

She stifled a laugh at the notion he thought he could fix anything, even the state of her muscles…and then she realized she had relaxed again after all.

"There you go." Jonah trailed his fingers down her spine. "That's more like it."

"It must be the sound of the water echoing in through the canyon, the closeness to nature at its most soothing and stark all at once. How could anyone stay tense?"

"So you like making love outdoors? I'm totally

on board with that. We could do this in any number of countries while I work restoration projects."

Her stomach backflipped. "Like showing me another infinity pool in Hong Kong?"

"Exactly. The possibilities are as limitless as the horizon."

It sounded exciting...and aimless for her. "I couldn't live my life that, just following you around the world." She pressed her fingers to his lips. "Don't even say it."

"Say what?"

"Something smug about—" she lowered her voice to mimic his "—having sex in different countries is a fabulous goal."

A tic started in the corner of his eye. "There you go again with negative assumptions about me. I can't help but wonder if you're using that excuse because you're nervous about what happened out there between us. You know damn well I have a job, a goal."

With an exasperated sigh, he plowed his fingers through his hair. "Every time I start falling for your down-to-earth strength and your passionate nature, you withdraw. Why?"

He was right, and it stung. Still she wondered, "You have a job, but how would I fit in with your plan? I need a purpose of my own."

That silenced him for the first time. She waited through at least a dozen clicks of the ceiling fan overhead and was almost ready to crack, to apologize so they could take a few steps back.

Her cell phone rang from inside her purse. He must have placed it in the room along with their refrigerated meal they'd never gotten around to eating. Not that it mattered in the least to her how it got there. She was just grateful for the distraction.

Eloisa tugged the cover with her as she stumbled from the bed for her bag resting on the trunk at the foot of the bed.

The display screen scrolled "UNKNOWN."

Averting her eyes from Jonah's obvious irritation, she thumbed the Talk button. "Hello?"

"Eloisa? This is your father."

Her stomach pitched at just the word "father" even though she recognized the voice—Harry Taylor, her step-dad. She was just too on edge since Duarte's surprise visit. "What do you need, Harry?"

She said his name in answer to Jonah's questioning look.

"It's about Audrey," Harry barked with unmistakable frustration.

Her stomach flipped faster. What could possibly be so wrong? Why had she let Jonah persuade her into running away? She should have known better than to leave when her sister was in such a fragile state. "Is she okay? Was she in an accident or something?"

Jonah sat up straighter, leaning closer and resting his hand on her back. His steady presence bolstered her as she gripped the phone and waited for her step-dad's reply.

"Audrey eloped with Joey."

Her sister had done what? Eloisa could barely wrap her brain around the very last thing she'd expected to hear.

"Oh...uh..." She struggled for words and could only come up with, "Oh."

"I can't believe she would act so impulsively, so

thoughtlessly after all I've done to make the perfect wedding for her, to give my daughter the social send off she always wanted."

Eloisa bit back the urge to note it was the send off *Harry* wanted. "I'm sorry about all the money you lost on down payments."

"You don't understand the worst of it," Harry rambled, the frustration in his voice rapidly turning to anger. "She says she and Joey are moving away, cutting ties to start fresh away from his family. She's going to throw away all the influence of his family name."

It sounded to her like her sister had wised up. Now that the shock was beginning to fade, she knew that Audrey was better off.

Jonah gave her a questioning look.

She held up a hand and spoke into the phone. "It's for the best Audrey gets her life in order now rather than risk a messy divorce later."

And didn't that hit a little close to home?

Harry's laugh hitched on a half sob. "Eloisa? Where are you? How soon can you get back, because I really need your help right now."

"Uh, I went out for a drive." And a flight. And a swim. Followed by a resounding realization that she and Jonah had very different expectations from life. While she'd more than enjoyed the peaceful aftermath of their lovemaking, she couldn't spend her entire life just floating alongside Jonah. "Don't worry, Harry. I'll be home as soon as I can."

She disconnected the phone.

Infinity had an end after all.

* * *

Jonah tugged on jeans and a button down, slicking his still-wet hair back.

God, things had gone south with Eloisa so fast.

Her family snapped their fingers and she was ready to run to their side. On the one hand, that could be an admirable trait. As a Landis, he would behave the same way in a crisis. When his brother's military plane had gone done in Afghanistan, the family had all pulled together to hold each other up until Kyle was found safely.

When Sebastian and his wife Marianna separated after their adopted daughter was reclaimed by her biological mother, the brothers had sat together through that first hellish night and poured drinks for Sebastian.

He could go on and on with the list.

Then why was he so damn irritated over this? Because no one was there for *her.* Yet they expected her to drop everything for manufactured crises that seemed a daily occurrence in Eloisa's household.

Jonah watched her yank on a fresh sundress and wished he could have enjoyed the moment more. But she was packing. Leaving. Determined to return home immediately to do heaven only knew what. Her sister had left and married some other guy. It was a done deal.

But still, Eloisa was tossing her clothes into her little bag a lot faster than she'd put them in there in the first place. What was really going on here?

Eloisa looked up sharply. "I thought you said we were alone?"

He stopped buttoning his shirt halfway up and looked around, listened. The elevator rumbled softly, then louder, closer. "Decorating staff is downstairs, but there's no reason for them to come up here, and they don't have an elevator key for the penthouse anyway."

A ding sounded just outside the suite.

His muscles tensed protectively. He checked to make sure she was dressed on his way out into the sitting area. "I said no one would bother us. Apparently I was wrong."

And he damn well wasn't happy about the interruption.

He opened the door into the hall just as a carefully coiffed woman stepped out of the private elevator. He would know those sweater sets and pearls paired with perfectly pressed jeans anywhere.

His mother, of all people, had arrived in the middle of nowhere just when he happened to be with Eloisa. His mother's arrival was too convenient. She must know something or at least sense something. He could swear his mom had some kind of special maternal radar.

Could this day go to crap any faster?

Closing the door to the penthouse quietly to seal off Eloisa from the catastrophe in the making, Jonah swore softly as he stepped toward the elevator. "Hi, Ma."

Ginger Landis Renshaw swatted his arm even as she hugged him. "Is that any way to welcome your mother? You may have gotten taller than me by the time you turned thirteen, but you will still watch the language, young man."

His mother was all protocol out in the political world, but with her family she still kept things real—even though she was now an ambassador to a small South American country.

He glanced over his shoulder at the closed door. He

could only keep Eloisa under wraps for so long. His best hope was to head off his mom long enough to go back into the suite and warn Eloisa. Prepare her for the meeting. Most women he dated either froze up around his family, or worse. They kissed up.

He was certain Eloisa wouldn't be the latter, but he worried about the former. And she sure as hell was more than a "date."

At least his brothers weren't here. "Mom, I have someone with me. This really isn't a convenient time."

"I know. Why do you think I'm here? I want to meet this Eloisa for myself rather than keep waiting for you to get around to it."

Nobody got jack by Ginger. The only question that remained? How much did she know? A lot, apparently, if she'd already learned Eloisa's name.

The door to the suite opened. His window to prepare anybody was over.

"Jonah," Eloisa called softly. "I'm packed and ready to leave, but if you're busy with work I can call a cab." She pulled up short at the sight of his famous mother. "Excuse me, ma'am."

"Eloisa, this is my mother," he said, although it seemed no introductions were needed, "Ginger Landis Renshaw."

His mother pushed past him, her eyes both sharp and welcoming. "Call me, Ginger, please. All those names are too much of a mouthful. It's nice to meet you, Eloisa."

"And you, too, ma'am," she said simply, taking his mother's hand lightly.

No shaking in her shoes.

Thus far she seemed to be silently holding her

ground and letting Ginger fill the silence with a running monologue about her trip out. Eloisa had a quiet elegance about her, a way of smoothing over even awkward situations. It was easy to see why she was the rock of her family, why both her fathers needed her by their sides right now.

God, she was mesmerizing.

"Jonah? Jonah!" his mother called.

"Huh?" Brilliant response. He peeled his eyes off Eloisa. "Uh, what did you say, Ma?"

Ginger smiled knowingly before answering. "I was just telling your delightful friend Eloisa how I had a stopover in the area to meet with a congressman friend of mine. Since I was in the States, I gave my other boys a call so we could all meet up here for a family overnight vacation."

What the— "My brothers? Are here?"

"Downstairs checking out your latest work. It's all quite lovely dear."

Apparently the evening *could* get worse.

Eloisa stepped back, as if dodging the brewing family conspiracy. "Jonah, it sounds like you and your mother have a lot to talk about. I'll just call to check in with my father while you meet with your family." She nodded toward Ginger. "It was lovely meeting you, ma'am."

She disappeared back into the suite before he could stop her. Although he appreciated the chance to find out what was up with his mother's surprise visit.

"Mom, what are you really doing here? No way in hell were you and Matthew and Sebastian *and* Kyle just in the neighborhood."

"Language." She swatted his arms again and tugged

him into the elevator. "Let's talk in here where it's more private."

"Did the General come along, too?" He could sense the family closing ranks. Something was up. And as much as he wanted to go comfort Eloisa, he needed to make sure she wasn't walking into some kind of ambush.

God, he'd thought Eloisa was quick to answer the call of her kin. The Landises could round up relatives faster than most people could put dinner on the table.

"Hank couldn't make it back from his meeting in Germany in time. He sends his best." The doors swooshed closed.

"Mom, this is nuts." And part of the reason he needed to travel. Frequently.

"This is being a mother. I can hear it in your voice when something's wrong. It's a mother's instinct, a gift I have for all of my children." She nailed the Stop button. "You asked about the Medinas and so I tapped into some resources. I found out quite a lot as a matter of fact, most of it about you and Eloisa."

Okay, she'd definitely captured his interest. For Eloisa's sake, he needed to find out every bit of information his mother had been able to unearth. "What did you learn?"

His mother pinned him with a stare she'd perfected on all four of her boys. "That you're married. And I decided that since you've been married for a year now, if I wanted to ever meet this new daughter-in-law of mine, I had better take matters into my own hands."

Twelve

Stunned, Jonah stared at his mother and processed her bombshell, along with all the repercussions it could have for Eloisa. How had his mom found out about his marriage…? "Sebastian."

Ginger nodded slowly. "I went to him with some questions when I started looking into the Medinas. He thought I already knew."

Their mother always had been good about pulling information out of them unawares. He couldn't even be mad at his brother.

Jonah pulled his thoughts back to the present. Things were still so unsure with Eloisa he needed to tread warily. "Mom, I understand your impatience, but I need for you to hold back just a little while longer." As much as he loved his family, Eloisa was his primary focus. What else had Ginger found out? "What were you able to uncover about the Medinas? Did you learn anything about the old king?"

She leaned back on the mirrored wall silently and chewed the tip of her glasses dangling on a chain around her neck.

"How much do you know about Eloisa?" he pressed again.

Ginger dropped her glasses back to rest on the chain. "I know who her real father is. A carefully kept secret for over twenty-five years, a secret that seems to be leaking out since your marriage, otherwise I never should have been able to uncover her identity."

He went stone-cold inside. He'd never for a second considered he'd put her at risk by marrying her. But of course he hadn't known her secret then. What a convoluted mess.

One he would fix. "No one will ever harm a hair on her head."

"You're that far gone, are you?" Her face creased with a deep and genuine smile. "Congratulations, Jonah."

Far gone? Hell yeah. "I'm married to her, aren't I?"

"There are problems, obviously, or you wouldn't have spent the year apart." She held up a manicured finger. "I'm not trying to pry. Only commenting on the obvious. Of course, I don't know her, but I would imagine she has reason to be wary."

"Eloisa freaks out about being in the spotlight." He glanced at the closed doors, thinking of her on the other side waiting with her suitcase. "When the time comes, this needs to be handled with a carefully worded press release."

"That's all well and good, but I meant she's wary

of being a part of a family. I obviously don't know her personally, but what I have learned makes me sad for her, and also gives me some thoughts on the subject of why you two haven't been enjoying marital bliss for the past year."

"We were doing okay a few hours ago until all the families started calling and showing up."

"Oh, really? Didn't look that way to me."

His gut churned over the fact Eloisa might have already phoned for a cab or made God only knew what arrangements while he was talking to his mom. He couldn't let her up and leave when he was distracted again, and how could he ever hope for a relationship with a woman he couldn't count on to stand still for more than a few hours at a time?

"Son, you've been blessed with family traditions so it seems simple to you. Not so much to others. Like Eloisa perhaps."

"I know that, Mom, and I don't take it for granted."

"I don't know that I agree with you there. Not that I'm condemning you and your brothers for it. Children should enjoy those traditions and be able to count on them over the years. That gives them roots to ground them when storms hit. Like when your father died. You carried a part of him with you in our traditions."

"What are you trying to say?" He was damn near turning backflips to figure Eloisa out and now his mom was going on about Thanksgiving turkeys and Christmas trees? "Mom, you're talking chick talk, and I'm a guy."

"If you want to keep her, you need to help her feel secure." Ginger released the Stop button and leaned to kiss her son on the cheek. "Now go take care of your wife. I look forward to talking with Eloisa more downstairs whenever the two of you are ready. Your brothers and I will be waiting."

A half hour later, Eloisa waited in the resort lounge with her luggage and Jonah's immense family. She was nervous, even lightly nauseated at this unexpected turn.

She and Jonah had barely had time to talk when he returned from the elevator. He'd simply apologized for his family's surprise intrusion and promised to get her to Audrey before her sister returned from Vegas. He would take care of everything, he'd assured her, giving her a quick but intense kiss before escorting her downstairs.

Fresh paint—mustard yellow—tinted the air and soured her stomach even more. Being with Jonah offered a world of excitement, but very few moments of peace, in spite of the panoramic setting.

Archways framed the two massive walls of windows showcasing the canyon. Stars twinkled in the night sky, the moon climbing. He'd promised they would still leave for Pensacola this evening. He vowed he understood her need to check on Audrey, even if his eyes seemed to say he thought she was overreacting.

Meanwhile, she was stuck in the middle of a very bizarre family reunion. She forced herself not to fidget in the mammoth tapestry wingback. He promised only his mother and lawyer brother knew the truth about their marriage and her family. Apparently the other brothers just thought she was a girlfriend. Having people learn the truth about her background scared Eloisa to the roots of her hair—but at least she didn't have to deal with everyone knowing.

Yet.

She stared at all four Landis men sprawled on red leather sofas, the only pieces of furniture, other than her chair, not wrapped in warehouse plastic. All four men shared the same blue eyes as their mother. Their hair was varying shades of brown. Jonah's was longer.

But there was no mistaking the strong family jaw. These were powerful men, most likely stubborn men. She suspected they got it from their mom.

Ginger Landis Renshaw paced on the lanai, taking a work call, her shoulder-length grey-blond hair perfectly styled. Eloisa recalled from news reports the woman was in her early fifties, but she carried the years well. Wearing a lilac lightweight sweater set with pearls—and blue jeans—Ginger Landis wasn't at all what Eloisa had expected. Thank goodness, because the woman she'd met appeared a little less intimidating.

She'd seen Ginger on the news often enough, reminding Eloisa that she'd followed press coverage of the Landis family all year with more than casual interest. From her attention to the news blogs and video snippets on television, Eloisa knew Ginger was poised and intelligent, sometimes steely determined. Today, a softer side showed as she glanced through the window at her son then over to Eloisa before she returned her attention to her business call.

The whole group was beyond handsome, their unity, happiness and deep sense of connectedness tangible even through the airwaves. And yes, she'd been searching for even a glimpse of Jonah in those photos and broadcasts all year long, too.

How had his mother managed to build such a cohesive family? She searched Ginger's every move through the glass as if somehow she could figure out the answer like a subject researched deeply enough in her library. Then one of his brothers stepped in front of the window, blocking her view. She searched her memory for which brother...

The oldest, Matthew Landis, was a South Carolina senator and the consummate charming politician. "Our baby brother, Jonah, here has always been good at playing things low-key, keeping a lookout in such a way nobody even knew you were watching, but even we didn't see this one coming." Matthew turned to Jonah. "Where have you been hiding this lovely woman?"

Jonah reached from the sofa to rest a hand on her arm. "We met in Spain last summer."

He kept it simple, uncomplicated. How surreal to sit here so casually in this serene retreat while her world exploded around her.

Audrey's life in upheaval.

Secrets with Jonah so close to exposure.

Nowhere to hide from the fact that she was falling hard for Jonah Landis.

She folded her shaking hands in her lap and kept up the pretense of calm conversation. If nothing else, she had a brief window with his brothers before they saw her differently. She could use this chance to learn more about Jonah—from someone else this time. "He kept the lookout how?"

Jonah interjected. "Let's not go there right now."

Kyle grinned. "Let's do. The odds are three to one in our favor, bro."

The world of brothers was fairly alien to her, other than a few brief days nearly twenty years ago.

Sebastian—the lawyer—stretched his arms along the

back of the sofa. "He kept Mom from discovering our tunnels."

"Tunnels?"

Kyle—the brother who'd served in the military—leaned forward, elbows on his knees. "When Sebastian, Jonah and I were kids, during summer vacation, we would pack up sandwiches and Kool-Aid and head out for the day."

"You played at the beach alone?" She glanced out at Ginger and couldn't imagine her tolerating that.

"Nope," Kyle continued, "we went into the more-wooded areas nearby. Sebastian and I dug underground tunnels. Jonah stood guard and warned us if any adults came near."

Sebastian's solemn expression lightened. "We would dig the trench, lay boards over the trough and cover the planks with dirt."

"What about your oldest brother?" She nodded toward Matthew.

Kyle elbowed the esteemed senator. "Too much of a rule follower. He wasn't invited. Although I guess our secret is out now."

"Secret?" Matthew extended his legs in front of him. "Did it ever occur to you to wonder why those tunnels never collapsed on top of you?"

Scowling, Kyle straightened indignantly. "We built damn good tunnels."

"Okay." Matthew spread his hands. "If that's what you want to believe."

"It's what happened." Kyle frowned. "Isn't it?"

The more contemplative Sebastian even shifted uncomfortably until Matthew shook his head, laughing.

"After you two went inside, Jonah would go back out and fix your tunnels. He had me stand guard."

The stunned looks on Sebastian and Kyle's faces were priceless.

Matthew continued, "He was an architect in the making, even then."

Brow furrowing suspiciously, Kyle scrubbed his jaw. "You're yanking our chain."

Sebastian said, "You two collaborated against us?"

"We collaborated *for* you. And if you hadn't excluded us from hanging out in your tunnels we probably would have showed you how to dig them right in the first place rather than laughing at you behind your back."

Kyle slugged his brother on the arm, which started a free-for-all of laughter and light payback punches between the siblings. Did her Medina brothers share moments and memories like this? Did she have the courage to find out? They had no real connection to her other than blood.

But her sister, Audrey? They may not have had the perfect family circle like the Landises, but she loved her sister and her sister loved her. She had to be there for her.

As Jonah had been there for his brothers all those years ago, protecting their secret while making sure they stayed safe. Even as a little kid, the youngest of the crew, he'd been a guardian, a protector, all things that made her fall even harder for him now.

Her throat clogged with emotion and tears, and God, she didn't know how much more enlightenment she could take in one day. Her emotions were already so raw.

And scary.

She turned to Jonah, caught his attention and lightly touched her watch. *We need to leave,* she said with her eyes.

For more reasons than just Audrey. She needed distance to think, because sitting here with the Landises, she wanted to be a part of Jonah's world so much it hurt. This wasn't a family who ran from responsibilities or commitments. *Jonah* was a man to depend on.

And right now, she wasn't so sure she was the kind of woman he deserved.

The next morning, Eloisa propped her elbows on her kitchen island, a mug of tea in her hands as she sat on a barstool next to her sister. Her *married* sister.

A thin silver band glinted on Audrey's finger.

Eloisa and Jonah had taken a red-eye flight back, arriving just at sunrise. She'd hoped they could talk on the plane but he'd received a call from the Peru developers who were working round the clock on plans for the project he would tackle after leaving here.

Leaving her.

After they'd landed, she'd been stunned to find her sister waiting at the town house. With Joey who now stood out on the patio with Jonah.

Eloisa covered her sister's hand. "I'm sorry I wasn't here for you when you needed me."

"I'm an adult, in spite of what our father thinks. I made this decision on my own." Her mouth pinched tight. "Joey wanted to elope and leave this town from the start. I never should have let Dad talk me into a big wedding."

"Don't be too hard on yourself. We want the people we love to be happy."

Audrey looked out the patio doors. "I really shouldn't be so tough on Dad. I was as guilty as him, being charmed by all the money. Dad was always so freaked out about having enough for Mom. I remember this one time he bought her a diamond-and-sapphire necklace. She loved it, but the whole time Dad kept apologizing that it wasn't bigger. He said he wanted her to feel like a queen."

A queen? Had her father known more than she realized? If so, this was rapidly turning into the worst-kept secret on the planet. "Mom loved him."

"I know. I want that for my own marriage." She clasped both her sister's hands, her whisper-pale hair falling to mix with Eloisa's jet black. "It just took me a while to realize it's not about the trappings. I know you probably think I'm crazy for running off."

She thought of her own elopement a year ago. It had seemed so right at the time, she could relate to how her sister felt. Guilt pinched at a corner of her heart. Maybe if she hadn't kept it secret all year long, Audrey might have been encouraged to make her decision earlier. "I may understand better than you think."

She looked out to the patio where Jonah and Joey chatted like old buds. How easily Jonah talked to people, how quick he was to put Joey at ease. Jonah might not embrace the public eye as much as his famous family, but he'd certainly inherited a winning way with people. He'd certainly won *her* over a year ago—and last night. He'd slid under her boundaries in a way no man ever had.

Audrey gazed out at Joey with a seriously love-sick look in her eyes. "I only wish I'd followed my instincts earlier. It would have saved you so much work and time."

Her sister appeared amazingly calm. It seemed all the drama had come from Harry.

Eloisa sipped her tea while her sister shared details about her hurried wedding in a Vegas chapel. "And Joey says we really can't build a life for ourselves here. His family would be involved in anything we try." She took a bracing breath. "So we're relocating. We don't know where yet. He says that's part of the adventure, figuring out where. Maybe we'll toss a dart at a map."

Audrey was embracing the same kind of future Eloisa could have with Jonah. Was that why her sister's words sent a bolt of envy through her? Not that she wasn't happy for Audrey, because this would be a wise move for her. But it would be difficult to see Audrey living the dreams Eloisa had walked away from.

Her eyes tracked back to Jonah again, his broad shoulders, his comfort in watching out for other people, whether it was his older brothers or her. She wanted this happiness for herself, too. She wanted to trust they could work out a way for her to fit her life with his.

She wanted to find the same surety she saw shining from Audrey. There was a vibrancy and strength of purpose in her sister that hadn't been there before. Audrey had gone from pale and ethereal to glittering like a diamond.

"You're really excited about the new adventure."

Ashley clutched Eloisa's hands. "Is that too selfish of me? You've always been here for me and now I'm leaving you."

A deeper truth, an understanding resonated inside her. "You're living your own life. You deserve that. We won't stop being sisters just because you're married, even if you live clear across country. I'll come see you. Pick somewhere interesting, okay?"

Audrey nodded, tears in her eyes as she opened her arms. Eloisa gathered her sister close, hope for her own future glinting ever so warily inside her.

Jonah pushed open the French doors to the patio, his shoulders, his unmistakable charisma filling the void, filling her. She looked into those clear blue eyes of his and knew in her heart. He wasn't out for revenge. He was here for her.

He'd stood by her today during a family crisis. Had intervened for her during her sister's awkward engagement party, had hidden their secret from most of his family. He was a great guy and she trusted him enough to take the next step. She didn't want him to leave for Peru. She wanted longer to test out what they had before it was too late. She deserved a future of her own with Jonah, and the time had come to claim it, obstacles and all.

Starting with telling him about their baby.

Thirteen

Eloisa closed the town house door after Audrey and Joey. Their laughter and playfulness out in the parking lot drifted through, teasing and tempting her with what a relationship could be.

Jonah walked up behind her, swept aside her hair and pressed his mouth to the sensitive curve of her neck. Her head fell back to give him better access. After the day they'd had, there was nothing she wanted more than to lose herself in the forgetfulness reliably found in his arms. Then she could curl up beside him and sleep like a regular married couple.

Except that would be hiding. That would be using sex to shield herself from making the tough step of opening herself totally to Jonah. Letting herself love him.

And even scarier, letting him love her.

She was actually pretty good at loving other people.

Not so good at letting them be there for her. And wasn't that a mind-blowing revelation she would have liked the time to mull over? Except she was out of time.

Deciding to do something and actually following through were two different matters. But she was determined to see this through before they landed in bed.

Eloisa stroked along the open collar of his simple button-down, wishing her nerves were as easily smoothed. "Thank you for being so understanding about coming back here for Audrey. I hated cutting short your visit with your family."

"They're the ones who showed up unannounced." He looped his hands low around her waist. "We can have more time with them soon if you want."

"I do."

His face kicked up in a one-sided smile. "Good, good."

Jonah tucked her against his side and strode deeper into the living area, out to the patio. He drew her down with him in the Adirondack chair, settling her in his lap with such an ease and rightness it took her breath away. How could such a big-boned, hard-bodied man make for such a comfortable resting spot?

Eloisa nestled her head on his shoulder and gazed outward. That would be easier than looking him in the face. The sky turned hazy shades of purple and grey as the sun surrendered and night muscled upward.

Jonah thumbed along the back of her neck, massaging tiny kinks. "I'm sorry for not taking into account your job, and your need for security. I can understand why following me from job to job may not sound like the best of lives for you. We'll work together to figure out a solution."

God, he made it sound possible to find a compromise. She wanted to trust it could be that simple.

"Is that what we're talking about?" She swallowed hard against the hope. "A life together?"

"I think we're most definitely moving in that direction." His chin rested on top of her head. "It would be a mistake to pretend otherwise."

"Okay then—" she inhaled a shaky breath, not nearly bolstering enough "—if we're being totally honest here, there's something I need to tell you, something that will be difficult to say and difficult to hear."

His arms stiffened around her, but he kept his chin resting in her hair. "Are you walking out again?"

"No, not unless you tell me to." Which could very well happen. A trickle of fear iced up her spine. What if she'd put this off until too late? Would he understand her reasons for waiting?

"That'll never happen."

"You sound so sure." She wanted to be as certain. But hadn't being with Jonah helped her see she couldn't plan for everything? "You're always full of absolutes, total confidence."

"I have a vision for our future and it's perfect." He tipped her face up to his. "You're perfect. We're going to be perfect together."

"You can't really believe I'm perfect. And if you think that even on some level, what are you going to do when my many flaws show?" Of course she was afraid of rejection after a lifetime of being shuffled aside through no fault of her own. A child didn't deserve that. Except now, she was an adult and had no one to blame but herself. "What if I don't fit into the beautiful world of no boundaries that you've engineered for yourself?"

"We'll work at it. Think about your graduate studies in Spain. You enjoyed your research contribution. Maybe that's a path to blending our worlds again. Or we split time, both making compromises."

He was offering her so much that she wasn't prepared to think about yet. Not until she'd taken care of this old hurt. "That's not what I'm talking about. It's something different, something bigger, a mistake I made."

He stroked her forehead. "You're such a serious person, and while I admire the way you care about the feelings of everyone around you, I'm a big boy. Now just cut to the chase and say it."

"I haven't been completely honest with you—" her heart pounded so hard her ribs hurt "—about more than just my father."

"Do you have a boyfriend on the side?"

"Good Lord, Jonah—" her hands fisted in his shirt "—I've spent the whole year aching for you. There's no room for anyone else."

"Then no worries." He winked.

Winked, damn it.

"Jonah, please don't joke. Not now. This is difficult enough as it is." She pushed the words up and out as fast as she could. "After we split up, after I left you, I found out I was pregnant with your child."

His hold on her loosened, his face swiped free of any expression. "You had a baby," he said slowly, his voice flat, neutral. "Our baby."

She nodded, her heart hammering all the harder through pools of tears bottled inside. The grief, the loneliness and regret splashed through her again with each thud of her pulse. She should have called him then. But she hadn't and now it was time to face the consequences for that decision. "I had a miscarriage."

"When?"

"Does it even matter?" She hated the way her voice hitched.

"I deserve to know when…how long."

She flinched with guilt. He was right. He deserved that and so much more. "I miscarried at four and a half months. Nobody knew except my doctor and my priest."

She wanted him to know that while she hadn't told him, she'd nurtured and honored that life even if he hadn't been there to witness it. Even if he was going to walk out, he deserved to know that.

The first shadows of emotion chased across his face—incredulity. "You didn't even tell your sister?"

"Audrey had just gotten engaged to Joey," she rushed to explain, and it sounded so lame now but had made such sense then. "I didn't want to spoil her special time."

"No," he said simply, his body shifting, tensing, no longer the welcoming place to land. Something had unmistakably changed between them. "I'm not buying the excuses."

She agreed, but still she'd hoped for some… understanding? Sympathy? Comfort after the fact? "What? I tell you my most heartbreaking secret and you just say 'no.' What's the matter with you?"

She couldn't bear to sit in his arms that had become so stone-cold. She rolled to her feet and backed away.

He stood slowly, his hands in his pockets. No warm reception for her revelation. "I think you didn't tell your sister because then you'd have to let someone get close to you, be a part of your life. Don't you think she would be hurt to know you didn't feel like you could turn to her?"

She hadn't thought of it that way before and she didn't know what to make of the notion now. Her confessions had churned up the loss for her, the retelling of it bringing to mind those dark hours when the blood loss started, then being in the hospital alone. The grief when the doctor told her the baby's heartbeat had stopped. The teeth-chattering cold after her D and C.

Would having her sister there have made the pain go away? Right now, with the memories fresh in her mind, she couldn't think of anything that would ease the loss for her.

And oh God, why hadn't she given more thought to how this would hurt Jonah? She forced herself to look in his eyes and confront the pain—and yes, the anger—she found there. "I should have told you then."

"Damn straight, you should have," he snapped, the anger seeping into his voice as well. "But you didn't. Because that would involve me being a part of your life and your family when it's easier to hide in your library with your books."

She gasped at the stab of his words. "You're being cruel."

"I'm being realistic for the first time, Eloisa." He paced the small stone patio restlessly, the frustration in his tone building with every step. "You talk about wanting a future together but you've been keeping this from me the whole time, even when we made love."

"I'm telling you the truth now. Just five minutes ago you said nothing could break us apart."

"Would you have told me if you weren't afraid I would find out anyway, now that all your secrets are coming out?" He pivoted back sharply to face her, the moonlight casting harsh shadows down his angry face. "When have you ever willingly let me into your life?"

She couldn't think of an answer. He'd led their relationship every step of the way.

He started toward her again. "All this time I've been wondering if you can trust me, and now I don't know if I can trust you. I don't know if I can be with you, always wondering when you're going to run again." He stopped pacing abruptly and plowed his hand through his hair. "This is too much. I can't wrap my brain around it. I need air."

He jammed his hands into his pockets again as if he couldn't even bear to touch her and left. The front door closed quietly but firmly behind him.

The first tear slipped free and pulled the plug out of the dam for the rest to come flooding down. Barely able to see, she walked back into her town house.

For the past year, she'd been immersed in her own pain and fears, never once thinking about how much she must have hurt Jonah when she'd left him. Now, standing alone with the echo of that lone door click in her ears, in her soul, she realized just how fully she'd screwed up in leaving him.

She was totally alone for the first time in her life. Harry was upset she hadn't persuaded Audrey to stay. Audrey was off enjoying marital bliss. And Jonah had left her. She had nowhere to turn.

Eloisa stood in the middle of her empty town house that had once felt like a haven and now seemed so very barren. She searched for something, any piece of comfort. Her fingers trailed over the glass paperweight, the one she'd made from shells and a dried flower, memorializing her baby's too-brief life. What would it have been like to share that grief with Jonah?

And now because of how she'd handled things, he was suffering the loss alone as well.

She gripped the cool paperweight in her hand—and revealed a plain white card with ten typed numbers, Duarte's number.

Perhaps there was at least one thing she could fix in her messed-up life after all. Perhaps she might as well make someone happy.

Jonah was going to get seriously trashed if his brothers didn't stop pouring drinks for him. But then that's why he'd come home to Hilton Head to be with his family.

Sitting on the balcony at the Landis beachside compound, he nudged away the latest shot glass on the iron outdoor table. He was still reeling from Eloisa's revelation about getting pregnant and losing their baby. Never once bothering to contact him about something so monumental.

Anger still chewed at his gut, along with grief for the child that could have been. And having a child with Eloisa? Even the possibility had his hands shaking so hard he couldn't have picked up the shot glass even if he'd wanted.

As much as he regretted not knowing about the life that had begun inside her a year ago, the knowledge of what happened made him realize the importance of getting things right with Eloisa this time. If birth control had failed a year ago, then it could fail again. He would not risk being on the other side of an ocean if Eloisa carried his child.

After their fight, he'd driven along the beach for about an hour until he'd calmed down enough to talk to her again. He hadn't known what he would say or how they could work through it. His ability to trust her had taken a serious blow. But he was willing to try.

Except once he returned to her town house, he found she'd already left. Her car was gone. Her suitcase was gone. Eloisa had run away again. Jonah had hopped the first plane to the only place he could think of to go. Home to hang out with his brothers.

Sebastian clanked down his crystal glass, the ocean wind kicking in off the waves. The surf crashed. Sailboat lines pinged against the double mast of the family yacht. "You have to figure out what speaks to her."

Frowning, Kyle leaned toward his brother with an almost imperceptible sway. "Marianna made you go to some kind of woo-woo, Zen-like couples retreat, didn't she?"

Sebastian reached for the bottle of vintage bourbon in the middle of the table. "What makes you say that?"

"'Figure out what speaks to her,'" Kyle mimicked in a spacey-sounding voice before laughing. "Really, dude, who are you and what have you done with my brother?"

Matthew clapped Kyle on the shoulder, the salty breeze filling their shirts, hinting at an incoming storm. "Don't knock it 'til you've tried it. There's something to be said for learning to speak their language on occasion. The benefits are amazing."

Sebastian smiled knowingly.

Jonah turned the glass around and around on the

table, a tic starting in the corner of his eye. He wondered for the first time how all his Neanderthal brothers had managed to find great women. What did they know that he didn't? What was he missing?

Hunger for making things work with Eloisa compelled him to flat-out ask. He sure as hell wasn't making headway alone. "You're going to have to 'speak' to me in regular-guy English if you expect me to understand."

Sebastian's face took on the lawyer look he assumed right before rolling out his best case. Of course the look was a little deflated by his cockeyed tie. "Okay, standard red roses and a heart-shaped box of chocolates are all well and good, and certainly better than not doing anything. But if you can think of something personal, something that says you know her...you'll be golden."

Kyle scratched the back of his head, his hair still worn short even after he'd finished his military commitment. "They really like to know we're thinking about them when they're not around."

Jonah eyed his brothers in disbelief. God, they were making his head hurt worse rather than helping. "Do you all get a group discount for the couples retreat?"

"Bro, make fun all you want," Matthew said. "You can have our advice or flounder around on your own."

"It's actually not that complicated," Sebastian explained. "Marianna adores our dogs." They both were nuts over their two mutts, Buddy and Holly. "One Valentine's Day, I bought Coach collars and leashes for the dogs, along with a donation to the local Humane Society."

Kyle jabbed a finger in his direction. "Remember when I got the laptop computer for Phoebe? Her squeal of excitement just about rattled every window."

Hearing how his brothers hit just the perfect note to make their wives happy offered up a special torture for him now that Eloisa had damn near ripped his heart out. "You had me tuck the wrapped computer where she would see it while you took her on a date."

Kyle smiled, his eyes taking on a distant air. "A late-night drive in a vintage Aston Martin convertible."

"Wow!" Matthew whistled low. "Nice move."

"Thanks." Kyle refilled his glass. "I'll give you the name of the guy who hooked me up. Now back to the computer." He turned toward Jonah, porch lights the only illumination, with the clouds covering the stars. "Phoebe was stretched too thin teaching her online classes and caring for the baby. I offered to take time off from work to watch Nina, even offered more nanny time, but she wasn't budging. The laptop gave her a way of working from anywhere."

His brother had done a damn fine job at blending two diverse lifestyles. Kyle and Phoebe might well have some good advice for Eloisa…if he hadn't walked out on her. If she hadn't followed up by walking out on him again as well.

It downright sucked being around these guys who practically oozed satisfaction and marital bliss.

Matthew snagged the bottle from his brother. "Extravagant is cool, too, you've just got to mix it up some with the practical."

Clinking the ice, Kyle lifted his glass for a refill. "What's Ashley's extravagance?"

Matthew's mouth twitched with a hint of a smile. "Don't think I can share that with you, my brother."

"Hey." Kyle raised his hands. "Fair enough."

The sound of a throat clearing reverberated behind them. They all four twisted in their seats.

Their mother's second husband—General Hank Renshaw—stood in the open French doors. His distinguished military bearing was still visible even after his retirement. His hair might be solid gray now, but he had a sharp brain that made him a major player in the national defense arena. "Hope you boys have saved at least one drink of my best alcohol for me."

"Yes, sir." Kyle snagged another glass from the tray they'd brought out with them and passed their stepfather—a lifetime family friend as well—a drink. "Maybe you can help Jonah here figure out how to get his wife back."

"Hmmm…" The General tipped back his glass with only a slight wince and dragged a chair over to the table. "Well, your mother likes it when I—"

"Whoa! Whoa! Hold on there a minute, General." The protests of all four brothers tumbled over each other.

Jonah agreed one hundred percent on that staying a secret. "That's our mom you're talking about. While I appreciate the offer to help, there are just some things a son doesn't need to know."

Matthew drained his glass. "The time we walked in on the two of you damn near gave me a heart attack."

"Okay, okay." The General chuckled lowly. "I get the picture." His laughter faded and he jabbed a thumb toward the door. "Now how about you three take the bottle and clear out so I can talk to Jonah?"

Chairs scraped back and his brothers abandoned ship. The slugging and laughs faded in the hall and up the stairs.

The General refilled both glasses. "Your dad was my best friend." He lifted his in toast. "He would be proud of you."

"Thank you. That means a lot to me." But not enough to clear away the frustration over failing when it counted most.

With Eloisa.

Why had she kept the news from him then? And now? He needed to understand that if they stood a chance at stopping this cycle of turning each other inside out, then running for opposite corners.

He didn't expect the General was going to be able to offer some magic bullet to fix everything any more than his brothers had. But still he appreciated the support. The General had been there for them after their dad died. He'd always vowed he was just helping out their mom the way she'd helped him after his wife died. But they'd all wondered how long it would take....

"It takes as long as it takes. But you don't quit."

How had the General known what he was thinking? "Have you added a mind reader medal to your already impressive collection?"

"Quit beating yourself up about the past and move forward," the General said with clipped, military efficiency. "Don't just curl up and admit defeat. You've got an opportunity now. Run with it."

"She's gone." Jonah reached into his pocket and pulled out the white card he'd found by her telephone, the same card he remembered Duarte Medina giving her. He flipped the number between his fingers. "She doesn't want to speak to me or see me again."

"And you're going to just quit? Give up on your marriage? Give up on her?"

His fingers slowed, the numbers on the vellum square coming into focus. His whole life coming into focus as well, because this time he wasn't letting Eloisa just walk away. There was a way to break this cycle after all. Show her how a real family came through for each other, everyone offering support rather than the one-sided deal she'd lived, always being the one giving. No wonder she hadn't reached out to him when she was hurting.

No one had ever given her reason to think her call for help would be answered.

This time he intended to show her that somebody loved her—*he* loved her—enough to follow and stay. "You have a point, General." He tapped the simple white card. "Lucky for me, I think I know exactly how to find her."

Fourteen

Eloisa sat on her father's garden patio overlooking the Atlantic, waiting. In minutes she would see Enrique Medina again. How surreal and confusing, and so not the joyful reunion she'd dreamed of as a child.

She turned to Duarte standing beside her somberly. "Thank you for arranging this meeting so quickly."

"Don't thank me," he answered with no warmth. "If it were up to me, we would all go about our lives separately. But this is how he wants it and, bottom line, it's his call to make."

His brusqueness made her edgier, as if she wasn't already about to jump out of her skin. She searched for something benign to diffuse the tension. "The rocky shoreline looks exactly like the one I remember from that single visit—magnificent. I often wondered if my memory was faulty."

"Apparently not."

And apparently Duarte would need more prodding to speak. "How strange to think our father has been so close all this time? In the same state even?"

Her biological father had taken up residence on a small private island off the coast of St. Augustine, Florida. One call to Duarte had set everything in motion. Her heart bruised beyond bearing, she'd been on a private jet, flying away from Jonah and the catastrophic mess she'd made of their second chance. Her throat clogged with more tears. She swallowed them and narrowed her attention to satisfying her curiosity about this place she'd thought of so often.

The towering white stucco house, rustling palm trees, massive archways and crashing waves… She could have been seven again, with her mother beside her, waiting for *him* to greet them.

Duarte touched her arm lightly, bringing her back to the moment. "Eloisa? He's here."

The lanai doors creaked opened. But no imposing king stepped out this time. An electric wheelchair hummed the only warning before Enrique came outside. Two large, lopey dogs followed in perfect sync. Confined to the chair, he was thin, gray and weary.

Duarte hadn't lied. Their father appeared near death. She stood but didn't reach out. A hug would have seemed strange, affected. The emotion forced. She didn't know what she felt for him. He'd needed her and beckoned. It was difficult not to resent all the times she'd needed him. Yes, he'd made contact through his lawyer over the years, but so infrequently and impersonally it seemed she was merely an afterthought. Her mind jetted back to that strange, but endearing, Landis family gathering at

Jonah's elegant Texas resort. This family reunion bore
no resemblance to that one.

"Hello, sir. You'll have to pardon me if I'm not quite
sure what to call you."

He waved dismissively, perspiration dotting his
forehead. "Call me Enrique." His body might be weak,
but his voice still commanded attention. The Spanish
accent was almost as thick as she remembered. "I do
not want formality or deserve any titles, king or father.
Now sit down, please. I feel like a rude old man for not
standing with a lovely lady present."

She took her seat again and he whirred the chair
into position in front of her. The two brown dogs—
Ridgebacks, perhaps?—settled on either side. He studied
her silently, his hands folded in his lap, veins bruised
from what appeared to be frequent IV needles.

Still, no matter the sallow pallor and thinner
frame, Enrique Medina's face was that of royalty. His
aristocratic nose and chiseled jaw spoke of his age-old
warrior heritage. There was strength in that face, despite
everything. And while his heavy blue robe with emerald-
green silk lapels was not the garb of a king in his prime,
the rich fabrics and sleek leather slippers reflected his
wealth.

The old king gestured toward the doors. "Duarte, you
can leave us now. I have some things to say to Eloisa
alone."

Duarte nodded, turning away without a word, walking
off with steps quieter than those of anyone she'd known.
But he wasn't her reason for being here today. She'd
come to see her father, to hopefully find some peace
and resolution inside herself.

"I'm sorry you're ill."

"So am I."

He didn't speak further, and she wondered if perhaps he'd started to lose his mental faculties. She glanced up at the male nurse waiting patiently at the doorway. No answers there.

She looked back at Enrique. "You asked to see me? You sent Duarte."

"Of course I did. I'm not losing my mind yet anyway." He straightened his lapels. "Please forgive me for being rude. I was merely struck by how much you resemble my mother. She was quite lovely, too."

"Thank you." It would have been nice to have met her grandmother or even see pictures like other kids growing up. Maybe it wasn't too late. "Do you have photos of her?"

"They were all lost when my home was burned to the ground."

She blinked fast. Not the answer she'd expected. She'd read what little was reported on the coup in San Rinaldo twenty-seven years ago. She knew her father had barely escaped with his life—his wife had not. He and his sons had gone into hiding. And while she understood the danger, she'd never truly thought of all he'd lost.

Certainly losing a picture wasn't the same as losing a person, but to have lost even those bits of comfort and reminders… "Then we'll have to make sure you have a picture of me to remember her by."

"Thank you, but I imagine I will be seeing her soon enough." He spoke of his death so matter-of-factly it stunned her. "Which brings me to why I called for you, *pequeña princesa*."

Little princess? Small princess? Either way, she'd never dared think of herself with that title. More than anything, her heart stumbled on the endearment that Harry had always applied to his biological daughter and never to her. Not that she would let mere words sway her after all this time.

Enrique steadied his breathing. "There are some things you need to know and time is short. Whether I die or someone finally finds me, our secret will come out someday. Even I can only hold back that tide for just so long."

The thought of that kind of exposure sent her reaching for the lemonade beside her. What if the king's enemies sought him out again? Sought her out? "Where will you hide then?"

If he was still alive.

"I am a king." His chin tipped. "I do not hide. I stay here for the people I love."

"I'm not sure I follow what you mean."

"By staying here, it keeps up the illusion that I—and my children—are in Argentina. No one bothers to look for them. No one can hurt them the way they went after my Beatriz."

Beatriz, his wife who'd been gunned down during the escape. "That must have been awful for you."

And her brothers.

His chin tipped higher as he looked away for a moment unblinking. Seeing the Herculean strength of will in a man so weak…

He focused his intense dark eyes on her again. "It was difficult meeting your mother so soon after my Beatriz was murdered. I did love your mother, as much as I could at that time. She told me if she could not have my full heart, she wanted nothing."

She'd always thought her mother stayed away because

of safety reasons. She'd never considered her mom acted out of emotion. Harry Taylor may not be anyone's idea of Prince Charming, but he had adored her mother. Eloisa sat back in her chair and let Enrique talk. He seemed to need to unload burdens. For the first time, she realized how much she needed to listen.

"I am sorry I did not get to watch you grow up. Nothing I can do now will make up for the fact I was not the father you deserved."

The humble honesty of that simple statement meant more to her than any amount of money. She'd been waiting a lifetime to hear him admit he should have been a father to her.

And while that didn't erase the past, it was a first step toward a healing. She brushed her fingers over his bruised hand, words escaping her.

"I did decide to ask your mother to marry me."

"What happened?"

"I finally looked past my grief to see a new chance at love waiting."

"She didn't want to live here?"

"Oh no, she wouldn't have minded staying here. She told me so. I just waited too long to ask."

Oh my God. "She'd already married Harry."

"I fought for her six months too late," he said simply. "Don't wait too long to fight, *pequeña princesa*."

But her chance was gone now.

This time, Jonah had left her. She wanted to shout her hurt and pain over the way he'd left, even knowing she'd brought it on herself. He was the one who'd walked out, not her. Enrique didn't understand. How could he? He didn't know her. He couldn't, not from detective reports or however he'd kept watch over her life.

She started to tell him just that but something in his eyes stopped her, a deep wisdom that came from experiences she couldn't begin to comprehend. This man knew what it meant to fight.

And his blood ran through her veins.

Eloisa gripped the arms of her chair with a newfound strength. She was through hiding in her library and in her fears. She loved Jonah Landis and wanted a life with him, wherever that life took them. He was hurting and angry now, and she couldn't blame him. She hadn't put her heart on the line for him. Taking cautious to a new level. But she would remedy that now. She was in this for the long haul.

She would fight for him so damn hard he wouldn't know what hit him.

Pushing to her feet, she cupped Enrique's face in her hands. "You certainly are a devious old man, but I do believe I like you."

His laugh rumbled as he gave her a smile and a regal nod.

Eloisa backed away slowly until her hands fell to her sides. "I have to go, but I will come back. I just need to clear up some things with Jonah first."

Her father raised his hand and twirled a finger. "Turn around."

What? Frowning, she glanced over her shoulder. And her heart lodged squarely in her throat.

Jonah stood waiting in the archway, his hair slicked back and flowers in his hand.

Jonah barely had time to nod to Eloisa's father before the old king vacated the porch, leaving him alone with her. He owed Duarte and Enrique for making this reunion happen.

And he intended to repay them by keeping Eloisa safe and happy for the rest of her life.

He closed the last few steps between them, flowers extended. "I don't know what specific kind of gift you would want that 'speaks' to your soul, so I had to settle for flowers. But they're pink tulips, like the picture on your wall. I figured you must have chosen it because you like them."

"They're perfect! Thank you." Taking the flowers in one hand, she pressed her fingers to his lips with her other. The ocean wind molded her sundress to her body just the way it had when he'd seen her again outside her sister's engagement party. They'd covered a lot of ground in a few short days.

"Jonah, I so was wrong when I said we don't know each other." She brought the tulips up just under her nose and inhaled. "The flowers are lovely but you've already given me exactly what speaks to my soul. You give me infinity pools and walk with me through dusty castles full of history. You coax me out of my dark office and you even compliment my apple-flavored lip gloss. You know everything about me except—" she arched up on her toes, the flowers crushed lightly between them "—how very deeply I love you."

He swept her hair back and cradled her head, the subtle scent of tulips mixing with the tangy salt air and the essence of *her*. "I know now—" thank God "—and look forward to telling you and showing you just how much I love you in every country around the world. If you're up for the adventure?"

"I like the sound of those ideas you discussed earlier

for blending our lives together. I think I'm more than ready to bring my library research world out into the field again. As long as you're there with me."

She angled her head to meet his kiss, the taste of apples and the touch of her tongue familiar and far too exciting when they could be interrupted at any second.

"We should speak to your father."

"Soon," she said, her smile fading. "But first I need you to know how sorry I am for not telling you about the baby right when I found out, and then for not telling you once we got involved again. That was wrong of me to keep it from you. You deserved to know."

"Thank you for that. You didn't have to say it, but I appreciate hearing it." The knowledge of that loss still hurt, and he suspected it would for a long time. But he understood how difficult it was for her to trust. He expected he would still have some work to do in easing away barriers she'd spent a lifetime erecting.

But he was damn good at renovations, at making something magnificent from the foundation already in place. "I brought something else for you besides the flowers."

"You didn't have to bring me anything. You're being here means more than I can say."

"I should have followed you before. I should have been there for you."

She cupped his face. "We're moving forward, remember?" Eloisa kissed him again, and once more, holding for three intense heartbeats. "Now what did you want to show me?"

He reached into his pocket and pulled out two gold bands. Theirs. He'd kept them the whole year. Her eyes bright with her smile and unshed tears, she held up her hand. He slid Eloisa's wedding ring onto her finger, and she slid his in place again as well, clasping his hand tightly in hers. This time, he knew, those rings weren't coming off again.

Jonah tugged one of the tulips from the bouquet and tucked it behind her ear. "Are you ready to go inside now, Mrs. Landis?"

She hooked her arm in his, like a bride with her bouquet. "I'm ready to go absolutely anywhere…with *you*."

Epilogue

Lima, Peru: Two Months Later

She had dreamed she was draped in jewels.

Languishing in twilight slumber, Eloisa Landis skimmed her fingers along the bare arm of the man sleeping next to her. She'd had the sweetest dream that her husband had showered her with emeralds and rubies and fat freshwater pearls while they'd made love. She stroked up Jonah's arms to face, his five-o'clock shadow rasping against her tender fingertips.

Eloisa flipped to her back and stretched, extending her arm so the sun refracted off her cushion-cut diamond ring to go alongside her wedding band. Early morning light streaked through the wrought-iron window grilles in the adobe manor home he'd rented for the summer. A gentle breeze rustled the linen draping over the bed.

What was it about this man that took her breath away?

His hand fell to her hip and she smiled.

Yeah, she knew exactly what drew her to him. Everything.

Growling low, he hauled her against his side. "The rubies, definitely the rubies," he said as he peeked through one eye, apparently not as asleep as she'd imagined. He flicked the dangling gems on her ears. "I've been dreaming of draping you in jewels for over a year."

"You certainly played out that fantasy last night." She reached underneath her to sweep free a sapphire bracelet that was poking into her back.

How delightfully ironic that he was the one giving her jewels and castles. Not that she needed any of it. She had peace and excitement, stability and adventure all at once with the man she loved. "You certainly brought along a king's ransom in jewels."

"Because you're a Landis, lady. That makes you American royalty." He rolled her underneath him, elbows propped.

Royalty. The word didn't make her wince anymore. She was coming to peace with that part of herself. She'd visited her father again. His health was still waning, his liver failing. She would have to face that, no more hiding for her. But thank goodness she had Jonah at her side to deal with the worst when it came around.

Jonah kissed her lightly, comforting, as if he read her thoughts, something he seemed to do more and more often these days.

Audrey and Joey were well on their way to opening a catering business in Maine, of all places. They said they planned to bring a little southern spice into lobster.

Harry planned to join them and manage the books, always looking out for his daughter's financial future.

Eloisa's family was expanding rapidly, with the Landises due in for a long weekend visit. Ginger had mandated they all needed to get to know their new relative better. Eloisa appreciated the overture. How silly to get so excited about being the belle of the ball.

But she couldn't help herself. The Landises had a way of making her feel special and welcome.

A part of their family.

Jonah toyed with the beaded pearls strung through her hair. "Have you given any thought to where you would like to live?"

"I figure when the right restoration project comes around for our home, we'll know it."

He gave her hair a light tug. "Can you narrow that down to a country for me?"

"Nope—" she threaded her fingers through his hair, drawing him down to her "—I'm through limiting my options out of preconceived notions." She nestled her leg more firmly between his, grazing him with the gold-flecked garter belt around her thigh. "Now, it's all about the possibilities."

* * * * *

A RING TO SECURE
HIS CROWN

KIM LAWRENCE

CHAPTER ONE

SABRINA CLOSED HER bedroom door with care, conscious of her two flatmates who were both doing a night rotation in Casualty. She had reached the front door, a piece of toast in one hand, her oversized bag in the other, when her phone rang.

She swore softly, and then again as her efforts at juggling caused her toast to land butter-side down on the carpet. Why did it *always* do that?

She dumped her bag, picked up the toast with a grimace and glanced at the caller ID before lifting the phone to her ear. The low-voiced conversation lasted a few moments as the junior lab assistant gave her the results she and the entire research team had been waiting for.

Consigning the toast to the waste-bin, Sabrina was smiling when she opened the door; the results were not what they had expected, they were better! Embracing the buzz of excitement, she hitched her bag over her shoulder, grabbed an apple from the fruit bowl to soothe her rumbling stomach and released the loose, heavy honey strands of hair that had got stuck down the collar of her jacket before backing out of the front door.

It was the noise that hit her first, like a solid wall

of sound; the voices calling her name seemed to come from everywhere.

Dropping the apple, she turned and was immediately blinded by flashing lights. She lifted a hand to shade her eyes and turned her head to avoid the microphones being thrust in her face.

Heart thudding like a piston, she tried to turn back but it was already too late. In seconds the weight of bodies pushing against her had already carried her several feet away and into the street and now she was surrounded.

'Lady Sabrina... Lady Sabrina... Lady Sabrina...! When is the wedding?'

'Will it happen before or after the island is reunified?'

'When did Prince Luis propose?'

'Is this a marriage of convenience?'

'What sort of message do you think you are sending to young women, Dr Summerville?'

The sound of her own name and the stream of questions coming from all directions felt like a physical assault. The conviction she had just walked into her own personal nightmare, the sense of galloping claustrophobia intensified along with the gut-freezing horror that literally paralyzed Sabrina. She couldn't breathe, she couldn't even think past the static buzz of panic in her head. She just closed her eyes, put her head down and waited for the ground to open up.

It didn't.

And then something did, though in amidst the confusion she didn't immediately register anything about what was happening until the grip on her wrist tightened and another hand slid around her waist. She was no longer being carried along by the media crush, she was being pulled in the opposite direction by someone who was strong enough to make it seem easy and to make her wild attempt to hit out at her abductor a joke.

It happened in a blur, one minute she was in the street trying to fight for her freedom and the next she was being unceremoniously dumped like a sack of potatoes into the back seat of a big sleek car that had been hidden from her view by the mass of bodies.

People didn't get kidnapped in front of the press and hundreds of cameras, she told herself while struggling to sit up. She managed it in time to see a camera being thrown at the crowd before the man who had climbed in beside her slammed the door on the noise outside. The mob were now pretty much hysterical.

'Drive, Charlie, if you would!' he drawled in an almost bored tone of voice.

The man in the driving seat reacted by doing just that. He pulled away from the kerb with a squeal of brakes and with scant regard for the lives of the bodies blocking their way.

Sabrina found her eyes connecting with the small, mean-looking eyes of the man in charge of the getaway in the rear-view mirror before she looked away. The tattoo in the shape of a dragon on the back of his thick neck was even less comforting.

Although she knew all about the physical and chemical processes that led the body to over-produce adrenaline, could answer, and actually *had* answered, an exam question on them, she had never, up to that point, personally experienced how compelling the flight-or-fight reflex was.

As the primitive survival response kicked in she literally threw herself at the door, pressing every button in a frantic effort to open it and sobbing with frustration when it didn't budge. She began to batter on the window, more in desperation than with any real hope of attracting attention—they were travelling at speed and the windows were blacked out.

'If you're trying to break it I should tell you that it's bulletproof, though that is quite a right hook you have, *cara*, and I consider myself lucky that you are not wearing heels.'

Her clenched fists slid down the glass and for a moment she rested her forehead against the coolness of the glass before she took a deep breath and turned to face her captor. She might have lost the fight to open the door but she'd won the fight to hide her fear behind a mask of cool disdain—well, as disdainful as you could look when your face was wet with tears and your mascara had most likely run.

'I am not your *cara*, I am not your anything, but if you don't let me go I will be your worst nightmare,' she promised. 'You will stop this car and let me out this instant or I will…' Her voice dried and her jaw hit her chest as she identified the man who was sitting in the corner, one arm resting along the padded backrest, the other holding a phone.

He smiled, looking like a fallen angel on performance-enhancing drugs. It had always made total sense to her that the devil would be good-looking or else where was the temptation?

Not that she was tempted in any way!

His electric-blue eyes glittering with amusement, Prince Sebastian Zorzi tipped his head and touched a gentle finger to her chin.

Shock zigzagged along her nerve endings as Sabrina pulled her head away breathing hard. The initial relief

she'd felt upon realising she was not actually being ab-
ducted, but in fact rescued, was swallowed up by a wave
of antipathy as she met the mockery in the eyes of her
future brother-in-law. His suit was beautifully cut and a
dark charcoal, the jacket stretched across broad shoulders, unbuttoned to reveal the white T-shirt he wore instead of a shirt and tie. The T-shirt clung just enough
to suggest the strong, well-developed contours of his
broad chest. It wasn't his tailoring that made her scalp
tingle though—under the laconic surface there was an
explosive quality about him. In the toughness stakes
Sebastian Zorzi could have given the bulletproof glass
a run for its money.

Obviously she had been aware that the brothers were
physically dissimilar. Nothing surprising about that; siblings often were. She and Chloe looked nothing alike,
after all.

But the Zorzi Princes were not just different, they
were total opposites in everything. It went beyond their
colouring or build, or even their smiles, actually *especially* their smiles! One's made you feel safe, the other?
She gave a little shudder. *Safe* was not a word she could
imagine many people using when it came to Sebastian
Zorzi!

'That's right, Lady Sabrina, I'm the rescue party.'
He lifted his hand and spoke into the phone cradled in
his palm. Sabrina noticed his fingers were very long,
the ends square-tipped and capable. They were definitely strong hands.

'Yes, I've got her. She's...' The dark lashes lifted
from the angular jut of his high carved cheekbones, his
blue eyes seemed to consider her for a moment—the
bone-stripping intensity making her shift in her seat before he responded to the question she couldn't hear. 'In

one piece, just about. She looks like she's been dragged through a hedge backwards, but she retains the ability to look down her well-bred little nose... So, yes, all right—if you like that sort of thing.'

His tone suggested that personally *he didn't like*, but then, having seen the sort of women Sebastian thought of as fine, Sabrina was actually quite glad.

He had a type.

And it had nothing to do with IQ points.

Hard to imagine that the endless succession of tall, leggy blondes whose names had been linked with his were universally dumb, but Sabrina had always imagined, with an uncharacteristic lack of charity, that they probably pretended to be dim! There was a type of man who just couldn't cope with a woman who could challenge them intellectually, and in her opinion the black sheep of the Zorzi family ticked all the boxes for that type!

He was the sort of royal prince who made republicans say smugly, *I told you so*...or they should do, she reflected grimly. It was just that somehow Sebastian made the unacceptable seem charming and no matter what his indiscretions everyone seemed to forgive him; and not only that, they *liked* him despite the fact he'd been sticking a finger up to authority all of his adult life.

It had always mystified Sabrina. Yet sitting a few feet away from him in an enclosed space, she began to understand it better. He didn't have to deliver a charm offensive, he just had to breathe!

The sensual shock wave of his presence had to be experienced to be believed! She had, and Sabrina no longer believed that any of the stories that circulated about him were exaggerated.

In the past it would not have been strange that they had never met. For many years relations between the two Velatian royal families had been, if not frigid, definitely cool.

Times had changed. No longer enemies, the two royal families had become the best of friends and co-conspirators, united in a common cause.

But at every social occasion where both families had been present, somehow Sebastian had always been absent. In fact, it wouldn't surprise her if Sebastian had been banned from such occasions. The only time Sabrina had even been in the same room as Sebastian Zorzi previously, it had been a very large room and he had vanished very early in the evening through a back exit, along with the much younger wife of an elderly diplomat, before they'd had the chance to be formally introduced.

Later that same evening she remembered the awe-inspiring and rather cold, or so it had always seemed to her, King Ricard coming to find his younger son. Luis, she recalled, had covered for his brother. It seemed to be the pattern of the siblings' relationship, his brother breaking the rules and Luis covering up for him.

If that meeting had ever happened she might have been prepared for the aura of raw masculinity Sebastian projected like a force field. It was primitive, raw sex appeal in its most concentrated form.

It made her skin prickle, her heart race and her limbs grow heavy and shakily weak. She didn't like it, but she accepted that she might well be in the minority there. A lot, if not most, might not exactly disapprove of the blatant sexuality of his wide, mobile mouth and the hard sculpted lines of his face. She took comfort in the knowledge that any second-year medical student, or, for that matter, sensible person, would have known her symptoms were caused by the after-effects of shock.

'Did anyone see us leave…?' He repeated the mystery caller's question. 'A few, I'd say.' His eyes, glittering with malicious amusement, found her own and she stopped the frenzied smoothing of her hair while he responded to the person on the other end of the line. 'I wasn't actually counting, but, no, she didn't give them any quotes, barring the curses. I learnt a few new ones!' He winced and lifted the phone away from his ear, waiting a moment, a smile playing across his lips until eventually he pressed it back into the angle of his jaw. 'Of course I'm not being serious. She was the epitome of inbred princess cool,' he soothed, before sliding the phone back into the breast pocket of his jacket.

Sabrina still didn't really know what was happening, but in that moment her desire to find out came second to her desire to react to his comments. 'The next time you accuse someone of being *inbred* I think maybe you should consult your own family tree.'

He gave a low throaty chuckle that alarmingly raised goosebumps over the surface of her skin. 'Point taken, though, as I'm sure you are aware, there was for some time a question mark over my genetic inheritance.'

Her eyes fell even though he displayed none of the awkwardness she immediately felt. Of course she knew. News of the late Queen's affair had found its way onto every front page after the love letters she had written to her lover had found their way into the public domain after the man's death.

Then soon after, in case anyone had missed the lurid headlines, there was the book written by the man's ex-wife and the nanny, who had been the first to connect the dates with the birth of the Queen's second son and shared her suspicions with a tabloid.

There had been a show of solidarity by the Zorzi royal family at the time too. The Queen had appeared looking beautiful and frail at the side of her husband, the two Princes with their hair slicked back and faces shiny.

'But nobody believes that now,' Sabrina said uncomfortably.

He threw her a sardonic look. 'Oh, plenty believe it, *cara*, and a lot more wish it was true...' One slanted brow arched as he shrugged his shoulders. 'Myself included.'

Distracted from her own situation by this statement, she could not hide her astonishment. 'You *wish* you were a bastard? I'm sorry, I...' She broke off, blushing furiously, but Sebastian Zorzi did not appear even slightly put out by being referred to as a bastard.

'Let's just say I don't wake up feeling lucky that Zorzi blood is running through my veins.'

'Well, Luis is proud of his heritage,' she countered defensively.

'My brother is more forgiving than I am.'

'Forgiving of who?'

The mockery left his eyes as he stared at her for a long moment. The expression on his face was hard to read. 'While I'm enjoying this deep and meaningful discussion, aren't there other questions you should be asking at this moment?'

She shook her head in confusion.

'Like, what just happened?'

She immediately felt stupid. 'So what did just happen?'

He gave a throaty chuckle that sounded cruel to Sabrina. 'Welcome to the rest of your life, *cara*.'

'I'm not spending the rest of my life with you.' Or even another second, if she had her way.

'My loss, I'm sure,' he drawled sarcastically.

She clenched her teeth. 'But *why* the cameras? The journalists? I don't understand.'

His dark brows lifted. 'Really? I'd heard you were bright. Ah, well, bright doesn't always equate with quick on the uptake, I suppose,' he conceded as she flushed angrily. 'There has been a leak.'

Crazily, all she could think about with those blue eyes mocking her was the leak in her bathroom that had occurred last winter, the one that had taken the landlord a month to fix.

He sighed, the sound the auditory equivalent of an eye roll. It was the last straw for Sabrina.

'Look, I'm sure having cameras and microphones thrust in your face is all part of a normal day in your life but it's not in mine, so shall we *pretend* just for a moment that you have an ounce of sensitivity? I'm badly traumatised and, like you said, not so quick on the uptake!'

A tense silence followed her outburst. *She never yelled!*

'Ever heard of volume control?'

She said nothing, afraid if she opened her mouth again she'd do something even more embarrassing like cry.

As he stared at her the humorous glint in his eyes completely faded, though there was certainly no softening in his blunt delivery as he spelt out the situation. 'Someone in the inner circle sold the story: wedding, reunification, the whole master plan.'

She shook her head and swallowed past the lump the size of a tennis ball that was lodged in her throat 'Why would anyone do that?'

'Oh, I don't know, maybe for *money*?'

She gnawed on her full lower lip, resenting the ease with which he made her feel gauche and naive.

'But don't worry, we know it wasn't you.'

Her eyes flew wide, the pallor that emphasised the sprinkling of freckles across the bridge of her small straight nose deepening. *'What?'*

'Well, first thought was that you might have got tired of waiting for Luis to pop the question and decided to nudge things along.'

'Why the hell would I want to do that?' In the hothouse emotional atmosphere her knee-jerk reaction emerged uncensored. 'I mean...' Her eyes fell from his searing stare. No, he couldn't see what was in her head; how the hell could he? At that moment *she* didn't even know what was in her head.

'I touched a nerve...interesting.'

'I am not a science experiment!'

One side of his mouth lifted in an incredibly attractive half-smile that made her fight to catch her breath while her skin prickled with antagonism.

'I am sensing that this is bad timing?'

'I don't know what you're talking about.' The bad timing was the twisting sensation in her stomach.

'No need to be coy. I'm assuming that there is a boyfriend in the wings you want to break the news to? Does this guy know that you've been tagged as a sacrifice to the great cause of reunification for years?'

'I am not a sacrifice!'

'Sorry, a willing victim, then. How many barrels of oil do you reckon marrying my brother is worth, just an estimate?'

She clenched her teeth. 'I am *not* a victim—'

'And the oil deposits in your rocky little kingdom

have nothing whatsoever to do with the sudden enthusiasm to reunify our lovely island state? Sorry, not actually *sudden*. How old were you when they told you the plan? That the feel-good factor of a royal wedding would silence the traditionalists on both sides of the border who cling to the good old days when we hated each other's guts.' He pushed his broad, muscular shoulders a little deeper into the leather backrest and let his head fall back. 'It must make you feel very special to know that you make up an entire chapter in a legal document that took two countries ten years to agree on.'

'You forgot one important factor...my family ran out of male heirs and, for the record, *some* guts,' she told him with grim sincerity, 'are easier to hate than others.'

His head lifted; he was grinning his insanely attractive smile. 'Go ahead,' he invited, tossing her his phone, which she caught on instinct. 'I'll pretend to be deaf.'

Lips clamped tight, she tossed it back. 'Thanks but I have my own phone and I don't have a boyfriend.' At university she'd dated a bit, but nothing serious, and then her best friend had met, fallen for and got engaged to a fellow student all in the space of a month. And though Sabrina could not imagine finding herself similarly smitten she had asked herself, *what if*?

Did she really want to find her soul mate only to be forced to walk away from him? The anger she hadn't even acknowledged to herself at the time suddenly found its voice—its *loud* voice.

'I don't date. You go on dates to hopefully get butterflies wondering if he is *the one*, right? So what would be the point?' She stopped, bringing her lashes down in a concealing curtain across her eyes, appalled as much by the bitter outburst as the person she had chosen to open up to. 'Besides, I've been far too busy with work for much else.'

'And now you're going to give that up too like a good little girl, anxious to please. I can see now why it never actually crossed anyone's mind that you were the leak. The general consensus being that you have never broken a rule in your life.'

His scorn stung, even if what he claimed was depressingly true. She had always been the good girl; she was not about to apologise for it. 'You make that sound like a vice.'

'As opposed to what…a *virtue*?' On the point of answering his own blighting question, he seemed to change his mind when after a short static pause he added, in an oddly flat voice, 'The culprit—and, *mea culpa*, he is one of ours—has been found, and he is, as we speak, being dealt with severely.'

'Dealt with?' It sounded sinister, especially when Sebastian said it.

His grin reappeared but it didn't reach his blue eyes. 'Don't worry, despite the bad press we get we haven't actually executed anyone for a century or so, as for thumbscrews we have found them not really that effective, so we just sacked him.'

'He lost his job?'

The air escaped through his clenched teeth in an irritated hiss. 'You're worried about the fate of a man who was responsible for throwing you to the wolves back there? Wow, you really are going to have to toughen up if you're joining our family, sweetheart!' he ground out. 'But if it makes you feel better the guy won't be penniless. His insider story of what goes on behind closed doors is pretty much guaranteed to make the bestseller list after it has been serialised in the Sunday papers.'

The colour that had been seeping back into her face retreated. 'That's terrible!'

'But hardly news,' he responded, sounding very relaxed about the situation. 'The fact my stepmother has a plastic surgeon on speed dial is not exactly the best-kept secret, neither is my father's tendency to throw the first thing that comes to hand when thwarted.'

It crossed Sabrina's mind that an outsider's view of the place could not be any more jaundiced than this cynical insider's.

'So what actually happens now?'

'Now you go get measured for your wedding dress.' His gaze slid down her body.

Smiling through clenched teeth, Sabrina struggled not to react to the calculated insolence in his scrutiny, sweat breaking out across her upper lip as she fought the impulse to lift a hand to shield her shamefully hardened nipples.

'Size eight, am I right? Or maybe a ten up top and an eight in the hips?' His eyes dropped to her legs where her ankles were neatly crossed one over the other, making her aware that she was rhythmically rubbing one calf against the other.

The abrupt cessation of movement brought his heavy-lidded gaze back to her face. 'I'm curious—did it ever occur to you to say no?'

'*No?*' she echoed, wondering if any woman ever had to say no to him. It seemed very unlikely.

Her sense of disorientation increased as his eyes narrowed on her face. 'Or are you actually content to be a pawn?'

'I don't know what you're talking about.'

'Really? Next you'll be telling me that you love Luis, that he is t*he one.*'

Her full lips thinned as she framed a carefully expressionless response to his contemptuous question. 'I'm not going to tell *you* anything…' Then spoilt the effect by instantly exploding resentfully, 'I wouldn't expect someone like *you* to understand.'

Sebastian levered his shoulders from the leather padded backrest and seat as he leaned forward, angling his body towards her. 'And what exactly wouldn't someone *like me* understand?'

She clamped her lips and shook her head, not that the action lessened the feeling of being cornered or the nerve-rattling impact of the aura of testosterone he exuded. If the option to crawl out of her skin had been offered at that moment she would have taken it.

'Duty,' she choked through clenched teeth.

His throaty laugh was mockingly ironic. 'Of course, *duty.*' His slow hand clap raised the levels of her animosity.

'What is funny about that?'

He widened his eyes. 'Sorry,' he said, sounding anything but. 'Was I meant to look impressed by your sacrifice? Oh, I don't think it's funny, *cara*, I think it's *tragic* that you are embracing martyrdom so enthusiastically. I'd blame the brainwashing but I think perhaps you were always the *good* little girl.'

The air left her lungs in a wrathful hiss. 'I have grown up, unlike *some* people, and I do not consider myself a martyr!' Her voice wavered; she was trembling inside and out with the violent rush of emotions his words had shaken loose.

It was a fact of life—or at least *her* life—that she had little control over a lot of things, but this was one occasion when she didn't have to take it—*or* him!

'You can mock the concept of duty and service, but

I'd prefer to be a good girl, as you put it, than a selfish, thrill-seeking, hedonistic waste of space. Has there ever been a moment in your life when you haven't put yourself and your pleasure above anything else?'

She probably imagined the flash of something that had looked like admiration before his head tilted to one side as he gave the appearance of considering her question. 'Probably not,' he conceded.

'Well, being a selfish waster is not a luxury we can all have even if we wanted it.'

'You enjoy your occupation of the moral high ground and in a few years' time, when you are wearing the crown, I just hope you will still think it was worth the things you gave up.'

'I haven't given anything up.'

'How about your work? Why did you waste time, effort and money to qualify as a doctor when you had no intention of ever using that skill?'

Her eyes fell. 'Research is important.'

'Granted, but it will have to survive without you, because my instructions are to deliver you to the embassy. Ours.'

'I'm not a parcel, I'm a person!'

'With feelings, of course—where are my manners? The shoulder to cry on...' He leaned towards her and her nostrils flared as the male, warm scent of his body, mingled with a faint fragrance, filled them. 'Feel free.'

'I do not require a shoulder and if I did—'

'I'm only the spare,' he cut in with an exaggerated sigh as she leaned heavily back. 'I get that totally. You're saving yourself for the man with the crown.'

Her hands clenched into fists as she looked at him with burning eyes. 'You are a really horrible man, you know that?'

'And you are a very beautiful woman.' A look of incredulity flickered across his face. 'Wait, are you...?' He put a finger to her chin and lifted her face towards him. 'Yes, you're blushing!'

'I am *not* blushing.' A sudden possibility had occurred to her, one that would explain his outrageous attitude and the reckless gleam in his eyes. 'Have you been drinking?'

'Not for at least two hours.' He raised his voice to reach the man in the driver's seat. 'Charlie, what time did we leave?'

'I believe it was four a.m., sir,' the man with the tattoo responded in a cultured voice.

'Really? Oh, well, I'm totally sober...well, maybe not totally,' he conceded. 'Oh, here we are.' The car drew up outside the embassy. 'Oh, and I almost forgot, Luis sent his love, and this.'

He leaned across and the sudden shock that had held her immobile as his lips covered hers faded into something else as the slow, sensuous exploration deepened. Sabrina was not sure how her arms came to be around Sebastian's neck but they were, and she was kissing him back as if he were water and she'd spent the last week in the desert. She had never before felt, never imagined anything like the sudden explosion of hot need inside her.

A need that intensified as she felt a shudder move through his lean body and felt the touch of his tongue between her parted lips. She moaned into his mouth and pushed her body into his as he kneaded his fingers into her hair. She felt on fire, filled with an aching need to...*what*?

Luckily, before she found the answer, as suddenly as it had started the kiss stopped.

She sat there, shivering, eyes wide, sucking in air in tiny laboured gasps as he leaned back in the seat staring at her, his hypnotic blue stare searing. Hot, dark streaks of colour emphasising the contours of his sharp cheekbones.

'How dare you?' The sound of her open palm making contact with his cheek was shocking.

He lifted a hand to his cheek and drawled, 'Don't slap the messenger, *cara.*'

'You are vile!' She choked, almost falling out of the car when the door was opened by someone wearing a military uniform.

She could hear his laughter as she walked stiffly up the shallow flight of embassy steps.

CHAPTER TWO

SEBASTIAN SET HIS shoulder to the stiff door that opened out onto a small Juliet balcony. It gave suddenly, filling the warm room with a welcome breeze. The view was as dramatic as the plumbing was idiosyncratic. His shower had run cold and then it had almost scalded him. Oh, well, maybe it was time he learnt how the other half lived, even if that half could claim a heritage as illustrious as his own, such as it was.

For a moment his lip curled into a cynical smile. For reasons obvious when you considered his nickname at school had been *the royal bastard*, Sebastian had never been able to take the whole heritage thing seriously.

A tap on the door made him turn, but before he could respond Luis walked into the room, his normal smile absent.

'Reading your body language I'd guess you were just told you've got weeks to live, or you've just had a heart to heart with our father. How is His Royal Highness?'

Luis's heavy sigh and despondent attitude would normally have evoked a sympathetic reaction from Sebastian, but today the only thing he felt was a surge of irritation. Didn't Luis realise that until he showed a bit of backbone the King was never going to stop trying to micromanage his life? Maybe not even then, Sebastian, a realist, conceded. If he were in his brother's shoes…

But you're not, are you, Seb?

Luis gets the crown and the girl.

'I didn't think you'd come, neither did…anyone.'

'You asked.'

Actually his father had ordered, which under normal circumstances would have guaranteed Sebastian's non-appearance, and yet he was here. *So why?* He rubbed the towel across his dripping hair and veered away from the question in his head before it formed.

'I asked the last three times I came to visit the Summervilles.'

'You know I have an allergy to duty.'

'So you keep telling everyone. Seriously—'

'It is a very serious allergy.'

'I wanted you to get to know Sabrina.'

'It's you she's marrying.' *And me she's kissing,* he thought, the sharp twinge of guilt he felt drowned out by the stronger slug of lusty heat that accompanied the memory of those soft, sweet-tasting lips. If Luis had kissed her more often maybe she wouldn't have melted in his arms.

That's right, Seb, because it's never your fault, is it?

He waited for the familiar hit of mingled frustration, sympathy and affection as he watched Luis walk, shoulders hunched in defeat, across the room. Instead, Sebastian found himself feeling anger and something that, had the circumstances been different, he would have called envy.

But of course it wasn't.

Envy would mean that his brother had something that he wanted, and Luis didn't.

Luis was welcome to the crown.

There *had* been a time when they were growing up that being pushed into the background and being referred to as the *spare* had got to Sebastian, but that had been before he had recognised that it was a lot worse for Luis, carrying the expectations of a country on his young shoulders. Luis had no choices—even his wife was picked out for him.

Luis was welcome to his bride; Sebastian had his freedom. His father had told both of his sons that privilege came with a price; well, so far he'd been proving his father wrong. Sebastian enjoyed the privileges that came with his title without any of the responsibilities.

And Sebastian didn't want to marry Sabrina—he didn't want to marry anyone—he just wanted to take her to bed. Even thinking about her now, and that miracle of a mouth of hers, made smoky desire slither hotly through him.

He ignored it. He'd kissed Sabrina and he wasn't going to do it again, even if the primal attraction that drew him to this woman was stronger than anything he could ever remember feeling. He knew himself well enough to know that it would pass—it always did.

And in the meantime there were plenty of women to kiss who were not about to marry his brother, who were not about to throw away their lives. *Her* business, he reminded himself, *her* choice.

Luckily he had recognised, before the entire kiss incident in the car had got out of perspective, the real danger of building it up into something it was not. She had an incredible mouth, beautiful lips and they made him hungry. The need to taste had swept away every other consideration in his head, but it had been what it was: a 'perfect storm' moment. Or maybe a perfect moment of madness, fuelled by the alcohol he'd imbibed much earlier in the morning at the nightclub, where he had been even more bored than usual.

The chances were, seeing Sabrina here, in her natural environment, as a woman who represented everything he had been rebelling against and rejecting all his life, that he would regain his normal objectivity.

'I didn't expect you to come, but I'm glad you did. I do appreciate the support.'

'Support?' Sebastian queried with a frown.

'I can't say I'm exactly looking forward to tonight.'

'Performance anxiety or…don't tell me you're having second thoughts?'

Luis turned away but not quickly enough to hide his flush of annoyance at the joke that presumably offended his highly developed sense of duty. If it *was* annoyance?

Guilt? Could he have hit a nerve? Was his brother having second thoughts? Sebastian dismissed the possibility almost straight away, no matter what his personal feelings. For Luis, duty, no matter what form it took, came first.

'So how is the blushing bride?'

'Fine… I guess.'

'You guess? You mean you didn't spend the night saying hello?' Sebastian said, immediately imagining himself saying a very long hello.

'I only just arrived and she…we… She doesn't blush.'

Sebastian's brows lifted. 'Oh?' he said, remembering the delicious rosy tinge that had washed over Sabrina's pale skin.

'Not that that is a *bad* thing.'

Sebastian's eyes narrowed in his brother's face. 'Which means that *you* think it is.'

Luis looked guilty. 'She just isn't always what you'd call very spontaneous.'

Sebastian cloaked his expression as he heard the echo of that soft little mewling cry as she'd opened her mouth to him. His body hardened helplessly at the memory of her soft breasts pushing into his ribcage.

The effort of fighting his way free of those intrusive memories delayed his response. 'Spontaneity can be overrated.' It could also be great...*she* would be great in bed.

Never going to find out, Seb.

He was a bastard but not *that* much of a bastard.

'Exactly, especially when your every move is being scrutinised. She has all the qualities to make the perfect Queen.'

The speculative furrow between Sebastian's dark brows deepened as he listened to his brother, sounding very much like a man who was trying desperately to convince himself that he believed in what he was saying.

'I'm sold,' he murmured drily. 'How about you?'

Luis dodged the soft question and his brother's speculative stare. 'Marriage is all about teamwork.'

'So I hear.' He had never given marriage much thought aside from concluding fairly early on that it was not for him, about the same time that he had nearly made a fatal error. 'I nearly proposed once,' he remembered, a rueful smile tugging the corners of his mouth upwards as he tried and failed to visualise the face of the woman who he had decided, at nineteen, was the love of his life.

'*You!*' His brother's jaw hit his chest before he recovered. '*You've* been in love?' Luis shook his head. 'Who? When? What happened?'

'What always happens—the glitter rubs off. I found out she snored and her laugh grated, but for a while I believed that she was perfect. Actually, I've believed quite a few were perfect since, the difference being I no longer expect it to last.'

In Sebastian's opinion, if you were looking for a formula for unhappiness it would be hard to come up with a more sure-fire method than tying yourself to one person for life based on a short-lived chemical high.

'Perfect? Like you, you mean?'

Sebastian winced and grinned, watching as Luis, his expression growing distracted, moved to one of the two chairs arranged at the foot of the bed. Sebastian held up a warning hand.

'I wouldn't do that. I made the same mistake. The leg dropped off. I've propped it.'

Luis made a detour to the other chair.

Sebastian's gaze moved around the room of faded grandeur. 'It's not what I was expecting. They really are strapped for cash. No wonder,' he observed cynically, 'they are so willing to sell their daughter off to the highest bidder.'

'They're not selling her!' Luis protested. 'Sabrina understands. She respects—'

'Our mother understood,' Sebastian interrupted, wondering if the anger he felt would ever go away. Anger at the system that had trapped his mother in a marriage that had, in the end, destroyed her. 'And that didn't turn out so well.'

'It's not the same!' his brother protested, flushing as he surged to his feet.

Sebastian arched a brow. 'From where I'm standing it looks like a classic case of history repeating itself.'

Luis's horrified rebuttal was immediate. 'I'm not like…him.'

Then break the blasted cycle!

Sebastian didn't voice his thought. What would be the point? He knew his brother would never challenge their father, and, if the positions were reversed, was he so damned sure that he would? Easy to criticise from where he stood.

'I wonder, Seb. What do you think he'd do if he knew…?'

Sebastian's irritation slipped away as he walked across to where his brother stood and laid a hand on Luis's shoulder. 'He won't,' he said firmly. 'We burnt the letters. No one knows they ever existed.'

The young brothers had not known at the time they discovered the love letters hidden under a floorboard that despite breaking off the affair after she discovered she was carrying her lover's child she had continued to see him after the child she had conceived with him had been born.

The irony was that they were right, there was a royal bastard, only it wasn't the son that the scandal-mongers had identified.

'As far as the world is concerned, the affair only started the year I was born.' Sebastian could see no reason anyone should ever know. 'We are the only two people who know, unless you plan on telling him?'

Luis shuddered. 'I stood by and watched you being bullied at school and then at home when we both know that you should be King. I have no legitimate claim to the throne. I'm not even his son.'

Sebastian shook his head. 'Be glad of that every day. Be glad of it, Luis!' he said, his voice gruff with ferocious sincerity. 'You've escaped the taint that I carry. *I'm* the son the bastard deserves. You will make a better King than I ever could be. You're the one who has made all the sacrifices…and you are still making them.' Sebastian straightened up, relaxing the grip on his brother's shoulders. 'You don't *have* to marry her, you know. You could say no.'

Luis shook his head and dodged his brother's gaze. 'Easy for you to say. I'm not—'

'Selfish as hell?' Sebastian thought of where being unselfish had got his mother. He'd choose selfish every time.

Luis's gaze lifted, just as his brother vanished into the bathroom. 'I'm not a rebel like you. I need to… I *care* about what people think about me.'

Sebastian re-emerged with a fresh towel, which he rubbed vigorously over his damp hair.

'And this marriage isn't about me, it's about bigger things. I'm realistic about it.'

'So how does *she* feel about it?'

Luis gave an uncomprehending shrug. 'How do you mean?'

'I mean what does *Sabrina* expect from this marriage? Is she realistic too?' He gave a sudden shrug, annoyed with himself for wasting time on a subject that was none of his business. 'Is the warm glow of doing the right thing enough for her too?' He began to vigorously rub his already towel-dried hair, asking himself where this swell of outrage was coming from. She'd made her bed and she seemed happy to lie in it…with his brother. 'Hell, Luis, do you two even talk?'

'We have a lifetime to talk,' Luis responded, not sounding as though the life he saw stretching ahead filled him with joy. 'But you mean sex, don't you? It's not like you to be so squeamish. Actually no, I haven't slept with her.'

'That's not what I meant, but as you've shared aren't

you taking this untouched virgin bride stuff a bit too far, Luis?'

Luis laughed. 'Even father doesn't expect that.'

'How incredibly liberal-minded of him.' Sebastian was still struggling with the implication of some of Sabrina's unguarded comments. Was it *really* possible that Sabrina had not had a lover, out of *fear* of falling in love?

'What if you're not compatible? Have you thought of that?'

Luis for once looked annoyed. 'For God's sake, Seb, this isn't about how good she is in bed!'

As the comment unlocked a stream of graphic images that flowed relentlessly through his head, Sebastian lowered his eyelids to half-mast. His jaw clenched as he struggled to stem the flow and pretended an amusement he was a long way from feeling. 'But it would help.'

It would help him even more, Sebastian mused darkly, if he could stop thinking of unfastening glossy honey hair and watching it fall over bare shoulders, pushing it back to reveal small firm breasts...

Oblivious to the tension underpinning his brother's taut delivery, Luis laughed. 'I really like her.'

'Like?'

Luis tipped his head in acknowledgment. 'She's sweet,' he began with the attitude of a man who was clutching at straws.

'And,' he ploughed on with determination, 'she has a lot of common sense.'

Were they even talking about the same woman? Sebastian wondered, thinking about the woman who had attempted to punch her way out of his locked car just to avoid being shut in there with him.

He recognised she'd been driven to this drastic move by desperation and fear and he had fully intended saying something to soothe her, but the expression on her face when she'd recognised him, the fact that she'd looked as though she had just discovered she had jumped into a car beside the Devil himself…he simply hadn't been able to resist playing up to her prejudices a little.

But then she had challenged his own firmly embedded prejudices. In the abstract he had been able to despise Sabrina Summerville, or at least the *idea* of her, a woman who, despite coming from a different generation, was just as willing as his own mother had been to be a compliant, political pawn.

The first surprise had been the desire that had twisted inside him when he'd found himself sitting just inches away from her, which shouldn't have happened. He had seen the photos. He already knew that she was good-looking, admittedly more classy than classically beautiful. But what those photos had not prepared him for was the crystal clarity of her skin, the sprinkling of freckles across the bridge of her small straight nose, the deep liquid darkness of her eyes that seemed to reflect her every mood like a mirror. And last, but definitely not least, the pink lushness of her amazing lips.

The blood-roaring primal intensity of his reaction had effectively blocked everything else from his mind for what might only have been seconds, but could have been an hour.

And the hits had just kept coming!

He'd expected a passive victim; he had got a feisty fighter, who clearly thought he was a total waste of space. What had got to him the most had been the conflict in her eyes, her vulnerability.

He'd just wanted to tell her not to do it. Not to marry

Luis. Instead he'd kissed her…a greedy response to a need that had been visceral in its intensity.

'I've never seen her lose her temper,' Luis said.

Sebastian could not control the bark of laughter that bubbled up from his chest as he lifted a hand to his cheek where the imprint of her fingers had lasted, but he didn't react to his brother's puzzled look.

'Perhaps you should try giving her cause and see what happens?'

'She's very pretty,' Luis added, his tone almost defensive as though he expected his brother to deny the fact.

Was Luis serious? The woman was beautiful. She wasn't his type, he had never leaned in the direction of cut-glass delicacy, but even *he* could recognise her natural beauty, the rare 'get out of bed with her hair mussed and still look knockout gorgeous' beauty, not that he would ever get the chance to prove his theory.

She was his brother's.

The reminder slowed the heat rising inside him but did not stop its slow, inexorable progress.

What are you, Seb? Fifteen? Get a grip, man!

'Are you asking me for an opinion?' Sebastian struggled hard to tap into the sympathy he normally felt for his brother, who was the one expected to make a marriage of convenience, the one looking ahead to a life of being the acceptable public face of the crown.

'No, yes? I suppose?' His brother produced one of his genuine smiles, seeming to suddenly shrug off his mood with an ease that Sebastian envied.

'Maybe you should go on a date.'

'With *Sabrina*?'

'Well, the dating ritual is kind of what people do before they get married, unless you have one of those "wake up in Vegas with a tattoo, a hangover and a wife" marriages. I can recommend the first two as a way of passing a weekend.'

Luis's eyes slid from his brother's as he sketched a smile. 'I haven't thanked you yet, for getting her out of that press scrum.'

'Glad to be of help,' Sebastian said, wondering about the change of subject and his brother's unusually evasive attitude. Luis, he decided as he studied his brother's face, looked positively shifty.

'I'm sure she took it all in her stride.'

Sebastian clamped his jaw as he fought a compulsion to defend Sabrina from the criticism he could hear behind this faint praise. 'You'd have preferred she'd have fallen apart?'

'Of course not.'

'Actually she was pretty shaken, but she came out fighting.' He saw no point adding that the fight had been mostly directed, quite deservedly, at him.

Luis got to his feet. 'She was lucky you were so close.'

'She might not agree... I'd been drinking.'

Luis looked amused. 'Fall asleep and snore, did you?'

Sebastian's eyes fell. 'Not exactly.'

Sabrina stubbornly refused to acknowledge the lump in her throat as she unpacked. The task didn't take long. There wasn't much, just a few pieces of clothing and personal items she had hastily crammed into a holdall.

They represented the majority of her things from the London flat she'd shared with a couple of girlfriends, or *had* up until two days ago.

The embassy staff hadn't wanted her to return at all that day, but in the end she'd been given the begrudging go-ahead for half an hour with what they'd termed a *discreet* security presence, which had turned out to consist of a team of four large dark-suited men.

Sabrina had retained enough of her natural sense of irony—*just*—to wonder what *non*-discreet looked like, as two of the silent, unsmiling figures had stared straight ahead as she'd packed and written a note for her flat-mates, who had both been sleeping after a long night shift. The other two minders had been, as they'd put it, *securing the exits*... She really didn't want to know what that involved! Though the dawning realisation that soon this bizarre would be her normal had made her lose whatever humour she might have seen in the situation.

When it had come to making a goodbye visit to the research unit where she had worked for just over the last year she'd changed tack, not requesting permission, instead just announcing her intention the next morning. Wait, no, it had been *this* morning. Things were happening so fast it was a struggle to retain any sense of time in this speeded-up version of her own life. She had hidden her surprise when the tactic had worked. Perhaps in the future she should stop saying please and simply demand?

Being the future Queen had to have some benefits.

You're getting ahead of yourself, Brina. You're not even a princess yet.

Her ironic grin barely surfaced before it vanished, because *soon* she *would* be.

She supposed she didn't really have the right to feel so shocked, it was hardly news, but in the past it had been a distant thing. Now it was all *very* real and there was no more pretending that her life was normal.

An expression of impatience drifted across her heart-shaped face, firming the lines of her delicate jaw and soft full lips as she cut off the self-pitying direction of her thoughts.

It is what it is, Brina, so get over it, she told herself sternly as she shook out the silky blouse she was clutching and put it on a hanger.

Was it actually worth the effort of unpacking?

The rate at which things were moving now would mean this wouldn't be her home for much longer. They were talking June wedding. Weeks away, not months or years. Once more she stubbornly ignored the flurry in her belly, less butterflies and more a buzzard's wings flapping this time in the pit of her stomach.

Her determined composure wobbled, as did her lower lip, as she pulled out the last item. The outline of the white lab coat she held up blurred as her dark eyes filled with hot tears.

She dashed a hand impatiently across the dampness on her cheeks and blinked hard as her thoughts were inexorably dragged back to when the colleagues she had worked beside for the past year had given her an impromptu leaving party. Some party poppers left from New Year had been pulled from a drawer and dutifully popped, exciting a mild overreaction from the security men, one of whom had flung her to the floor.

Someone whose name she didn't even know was willing to put himself between her and a bullet. She could see the surreal realisation hit her friends almost as hard as it did her.

In the subsequent dampened party atmosphere someone had handed around sausage rolls hastily bought from the twenty-four-hour mini-mart on the corner, and then they had presented her with the lab coat, a crown emblem sewn onto the breast pocket.

She had struggled to smile at the joke while accepting the leaving present and hugs of colleagues, who'd all said how much they were going to miss her, while she had tried hard not to think about how much she would miss them. She'd miss, too, the challenge of her work—unlike the challenges that lay ahead, this one had been of her own choosing.

Despite the hugs she'd been able to see they were looking at her differently, *thinking* about her differently. The realisation had saddened but not surprised her. Experience had taught her to expect no less. It was why once she'd had a choice in such things she had never advertised her title or background. She'd wanted to be accepted for who she was with no preconceptions.

She would always treasure her time at university, both as a medical student and then staff member at the prestigious research unit. Dr Summerville was a title she had earned and was proud of. *Lady* Sabrina, daughter of the Duke and Duchess of East Vela, was simply an accident of birth, the same accident that would see her promotion to Princess and one day Queen of the soon-to-be-reunified island kingdom.

She had relished the opportunity to be judged for her ability and not who her parents were. She had liked that when people had asked her where she was from, *East Vela* had drawn a puzzled frown and an inevitable, *where is that?* Or, *don't you mean Vela Main?*

There were big advantages for someone who did not like attention of being a royal from somewhere so obscure, the main one being that a third-division royal did not rate heavy security—one of those things she was learning that you did not fully appreciate until it vanished.

For the last few years Velatian politics had seemed a long way away, and she had kept it there, enjoying her freedom, her taste of real life. Sure, she'd been able to hear the clock ticking down, and the knowledge of what lay ahead had never vanished, but she had always known that her parents would make sure she was eased gently into her future role.

But there had been no gentle easing, more like a total immersion. A sink-or-swim introduction of what it meant to be Queen-in-waiting.

One day she had gone to bed as Dr Summerville, an invisible white coat in a laboratory, and had walked out into the street the next morning to calls of, *'Lady Sabrina, when is the wedding?'*

Her eyes clouded with memories as she rubbed her arm where the imprint of his fingers was beginning to turn from black to a more mellow yellow. She squeezed her eyes shut but couldn't block out his face…or her guilt, or the feeling in the pit of her stomach when she remembered how his mouth had felt against hers, his taste, the raw sexual energy he exuded.

She lifted both hands to her head and yelled, 'Go away!'

'Why? What have I done?' Sabrina's eyes flew open as her sister walked into the room and flung herself face down on the bed.

'There's a wasp…do you mind?' Sabrina said, pretending a crossness she didn't feel because she was glad to see her sister. She eased a dress out from under Chloe's prone form. 'I am wearing this tonight.'

Chloe propped her chin on her steepled fingers and scanned the garment that Sabrina hung on a coat hanger and hooked over her wardrobe door.

Chloe gave her verdict. 'Nice, love the fifties vibe, but you could show a bit more cleavage.'

Sabrina raised a brow.

'You did ask,' her sister said.

'No, actually I didn't.'

'Well, you should. Have you any idea how many people read my fashion blog? I am considered a fashion guru.'

'And what do you think Dad is going to consider about *that*?'

Sabrina angled a nod in the direction of the micro miniskirt her sister was wearing in neon green.

'He won't see it,' Chloe said with a grin as she rolled over and pulled herself into a sitting position, her long legs tucked under her.

It was then Sabrina saw what her sister was wearing on top.

Chloe gave another million-voltage smile and held her arms wide to proudly show off the T-shirt. Sabrina had seen identical ones in the tourist shops in the capital of Vela Main, where the iconic image was reproduced on everything from tea towels to mugs. It was of the Venetian Prince who had fought for, and gained, independence for Vela.

'You like? I'm showing my hands-across-the-border solidarity. They say his eyes follow you round the room.'

'They do,' Sabrina said shortly. She had seen the original on the wall of the great hall in the royal palace.

'Don't you think their Pirate Prince looks like the bad brother? I can't see how anyone could have thought he was a bastard,' Chloe added, pulling the fabric outwards to look at the face of the Venetian Prince famous for being the man who had fought dirty to secure Vela Main's independence from Venice. That, and his career as a successful pirate.

It was Luis who had pointed out the similarity during a day trip her family had made the previous year to take lunch with the royal family at Vela Main.

'His eyes really do follow you around the room,' she

had said, staring at the original of the much-reproduced image.

'Sebastian has the same trick,' Luis had said.

'He was very handsome. Him,' she'd added, pointing at the portrait and adding hastily, 'Not your brother.'

Luis had laughed at her embarrassment. 'You might change your mind when you two finally meet. I'd like to say Seb got the looks and I got the brains, but...'

'I think you're very smart, modest and good-looking.'

Whenever doubts had crept in Sabrina had reminded herself that Luis couldn't have been more unlike his hateful brother if he'd tried.

They were day and night, Sebastian definitely being night, even though his eyes had made her think of the brightest, most blindingly blue summer sky when he'd bent his head and fitted his cool, firm lips to hers.

She felt the guilty heat rise through her body as she reminded herself that she *could* have stopped it from happening!

Belatedly aware that Chloe was staring at her, she shook her head.

'A bit,' she conceded before changing the subject. 'God, you look like an advert for something healthy... or toothpaste?'

'And you, sweetie, look like you were doorstepped by the national media.' She held out her arms. 'Hug?'

'Yes, please.'

Sisterly hug exchanged, they sat down on the window seat side by side.

'I'm quite jealous of the number of hits you got... did you watch it?'

Sabrina did not pretend not to understand; she had heard she had gone viral. 'No, I was there.'

'Don't look so gloomy. I know many women who

would pay to get chucked into the back seat by Sebastian Zorzi, and you were wearing nice undies.'

Sabrina's eyes widened. 'You couldn't…?'

Chloe chuckled at the shocked reaction. 'No, just a lot of leg.' Her expression sobered. 'Seriously, though…?'

Sabrina angled an enquiring look at her sister's face.

The grin re-emerged. 'He is seriously gorgeous! How about a double wedding? I'm up for it if you are!'

'What, and share my day in the spotlight?' Sabrina said, struggling to reply in kind because the image of her sister, dressed in white, standing beside a tall, lean, handsome figure made her feel a little queasy.

'Because we all know how much you love that.' Chloe's smile vanished. 'Brina, are you all right? I'm just trying to lighten the mood, you know. Are you really going to do it?'

'Do what?'

'Go through with this crazy medieval marriage of convenience? You can't let yourself be used this way, Brina. It's so wrong.'

'I don't have a choice.'

'There is always a choice, Brina.'

Sabrina shook her head and veiled her eyes with her lashes. It was true, but now the time was here she wished she believed it. 'I want to marry Luis. He's a nice guy.'

Chloe's expression grew serious as she took her sister's hands in hers and said gravely, 'Don't you think you deserve better than *nice*? A husband who thinks you are more important than anything?'

After a shocked moment Sabrina brought her lashes down in a protective sweep as she swallowed the emotional lump in her throat. Chloe had voiced the thoughts she didn't dare even allow herself to think.

'Since when did you become a paid-up member of the soppy romantic club?'

Chloe's smile was back as she jumped to her feet. 'I hide it well. So how about I do wear this tonight?' She moved her hand down the tiny skirt she wore. 'And flirt with the sexy Sebastian?'

Sabrina struggled to respond to her sister's teasing smile, managing some sickly approximation of an answering smile despite the tight feeling of rejection in her stomach.

'Chloe, be careful. Sebastian Zorzi, he isn't the sort of man you play with.'

She thought of eyes so blue they took your breath away and felt a little shiver trace a sinuous path down her spine as the memory surfaced, both terrifying and seductive. She didn't want Chloe to be exposed to the danger he represented.

Or maybe you don't want her to be kissed.

'He's dangerous.'

Chloe laughed. 'He sounds better and better. Now how about a glass of wine to get us in the mood, or to at least prepare me for the undoubted cold shower that awaits me when I go to my room? Perhaps when you've sold your body for the good of the country we can get the plumbing fixed?' She grinned and produced a bottle from the capacious handbag she had dumped by the door. 'Glasses?'

CHAPTER THREE

HER MOTHER ENTERED her bedroom with dramatic abruptness just as Sabrina was fitting the last hair in the smooth twist she had wound her hair into.

'There has been a disaster with the meal. Don't ask!'

Sabrina didn't but the harassed Duchess told her anyway. 'I found out an hour ago that the Queen is gluten and lactose intolerant. Half the menu had to be revised. The chef is not happy.'

'I'm sure it will be fine,' Sabrina soothed, getting to her feet. Focusing on her mother's panic made it somehow easier to deal with her own nerves. 'Just breathe, Mum.' She laid a hand on her parent's arm.

The Duchess took a deep breath. 'Yes, I'm sure you're right, but I'm running terribly late. I haven't even started getting ready, not that it really matters. The Queen—' she lowered her voice and glanced over her shoulder, as though someone might be listening, before adding in a note of mingled envy and despair '—always makes me feel inadequate. I swear the woman gets younger every year!'

'Mum, you always look lovely!' Sabrina protested.

Her mother smiled. 'You're a good girl, Brina. And you're right, of course, at my age it's silly to worry about what I look like.'

'I didn't say that,' Sabrina protested. 'There's plenty of time for you to go and get ready.'

'I can't. I promised Walter that I'd run through the final details with him and speak to the staff.'

'Leave it to me,' Sabrina said, pretty sure she would regret the offer. The major-domo, Walter, always made her feel as though she were ten again and he'd just caught her trying to glue together a piece of porcelain she had broken. 'You go and get ready.'

'Really?'

Sabrina nodded.

The Duchess gave her daughter a gentle hug. 'You're an angel. I really don't know what I'll do without you when you're married.'

'Pretty much what you've been doing for the past seven years while I've been living in London, except from now on I'll be closer.

'Of course. You're such a sensible girl. You've never given us a moment's worry, unlike your sister! Speaking of Chloe, I'm going to check what she's wearing.' Reaching the door, she stopped and turned back. 'You look very beautiful tonight.'

Sabrina grinned and smoothed the full skirt of the calf-length fifties-style pale blue silk dress she wore. 'Oh, this old thing?'

'And you're wearing your grandmother's pearls,' the Duchess said, an emotional crack in her voice, as Sabrina touched the string of antique pearls wound around her slender neck. 'You do know we are both very proud of you, don't you? I wish there was another way. That you could—'

'Nobody is forcing me to do anything. Luis is a lovely guy and I plan on being very happy.' She took her mother by the shoulders and propelled her out of the door. It was only when the door had closed again that her forced smile faded. Happiness, she reminded herself, was not a right; in her case it was more a hope.

Sabrina didn't search out the major domo; she knew he'd find her. She relayed her mother's concerns, being careful not to tread on Walter's toes. He responded with his habitual air of statuesque calm to her queries. It was at his suggestion she had a few words with the staff, mainly to thank them for their efforts in hosting the royal party at such short notice.

Then, with Walter, she checked out the table setting in the formal dining room. It was a room they rarely used as a family, but tonight the table groaned with silver and crystal, and happily the candlelight hid a multitude of sins—including the massive crack in the ceiling, which the engineer's report had ominously re-ferred to as significant.

There was, it seemed, only one decision for her to make.

'Her Grace had not decided if we should serve the aperitifs in here, or the small salon?'

It was a courtesy, she knew, because Sabrina had already seen the scene set in the salon as she'd walked past, but she happily maintained the illusion that it was her decision and responded to the courtesy enquiry gravely. 'I think, the small salon.'

The major-domo tipped his head in stately approval of her response. 'I will see to it. If there is nothing else…?'

'Nothing, thank you, Walter.' About to follow him from the room herself, Sabrina paused and turned back. She walked across to the row of French doors that lined one wall and she began to open them up. The last one stubbornly refused to budge, causing her to curse softly. She aimed an irritated kick at it with one narrow, elegantly shod foot, before she paused to get her breath.

The same cool draught of mountain air that Sebastian felt on his face as he reached the open doorway made the full skirt of Sabrina's dress billow around her slender legs. He watched as, eyes closed, long lashes fanning darkly against her smooth cheeks, eyes squeezed closed, she let out a long sibilant sigh through parted pink lips as she turned her face into the breeze, making no attempt to tame the fabric as it lifted and fluttered some more.

The tilt of her chin and the elegant placement of her arms made him think of a ballet dancer. An idea that was reinforced as her head fell back revealing the long, lovely line of her neck and throat and the angles of her collarbones. Though high to the throat, at the back the bodice of the dress she wore was cut into a deep vee that exposed a half-moon-shaped mole on the crest of one delicate shoulder blade.

Sebastian felt the heat rise through him and forgot to breathe, forgot *how* to breathe as the graceful image burned deep into his brain. Hunger tightened its grip, a primal pleasure/pain presence low in his belly and all points south. There were so many warning bells ringing in his head that he was deaf to everything but the heavy thud of his heart, the ache in his body and the whisper of sound as the fabric brushed against her legs.

Then she opened her eyes and gave a tiny sigh. The sound snapped the sensual spell that had held him transfixed, leaving behind something that he refused to recognise as tenderness. That sigh had sounded so damn *wistful*.

She remained oblivious to his presence as he crossed

the room. She had both hands braced against the door frame and was pushing against the stubborn door, when he placed a hand above her head on the door jamb.

The door gave with a shudder.

'Thank you.' Sabrina turned, the corners of her soft mouth lifted in a smile of gratitude, which melded into one of dismay as she saw that it was him.

Sabrina stepped back so quickly that she almost lost her balance. The impact of his physical proximity acted like a live current, her quivering stomach vanished into a bottomless black hole and it took every ounce of her willpower to stop herself backing through the open door, which would have been impossible anyway because her limbs were paralyzed with shock. *They call it lust, Brina.*

Ignoring the mocking voice in her head, she lifted her softly rounded chin to a warily aggressive angle and directed a cool look up at the tall figure of the Zorzi black sheep. Sebastian just stood there in his formal black tie and tux, looking as if he had just stepped off a glossy Hollywood set.

'You're too early!' Panic made her voice sharp.

'I could hardly wait to sample the well-known hospitality of East Vela,' he countered sardonically as his heavy-lidded stare travelled from the top of her glossy head to her heels and back. Sabrina fingered the pearls at her throat, trying desperately to ignore how his assessing and overtly sensual gaze made her whole body tingle.

The nervous action drew his stare to her throat, where a blue-veined pulse pushed against the pale skin.

'You startled me. I thought you were Walter.'

So the smile was for Walter. 'You look…good.'

No smile came with the compliment, which was delivered in an expressionless voice.

'So, should I?'

'What?'

'Go away and come back.'

Sabrina flushed and moved her head slightly to look past his shoulder willing someone, anyone, to appear.

They didn't.

'If you were expecting Luis he's waiting on an important call.'

She firmed her shoulders and reminded herself that being pleasant to people she didn't like was part of her future job. She could not allow personal feelings to enter into it. 'No, of course not. You just took me by surprise and this is a bit...awkward.'

'Why?'

She tightened her lips and glared at him. 'I have no pleasant memories of our last encounter.'

'I can think of one,' he teased, looking at her mouth.

The longer their glances held, the thicker the atmosphere in the air became. Sabrina was the first to look away, fixing her eyes on a point over his shoulder as she fiddled with the pearls. 'I had assumed you were drunk but I can see now that you're always...' Her words faded as the vivid memory resurfaced. His breath the other day had not actually tasted of booze, just mint and... No, she was not going to go there!

'Irresistible?'

Before she could react to the suggestion the antique string of pearls she was playing with snapped.

Sabrina immediately fell to her knees, trying to grab the pearls, which were bouncing across the polished wooden floor in all directions. 'Oh, no! No, no, no.'

'Relax, they're not the crown jewels...' He stopped, his teasing look vanishing from his face as she lifted her head and he saw that she was close to tears.

'Just go away!' she hissed. 'I don't give a damn about the crown jewels. They were my grandmother's pearls.'

With a frown he dropped down, squatting on his heels beside her. He saw the little tremors that shook her shoulders and felt something twist hard in his chest. He did his best to ignore it, telling himself it was either indigestion or the threat of tears that had caused it. He'd never liked seeing women crying.

'She left them to me. She always wore them and now they're ruined! *Everything* is ruined...' Dignity forgotten, on all fours now, she stretched to retrieve a pearl that had slipped under a chair, but as her finger touched it it bounced away. 'I can't do this! It's so, so... No, I just can't!'

'What we need is a system. An inch-by-inch search. What do they call it—a fingertip search?'

The image that drifted into her head involved his fingertips moving very slowly, but the surface they were exploring, the secret crevices they were discovering, had nothing to do with the wooden floor! What was happening to her?

'You count and I'll retrieve.'

She struggled to drag her thoughts back to the present. The process felt like swimming through warm honey. There was a horrible temptation to taste it.

'That really isn't necessary,' she managed finally, her voice carrying nowhere near the level of conviction she was hoping for. 'I'm really not that sentimental.'

He had already lifted the heavy starched linen table-cloth; at her comment he glanced back over his shoulder. 'Yes, you are, which is fine. Make yourself useful and hold this up. There are some under here.'

After a pause she did as he requested and lifted the heavy starched linen cloth while he reached under. A moment later several more pearls were dropped into her open hand.

She glanced at him from under her lashes. His dark hair was ruffled and there was a dusty smudge on the dark lapel of his jacket. Without thinking she reached out to brush it away. 'You don't have to do this, you know.'

'I know.'

She had never seen anything as blue as his eyes; they were compellingly hypnotic. She fought a short internal battle and dropped her hand away, escaping the full impact of his eyes by looking up through the mesh of her lashes. 'Well, thank you, I think that's all of them,' she said at last, closing her hand that was now full of the smooth pearls.

Sebastian rose to his feet before her and reached out a hand. After a pause Sabrina took it and allowed him to pull her to her feet. Her stomach made an unscheduled dive as her quivering nostrils picked up the scent of his warm body, the clean fragrance, the *maleness*.

He immediately released her hand but she could still feel the warmth of his fingers as she rubbed her hand along her silk-covered thigh. The stab of sexual desire that pierced her was so tangible it seemed to her guilty mind that it echoed off the walls like an accusation.

'I've been meaning to get them restrung for ages.' She began to babble. What was he trying to do to her? Nothing, came the depressing and shaming answer, he didn't have to do a thing.

'Lady Sabrina?'

She responded with relief to the sound of her name and the familiar respectful voice. 'Yes, Walter?' she said, moving towards the door where the major-domo stood.

'I just wanted to let you know that the Duke and Duchess are in the small salon.' He turned towards Sebastian and bent forward at the waist. 'Sir, I believe that the royal party will be joining them there directly.'

'I'll be right there, Walter,' Sabrina said, shifting the pearls from one slightly sticky hand to the other.

'May I help?'

'These are my—'

'The late Duchess's pearls.' The major-domo gave one of his rare smiles and held out a hand. 'I never saw her without them,' he added when Sabrina looked reluctant. 'They will be safe with me.'

Sabrina acknowledged the reassurance with a smile and tipped the pearls into his hand. 'Thank you.' She stood there, hopefully not looking as awkward as she felt as she turned back to Sebastian, who had watched the interchange in silence. Not quite meeting his eyes—some might call it cowardly but she called it sensible—she gestured towards the door. 'I'll show you the way, shall I?' Without waiting to see if he accepted the invitation, she left the room, not caring if she gave the impression of running away. Any woman with an ounce of common sense would run in the opposite direction when they saw Sebastian Zorzi, though she doubted there were many who did. Luckily she had never been one of the number who were drawn to danger, even when it wore a suit as well as he did. He probably looked even better without the suit!

Face flushed with shame, she speeded up, but she had only gone a few yards before he fell into step beside her.

'I never met your grandmother. But I've heard a lot about her. She sounds like quite a character.'

'She always said exactly what she thought.' And her outspoken grandparent had thought that the plan to marry her granddaughter off to seal the reunification deal was an appalling plan and she had said so, often. 'Chloe is very like her. Not in looks obviously.' Her grandmother had been tiny and delicate while her sister would not have looked out of place in an Olympic rowing team.

'But not you?'

'Gran was a rebel,' Sabrina said, aware of the emotional ache in her throat but not of the wistful quality to her observation as she thought of the old lady who had been such a big part of her early years. 'So, no, we are not alike. I'm a *good* girl, remember?' she said, forgetting her intention not to look at him and angling a resentful look up at his dark, lean, *insanely* handsome face.

Sebastian intercepted the glare and held her eyes as he raised a dark sardonic brow before allowing his stare to sink to her mouth, heat sparking in his heavy-lidded eyes as they moved across the full soft curves. 'Not always,' he purred throatily.

She looked away quickly, feeling the heat climb to her cheeks as the volume of the background hum of sexual awareness that she had been successfully dealing with up until now became a deafening clamour.

'We all make mistakes. I think the trick is in not repeating them,' she said. Two could play the innuendo game! 'Here we are,' she added, as a young maid carrying a tray bobbed a little curtsy. The younger woman's wide appreciative eyes stayed firmly on Sebastian as she almost bumped into the full suit of armour that was positioned beside the door they had reached before walking through, head down now to hide her burning cheeks.

Sabrina angled a sideways look at Sebastian, who didn't even seem to have noticed. Presumably, she thought bitterly, he was used to women falling over when they saw him.

Glass houses, Brina?

Ignoring the sly contribution of the voice in her head, she walked ahead of him into the room, where her parents greeted her with an exchange of relieved looks before glaring at Chloe, who sat twirling an olive on a stick in her drink.

'I only said she *might* have had second thoughts,' her sister defended, opening her eyes innocently wide. Her eyes widened further, only not so innocently this time, as Sebastian appeared behind her sister.

Her father, his hand extended, immediately moved to greet the younger man, assuring him how delighted they were that he was able to join them.

'And I must tell you how grateful we were that you were able to extract Sabrina here from that unpleasant situation earlier in the week.'

'Oh, for heaven's sake, Dad, you make it sound as though he led a black ops rescue mission. He merely gave me a lift in his car!'

Her horrified parents turned, twin expressions of embarrassed disapproval on both their faces.

'Sabrina!'

Wishing she had kept her mouth shut but equally unable to back down, she shrugged. 'Well, it's true. I could have got a taxi and there would have been less fuss.' And no guilty secrets.

'What has come over you, Sabrina?' her mother asked, regarding her elder daughter with horror. 'I apologise, Sebastian, for—'

'No need at all. Sabrina is right—it was no bother. I was in the area.'

'You mean you were falling out of a nightclub!'

That's the way to go, Brina, because the hole you had dug was not deep enough.

'Oh, the new one that everyone is talking about? Is it really as gloriously debauched as everyone said, and did Laura really dance topless on the table?' Chloe asked, winking at Sabrina as she drew the parental fire onto her own head. But before she got a response to any of her questions Luis entered the room ahead of his parents.

Sabrina, her eyes lowered, performed a curtsy when her turn came.

The Queen, enveloped in a cloud of perfume, put a hand under her chin and while Sabrina fought the urge to snatch it away she turned her chin to the light.

'She is so pretty. Isn't she pretty, Ricard?' She appealed to her husband who, after raising a brow at the presence of his younger son, was accepting the glass of champagne that had been offered him. 'Lovely cheekbones.'

'Delightful,' the King responded, not looking at Sabrina or her cheekbones or, to her relief, her child-bearing hips, which were probably the only attribute in his future daughter-in-law that interested him, but staring at the glass of champagne he held.

He wasn't holding it for long. The Queen released Sabrina and promptly removed it from his hand.

'Doctor's orders,' she explained, and handed him an orange-juice-filled flute.

Aware that Luis had come to stand beside her, Sabrina turned with a smile.

'Did you have a good journey?' she asked, hearing the fake bright note in her voice. If she couldn't think of something to say to him now, what would it be like in twenty years' time? She let her eyes drift to where Sebastian stood talking to her sister, knowing there was no logic to it but blaming him for the horrid sinking feeling in the pit of her stomach anyway.

'Pretty good considering.'

Chloe had moved away but she could still hear her sister's laughter as Sebastian, who followed her, spoke in a low rumble, his words inaudible.

'And did your call go well, Luis?'

'Call?' Luis repeated, his expression suddenly guarded, even, weirdly, *suspicious*...

'Your brother said that you were waiting on an important call.'

Luis seemed to relax a little and Sabrina decided she had misread his veiled expression. 'Oh, yes, sure, it was not really important. Sebastian must have got the wrong idea.'

When five minutes later dinner was announced the small gathering left the room. Protocol demanded that the King, with the Duchess on his arm, led the party, followed by the Queen and the Duke. Before Luis could take her own arm and fall into place behind them, Chloe slid between them, taking Luis's arm.

'Your bad brother has been telling me some things—' she flung a laughing glance over her shoulder '—and I really don't know if they're true. Tell me, how do you know if he's lying?'

'I'm hurt at the accusation I would ever tell an untruth,' Sebastian protested as Chloe led his brother away.

Watching the little interchange Sabrina felt a stab of something that resembled jealousy, enough to increase the level of conflict swirling in her head by several uncomfortable, confusing notches.

'Shall we?'

Looking from the arm presented to her to his face,

she gave a quick nod and placed her hand lightly on it. While the couples ahead made light conversation, in contrast they walked in silence down the hallway until they reached the dining-room doorway.

'What is it?' Sebastian asked, refusing to acknowledge the stab of sympathy as she stood there, her slim body in an attitude that made him think of a scared animal trying to work up the courage to move out of the headlights. Or in Sabrina's case, he supposed, to step into the spotlight.

'Nothing,' she said, forcing the word through pale lips. 'Just…just give me a minute, would you?'

The sympathy he'd held in check turned into anger as he watched her.

'Is it worth it?'

The harsh scorn in his voice forced her gaze upwards. She felt her anger rise, hot and resentful. 'Financial stability, a reduction in the unemployment rate, an education system that is fit for purpose…funding for—' She took a deep breath, her expression hard with contempt when she finished. 'Is that worth me marrying a man I respect and like? Yes, I think so.' She let go of his arm and, chin up, shoulders firm, she walked in ahead of him.

Sebastian watched her queenly progress and felt a stab of something that he refused to recognise as respect.

CHAPTER FOUR

TAKING HER OWN SEAT, Sabrina watched as Chloe, already seated, said something to make the normally severe guest of honour laugh. Sabrina felt a stab of envy for the social ease that came so naturally to her sister, who tonight looked particularly stunning in a slim-fitting flame-red shift. Sabrina could work the room with the best of them when required, but it had been a learnt process. With Chloe it came naturally.

As the waiting staff began to circulate the table Sabrina struggled to force her mind back to Luis, seated to her right, responding with an ambiguous nod because she didn't have a clue as to what he'd just said before. Her eyes were drawn across the table where Chloe was now talking to Sebastian.

Then, as a waiter moved between them, Sebastian's gaze shifted. Caught staring, Sabrina looked away quickly and grabbed Luis's hand.

She ignored the mortifying fact that Luis's first instinct was to pull away and she couldn't ignore the look of alarm in his eyes when she'd laughed quite inanely, as though he'd just said something desperately amusing.

'Sabrina dear,' her mother said. 'They are trying to serve the soup. If you must hold hands...'

Everyone looked and Sabrina let go of Luis's hand,

keeping the blush at bay by sheer force of will. Rather to her surprise he kept hold of it. He actually turned it over, then she realised what he was looking at.

She should either have put on some make-up to cover the bruises on the inside of her forearm or worn long sleeves.

'How did that happen?' Luis said, directing a concerned frown at the darkening patches either side of her arm.

'I bruise easily,' she said quickly, putting her hand across her middle.

'Since when?' Chloe asked.

'Let me see that, Sabrina.'

'It's fine, Mum, it probably happened when I was jostled by the press.'

'Those animals!' her protective father rumbled, his face dark with anger as he surged awkwardly to his feet.

'Arnica,' her mother said, her eyes on her husband, who after a moment subsided in his seat. 'It really helps bruising. I wonder if we have any...'

'I'm fine!' Sabrina said, her smile strained. 'Just fine, it's nothing and—' She took a deep breath and addressed the rest of her comment directly to Sebastian. 'I'd like to put what happened behind me, to forget about it and move on.'

A three-year-old could have read the coded message but she found it frustratingly impossible to tell from his expression if *he* had understood.

It was the King, who was seated at the head of the table, who picked up her theme. 'We'd *all* like to move on,' he pronounced suddenly.

It was rare that he and his father were on the same page but on this occasion moving on seemed an excellent idea and one Sebastian realised he needed to put into action at the first possible opportunity.

He felt as if a protective layer had been stripped from his skin. It wasn't just what he felt, it was how *much* he felt.

He'd made the connection between those finger marks on Sabrina's arm and his rough and ready extraction method the moment Luis had drawn everyone's attention to them. Knowing he was responsible had shaken loose this painful cascade of emotions he could not identify, emotions he had never come close to feeling in his life before. The depth of the self-loathing he felt was visceral in its intensity.

Having waited until he had everyone's attention, the King continued, in a deeply disgruntled tone. 'Though there seems little chance of that when we have that damned book to look forward to. If the legal team had not been persuaded by a *certain someone*.' The direction of his poisonous glare left little doubt who the *someone* in question was.

The only person who didn't look uncomfortable was the target of the King's venom.

Sebastian's broad shoulders lifted in the slightest of shrugs, the cool in his eyes as icy as his father's barely concealed antagonism was hot.

'I was asked for my opinion and I gave it, Father,' Sebastian responded calmly. 'I have no idea if it influenced the advice you were given, but I thought and I still do think that though a gagging injunction might have prevented the book being published in the UK, it would have been nothing more than a delay. And with people being able to access the details and the book online it would simply have been good publicity for the author.'

'Why *did* the lawyers ask you?' Chloe, who had been listening with curiosity to the interchange, asked.

The King gave a laugh and, ignoring his wife's speaking look, nodded to have his wine glass filled. 'Good question, young lady.'

'It was a field that I worked in for a while.'

'You're a lawyer? Why didn't I know that?' Chloe asked the table in general. 'I thought I'd read everything there was to know about you.'

Sabrina, who had felt the tension that had been building in Luis while his brother and father faced off, was less surprised than the others when he replied to Chloe's question.

'You tend to read about my little brother falling out of nightclubs, Chloe, but before he became the playboy of the western world he graduated top of his class at Harvard law and worked for the best legal firm in New York. He was even offered a partnership.'

Glancing towards Sebastian, Sabrina glimpsed an expression that on anyone else she would have labelled embarrassment.

The King, looking annoyed at the interruption, took over the story. 'But he chose to risk everything and—'

'I'm not really a team-player, Father,' Sebastian interrupted.

'You're a gambler!' his father condemned.

'Father!' Luis protested.

'It's all right, Luis, stock speculators are frequently called worse.'

'Gamblers lose money, Seb, you don't. And,' Luis added, addressing his remark to the rest of the table, 'Sebastian does pro bono work for at least one charity that helps…'

His heated defence came to a stumbling halt when

the King, whose normally florid colouring had taken on an alarming purplish hue, cleared his throat loudly and drawled contemptuously, 'I'm sure we feel honoured to have a financial genius and altruist in our family.'

The Queen reached out and laid her hand over her husband's. 'Not the time, Ricard,' she murmured softly.

The effort to respond to her warning glance deepened the unhealthy ruddiness another couple of shades before the table was engulfed in a painfully awkward silence, broken after a few uncomfortable moments by the Duchess.

'Sabrina, I thought you were wearing your grandmother's pearls earlier?'

Sabrina shook her head as the knot of anger in her chest grew. She struggled, and failed, to dampen the tide of righteous fury that was making her head spin. She took a deep breath and exhaled it slowly through flared nostrils. King Ricard, in her opinion, was a poor excuse for a parent—he was in fact a *bully*!

'A slight mishap,' she managed finally, unable to stop her glance flickering towards Sebastian. There had been no *mishap* involved in the King's attempt to belittle his son. Sebastian might not need looking after now, but he didn't deserve—*nobody* deserved—his parent trying to humiliate him in public, and there was no doubt that that was what the King had been trying to do.

It hadn't worked but she could imagine a time in the past that it had, probably when Sebastian had been young. Oh, but she *hated* bullies! An image of Sebastian as a child floated into her head.

Had Luis been defending him then, too?

There was warmth in her eyes as she flashed her future husband a smile. She had really admired the way he had defended his brother and if she was honest she'd been surprised by it. She felt a little ashamed that she'd had such low expectations of him.

'What happened to the pearls, Sabrina?' her mother pushed for details. 'You haven't lost them?'

'Of course not, they need restringing.' She closed her mouth, not intending to say anything but her wretched imagination had taken hold and that image in her head just wouldn't go away. Two brothers united in fear of their father, and she couldn't stop herself. 'You must be really proud...'

During the seconds it took the King to realise she was talking to him, Sabrina felt her mother's alarm and deliberately didn't look her way.

'Proud of your sons,' she clarified with another brilliant smile that hid not just her anger but the fact that she wished she had not started this. It wasn't as if Sebastian weren't big and beautiful enough to look after himself.

He hadn't always been big but that he'd always been beautiful was a given. As hard as it might be to imagine now, she could see the boy he had been without the armour he possessed now taking what amounted to mental abuse from his father, who somehow and unfairly blamed him for his mother's infidelities. There was no excuse in Sabrina's mind.

'And what they have achieved.'

Despite you, she thought, meeting his icy glare and, realising that if she let him think he could intimidate her she'd set the pattern for the next years of her life, she didn't look away. 'They are a credit to you,' she said, daring him to deny it.

After a pause during which it felt as if the entire table held their collective breath, though that might have only been her because she had realised that in challenging the King she might just have caused a diplomatic incident, the King nodded his head and grunted.

So no diplomatic incident, just a very, *very* unfriendly look… It could have been worse, though maybe not much.

'My mother,' the Duchess said, her voice bright. 'My mother always wore those pearls. They were her signature. Really, Sabrina, you should have taken more care. Are you *sure* you didn't lose any?'

By the time the subject of the pearls had been exhausted the King's colour had returned to normal and the rest of the meal passed without incident, though the King quite pointedly did not address his younger son. Not that the silent treatment seemed to bother the object of his disapproval.

The meal over, it seemed like an age to Sabrina before the King rose and gestured to Luis. 'A word,' he instructed, before nodding to his hosts and sweeping out, leaving the Queen behind.

As he was about to leave Luis leaned in. 'I wonder if you'd take a walk in the rose garden with me later, Sabrina?'

So I can sign away the rest of my life and become an invisible helpmate and mother of your children—why not? Then she felt guilty because Luis looked as miserable and tense as she felt.

'That would be lovely,' she said politely.

This is not about you, Brina. This is about more important things like the future, schools, people's jobs.

And it could work. They could skip the entire 'falling out of love' part so often involved in marriage by never being in love to begin with.

Her father's voice broke into her introspection.

'Shall we leave the ladies, Sebastian? I have an excellent brandy in my study.'

Sabrina was surprised; her father's study was his sanctuary. She couldn't recall him inviting anyone into it. He must have taken a liking to the black sheep, or more likely he was trying to compensate for the way Sebastian's father had treated him. Perhaps like her he had noticed how quiet Sebastian had been for the remainder of the meal.

The tension that hummed inside Sebastian as he left the room behind the Duke had nothing to do with his father's open hostility but the fact that Sabrina had stood up to the King, defending both him and Luis.

Nobody had *ever* done that, and in doing so she had probably made herself a target. His jaw clenched. Didn't she see that men like his father responded to flattery, not a challenge to their authority? Chloe knew that, the Duchess knew that, yet Sabrina had just stuck out her chin. Did she think he needed a champion? Did she think he couldn't look after himself?

He'd seen her shaking, whether from anger or fear he'd been unable to tell, but she'd been pretty damned magnificent. An idiot, but a beautiful, brave idiot!

Sabrina went to get herself a wrap before she ventured out into the gardens. She had not reached the rose garden when Luis appeared on the path ahead.

'I didn't actually find the rose gardens. I got a bit lost.'

'That's fine, it's over that way, beyond the tennis courts, but we really don't have to go that far. Here is fine, unless you are really that interested in the roses? Or am I making an assumption?'

Luis lowered his gaze from her direct look. 'No, you're not,' he admitted, dragging a hand through his fairish hair. He had inherited his mother's colouring.

She tried to visualise him in ten, twenty years' time and found she couldn't, though oddly she could see Sebastian. Perhaps a few more lines around his eyes, a little more cynicism in their depths, maybe a strand of grey or two, but his incredible bone structure virtually guaranteed that he would look essentially the same.

You are about to be proposed to by one brother and you're thinking about the other, Sabrina.

'We've never…' She stopped, realising she couldn't ask him to kiss her so she could forget being kissed by his brother. 'Can I ask you to do something for me?'

She watched a look of caution drift across his face.

'Don't worry, I'm not going to ask you to say you love me.' His flush suggested she had correctly interpreted his alarm, but this wasn't about love. She didn't love either of the Zorzi brothers.

With Sebastian it was simply sex, or it would be, and with Luis it was respect. Respect lasted longer and was, she told herself, a much sounder basis for marriage.

'Sorry, I've never been proposed to before and I'm— Oh, no—look you don't have to—' She stopped because Luis had already dropped to his knees.

'Will you do me the honour of—?'

'For God's sake, yes—get up, please! Sorry, I—' On his feet, Luis held out a ring in a velvet-lined box. The diamond looked bigger than most continents as it flashed in the moonlight. 'Wow, how…very…large. I'm—' She stopped as the ring was slid onto her finger. 'I suppose as it's already there I should say…well… I suppose…yes.'

Not exactly a ringing endorsement but her husband-to-be looked satisfied, or that might have been relief that it was all over. 'That's great. We can make this work, can't we, Sabrina?'

She met his earnest gaze, noticed the beads of moisture along his upper lip. 'Everyone needs to work at marriage.'

'That's true,' he said, acting as though her clenched response were actually wisdom and not desperation. 'Would you like to come with me while I tell my father?'

'I'll wait here.' She caught his arm as he turned to go. 'Aren't you forgetting something?'

He looked bemused.

'A kiss?' She had been half joking but Luis's expression became serious.

'Of course.' He took her shoulders and leaned in.

Sabrina closed her eyes and held her breath. The brush of his lips across her mouth hardly constituted a kiss. She opened her eyes and endured an awkward pause.

'We really should go and tell the families together, present a united front.'

'You go ahead. I'll… I'll just take a moment.' A moment to appreciate that she was marrying a man whose kiss had had absolutely no effect on her—unlike the response a kiss from his brother had drawn. She expelled a long sigh, her glance drifting to the ring on her finger.

Her dark eyes flickered wide as the full implication of its presence there sank in, or rather seeped out from the pit of her stomach until her entire body was ice cold.

Now it was just a matter of waiting for someone to realise how not up to the task she was.

She stood there breathing through the moment of sheer panic, willing calmness to flow through her body.

Then her chin lifted. 'Time to step up, Sabrina.'

* * *

'For a woman who is about to live every little girl's dream, you don't sound very happy.'

He was here, of *course* he was here. She must have done something very bad in a previous life and she was paying for it now.

Heart thudding heavily, she turned around just as Sebastian appeared, a dark shadow surrounded by the darker shadow of the undergrowth.

'Happiness is not a right and I am not a little girl.'

He stopped being shadow and stepped forward into the light.

At some point since he'd left the table he had discarded his jacket, his unfastened tie hung around his neck and the top three buttons of his shirt were open. She could see the faint shadow of dark chest hair and it made her insides quiver.

Stop, she told herself firmly. There was no point wanting something you couldn't have. And she should be glad of it; he'd have used her as he used all women, except, *maybe she wanted to be used*?

Unwilling to deal with the sight of him standing there, the sheer physicality of his presence, she took refuge in spitting anger.

'How long have you been standing there?' If he had seen the awful, miserable proposal she would die.

'Relax,' he drawled. 'It's not like I saw you making mad, passionate love in the shrubbery.' His eyes drifted over her head to the stone wall with clematis clinging to it. 'Or up against the wall.'

The suggestive rasp in his voice sent a deep shudder through Sabrina's body. 'How *dare* you spy on me?' she squeaked, making the mistake of telling herself she wouldn't think about the wall. So obviously that was all she could think of…being pressed up against it, his hands on her body, on her skin.

'Spy? I almost drifted off. How was I to know my brother would not bother to go more than two steps from the back door to propose?' The indents between his eyebrows deepened as his dark brows drew together in a straight line above his heavy-lidded eyes. 'If that actually constituted a proposal!'

His flaying scorn at least threw cold water on the fantasy images in her head.

'Your brother is worth ten of you!'

'Oh, more, angel, much, *much* more.'

'And just because he treats me with some respect and doesn't grope me.'

'If memory serves, you groped me right back.'

She compressed her lips. 'Go to hell!'

'Language…'

'What can I say? I was taught by nuns.'

'They must be very proud of how you've turned out. Actually, hell is a bit warm for me at this time of year. I thought Paris, you know what they say, Paris in the springtime…though it's bit late for that.'

His contemptuous attitude stung. 'I wouldn't expect you to understand the concept of duty. I wouldn't expect you to understand anything except your own selfish—' Breathing hard, she broke off. 'I have no idea why I'm even trying. Have you *ever* in your life done anything that wasn't selfish?'

'My lifestyle is not the issue. It's the thought of yours that is scaring you. You can see the rest of your life stretching out in front of you and you don't like it. This is your choice, *cara*, so don't blame me!'

Her chin went up and she took a step towards him. 'My life will be a hell of a lot more fulfilling than yours, unless of course you count chasing anything in a skirt fulfilling. And I will have a husband I can respect!'

He clenched his jaw, the tension causing a quiver of muscles under the surface of his skin as he held his breath until the stab of pain that felt like a dull blade sliding between his ribs became a manageable dull ache.

Acknowledging it as jealousy would take him to a place he didn't want to go, so instead he turned his frustration on the woman standing there.

'And Luis is going to *respect* you right back. Every girl's dream, I suppose, but then a crown *is* worth a few compromises.' Even as he tossed the accusation at her he recognised the unfairness of it. He was probably one of the few people in a position to understand how trapped she was. 'I pity you.'

She clenched her teeth. 'Don't you *dare* feel sorry for me!' she blazed up at him, her dark eyes flashing.

'I don't feel sorry for you! I feel…' The waste of it, he thought, his eyes sinking to her mouth. All that passion and fire and, despite the alarm bells ringing in his head, he stepped in closer. The moment coincided with the lights from the room that had illuminated the paved area where they stood being switched off.

The moon was behind a cloud and the darkness was total.

Sabrina blinked in the darkness. It was like being wrapped in inky velvet. A thrill of illicit excitement made her stomach clench and raised a rash of goosebumps on her skin.

She made herself think past her thudding heart, recognising the danger. Darkness gave a sense of anonymity; people did things in the darkness that they would not in the light. Except for Sebastian, who did what he liked, when he liked.

What would it feel like, she wondered, to be like that?

'Are you all right?' His deep voice was huskily concerned.

The disembodied question drew a sharp laugh from her. *All right?* So now he was concerned after throwing her into an emotional tsunami, after making her question things that she had never questioned? He had made her want what she could not have *ever*.

Suddenly the fight drained out of her, as she realised she would never be happy, or at least content, until she let go of that tiny grain of irrational hope that the marriage wouldn't really happen, that there would be a last-minute reprieve.

She just had to accept it and not fight, not want more.

'I'm fine. I'm going in. Luis is expecting me to join him.'

'I'll see you in.'

He was closer.

'So suddenly you're the perfect gentleman,' she mocked unsteadily.

Sebastian's eyes had adjusted to the light and her face was a pale blur, her body less distinct. The compulsion to reach for her in the darkness was so strong the effort of fighting it made him quiver like someone with a fever. 'I deserved that, but you deserved a better proposal.'

'Not everyone has your way with words. I suspect the only proposals you have any working knowledge of are of the indecent variety.'

'I may not know much about duty, but you have now agreed to marry my brother so you are totally out of bounds. Even to a total sleaze like me, so you can stop looking at me like that.'

'You don't know how I'm looking at you.'

'I know those big hungry eyes. Just go inside while you still can.'

She shivered, a thrill of excitement shimmering through her body at the message in his dark voice. 'What happens if I don't go inside?'

'You are killing me, you know that, don't you?'

She felt a tide of hot shame wash over her. 'Sorry.'

'Me too.' He heard the swish of her dress as she turned and ran away in the darkness. 'See you at the church, *cara*,' he called softly after her.

CHAPTER FIVE

SEBASTIAN ARRIVED AT the cathedral early. The place was empty but for a group putting the final touches to the flower arrangements that filled the massive space with the overpowering fragrance of orange blossoms.

He hated the pervasive smell but it was better than the alternative—being outside for the orgy of meet-and-greet, hand-wringing, air-kissing formality to be endured when the guests ranged from obscure European royalty to heads of state and the elite of Europe.

For one day the eyes of the world were focused on Vela Main, though not ones in helicopters. The capital had been designated a no-fly zone for the duration. The security was so extreme that he was surprised the sun got to shine without a permit. This was a day that might have looked to have been miraculously thrown together in two weeks, but in reality it had been planned in the minutest of details for the past five years. The only thing they'd needed was a date for the wedding machine to swing into action. There was a contingency plan for everything, including the possibility that the bride might have put on a hundred pounds or was six months pregnant.

The only point of friction was the presence of the television cameras. Just how much did they want to share with the world's media? How much of an air of mystery did they want to retain? In the end a compromise had been reached—it had been decided the cameras would not be allowed to film the service itself. A small blessing considering they would film everything else.

His head lifted from his contemplation of the floor and his private reflections on the general awfulness of weddings, and this one in particular, when a side door closed behind the last of the florists.

Was it the silence or the atmosphere? He had no idea, but suddenly there was no hiding place for the thoughts that he had been running from. The ones he had refused to acknowledge.

Suddenly the thing he was running from was right there, an inescapable fact, the reason he had moved heaven and earth not to be here today, had actually *invited* his father's wrath. The fact of the matter was that he could barely look at his brother without wanting to knock him down. He was jealous.

Sebastian believed all things to be transitory but that didn't alter the fact that he *wanted* Sabrina. It actually went beyond wanting; it was a *yearning*! Hell, he had less control than he'd had as a hormonal teenager!

Was there some perversity in his DNA that made him want the things he could not have? And then, when forced to recognise it, going out of his way to prove to himself and the world that he didn't want it?

It was a lot less painful than being told you couldn't have something.

His wry smile was tinged with sadness as his father's voice drifted into his head, not just the words but the intonation preserved perfectly in his memory from years ago. He'd just turned fifteen and his brother seventeen…

'Sebastian, you will not go to the briefing next week with your brother.'

He could recall the kick-in-the-gut feeling; he had been hoping for a paternal pat on the back.

'He will ask you and you will say no. Do you understand?'

Sebastian hadn't understood. Luis had begged him to go with him in the first place, after the first weekly briefing he'd attended had, as he'd gloomily told his younger brother, been a nightmare. It had gone on for hours, been so boring that Luis had almost fallen asleep, but he hadn't been able to because the senior palace officials had kept asking him what he thought.

Luis had thought it a massive waste of time.

Sebastian had loyally tagged along, expecting the worst, and it was true that some of the discussions had gone over Sebastian's head, but the complexities discussed had not intimidated him, and he had been a lot less reticent than Luis when asked for an opinion.

His father had come into the room halfway through and sat as a silent observer. Hadn't he seen how well he'd done?

'These meetings are for your brother. They're part of *his* training. One day he will be King, our people will look to him. He needs to stand on his own feet. Do you think he did that today?'

'No, Father. Actually I'd prefer to play cricket anyway. Poor Luis, I expect he'd prefer that as well.' He'd made himself believe it because lying to himself was better than envying his brother.

Well, he hadn't been playing cricket for the last two weeks, but he had thrown himself wholeheartedly into enjoying the pleasures his brother could not. He had made a point of being photographed falling out of exclusive night spots in several time zones.

The media had loved it: headlines spoke of his debauchery; there had been two kiss-and-tell stories that he had been asked to confirm or deny. The truth was, neither of the enterprising ladies in question had made it as far as his bed, and neither had any of the other women snapped falling out of nightclubs and climbing into the back of limos with him.

Sebastian had slept solo, despite the seething sexual frustration that dominated his every waking moment.

The more he tried not to think of Sabrina, the more she dominated his thoughts. Her face, her lips, her body. Under normal circumstances the solution would have been simple, but, as taking her to bed was not an option, instead he focused on her faults, calling her dedication to duty an inclination towards martyrdom, her innocent air artificial, her stubbornness infuriating. But the exercise simply made him more aware of his own faults—the difference being his were real.

She was a person ruled by duty and he was a person ruled by selfishness.

It would have made life a lot easier if he could have seen what Luis appeared to when he looked at Sabrina. The problem was he didn't see what Luis saw—in fact his brother's blindness was another source of frustration. The man had been handed a gift and he acted as if he were some sort of victim. There was a black irony—his brother did not appear to really want her, while he... He shook his head. It really didn't matter what he wanted; the bottom line was he couldn't have it.

'Sir?' So deep in his own thoughts, Sebastian hadn't heard the door open.

He turned his head and saw one of his brother's newer aides standing there. He read nothing into the man's worried frown. For all he knew impending doom might be the man's natural expression.

'Your brother asked that I should deliver this to you by hand.'

Sebastian looked at the handwritten envelope the man was holding out to him.

'Thank you.' A note from Luis? When he would be here soon? He glanced at his watch and realised that his brother should be here now.

Refusing to acknowledge the stirrings of unease in the pit of his stomach, Sebastian slid a finger under the seal and withdrew the single piece of paper.

By the time you read this I will be married. It is better that you don't know where I am.

Sebastian's eyes moved rapidly over the handwritten lines, his emotions shifting from disbelief to shock to fury.

White under his tan, a pulse beating like a sledgehammer in his temple, he got halfway through the rest of the letter before a growl escaped the confines of his throat. He screwed the paper up and tossed it away and stood there, eyes closed, his breath dragging in and out. Only respect for where he was keeping the litany of curses inside his head as he clawed his way back to some sort of control.

His brother had *skipped town*!

Sebastian's gaze went to the altar, where moments before he had imagined his brother kneeling beside a veiled Sabrina.

He felt a stab of guilt. He had wanted it not to happen and now it wasn't, but the cost of his wishes coming true was Sabrina's humiliation.

Sabrina! Did she know? Had his brother sent her a handwritten note too? He was suddenly ready to punch his brother, except Luis was somewhere else, with the love of his life, leaving the rest of them to pick up the pieces.

He bent to pick up the rejected missive, uncreased the paper before he read it again, skimming over the initial sentences.

Better that he didn't know? *Better for you,* thought Sebastian, *because if I did know I would follow you and throttle you, brother!*

He skimmed over the next section, which basically praised and defended the woman his brother had eloped with.

> *Gretchen is a marvellous woman—you'd love her—but people will tell you things about her. She's had a hard life...the drugs were her escape from abuse. She has never tried to hide anything from me.*

Pity, Sebastian thought, directing his silent response to his absent brother, *you cannot say the same!* But of course there had been clues. It no longer seemed incomprehensible that Luis had seemed determined to find fault with Sabrina when clearly she was everything a man could wish for.

His brother, his *dutiful* brother, had been clinging to his forbidden love. Ironic really, he'd been guilty as hell for having feelings he wasn't allowed for his brother's bride while his brother had been pining for another woman. Presumably more than pining.

I didn't want to hurt anyone, but in the end it was simple. I can't live without her. By now Dad will have received my letter of official abdication. He'll need you.

I've told him, Seb, that I'm not his biological son. I hope that will make it easier for him. For both of you.

I know you never understood how I'd begun to forgive him for the way he treated Mother, but I didn't forgive him. I forgave myself for not being able to protect her—you never did.

Abdication. The word jumped out at him from the page as Sebastian felt a totally unexpected stab of sympathy for his parent. His father was going to be devastated. Luis had always been the real son, the one he had put all his hopes for the future in.

Everything I do is an act, it always has been, and I can't do it any more. I would have made a terrible king, it always should have been you, and now it is.

You can stop pretending that you can't do everything better than me. I've been pretending. But so have you, Seb.

Sebastian's chest heaved even after he had read the words. He hardly took in the full implication of his brother's letter, not realising even now that his own life was about to change for ever. Instead what struck him was the omission in the note.

Sebastian turned the page over, unable to believe that his brother had not spared a single sentiment of regret about Sabrina, the woman he had left very publicly standing at the altar.

'Highness.'

Sebastian turned to find one of his father's private secretaries standing in the place that had moments earlier been occupied by his brother's staffer.

'Your father wishes to speak to you.'

Sebastian got to his feet. 'He knows?'

The man tipped his head.

'And how is he?'

'He is most…distressed.'

The last occasion he had been summoned to his father's offices Sebastian had been left to cool his heels in an outer office for half an hour. On this occasion the doors to his father's rooms were open and he was shown straight in.

Sebastian struggled to contain his shock. King Ricard had always worn his sixty years comfortably, and, other than the thickening around his middle and the grey showing in his neatly trimmed beard, he looked much as he had done twenty years ago, but he seemed to have aged visibly since the previous evening.

'Luis—'

'I no longer have a son called Luis, and you have no brother.' The King brought his fist down on the desk, glared at his younger son then turned away but not before Sebastian, who had initially stiffened at the autocratic decree, had seen the sheen of tears in his father's eyes.

Hell, the old man had lost his favourite son and the

legacy he wanted to leave in one fell swoop! He wanted to be remembered by history as the King who had re-unified the island, and he could see that dream slipping away.

'Are you all right?'

His attempt at sympathy was greeted with a pithy retort. 'A bit late in the day to show concern for my well-being. But how I am feeling is not important. The future of our line, my legacy, the reunification is what is important. You and he, you connived...*you* knew he was not my son. I suppose you both thought it was a revenge for your mother. I know you both blamed me... that woman... *I loved her*!'

The last anguished words seemed ripped from him, leaving a shocked silence in their wake.

Sebastian had thought that this day couldn't hold more shocks and now this?

'Yet, you made her miserable.' Luis was right: of all the things their father had done, that was the *one* that Sebastian had never been able to forgive. As for forgiving himself, how could he? Why should he? He had watched his mother die, slowly, by inches and had been helpless to stop what was happening. He *should* have been stronger.

'Do you think *I* was happy? She never loved me. I knew that. I was willing to turn a blind eye to the affair and then it was out and I... None of this is important now. What is important is saving our plans. Reunification is the only thing that matters. We must think ahead—delay would be disastrous.'

'The Summervilles—have they been told?'

'The Duke is furious, and I don't blame him.'

'How is Sabrina?'

His father's heavy brows knitted. 'Who?'

His jaw clenched. 'The bride.'

'Oh, well, upset, I assume. I doubt if she knew about this woman so it must have come as a shock.'

The implication took a few moments to sink in. 'But you did?'

An expression of irritation flicked across the older man's face. 'Do you think I do not always have eyes on you both?' he sneered. 'I *know* you did not actually have an affair with that married woman last year, though you seemed content to allow the world to think the worst of you,' he observed drily.

Sebastian gave an impatient shrug; none of this was news to him. 'This isn't having your spies report back on my love life so you can stay ahead of the game. You knew that Luis was in love with someone else and still you pushed him into marriage.'

The condemnation made no impact on the King. 'I knew he'd had an affair with a woman with an unsavoury past. I asked him to stop. I knew he had slipped,' he admitted. 'He actually wanted to tell the... Sabrina, but we talked him off the ledge.'

'How long has this been going on?'

'Around two years.'

Sebastian sat down in a chair. 'I don't believe this.'

'Unlike you, he was discreet.'

Sebastian's head lifted. 'So it's all right so long as no one finds out? You pushed him into marriage. Did it never strike you as unfair to—?'

His father flashed him a look from under lowered brows. 'He promised me it was over and I believed him.'

Sebastian's anger vanished as his father swayed, the pallor of his face acquiring a grey tinge that sent a slug of fear through Sebastian. 'Are you all right?'

'I'm fine.' The older man sank into a chair, shrugging off his son's helping hand irritably. 'I am not about to hand over my crown any time soon.'

'I don't want your crown.'

The King gave a laugh that ended with a wheeze. 'Are you so sure about that? You were always the one that people looked to. Your brother... No, you have no brother. I have no son...the *bastard* is gone!' He broke off, gasping as his lips turned bluish.

'I'm going to call a doctor.' Before he could raise his voice to call for the help that would undoubtedly be stationed outside the door, his father grabbed Sebastian's arm to get his attention. The fact that his hand was shaking shocked Sebastian in some way more than every other shock the day had delivered.

'No, just get me the bottle out of that drawer.'

Sebastian opened the drawer. 'This?'

His father nodded. 'One under my tongue.' After a moment he nodded. 'That's better.'

'How long have you been ill?'

'I am not ill.'

Sebastian handed him a glass of water. 'How long?'

'It is just angina.'

It seemed to Sebastian that *just* and *angina* were not two words that ought to be used in the same sentence.

'Did Luis know?' He hoped bleakly that the reply would be no, because the brother he loved and admired could not do what he had knowing their father had a heart complaint.

'He needed to know. He was the heir.'

'And I did not?'

'You didn't want to know, but now you have no choice. You, God help us, you are the future of our country.'

Sebastian's gaze lifted upwards but the elaborate

ceiling with its raised relief panels stayed where it was thirty feet above his head. The impression that it was inexorably lowering was an illusion; his cage had no bars, no locks. He would be expected to enter of his own free will. The devil had come to claim him.

'So no pressure, then.'

'Do not be flippant, Sebastian.'

The comment wrenched a hard laugh from Sebastian. 'You expect me to step up, just like that?'

'I expect you will do your duty. Your trouble is everything came too easily to you. Unlike your *brother* you never had to work at anything. That, and your problem with authority.' A laugh rumbled in his chest. 'You *are* the authority now.' The thought seemed to amuse the King for a moment at least before he turned to the matter in hand.

'Count Hugo is briefing the press now. I want you to make an announcement to the guests. It is very important that we are on the same page to minimise the damage, so we will liaise with the Summervilles, smooth things over. Your stepmother is with them now, then, after a decent interval, it can be announced that you and the girl... Sabrina...have decided to get married.'

'I always knew you were ruthless but the human factor, does it actually matter?'

'The *human factor* as you call it is a luxury we do not have. It is one of the things we sacrifice for the privilege of being who we are.'

'Don't you think that after this Sabrina might have other ideas? That she might not like to be moved like a pawn on a board?'

'She is not a pawn, she will be Queen, and if you think her parents are less committed to this than we are, you are wrong.'

Sebastian turned his head from his father to stare at the wall beyond, where light filtered through stained-glass panels of the window left a shifting, shimmering rainbow effect on the stone wall. He took a deep breath and pushed beyond the static buzz of adrenaline over-load, fighting to contain the sense of helpless anger he felt surging inside him.

It was ironic—in some ways this was the opportunity he had always imagined, the definitive moment when he could throw his father's expectations and duty back in his face!

Now it was happening and as much as he wanted to reject his father's certainty, as much as he wanted to yell, *'To hell with duty,'* and walk away, he couldn't. He could fight against the duty, but in the end he would do what was expected. The realisation came with a crushing sense of dread…and not just for him.

'Did anyone ask Sabrina what she wants to do?'

'She knows her duty, just as you do, right?' The King did not pause to allow Sebastian space to answer. 'Right now this is about damage limitation. Do you know where your brother is?'

'I thought I had no brother.'

'If he is going to speak to the press I need to know.'

'You mean you need to silence him.'

'I mean to reason with him through an intermediary. I might be willing to continue his generous allowance. Not everyone is as pig-headed as you are, Sebastian.'

CHAPTER SIX

SABRINA STOOD IN a corner.

Her mother stood in the middle of the room in floods of tears and Chloe was providing a shoulder to cry on. Queen Katherine was offering her a glass of brandy, almost as large as the one she was drinking herself.

Her father was standing, his back turned to her, deep in conversation with Luis's private secretary and a group of palace officials. The conversation was not private; her father's comments could probably be heard a mile away.

People seemed to have forgotten she was there.

She really wished she weren't. She closed her eyes and imagined herself in the mountains, the wind in her face, the… A throb of pain in her hand dragged her back to the moment.

Her fingers, which were curled in a death grip around the scrunched-up paper, were white. She lifted her hand to her chest and flexed them to encourage blood back into the cold extremities.

With no pockets in her wedding dress to tuck the letter into, she transferred it to her other hand. She had read it three times before it had made any sense. Actually it still didn't, but she had finally gone to her mother's room and announced that the wedding was off, would someone tell the guests?

'Last-minute nerves, darling. I remember it well. Oh, my, you look beautiful and that shade of lipstick really suits you. The flowers will be—'

'No, Mum, it's really off. Luis has left—there's a letter. He loves someone else apparently and he can't live without her.' She didn't add that Luis had revealed the secret of his parentage, that he and not Sebastian was the bastard.

'Don't be silly, darling.'

'He's abdicated.'

The word seemed to penetrate. It had done the same for Sabrina when it had leapt out from the page; it had made her go back and read it again. The shocking contents evoked a multitude of emotions; humiliation was there and with it relief, a relief that made her feel guilty. She had been given her life back, her freedom, but at what cost?

'But he can't do that. You're going to be the next Queen.' Her voice rose with each successive word until *Queen* emerged as a screech that hurt Sabrina's ears. And not just her ears; belatedly aware of the open-mouthed audience, Sabrina got to her feet, shooing away the team of make-up artists who were putting the finishing touches to the Duchess's face.

Her mother didn't react to their expulsion. 'Dame Olga is singing at the service. She turned down a concert at the Met to be here. Call your father—let him sort things out.'

'I don't think it can be sorted out, Mum.'

'What did you do?'

The unexpected attack made Sabrina back away.

'What did you say to make him do this? Did you say you wanted to carry on working? I knew it! I said to your father that it was a mistake to allow you to have a career… Here he is now.' She gave a sigh of relief as the door opened.

Her father, flanked by senior members of his staff, stood in the doorway. The expression on his florid, good-natured face was grim.

The Duchess's wail was muffled by the hands she pressed to her face.

'Pull yourself together, Olivia,' her husband snapped unsympathetically. 'We need to limit the damage. Where is…? Oh, there you are, Sabrina. At least one person isn't falling apart,' he approved. 'We can't talk here. Come down to the…?' He raised a stern questioning brow at one of the palace staff that had entered with him.

'The King instructed me to make the south salon available, Your Grace.'

So here they all were in the south salon and after half an hour all the talk was going pretty much nowhere.

Sabrina looked at the clock ticking away in a corner, her eyes fixed on the hypnotic swing of the pendulum. She knew she should be feeling more; she was after all the person who had been humiliated. Something she was not likely to forget as her mother kept screeching the information at her every few minutes.

Would anyone even notice if she weren't here?

She unclipped the veil—a family heirloom—and dropped it to the floor. She would have stripped off her finery there and then if she could have but then someone might notice she was there. A naked woman in the room generally got attention.

She fought the temptation to tear at the tiara that felt heavy on her head, and the saucy blue garter, her sister's contribution, had slipped down her thigh. It was all so wrong, even before Luis had followed his heart.

And now, even though she knew it would be considered treasonous by many to even think it, she admired him for having had the guts to walk away. His dumped bride was probably the only person in the room who felt some sympathy for his decision.

But then she knew what it felt like to agree when you wanted to scream no. She knew what it felt like to do your duty. Luis had done what she hadn't had the strength to do. He'd been honest, but how would he live with the guilt?

Suddenly the need to escape the room became overwhelming. If she stayed in it any longer she'd *explode*!

The men stationed outside the door continued to look ahead as she slipped past.

She wanted to go home.

'Sabrina!'

She ignored the voice and began a perilous descent of the spiral steps, going far too fast for someone wearing three-inch heels.

The palace was a maze and built on a massive scale but she was pretty sure that she was headed for the stables. After that her plan was a little hazy but so far plans had not worked out so well for her—maybe it was time to wing it.

'Sabrina, stop!'

She heaved a sigh, grabbed the wooden balustrade and tilted her head back to view her sister, who stood resplendent in the sea-green silk froth of her bridesmaid dress.

'Sabrina, what are you doing?'

'I don't know.' Her expression blank, she looked at the piece of crumpled paper in her hand—actually, she felt blank inside. She cleared her throat. 'It was getting a bit…hot in there for me. I need some fresh air.'

'Outside is probably not the best place to be. There are several hundred guests being—'

'Told the groom has bolted before the stable door closed and, speaking of stables, I think this staircase leads to the stables. There aren't going to be any guests there.'

'It does, but you should come back. They are—'

Sabrina shook her head, cutting her sister off. 'Whatever *they* want me to do the answer is no. Just for today I want a day off from doing and saying the responsible thing.'

Chloe, her skirt hitched high, skipped lightly down the stairs to join her. 'Fair enough. Well, I'd be delighted to tell them to go and stuff it, or I could run away with you. Are you up for this?'

'Why not?'

Her sister's eyes widened. 'I never expected you to say yes,' she admitted.

'So you didn't mean it?'

Chloe laid a hand on her arm. 'Oh, I meant it!' She took the next step herself and paused. 'Mum is sorry, you know, that she yelled. She just panicked.'

'Like Luis—actually, not like Luis. I don't think he panicked. I think he came to his senses. He loves someone else.'

'Fair enough, and, for the record, in your place I wouldn't be so understanding. If he was going to come to his senses why didn't he do it last week or last year or even yesterday? Why leave it until now? It's—'

'A total nightmare,' Sabrina agreed, thinking guiltily of the light at the end of the tunnel.

'Did you guess that he was going to?'

Sabrina shook her head. 'I didn't have a clue.' She expelled a sigh. 'I just need some breathing space.'

'I can do better than that.' Chloe made a grand-reveal gesture as they walked around the corner. 'I always have an escape route. I had a date with a couple of friends last night…after Mum's curfew. We parked here. You fancy a drive?'

'They are not cars,' Sabrina said, looking at the two shiny monsters sitting there. It didn't even occur to her to ask where the owners were as she stared at the dazzling chrome.

'Didn't I tell you I've been learning?' Chloe picked a helmet off the first motorcycle and began to clip it on. 'It's actually quite easy.'

'You want me to sit on the back of that wearing this?' She gestured down at the acres of fitted white silk moulded to her body.

Chloe, hitching up her green skirt, was already clambering onto the first machine. She tossed her sister a set of keys and nodded to the second helmet. 'No, I expect you to follow me on that one,' she retorted, revving the engine of the bike she had climbed onto.

'That's mad, Chloe.'

'True, but if you're not going to be mad today when are you going to be mad, Brina? Come on!'

Sabrina stood there, shaking her head. 'I couldn't.' Her eyes lifted to her sister. *'Could I?'*

'Last night we went for a swim at a little beach just along from the Roman ruins where you opened that yawn-a-minute exhibition on Saturday.'

'Swimming?'

She knew there had to be several dozen legitimate reasons that this was a bad idea but at that moment her brain could only come up with one. 'I don't have a swimsuit.'

Chloe grinned. 'We didn't have swimsuits last night. It is a very private beach.'

* * *

His father had made it as far as the door when his breathing got a lot worse. The doctor, called against his father's wishes, said that bed rest was called for as a *precaution*.

It was half an hour later when Sebastian, deputising for the King, a first, was leaving the room when he encountered someone he vaguely recognised as the Duke's aide, a man who bowed excessively and smiled a lot.

'Highness.' The man sounded breathless, his bow perfunctory and big politician's smile absent. 'Are they here?'

'Are who here?'

'Lady Sabrina and Lady Chloe? We have no idea where they have gone and the Duchess is quite distressed. She has decided they have been kidnapped.'

'Considering the level of security here I seriously doubt it. I have an idea, though. Leave it to me,' he said, leaving the gasping man standing there staring after him as he strode off purposefully down the corridor, punching in the number of the head of security as he walked.

It was picked up immediately.

'The *delicate* security breach we discussed last night?'

'Lady Chloe and the other bridesmaids reached their rooms safely, sir. They remained unaware of the security presence.'

'And you left the motorbikes where they were?'

'We did. Is there a problem?'

One problem? Now that really would be a luxury, Sebastian thought as he took the staircase on his left. It led directly to the stables, where last night Chloe and her friends had naively imagined they had foiled the palace security.

The oil spots on the floor showed where the motor-bikes had stood and the wheel treads in the dusty straw the direction they had gone.

Jaw clenched in frustration, he closed his eyes, but before the curse could leave his lips a muffled sound brought his eyes open. Head tilted to one side, he waited and was rewarded by another noise. It took him a few seconds to track the sound to its source.

He found a piece of torn silk before the rest of the dress and the person wearing it. His initial flare of gut-tightening alarm faded as he realised that Sabrina, who stood beside a motorbike that was lying on its side, hav-ing first collided with a wall, was not injured. The same could not be said of the motorbike.

'I hope you're insured?'

Sabrina jumped as though she'd been shot and spun round, brushing the sections of her hair that had es-caped the carefully constructed top knot from her eyes as she adopted a defensive attitude. 'It's not mine,' she said, fighting the weirdest compulsion to walk straight into his arms. Skinny dipping was one thing, giving into that impulse would have been taking recklessness to another level.

Still, she'd thought about it, which was bad enough.

I am clearly in a worse condition than I thought, she realised, because any woman who thought safety and comfort lay within those strong arms needed therapy and lots of it!

'Chloe said it was easy.' She sniffed, casting a look of loathing at the motorbike. 'It isn't. I can't do anything right, not even run away…' Her voice quivered with self-pity as she felt an angry splash of tear on her cheek. She swiped it away with a hand and glared at him.

His lips twisted into an ironic half-smile. 'You just

thought you'd slip quietly away on the back of a motor-bike wearing *that*?'

Following the direction of his gaze, Sabrina looked down and felt a stab of guilt when she thought of the skilled women who had sewn the thousands of seed pearls onto the acres of white silk. The beautiful dress was trashed! There were several smears of dirt, oil or both on the bodice and a massive rip in the skirt from when she had tried and failed to mount the motorbike before it had taken off without her.

'Chloe managed it.' Her dismay spiked again when she thought of her sister. 'She's going to be wondering where I am. She'll be worried. She'll think I've done something stupid.'

'As opposed to riding on a motorbike in your wedding dress? Don't worry, I'll send someone to tell her you're all right.'

Sabrina shook her head, her lips firming into a mutinous line. 'I don't want to *send* someone. I want to go with her. I know they've sent you to take me back.' She folded her arms across her heaving chest and looked up at him, defiance shining in her brown eyes. 'But I won't go.'

He studied her, reading the determination in her tear-stained face, and felt a strong beat of sympathy.

'Did you know?' she asked suddenly. 'That he was going to do it?'

'No, I got a note.'

She nodded. 'So did I.' She held out the crumpled piece of paper. 'Did you know there was someone else?'

His jaw tightened. 'No.'

'Ah, well,' she sighed. 'It's over now.'

Maybe it was a blessing that she actually believed that; he doubted she could cope with the truth. The question was, could he? 'Come on,' he heard himself say.

She blinked. 'Where?'

'Where did you plan to run away to with Chloe?'

'The beach…the one past the Roman dig. We were going swimming.'

'OK.'

She blinked. 'What do you mean?'

'I mean,' he said, 'that I will take you to join Chloe.' He spread his hands wide as she continued to look at him with suspicion. 'No catch.' Without waiting to see if she followed him, he headed for the row of garages where his brother kept his cars. The doors were open and he approached the first one.

He pulled the dust cover off a sporty two-seater. 'It's Luis's,' he said without turning. He had heard the sound of her heels on the cobbles behind him. 'He never locks it.' Sebastian had no compunction about taking it. Luis had gifted him his life and his bride, not that she realised it yet, so he supposed the car was his too.

As she followed Sebastian the irresponsibility of this course of action was beginning to hit home. Running away achieved nothing.

He turned and arched a brow. 'You coming?'

She rocked back a little on her spiky heels as they sank into the gravel. 'I should really go back.'

He didn't proffer an opinion, just stood there looking at her. She took a deep breath and made a choice of the middle ground. 'All right, we'll go and find Chloe and then come back.'

The engine purred into life while she was still manoeuvring herself into the low seat and she released a small squeal as it sped off as she closed the door.

Avoiding the chaos that it seemed safe to assume

surrounded the main entrances to the palace, Sebastian drove through the unguarded stable entrance, past the neatly fenced paddocks, empty today while the staff were attending the celebrations.

Sabrina stayed silent until they reached the hairpin bends that surrounded this part of the island's coast. 'Luis said something in his letter.'

His blue eyes flickered briefly her way.

'Is it true? The King isn't his father?'

'Does it matter now?' He dismissed the question with a curt flick of his head. 'And Luis was an idiot for telling you and…telling anyone,' he condemned.

She was bemused by his attitude. She had seen with her own eyes how his father behaved towards him and she could imagine what effect the headlines about his mother's affair and the rumours of his birth had had on the life of a boy at public school.

'But people said things about you, wrote things. You could have told them the truth.'

'I have a thick skin and I totally believe the old adage what doesn't kill you makes you stronger. It doesn't bother me what people say, or think. They will always find something to write. It would have been harder for Luis.'

She shook her head and wondered if he had told himself that so many times he actually believed it.

'What's happening?' she asked, sliding down in her seat, feeling conspicuous in her white wedding dress as the car slowed to a crawl. Before Sebastian responded to the question they came to a complete standstill.

'I'm not sure,' Sebastian admitted, tapping his fingers on the steering wheel before he opened the window and leaned out. That was when he smelt the smoke… acrid and unmistakable.

'Wait there.'

She craned her neck as Sebastian, with long-legged ease, exited the car and approached one of the several people who had already left their cars. Some were pointing, and then she saw the plumes of smoke rising from behind the hill ahead. Sabrina's stomach muscles quivered as she clambered out and, skirt in hand, ran towards Sebastian, oblivious to the stares her outfit was attracting.

Sebastian stopped, suggesting to drivers they pull their cars as far to the side of the road as possible to give access to rescue vehicles, and turned to her. 'I said to wait inside the car.'

She ignored the statement. 'What's happening? Do you think Chloe…?'

He laid both hands on her shoulders; the heavy contact was somehow comforting. 'There is nothing to be gained from jumping to conclusions. I'm just going to go find out what's happening. You wait here. I'll be back as soon as I can.'

Several other drivers were already jogging down the road but Sebastian hit the ground running, passing them all in moments.

It didn't cross her mind to obey his instructions, but by the time she had rounded the bend ahead and the scene of devastation several hundred yards on was revealed there was no sign of him among the wreckage.

Was Chloe in that?

Battered by fear, her heart thudding, the sound of distant sirens in her ears, Sabrina ran on past a large tanker that was slewed across the road, totally blocking it both ways. She stopped and looked around. It was like some sort of war scene you saw on the TV. Some of the people from the concertina of cars either side of the tanker that were lining the road were standing in the road looking dazed and some were stretched out on the floor. Underfoot was the crunch of broken glass, everything grey in the pall of smoke that made her throat ache and eyes sting.

One distant car was already on fire, sending plumes of orange into the air, increasing the stench of smoke and fuel. If the fire reached the tanker... She pushed away the tendrils of panic and tried to think as, icy cold inside, she ran on past the groaning, blood-spattered victims.

The air left her lungs in one long hissing sigh of relief when she spotted Sebastian; even at fifty feet his tall, commanding figure was easy to spot. It was a couple of seconds later before she saw that he was carrying a figure. She had barely registered the green dress when there was a loud explosion, strong enough to knock one of the men standing close to Sebastian off his feet.

Sebastian swayed but managed to keep on his feet, not really registering the pain of the metal shard that sliced through his cheek. It wasn't until he pushed himself forward that he saw the spark. Before he could brush it away it ignited Chloe's dress.

He dropped her down on the ground and tore off his jacket, smothering the flames before they took hold. Another man joined him until the fire was extinguished.

Chloe opened her eyes and looked up. 'Wow, you look awful...is that smell me? Mum is going to be furious about the dress.'

'It's OK. You're OK,' he said, hoping that it was the truth but in reality he didn't have a clue.

'Sebastian!'

The sound was almost drowned out by the whirr of helicopter blades above their heads.

Sebastian turned his head towards the cry and saw her running, stumbling, dodging the obstacles in her path. Sabrina was yelling something but he couldn't make out the words above the helicopter and roar in his ears.

He got to his feet and swayed; he could make out Sabrina's face now. See her mouth move, but the words and sounds of sobs and everything else were drowned out by the shrill whine of sirens as a fleet of ambulances and fire engines arrived on the scene en masse.

That was the last thing he heard before the ground came up quite quickly to meet him.

CHAPTER SEVEN

LATER THE SEQUENCE remained blurred in her mind. She remembered seeing Sebastian, then the blood that covered half his face, and she watched him fall, and then in her head it happened again and again until finally she got his name out.

'Sebastian!' Her cry sounded that way in her head but came out as a croak as she began to stumble past the debris that littered the area, her progress frustratingly slow across to where he lay—where he lay very still.

Heart drumming, dread like an icy hand around her heart, she knelt down to where he was lying face down, his head turned away from her. One arm was curved above his head, the other trapped under him.

He groaned and she felt a rush of relief that made her sob. 'You're alive. Oh, God, don't die, don't die...please, Sebastian! Help, someone, please, he's...'

A wave of horror rolled over her; the extent of the destruction was too much for her to take in...too much... It was like the set of a disaster movie's big scene only it wasn't a movie—it was *real*.

On her knees she moved towards where her sister lay a few feet away, her eyes closed. Nobody had heard her cry for help, they were busy crying, wailing, bleeding or dying, but she tried again.

'Help!'

Her throat was raw by the time someone heeded her cry.

A man with a torn shirt, his face smoke-blackened, appeared.

He dropped down beside Sabrina and felt her pulse. She shook away his hand—couldn't he see she was fine?

'You're going to be OK.'

'My sister... Sebastian...' She touched her sister's hair and nodded to where Sebastian lay close by.

She watched, her fingers on Chloe's comfortingly strong pulse, as the Good Samaritan began to turn Sebastian over. He was halfway through the procedure before she realised what even someone with a scrap of first aid knew—and she was a doctor.

She was a doctor!

She left Chloe and grabbed the man's arm. 'No, don't! He might have a spinal injury. He needs to be—'

The man stopped, not in response to Sabrina's urgent plea but at the terrible groan that issued from Sebastian.

The sound cut through Sabrina like glass. 'You're hurting him!' she wailed.

His hand fell away. 'Sorry. I was only trying to help.'

They both turned as Sebastian completed the manoeuvre himself before sliding back into unconsciousness.

The man beside her swore as he stared at Sebastian's face. 'That's a mess.'

Sabrina clenched her fists and hissed a fiercely protective denial. 'He's fine...oh, your poor face.' She lifted a shaking hand and, on her knees in the dirt, touched the side of his face that wasn't shredded and bleeding and stroked the dark hair back from his brow.

The man moved away.

'Hey, he's the guy who got the girl from the cliff.'

Two men walking past supporting a staggering woman between them stopped and looked down at Sabrina and Sebastian.

'Hold on, they'll be with you soon…'

'I'm fine, but they—' She stopped, her voice cracking with fear.

The man nearest nodded and raised his voice and yelled, 'One over here, one for triage, severe facial lacs, blood loss, head injury!'

'Brina!'

'Chloe.' Before Sabrina could react to her sister's hoarse whisper two jumpsuit-clad figures reached them. She shuffled out of the way, watching as they examined her sister, inserted a venous line before lifting her onto a stretcher.

When Chloe saw Sabrina she struggled to pull the oxygen mask off her face.

Sabrina covered her sister's hand with her own. 'No, leave it.' Chloe's eyes closed. 'She's my sister,' she explained to the two paramedics as she ran along beside them.

'We'll look after her,' one said. 'She's being airlifted.'

She walked back to where Sebastian lay and stood there watching as her sister was stretchered away to the waiting helicopter. The explosion was deafening.

Sabrina reacted on instinct, throwing herself over Sebastian. She had no idea how long she lay there; her ears were still ringing when two paramedics pulled her off.

One began to examine Sebastian, the other shone a torch in Sabrina's eyes. She pushed his hand away. 'Can you walk?' She nodded.

'Great.' He draped a foil blanket over her shoulders and shouted out, 'A walking wounded over here, guys.'

She lifted her chin. 'No, I'm not leaving him.' She'd let them take Chloe away but enough, she decided, was enough. 'I'm staying with him.'

The tired-looking paramedic sounded irritated by her attitude. 'Look, there are people here who actually do need my help and—'

The young woman crouched beside Sebastian, adjusting the line she had just put in his arm, looked up. 'Have a heart, man, can't you see that they just got married?' She indicated Sabrina's torn and dirty wedding dress.

'This is your wedding day?'

'It was meant to be,' she answered truthfully, thinking that it seemed like a lifetime ago since she had put on her wedding dress.

He swore in sympathy and looked down at his colleague, who was still kneeling beside Sebastian. 'That one ready to move?'

She nodded. 'He's stable, and sats are up to ninety-five…tough guy.'

The man with Sabrina took her arm. 'You can go with him.'

'Thank you,' Sabrina said. Her gratitude even greater when, on the way to the hospital in the back of the ambulance, Sebastian regained consciousness twice and each time it was the sound of her voice that stopped him fighting to free himself from the safety restraints before they had a chance to administer sedation.

Sabrina had not expected their anonymity to last. Admittedly her face, even without the walking-wounded look, was less well known but it seemed inevitable that someone would at some point make the connection between the anonymous injured figure who lay, his famous features swathed in bandages, on the stretcher and their Prince.

But so far no one had and, as it was hard to imagine that their treatment could have been better if the hospital staff had realised they were treating their Prince, it hadn't seemed a priority to explain or correct the myth that they were a newly married couple, which had obviously followed them to the casualty department. While she waited to be seen herself, she was kept up to date with Sebastian's progress. Sabrina knew she would not have been told the results of his CT or any of the other tests if they had known the truth.

As someone who was not his wife or family she would have been told nothing, so she silenced the twangs of conscience, and took comfort from the technicality that she hadn't lied—yet. Unless staying silent could be counted as lying. Should she reveal that under the dirt, blood and injuries the man they were treating was their Prince?

People were kind even rushed off their feet. The staff she asked took time to try and find details about Chloe for her, though on each occasion they had not been able to locate her sister in the system, but then the system had to be at breaking point.

The island boasted some pretty impressive medical facilities, but a major disaster had stretched their resources to the limit.

It remained frustrating that nobody seemed to be able to tell her where her sister was, but her own injuries were minor. She hadn't even known she had any, but the blood seeping from the head wound had caught the attention of a passing nurse. It needed stitching and they insisted on keeping her in overnight.

'I hope you don't mind sharing,' the nurse said as she manoeuvred Sabrina's bed into place beside the occupied one in the room obviously only ever intended to hold one bed.

'Of course not.'

The nurse smiled. 'Not really the way you intended to spend your honeymoon, but we thought…'

Sabrina's eyes flew to the person lying in the bed next to hers.

It was Sebastian, looking much better than when she had last seen him despite the livid bruises visible around the dressing that covered the wound on his face. His hands above the sheet were swathed in bandages too.

'Is he in pain?' she whispered, knowing full well they would have pumped him up with painkillers but needing the reassurance of hearing someone say it.

'No, he's dosed up to the eyeballs so he might be a bit groggy when he wakes up,' the nurse warned. 'The drip is just giving him fluids,' she went on to explain.

Sabrina nodded, glancing at the label on the bag.

The nurse gave her hand an encouraging squeeze. 'He was lucky really. The surgeon who repaired your husband's face is one of the best plastic surgeons there is—not that we don't have good doctors here, but Mr Clare is *the* man. And he was only on the island for the royal wedding, apparently. I wonder how that went. Anyhow, he just turned up here and offered to help out after he heard about what had happened.

'I just thought you should know that your husband had the very best care. I'm sure a doctor will be along to fill you in later but, as you can imagine, we are a bit stretched.'

'Thank you. His hands…?'

'Superficial.'

Her lowering of tension was fleeting as she asked a moment later, 'My sister, Chloe, did anyone...?'

Sabrina read bad news in the girl's hesitation so she was prepared as much as she could be for bad news when it came.

'That would be *Lady* Chloe Summerville?'

Sabrina nodded.

The girl's eyes widened. 'So you're...?'

'I'd kind of prefer to stay below the radar for now.'

The nurse responded to the appeal with a nod and a smile. 'They airlifted your sister to a specialist burns unit on the mainland. I believe your parents went with her...' The girl laid a buzzer on the bed beside her. 'You just ring if you want anything, La— Sabrina.'

Sabrina looked at the buzzer. What she really wanted was to go back to that moment on the staircase when she could have gone, no, *should* have gone back. But that wasn't going to happen because the world was not fair. If it were *she* would be the one living with the consequences of her actions, not Chloe, not Sebastian.

If she could have swopped places she would have in a heartbeat.

That's easy to say, Brina, mocked the voice in her head, *when you know you can't.*

Nurses came in and out during the night to record Sebastian's observations and when they saw she was awake all they told her was that he was *doing fine*.

She lay there counting down the hours on the clock on the wall opposite. It was two in the morning when a dapper man she recognised as the King's private secretary appeared.

He didn't seem to notice Sabrina at first, he was so transfixed by the sight of Sebastian.

He shook his head and gasped, 'Lady Sabrina! You

here, this is…well, it is simply intolerable to expect either you or His Highness to share a room with *any-one* at all.'

'It's fine,' Sabrina said. 'They are pushed for space and I'm going home in the morning. But if there is any news of my sister could you let me know?'

'Of course, so sad, and when we were still reeling from this morning's events. The King is… Well, he wanted to come, but he had an…an event when he heard.'

'Event?'

'A heart event. Not an attack, you understand, but the Queen is at his side and he is comfortable,' he added as if he were reading out a press release—actually he had probably already done so. 'They wanted to be here, but it is lucky they are not here to see their son being treated like an ordinary— Of course, if he had not gone out without his security presence… But, no matter, I will set wheels in motion.'

'At least there are no press hiding behind bedpans to take a snap.'

The man rubbed his chin as he took on board her comments. 'That is certainly a benefit of anonymity, and the idea of the Prince being treated like any of his subjects would be good for his image, presenting him as a man of the people. Well, perhaps for tonight at least we might leave things as they are.' He tipped his head towards the bed where Sebastian slept on. 'Do you know if there will be any scars?'

'I should think so,' she said evenly and closed her eyes. If she had to hear the man thinking out loud of how to put a positive spin on Sebastian being marked for life she would have to throw something at him.

She was so tired of people who thought that the truth

was a dirty word, people who thought through every syllable they uttered, always choosing appearances above honesty.

Sometimes the truth was just the truth, no matter how much you manipulated it, and the truth was that two people she cared for deeply were in pain because of her!

Her eyelids flickered as a series of images ran through her head. Sebastian mocking her, Sebastian aloof, Sebastian kissing her, Sebastian smiling and on and on, always Sebastian.

Was she in any position to condemn anyone for being economical with the truth?

Truth?

Didn't you have to ask the right question first to hear the answer, the truth?

When she opened her eyes the King's private secretary had gone. She looked at the man in the bed beside her own and saw that Sebastian was awake and looking at her, his blue eyes clouded by the drugs in his system. The ache of empathy was so strong that she forgot all about truths and answers.

'Hello,' she said softly.

'I...' He paused and moistened his lips. 'I was looking for Chloe,' he slurred.

She felt tears spring to her eyes. 'You found her.'

'Where is this...?'

'Hospital. You were hurt but you're going to be all right. The room, it's funny...' she said, ignoring the odd aching feeling inside her when she laughed, 'but they think we're married.'

'We are married? Yes, I remember now. I was dreaming about it. I kissed you.' He smiled. 'I remember now you looked beautiful.' Still smiling, he closed his eyes and his breathing showed he was asleep.

Satisfied that he was resting comfortably, she had just drifted off to sleep herself when she was woken.

The man wheeling the chair told her that he had come to take her to CT before discharge.

She glanced towards Sebastian, who was still sound asleep.

'I don't need one.'

'I'm not a doctor, are you?'

She could have said yes but she didn't. 'I could walk.'

'You could, but if you fall over I'm the one who'll get the boot...so...?'

She got in, holding the open back of her gown in place to cover her modesty and her behind.

'I've seen worse,' wisecracked her driver. 'You two the honeymooners? Don't worry, it won't take long and he'll still be here when you get back.'

He was, but not in bed when she walked into the room past the security guards who had been there when she'd left. Her brief flurry of irrational panic subsided when she saw the figure standing in a narrow open door that was a tight squeeze for a broad-shouldered man plus a portable drip stand.

In her absence the big bulky dressing had been removed. In its place was a narrow, almost transparent strip that showed the full extent of his repaired wound. Sabrina was relieved by what she saw. The man who had operated had clearly been as good as the nurse had claimed. Her professional eye could see beyond the bruising and swelling that made his face unrecognisable, and she knew that the healing process would fade the livid raised red scar to silver.

The professional in her saw a good job; the woman in her saw not ugliness, but pain and she winced, her empathy shifting uneasily to dismay. What she was feeling went beyond normal empathy. It wasn't even guilt that she felt; it was more…it was… The name for what she was feeling remained there, just out of reach.

As their eyes met Sebastian's were dark with pain and exhaustion. She ironed her expression out into a smile as her eyes moved in a covetous sweep up the long, lean length of his body. Unlike her he was not wearing hospital issue, although someone kind in the CT department had given her a big towelling dressing gown to cover the open-backed theatre gown. Sebastian, by contrast, was wearing a pair of dark sweats and a T-shirt that revealed the incredible lean muscles of his torso and his powerful biceps. Fighting the hormonal rush, she lowered her eyes.

'Should you be out of bed?'

Sebastian took hold of the drip stand awkwardly in one lightly bandaged hand and began to walk towards her, feeling her eyes on him and knowing what she saw when she looked at him. It had been there in her face in that unguarded moment—he had become a man with a ruined face, someone to pity, someone she would soon learn it was her *duty* to be with, to lie in bed with even if inside she felt disgust.

And Sabrina would never turn her back on her duty.

He turned away as he felt the fury and outraged pride rise in him.

'Well, as you see, I am. The surgeon is apparently due to arrive in…' He glanced towards his wrist and swore, then swore again as he banged the drip stand into the table positioned at the bottom of the bed.

'What's wrong?'

'Nothing is wrong. I've left my watch in the bath-room and this thing is—'

'I'll get it.' Sabrina moved past him into what was little more than a cubicle, clean but utilitarian with a basin, lavatory and shower.

'How are you feeling, really?' she called out as she lifted the metal-banded watch from where he'd left it on the edge of the washbasin.

'Pretty much the way I look. Maybe under the circumstances *pretty* is not the right word.'

The bitterness in his voice made her pause; he could not blame her for what had happened any more than she was blaming herself. If she hadn't run away from her responsibilities her sister and Sebastian would have read about the pile-up in the newspaper.

'The scar will fade, you know.' It sounded like a platitude and one it seemed he had no intention of responding to. Taking a deep breath, she prepared to go back and face his pretty justified anger when the sound of a new voice made her pause.

'Outside, all of you!'

Poised on the point of walking out of the small bathroom, Sabrina instinctively shrank back into the room. The voice was unmistakably that of King Ricard.

'I thought you'd had a heart attack, Father.'

'A slight cardiac *incident*, that's all,' she heard the King correct. 'You look like hell. What were you doing on that road with the Summerville sisters?'

'Going for a swim.'

'Do not t...t...try me, Sebastian.'

'Shall I get that nurse back in here?' No sarcasm this time, but concern roughened the edge of Sebastian's deep voice as his father wiped beads of sweat from his upper lip.

'She's a doctor, not a nurse, and no, it's just overly warm in here.'

'You didn't need to come in person. You could have just sent flowers but I'm touched. I really am.'

'Why is everything a joke with you? This is the sort of attitude that made it necessary for me to come in person. The news that you and the Summerville girls were involved in the pile-up has leaked—inevitable, but annoying. However, there is some good news. They have decided that you were a hero. Don't look at me like that. I don't care if you were not—this is the way people will see you.'

Her back pressed against the white-tiled wall, she could hear the satisfaction in the monarch's voice. An image of her parents sitting beside her sister's bed drifted into her head. The last thing they would be thinking about was how the media spun the story. While in the other room the King had not even asked his son how he was!

'And that is all that matters, the perception not the truth.'

Her eyes widened. It was as if Sebastian had picked up on her own thoughts, though he sounded more warily resigned than angry.

'Do not take that sanctimonious tone with me, Sebastian. You are not some innocent. The royal family is a product and it is our job to promote it. You are my heir.'

'You make it sound so attractive, Father,' she heard Sebastian drawl. 'Has it occurred to you that I might say thanks, but no, thanks?'

'You always thought you could do the job better than me. Now is your chance to prove it.'

'Spoken like a true manipulator.'

'So is there anyone in your life at the moment—a woman?' From her hiding place the King's deep sigh of irritation was audible. 'Fine, it makes no difference, but if there is get rid of her. Later on if you are discreet I see no reason you shouldn't enjoy liaisons, but until you are safely married I want no sniff of scandal. Getting her on side is going to take delicate handling after what your brother did.'

'I thought I did not have a brother.'

The King ignored the interjection. 'The Duke and Duchess,' he continued, 'have become very *sentimental*. Their attitude is most disappointing. I suppose with the other girl in hospital…but hopefully they will rethink in due course. However, as it stands, they say they are not going to force Sabrina to marry you. They say it is *her* choice. So it is your job to make sure she makes the *right* choice. It should not be too hard for you—she has a sense of duty and you have a way with women. Do I make myself clear?'

'Crystal.'

From her hiding place she heard the sneer in Sebastian's voice but his father seemed oblivious to it.

'In some way, you know, this accident could be a blessing. It will keep the wedding story off the front page at least.'

'Spoken like a true narcissist. Pain, suffering and loss—who cares so long as it's useful for us?'

'At least you recognise that there is an *us*… Finally. This royal business we are in, *love* is best kept out of it.'

'You told me you loved my mother.'

'And it never gave me a moment's happiness. What do you want? Oh, for God's sake…'

'Five minutes, I said, Your Majesty.'

'All right, just watch what you are doing with that chair. Sebastian, we will speak later. Do not say anything to the press until you have spoken to Hugo and if anyone calls you a hero try to look modest. Who knows? That scar might even be useful.'

Sebastian waited until the royal party had exited, leaving the original guards outside, and went into the bathroom. Sabrina was sitting on the floor, her knees drawn up to her chin, her back pressed against the tiles as though she had slid down them.

'I am assuming you heard all of that.'

Sabrina lifted her head, pushing her hair back from her face with both hands as she angled a look up at him. There was a remoteness in his face that she found chilling.

'So, I'm going to be passed on to the next brother.'

Who doesn't want me any more than the first one did...

She recognised it was irrational, but for some reason this knowledge was far more painful to her than the humiliation she had suffered at Luis's hands.

The belief that she was doing the right thing had enabled her to take a pragmatic approach to the prospect of a loveless marriage to Luis, but when it came to Sebastian being coerced into taking his brother's reject, Sabrina couldn't be objective. Everything inside her just shrivelled up with horror at the prospect of living a lie with Sebastian; she hated the idea of him resenting her and their life together.

How long would it be before he did as his father had suggested and had a discreet affair?

'You heard him.' Their glances connected. 'You could refuse. It sounds as though your parents have had a change of heart. They have realised perhaps that their daughters' lives are more important than political machinations?' He looked at her and saw the sadness in her dark eyes. 'But you won't, will you? The fact is you won't because you have been brainwashed from birth to be *the sacrifice*. You didn't want to marry Luis but you were prepared to, you were prepared to lie in his bed, let him make love to you while you planned next week's dinner menu.'

'I tried not to think that far ahead.'

She didn't realise until she said it that this was true; she had never once imagined herself in bed with Luis. She had never thought about his naked body, or his mouth or how his skin would feel against hers. But since the first moment she'd seen Sebastian she had not stopped thinking about *all* of those things about him, and a lot more!

She was thinking about them now, and the rise in her core temperature made her glad of the cool of the tiles as she pushed herself up the wall into a standing position. The ache low in her pelvis mocked her weakness while his double standards and his contemptuous attitude made her angry enough to ignore the grey tinge to his skin, the lines of pain bracketing his mouth.

'I don't know why you're angry with me. I didn't hear *you* say no to your father! You have to do something you don't want to—oh, well…boo-hoo! Do you think I *enjoy* feeling like some hand-me-down pair of shoes that never quite fitted to begin with? But, what the hell, they look the part if they cripple you…!'

During her outburst he had stared down at her, then after a couple of beats of silence he laughed, the hard sound devoid of humour.

'No, I didn't, did I?' he drawled slowly, the anger in his cobalt-blue eyes replaced now by a glitter of self-derision. 'I'm actually as surprised as you to discover that I'm not about to take advantage of this heaven-sent opportunity to kick my father when he's down.'

As he inhaled through flared nostrils his chest lifted dramatically, drawing her attention to the telltale triangle of sweat on his T-shirt. Her self-righteous tirade still echoing in her ears, she winced as guilt sliced through her. She had made zero allowances at all for the fact he was clearly in considerable pain, even if he was too damn stubborn to admit it.

He released a long, hissing breath as his glance settled on her face; the look in his eyes made her own breath catch.

If her life had depended on it she could not have broken free of that hypnotic azure stare.

'Shoes…mmm…' Inside her hospital-issued slippers Sabrina's toes curled. 'I don't think so—not even the high-heeled spiky, sexy ones, though I *can* see you in them. Actually you make me think of…' his glance sank to her mouth '…*silk*…' the way he curled the word around his tongue made her shiver '…and I think we could fit very well indeed.' His bandaged hand lifted to the bandaged side of his face. 'If, of course, you are able to overlook this in the dark.'

The last comment shook her violently free of the dry-throated, breathless floating sensation that had gripped her during his earlier throaty comments.

She closed her eyes and clenched her fists, hissing through clenched teeth, 'Yes, because I am a shallow, superficial… Be glad you are injured or, so help me, I'd be kicking you.' She pushed past him and back into the hospital room.

She missed the startled look on his face but heard his laughter and sensed him moving back into the room they had shared last night as she went across to the bed she had slept in and grabbed the plastic bag containing the clothes she had been wearing when she'd arrived.

Clutching the bag to her chest, she slowly turned and instantly forgot what she was about to say. 'Get back into bed.'

'That's a very wifely thing to say.'

She fought the urge to help him, keeping her expression carefully neutral at a grunt of pain that escaped his clamped lips as he eased himself onto the bed.

He pulled out a pillow before easing his long lean length down slowly. By the time he had accomplished the task his skin gleamed with a thin layer of perspiration. 'What, you're not going to plump my pillows?'

'When did you last have analgesia?'

'Does it matter?'

'Being in pain,' she retorted tartly, 'when there is pain relief available does not make you manly, it makes you pretty stupid.'

Privately he conceded she probably had a point. 'Not big on the bedside manner, then.'

I could be.

Shocked by the thought that jumped into her head, she veiled her gaze, clearing her throat before she responded.

'Shall I call a nurse for you?'

'As it's been a full thirty seconds since one applied a cool soothing hand to my brow I think we can assume we won't have to wait long until one appears,' he observed, not sounding very grateful for the attention. 'How about you?'

'I'm fine, barely a scratch,' she admitted guiltily.

'And Chloe?'

'I don't know. She's been transferred to a burns unit.' It certainly put her own problems in perspective. 'It's so unfair. I caused this and Chloe and you are both paying for it.'

He arched a brow. 'How exactly is this your fault?'

'I ran away.' She blinked as her eyes filled with the sting of unshed tears burning.

'It was an accident, Sabrina, a freak set of circumstances. Beat yourself up by all means if you want to, but I suspect that Chloe would benefit from a slightly less self-indulgent response.'

She flinched, the initial flare of indignation at his callous attitude vanishing as she recognised he had a point. She scrubbed her eyes with her knuckles and took a deep breath. 'You're right,' she admitted. 'Mum and Dad are with Chloe. It's where I should be.' Her jaw firmed as she wondered how quickly she could get to them.

Disarmed by the admission that he could not imagine any woman finding herself in Sabrina's position, he studied her face. The tear stains, the bruised smudges beneath her eyes, the honey hair lying loose and tangled—and yet she still looked beautiful. His body, bruised, battered and broken even as it was, reacted to that beauty, the lust tempered with tenderness that struck a chord of shock through him.

'Family loyalty?'

Sabrina's eyes lifted at the soft comment. Her slender shoulders rose in a tiny shrug. 'It's what families do.'

'Your family maybe.'

'Have you and your father...?' she began tentatively.

'Always hated one another?'

She met his gaze steadily. 'I wasn't going to say that.'

'No, I'm sure you were going to be more tactful. My father never forgave me for being born even after he discovered I was actually his son and, unlike Luis, I never forgave him for killing my mother. Oh, not literally,' he admitted in response to her wide-eyed reaction. 'He didn't need to. Perhaps he did *love* her, or his version of it, I don't know, but he sealed her fate the day he married her. She was very young and the marriage was—'

Across the space that separated them Sabrina could feel the emotion rolling off him. Years of anger and resentment that had dominated his childhood and shaped his adult life. 'Convenient,' she inserted quietly. 'What was she like?'

A flicker of surprise crossed his face and for a moment he was silent, as if considering the question. 'Didn't Luis ever speak to you about her?'

She shook her head. 'We never talked much at all.'

He stayed silent as he absorbed this information; something in his expression made her wish she had been less open. 'Delicate,' he said eventually. 'And sensitive, shy. I used to *will* her to stand up to him.' His jaw clenched as he admitted with an air of acceptance she sensed had been a long time coming, 'But she couldn't, it wasn't in her. Ironic really—Luis did what we always wanted her to do: he escaped. But she never did. It was like seeing a wild bird trapped in a cage. Painful, heartbreaking, but you know deep down that even if someone opened the door for her she'd be too scared to fly away.'

The poignant image his words drew made her eyes fill, but as much as she felt for the sad, unhappy woman he described Sabrina felt *more* for her sons. She strongly believed that a mother's job was to protect her children but it seemed the roles had been reversed with Sebastian and his brother. She sucked in a deep breath as she silently vowed that no child of hers would ever feel like that.

'Or, she knew it was her duty to stay,' she suggested quietly. 'I know you think it's a dirty word, but isn't that what you're doing by marrying me?'

'Did you just propose to me, Sabrina?'

Her delicate jaw quivered. 'I expect that that will happen when we're not in the same room by someone who is working on the press release now and it's better that way, isn't it? No pretending, given the circumstances.'

There was no trace of the relief she had anticipated in his expression, but then he was most probably in pain. He certainly didn't object when a nurse bustled in and offered to top up his pain relief.

The effects of the analgesia hit Sebastian almost straight away; within seconds his eyelids were closing, and before a second nurse appeared with a holdall that had arrived with fresh clothes for Sabrina he was asleep.

She changed quietly in the bathroom so as not to disturb Sebastian. On her way to the door she paused and looked down at him. Asleep he looked younger, the lines of cynicism ironed out.

Unable to fight the impulse, she reached out and found her fingers halfway to his cheek before she stopped herself. A quiver of sensation radiated out from the pit of her stomach…not her heart. Gratitude was natural. He had saved Chloe. They had gone through a trauma together.

This was a merger, not a marriage.

CHAPTER EIGHT

LOW-KEY, IT HAD been agreed, was appropriate under the circumstances, and the civil ceremony was just that, a handful of people beyond the immediate family. There were photographs, which would be released along with an official statement to be issued later that week.

So she was married. Sabrina could not decide if she was meant to feel different. She glanced to the man, her husband, who sat beside her. There was a remote, untouchable quality about him that even had she wanted to make conversation would have made her think twice. Sabrina didn't want to.

They were physically inches apart but in every other way worlds apart; the journey passed in total silence, not the companionable variety. He was making no effort to change that.

The only time he had spoken was when they'd got in the car and she had told him that she wanted to go to the hospital to see Chloe. He'd nodded and issued a curt instruction to the driver. Then, when they'd arrived at the hospital, he'd pulled out a laptop.

'I'll wait here.'

So Sabrina had gone into the private London hospital her sister had been transferred to, flanked by two security men, to the room where her sister had spent the last few weeks. Chloe had been scheduled to leave before the wedding, but an infection had meant that the skin grafts on her leg that had sustained injury had not taken and the entire painful process had had to begin all over again.

The amount of suffering her sister had endured made her own situation seem insignificant. She took a deep breath before she went in, donning a smile along with a sterile gown. The guilt she felt was her problem. It was not something she was about to burden Chloe with; her sister had enough to contend with but Sabrina knew it was her fault. If she hadn't run away Chloe would not be lying in a hospital bed.

'Hello, you!'

Chloe was lying in bed, her lower body beneath a cradle arrangement that held the sheet off her skin, her face a little thinner than it had been a few months ago and a lot paler, but her smile was just as bright.

'So, how did it go?'.

Sabrina pulled up a chair and did her best to soften the truth with humour.

'Oh, you know—your usual shotgun wedding atmosphere. Without the pregnancy, of course. Lots of glaring and suspicion and a man…actually, four…guarding the door to stop anyone from legging it.'

'Sounds a laugh a minute.'

'It was pretty much what I'd expected and this time the groom turned up, which most people seemed to think a plus,' Sabrina added drily.

'Well, I think you had a lucky escape. Imagine living your life with a man who was in love with someone else.'

The way Chloe was talking it was almost as if she believed that Sebastian loved her. If it made her happy Sabrina saw no reason to correct her.

'So where is the man himself? I forgot to thank him for the fruit basket he brought this morning, so send my love.'

'You saw Sebastian this morning?'

'Didn't he say?'

Say? She swallowed a bubble of hysteria in her throat. 'He must have forgotten.' She was not about to tell her sister that they barely communicated at all.

Had it really been two months since that strange twenty four hours when they had shared a hospital room the night after the accident? She had barely been alone with Sebastian since.

'He comes most mornings—has all the nurses drooling. You do know that if you hadn't married him I would have had him myself, don't you? If he hadn't got me off that cliff I couldn't have held on any longer.' She shuddered. 'I know that nowadays it would be sympathy sex, but—'

'Chloe, don't say that!' Sabrina said, her voice husky with tears. 'The doctors say that the scars will be—'

'They will be scars, and, unlike your husband's, they will not be sexy ones. And while we all know that it's what you're like inside that counts, back in the real world, well...' She gave a sudden deep sigh and wiped her hands across her eyes. She smiled. 'Ignore me, Brina. I'm just having a self-pity day, but Sebastian is a good man, you know, and we have kind of bonded over our scars.'

Sabrina stayed for half an hour before reluctantly leaving her sister.

The sight of the streaks left by dried tears on Sabrina's cheeks when she returned to the car elicited an involuntary stab of protective warmth in Sebastian's chest.

'How is Chloe?' he asked.

'Being brave, but I think she's in pain, though she says not. She thanked you for the fruit.'

He gave a grunt of assent and nodded.

'I'm grateful, Sebastian.'

He stiffened. 'I do not want your gratitude.'

She could almost feel the dignity and calm that she had fought hard to retain all day slipping like sand through her fingers. Except her fingers were clenched so tightly into fists that nothing could have escaped them.

'You don't want a wife,' she blurted, hearing the heavy thud of her pulse like a hammer in her temples as her suppressed anger surged hotly.

Even as she acknowledged it she realised that she had no legitimate right to feel this way. It was no more rational to feel angry now than it had been to imagine that they had made some sort of *connection* that night when they had shared a hospital room.

What had happened since had shown pretty clearly that the only time they were ever going to be *connected* was when he was heavily medicated. She smothered a hysterical bubble of laughter and coaxed some calm into her manner.

'But you've got one. Me, actually, and it's kind of obligatory to talk to her.'

He closed the laptop, the tension of the day and the days that had preceded it stretching the skin tight across his perfect bone structure, a perfection that was emphasised not marred by the scar, already fading to silver, along the right side of his face.

He read the unhappiness and anger in her face and felt a fresh surge of the guilt that had been his ever-present companion over the last weeks. Weeks when he had been the recipient of an immersion programme in all that being the heir apparent involved, and, in the process, feeling a new respect for his brother.

At least he now knew what he was letting himself in for. Sabrina? She was totally unprepared for what was coming, just as his mother had been, and yet had he warned her? Had he opened the door of the golden cage that had now closed? He felt a fresh surge of loathing; he was no better than his father.

'What do you want me to say?' He could have said he wanted her, that he had wanted her from the outset more than he had ever wanted another woman, but wanting did not excuse the fact he had taken advantage of her ignorance. Because he didn't want to do this alone. He felt a flash of guilt.

Pride brought her chin up, but the coldness in his voice hurt more than she was prepared to admit. It was becoming pretty obvious that he didn't require anything from her.

'I think you've said enough.'

Sabrina glanced his way occasionally during the rest of the journey; his stillness was as impregnable as his profile, the shadows as they travelled through the darkness adding emphasis to the strong, sculpted planes as he stared out of the window.

What was he thinking?

It was impossible to tell. Nothing seeped through his mask, only the occasional Arctic-wolf flicker in his arresting blue eyes reminding her of the man he had been two months before. Two months being the time that had finally been considered a *decent* interval between being dumped by one brother and getting married to the next.

She found herself wondering what had happened to, and amazingly feeling a stab of nostalgia for, the *Playboy Prince* who was guaranteed to be in the *right* place saying the *wrong* thing for the cameras, smiling as he put two fingers up to the world in general and the press in particular.

Had that man, the one whose life choices kept the damage-control experts in work, gone for ever? She recalled the soft words he had murmured for her ears only when he had observed her hand shaking while they waited for the registrar's arrival.

'Relax, just treat this day like any other, no different than yesterday, no different than tomorrow. Don't have any expectations—I don't. I expect nothing of you.'

He might not but others did. The King's senior advisor, who had taken her to one side just before the actual ceremony, had reminded her that the fate of a nation was pretty much on her shoulders.

'Prince Sebastian is an unknown factor. He is making an effort but we all know that he is volatile, his history... I know we can trust you, Lady Sabrina, to be a steadying influence.'

'I think it might be better if you trusted the Prince. I will not mention your comments on this occasion, but in future...' She had taken some pleasure from the aide's embarrassed retreat and hoped the message had reached the King that if he wanted to undermine his son she would not be party to it.

The words of an article she had read the previous week profiling the men with power in Europe came back to her. The new Crown Prince was *complex*, the smitten writer had claimed, referring to the glimpses of the barbaric pagan behind the urbane exterior.

Pagan? Not helping, Sabrina, she told herself, pushing away the words. The car suddenly turned off the minor road they had been travelling on for several miles and through big gates that swung open at their approach. The uneasiness in her stomach gave an extra-hard kick as the gates closed behind the car that had travelled at a discreet distance behind them since they'd left London.

The driveway, illuminated at ground level by rows of lights, seemed to go on for miles. Sabrina didn't mind; she was in no hurry to arrive!

Finally they stopped, the uniformed driver pulling up in front of a building with a Georgian façade. This was a private house, not a hotel. Someone had told her who the house belonged to—not that the owners would be here for the duration of their stay. They had been guests at the small ceremony today. Sabrina had been introduced but she couldn't remember their faces or names; it was all part of the blur.

For a full thirty seconds nobody moved except the man who was sitting beside the driver, who spoke into a device attached to his wrist, then he nodded and it seemed as though dark suited and booted figures appeared from everywhere.

Sebastian was already being greeted at the porticoed entrance when someone eventually came and opened the car door for her. By that point, aside from the alert-looking suited figures either side of the entrance, the security presence had vanished.

As she made her own exit she imagined them hidden in the bushes. It wasn't a particularly comforting thought. As she approached the house the feeling that had been with her all day persisted. A weird sense of out-of-body disconnection, as though this were happening to someone else and she were watching. And now she was listening to someone else's heels crunching on the gravel, someone else was feeling the evening breeze carrying the tang of the sea on her face.

But it hadn't been someone else that had said *I do* today. That had been her.

Inside the hall of the house, a magnificent marble-floored space dominated by a great sweeping staircase and lit by several chandeliers, stood *her husband*, his back turned to her. He was deep in conversation with three other men and a woman who was taller than two of the men, and striking with close-cropped white blonde hair set off dramatically against the black trouser suit she wore.

Sabrina could not hear what they were saying but it didn't seem to make Sebastian happy, though he heard them out before he fired off a staccato stream of sentences.

Weirdly she almost envied them—at least he was communicating with them in entire sentences, not gruff monosyllables.

Fighting was better than indifference; she was beginning to wonder if she had ever imagined that he had been attracted to her. It made the fact that just looking at him made her tremble all the more hard to come to terms with—to live with on a daily basis.

Maybe that was what it was. She represented the duty that he resented and there was nothing attractive about duty. She didn't know and quite frankly she was tired of trying to figure it out. Her head ached with the constant questions whirling around inside it.

Suddenly her patience, worn paper-thin, snapped. She was done with waiting. She cleared her throat. 'Sebastian.' Her voice, pitched low, carried.

There was a perceptible pause before Sebastian turned around long enough for her cheeks to begin to burn at the prospect of being humiliated.

An unexpected rush of anger-fuelled adrenaline kept the tears she felt burning behind her eyelids at bay.

She watched, the sinking feeling not improving as he said something that made the trio with him nod, and he began to walk towards her, his dark hair gleaming glossy blue under the light cast by the chandeliers, his scar made to appear darker by the same trick of the light.

In profile during the journey it had been hidden, but now, full face, the thin angry line on the left cheek of his lean face was revealed. The sight made her shiver as it always did, not because she found the blemish on his perfect face repulsive but because of how he had received it.

Her fault.

She straightened her spine, the reaction involuntary as he walked towards her with the long strides of someone who possessed natural athletic grace. Power refined and controlled that sent a visceral little shudder through her body.

He paused a few feet away and swept her face with his gaze. She thought she saw emotion move beneath the azure surface before his long dark lashes half lowered, making it impossible to read any further clues, and when he spoke his voice held no discernible inflection.

'You look tired.' The edge of roughness to the husky texture of his voice added depth to the velvet.

Realising after a lengthening silence that the comment hadn't been rhetorical and he expected her to respond, Sabrina tipped her head. 'Yes,' she agreed. Tired hardly came close to describing the bone-deep weariness she felt.

'You should go up.' His eyes moved beyond her and a woman appeared, as if by magic, smartly dressed in a blouse and tweed skirt. She dipped her head deferentially towards Sabrina.

'Mrs Reid will show you to your room if you need anything…? I will join you presently.'

Her liquid dark brown eyes flickered wider at the statement, alarm bleeping briefly through the horrible *flatness* of her emotions. Then it was gone and so was he, moving towards the waiting group. She could see that he had already dismissed her from his mind.

Simultaneously recognising the tightness in her chest as hurt, utterly irrational given their circumstances, she asked herself if she'd prefer he acted a part? Yes, actually she would. She was all for pretence if it stopped someone feeling wretched.

'I hope you like your rooms. His Highness usually has the West Wing suite when he stays with us. He said it would be fine.'

'What?' Sabrina paused, the light-headed feeling made her wonder if she had eaten anything today. The woman with her paused too, as had the group in the hall. Her husband was the only one *not* watching their progress.

What were they all thinking?

Were they asking themselves what sort of marriage this was where the husband needed to be reminded that his wife was there? She experienced a sudden flash of anger.

He could, with a minimum of effort, have made this day slightly less awful.

She hadn't been expecting him to serenade her or carry her over the threshold, even. But would it be *too* much to ask that he acknowledged her existence, show some degree of basic courtesy instead of behaving with the charm and charisma of an adolescent being forced to attend a family function when he would rather hang out with his friends? Of course, Sebastian was not an adolescent and the friends he probably wished he were hanging out with were six-foot blondes in tiny bikinis, but essentially the situation was the same. He was clearly, 'Sulking.'

She could almost hear her elocution teacher, the poor man who had been brought in by her parents when her first attempt at public speaking had not only brought her out in hives but been inaudible, applauding her projection.

Her stomach clenched in horror, the rest of her froze, as thanks to the excellent acoustics the angry accusation echoed once, twice, three times before fading away.

In the hall you could hear in the pin-drop silence Sebastian's voice sounding tersely impatient. 'So does anyone have the financial projections I asked for?'

In her head Sabrina could hear her mother's voice as she coaxed her out from the cupboard she had retreated to after she'd admitted to her best friend that she fancied the captain of the football team, unaware that she was standing close enough to the live mic to have the entire assembled school hear her.

'You have two choices when you make a public faux pas, Brina—you can either make a joke of it or act as though it never happened.'

Sabrina went for the latter and turned to the woman who was escorting her, comforting herself with the fact her new husband had the sort of attention span that meant unless you were six feet and blonde—and she was five six and fairish—he had pretty much deleted you from memory five seconds after you went out of his line of vision.

She lifted her chin. She would not vie for his attention but she would not be treated as though she were invisible either.

She produced a smile that said she was actually interested. 'I'm sure the rooms will be perfect, thank you. This is a beautiful house.'

She'd said the right thing. The housekeeper was very proud of her employers' historic home. She went on to regale Sabrina with a history that revolved mostly around the famous and infamous figures who had stayed there over the centuries.

CHAPTER NINE

THEY RESPONDED TO his question in a respectful way, even though they had just given the said information to him ten seconds earlier. Still, the respect was as yet only skin deep. He was perfectly well aware that he had yet to earn this. They, and in fact the world, were still waiting and maybe, in some cases, hoping that the day would come when he'd roll up for a scheduled conference late, hungover or possibly both.

Sometimes their doubts, never voiced, felt like a shout, but he knew that he could not allow self-doubt to creep in, so the extra hours he put in were not to prove anything to the doubters, but to himself.

'This could wait until the morning if you prefer, Highness,' said Ramon, the accountant.

'You have somewhere else you'd prefer to be, Ramon?'

The man adopted an expression that suggested he wanted nothing more than to discuss a report on the financial benefits to be gained from amalgamating the tourist boards of both sides of the reunified island!

'Fine, I believe there is coffee provided for us in the study.'

Sebastian could feel their resentment as they filed past him. They all had places they would prefer to be, whereas he had a place he did not want to be.

Keeping his libido on a leash around her was driving him closer to the edge on the occasions when he was unable to avoid contact, but as hard as it was, as much as he wanted her, his guilt—or was that his pride?—would not allow him to act on it.

He didn't want her *available* or *willing* or *dutiful*. Sebastian wanted her mad, crazy, hungry for him. In his dreams she begged him to come to her and he would wake up bathed in sweat and aching.

Sebastian's jaw clenched as he lost his battle not to look towards the staircase in time to see her vanish from view.

'Highness, is there anything I can get you?'

The form of address dragged Sabrina's wandering thoughts back from the dark place they had drifted to. She was barely aware that they had reached the suite of rooms that they had been allocated. The woman walked her through them, opening the doors to two en-suite bedrooms that opened off a large, comfortable central sitting room.

'Would you like a fire lit?'

Sabrina's eyes went to the fireplace. 'No, that's fine, thank you,' she murmured, waiting until the woman had left before leaning against the closed door.

She stood there, eyes closed for a few moments, before levering herself away from the surface and giving herself a mental shake before she looked around the room. Even without an audience she found herself feigning an interest she was far from feeling, a *lifetime's training kicking in*.

They were only scheduled to spend one night here but someone had gone to a lot of trouble. Or more likely an army of 'someones' had. There were the welcoming touches, like the flower arrangements, the iced champagne. Opening one of the doors that led off the sitting room, Sabrina stared at the neatly turned down four-poster that took centre stage. The bed in the second, equally grand bedroom was turned down too. Not letting her mind go there, she continued to deal with the moment and not think beyond it, preferring to deal with each situation as it arose before moving on to the next hurdle.

Hurdle—was that what her married life was going to be?

She frowned. If you started thinking of yourself as some sort of helpless victim, inevitably you became one. She turned her back on the bed and opened one of the numerous fitted cupboards that lined one wall, where she found a selection of her own clothes hanging neatly on hangers, along with a row of shoes.

It wasn't until she opened it fully and caught a glimpse of herself in the mirror-lined door that she saw she was still clutching a sad-looking bouquet in her gloved hand.

Peeling off her silk gloves, she walked back into the sitting room and sat down, loosening the top button of the blouse she wore beneath her cream silk suit. It didn't help the restricted feeling in her chest. There was still that cold, heavy weight behind her breastbone that she had spent the day pretending wasn't there.

Sitting upright again, she kicked off the heels she wore and flexed her fingers, staring as she did at the rings that felt cold, the wide gold band above the square-cut emerald engagement ring, and fought a sudden compulsion to tear them off.

The act would have been both pointless and childish and now was the moment to behave like an adult, so instead, to distract herself from the feelings that were building inside her, she reached for the TV remote, pressed the on button and began to scroll through the channels.

She closed her eyes and let her head fall back. She allowed the husky diction of a well-known female news-reader to wash over her.

The woman actually had quite a pleasant voice, soothing, until that one phrase made her jolt into a tense upright position—*Princess Sabrina*!

On the screen the newsreader's face was replaced by a scene of the wedding guests, the camera zooming in close-up on a few famous faces.

'It is believed that after being left quite literally at the altar last June by the then Crown Prince Luis, his jilted bride, Lady Sabrina Summerville, has married his brother, Prince Sebastian, at a private ceremony. The couple and the bride's sister were both involved in the tragic accident on Vela Main on the day of the wedding.'

The images of the wedding guests vanished and in their place was footage of helicopters circling and am-bulances with wailing sirens, their flashing lights illu-minating wreckage strewn across a road.

Sabrina stared transfixed at the nightmare scene of twisted metal and bodies, unaware as the remote slipped from her nerveless fingers.

She hoped that Chloe was not watching this.

She gave a sigh of relief as the crash scene van-ished, though the tension climbed straight back into her shoulders as Sebastian appeared on the screen, tall and tanned, looking like the hero of an action movie. Over one broad shoulder he carried skis while the other shoul-der was occupied by the fashionably tousled blonde head of a leggy soap actress who had both her arms around his middle as she smiled for the cameras that surrounded them. Sebastian looked down at her with an expression of amused indulgence before turning to the camera crews as he made a gesture that ensured the photo being plastered over front pages the next day.

'Sabrina…'

She leapt at the touch of his hand on her shoulder and fumbled for the remote.

'What rubbish are you watching?' he asked, sounding impatient.

'I'm not watching,' she denied, annoyed with herself for feeling inexplicably guilty, then almost immediately embarrassed as a picture of herself looking solemn with pigtails and no front teeth, one from the family album, filled the screen.

Her fingers had closed over the remote but just as she was about to press the off button Count Hugo appeared, looking sincere as he stared into the camera.

'What the…?'

Behind her Sebastian drawled, 'I think it might be a good idea to watch this.'

'You realise, Count,' said the man holding the microphone, 'that many will believe this marriage is one of political expedience? Prince Luis was a popular figure both sides of the border. Many question his brother's ability to fill his shoes, and this marriage today—this rather low-key marriage—is it not true to say that it is nothing more than a cynical stunt to shore up crumbling support for the reunification project?'

The Count, who had continued to smile benignly into the camera through the comments, remained unflustered as he posed his own question.

'Donald, I ask you, if it was a "stunt", as you call it,

would it be low-key? One can never silence the cynics, but the facts are, whether you choose to believe them or not, that the Prince and his bride have known one another for years, and have been…close in the past. After the events of last June the respect they have always felt for one another has turned into love.'

The newsreader's face appeared as the Count vanished.

'You can see the full report tomorrow night at nine, when the reunification is discussed by a panel of experts—but here is a—'

Sabrina pressed the 'off' button and turned, her expression accusing as she faced her husband.

'Did you know about this?'

'No…'

She arched a sceptical brow. She could not believe that the Count would have gone ahead with something like that without running it past Sebastian first.

'But I'm not exactly surprised, and I'm not really sure why you are.'

'You're not surprised to hear that *you're* one half of one of the greatest love stories of the decade?' She folded her arms across her chest and glared up at him. 'Well, it came as news to me.'

Sebastian reacted to the spiky sarcasm in her voice with a negligent shrug. 'The question is, did he have you convinced? I thought he came across as surprisingly sincere,' he mused, tugging off the tie that was looped around his neck.

'Does it not bother you that he was lying his head off?' she squeaked incredulously.

Sebastian gave a cynical smile. 'Yes, he was lying. He is a diplomat. It is what he does.'

'And he just goes ahead and does it? He doesn't run it past anyone?'

'He has a level of autonomy.'

She could tell that was only half the story. 'You're just as bad as he is!' she accused. But Sebastian was much better to look at. 'Is there some special class where they teach you how to dodge a question?'

'Actually, yes.' He removed his eyes from the pouting outline of her lips. 'I asked him to handle the press. I don't micromanage but I think the brief I gave him was too…broad.'

She rolled her eyes. 'Finally! And you're all right with what he did?' Her voice shook with the sense of outrage she felt.

He gave her a very direct look and a surprisingly straight answer. 'I am not happy.'

Something in the clipped delivery made her look at him. Sabrina became aware for the first time that he was actually pretty angry. She felt an unexpected stab of sympathy for the Count.

Sebastian glanced at the blank screen of the television. 'It was…tasteless. He overstepped the mark, but that's politics for you.'

She subsided with a sigh into a chair. 'I don't like politics.'

He flashed a bleak grin. 'It's not going to go away any time soon.' He walked across to the table and picked up the bottle from the ice bucket. 'You look like you need a drink.'

She shook her head automatically and wrapped her arms around herself, squeezing tight until her fingers dug into her ribcage, hard enough to bruise. Her chin rested against her chest as she closed her eyes.

'Well, I do.' He put both the champagne flutes he had filled down on the polished surface.

'Do you ever have flashbacks…?' she asked. He looked at her as she shook her head. 'It doesn't matter.'

His frown deepened. 'How do you mean flashbacks?'

'The accident.'

'Do you?'

'It's got better. The therapist said—'

'You have seen a therapist?'

'My parents insisted.'

'Does anyone else know this?'

'Anyone?' she countered, her brow pleating into a puzzled frown.

'Anyone other than your parents?' he pressed. 'Did you discuss it with friends or—?'

Her sudden shocked laugh cut him off. 'You think there is some sort of *stigma* attached to having counselling for post-traumatic stress?'

'What I think is not relevant.'

She felt her anger and, yes, disappointment, swell a tight knot in her chest. 'Actually I think it's *very* relevant.'

'In our position it pays to be aware, anticipate the effect our actions will have. We must always be conscious of how the public perceive them. From this point on our lives, everything we do, is going to be scrutinised.'

'What do you mean,' she asked, 'from this point on? You have spent your life playing for the cameras.'

Spasms of irritation flickered across his face. 'Mental health is a sensitive issue and the press can spin—'

'You're afraid that people will say you've married someone unstable? You know something, Sebastian? I actually don't care what you think,' she shouted. How much simpler her life would be if that were true! 'I had a problem. I couldn't sleep and I got help.' She drew a slicing motion with her hand. 'End of story.'

'Don't overreact!'

His dismissive attitude made her jaw quiver. 'I'm not the one overreacting. You can't deal with it—*tough*, Sebastian! But you know what I think? *You're* the one with the problem,' she charged, her brown eyes sparking with contemptuous accusation.

He watched, jaw clenched, his anger slipping away as Sabrina bent and picked up the slingback heels she had been wearing, pulling the silk across her deliciously rounded bottom tight before she straightened up and flung him a look of contempt over her shoulder. Then, shoes dangling from the fingers of one hand, her slender back rigid, she flounced in a dignified fashion from the room.

He winced at the sound of the door slamming.

Eyes squeezed closed, he lifted one of the glasses he had filled to his lips. The fizz slid smoothly down his throat but didn't produce any lightening of his mood as the bubbles seeped into his bloodstream.

With a curse he slammed the glass down, before he began to pace across the room. He was furious with her for being unforgivably right. He exhaled, his chest lifting as he came to a halt, eyes closed, a low grunt of self-directed anger rumbling in his chest.

She was right and he had never felt more ashamed of himself. What the hell was wrong with him? He had responded to her confidence like the sort of narrow-minded bigot he despised. She wouldn't be doing any confiding in him again in a hurry.

Maybe that was why he'd done it, as another way to push her away?

How many times had he sneered when his father had

adopted a similar attitude? Truth was disposable; unfairness could always be spun in your favour.

After a moment he walked towards the recently closed door.

The room was empty. One lamp beside the bed was switched on, illuminating the darkness. He could hear the sound of running water in the bathroom. Calling Sabrina's name, he walked across the room. The bathroom door was open and she stood barefooted in a silk slip at the marble washbasin, her hands under the running tap as she stared at her reflection in the mirror.

'Sabrina.'

She reacted to the sound of her name like a startled deer and spun around, wary-eyed, to face him. Their eyes connected and her chin lifted to a haughty angle, despite the blue-veined pulse he could see leaping at the base of her creamy throat. 'Do you mind knocking before you come into my room?'

'Yes, as a matter of fact I do, and I'm damned if I'm going to start off this marriage with sulks and closed doors.'

She switched off the water and stalked past him. 'Fine, next time I'll lock it. And I'm not sulking.'

'I'm sorry…'

She had been ready to counter anything he threw at her except that…an apology! It crossed her mind she had misheard him. 'What did you say?'

'I'm sorry. That was…' He hefted a sigh and dragged a hand back and forth across his already mussed hair. 'I'm so busy pretending to be the Prince everyone wants that it's hard to switch off.'

That was the way he operated. He focused on the task at hand. It had never mattered what the task was; he gave all the same commitment and he didn't carry baggage to weigh him down. Because he had shrugged off the accident it had not even crossed his mind to consider that it might not be so easy for Sabrina.

Her dark eyes widened. 'You don't have to prove anything to anyone.'

He shrugged, an ironic half-smile quivering the corners of his mouth. 'Only myself maybe. You must be aware that people are waiting for me to fail?'

She shifted uneasily, feeling an unexpected stab of sympathy for Sebastian as she remembered the comments earlier that day of his father's aide.

Her fingers playing with the thin spaghetti strap of her silk slip drew his eyes to the smooth curve of her shoulder.

'Well, you have worked pretty hard at establishing yourself as the Playboy Prince, haven't you?'

He gave a hard grin, the gleam in his blue eyes and the flash of white teeth making her stomach flip. 'That was not all hard work—some of it came naturally. Look, I am not going to pretend I am something I am not. I am not a romantic...which, considering our circumstances, might not in itself be a drawback. I was never looking for a soulmate—'

'Or a wife.'

He blinked; she could see that her comment had caught him unawares. 'True, but marriage is a contract and I understand contracts.'

But not love.

Sebastian didn't believe in love and maybe that made it easier than believing in it as she did, and knowing that it was something she could never have.

Don't think about the things you can't have, Brina, she told herself. *Focus on the things you can have, the things you can achieve...you can have children...* Something she had always considered one of the greatest gifts a woman could be blessed with. Beyond that she had allowed herself to believe that she might be in a position one day to have influence on things she cared about: health care, women's education… She might be able to leave a legacy even if she could not have love.

'People aren't always looking. Luis wasn't looking and he found his soulmate.'

'I am not Luis, Sabrina.'

'No, you didn't run, but you wanted to!' she countered, knowing the accusation was unfair but unable to repress the great sense of frustration she felt.

'I am not a romantic. I do not believe that I will be walking down a street and be struck by the emotional version of a lightning bolt when I find my soulmate. You regret that you have not had your time out there kissing frogs and waiting for one to turn into a prince. The fact is, the only Prince you will have is me…but I promise you, *cara*,' he continued, his voice softening to a low, throaty, toe-curling purr as he took another step towards her, 'those butterflies you spoke of do not require a soulmate. You can feel them. You *will* feel them.'

Heart racing, her blood pounding, she quivered but didn't evade his hand as his fingers trailed down her cheek, the light touch sparking nerve endings to life before his hand fell away.

'You sound very confident.'

'There has been an attraction between us from the first moment we met. I really don't want our married life to start with closed doors. How about we push those doors open?'

Their eyes locked, neither spoke; the touch of his hand on the bare skin of her shoulder made her jump.

She moved to pull the strap of her slip up but his free hand caught her wrist.

Her heart was thudding a wild drumbeat in her chest as her glance moved from the fingers circling her wrist to his big hand, brown against her skin. She swallowed and looked back up into the burning blue of his eyes and she felt her resistance slipping away like sand through her fingers.

She managed a sensible smile, hard when he was close, so impossibly male. 'Sebastian, this is not a good—'

His grin sizzled away her sensible thoughts.

'To hell with good!' he growled throatily, then, still holding her gaze, he let go of her hand and took hold of the hem of her slip, which he pulled over her head in one slick motion.

She didn't move.

The sexual tension had reached screaming point in one slam of a heartbeat.

His hands followed the path of his eyes as they slid down her neck, over her shoulders then down to her quivering breasts. His fingers splaying to cup them, as his thumbs teased the hot, aching peaks.

Her eyes squeezed tight shut as she stood, head back, hands clenched into white-knuckled fists as she focused on the incredible sensations coursing through her body, opening only when he spread his hands under her rib-cage around her waist.

He bent his head and covered her mouth, the kiss slow and sensual. She could see the sensuous glitter in his eyes through the screen of his long lashes. When he pulled back, desire, hot and fierce, roared inside her.

He rubbed his nose up against hers, blowing wisps of

hair from her eyes before he moved in again. This time the kisses were not slow, they were hard and hungry.

Still kissing her on her lips, her neck, her eyes... everywhere, he picked her up and carried her over to the bed. Lying there, she watched as he stripped, holding her eyes as he fought his way out of his clothes, revealing a lean and muscled body, his golden skin dusted with strategic drifts of dusky hair.

And he was really, really aroused.

The image of primitive male beauty sent a fresh surge of breathless excitement through Sabrina's body. One hand on the mattress beside her, he bent forward. Greedy, she looped her arms around his neck and dragged him down onto the bed beside her.

The first skin-to-skin contact drew a shocked cry of pleasure from her throat. His skin was like silk, his body hard, the lean strength of it different and intensely thrilling.

His hands moved in long sweeping movements down her sides, her quivering thighs, before moving to her bottom. He kneaded the tight flesh with his fingers, dragging her in hard against his body as she pushed up and into him, opening her mouth to the invasion of his tongue. Wanting to open herself to him so much at one level it scared her, but the fear was lost in the need; the deep, driving, relentless throb of need that had invaded every cell of her body.

'Hell, Sabrina!' he breathed against her mouth.

'Hell, back,' she teased, kissing the scar on his face, letting her tongue run down the length of it before framing his face between her small hands and saying fiercely, 'I hated you hurting.'

He groaned. He was hurting now!

Was it always like this, or was this hot make-up sex?

he wondered as he slid down her body. His thought processes stopped as he fitted his mouth hungrily to one
perfect tight nipple and felt her moan and arch under
him.

He tipped her over, sliding up her body until they
were lying side by side. Her skin was hot to the touch
and felt like silk…he couldn't believe how soft.

'Incredible,' he murmured as he slid a hand down
behind her knee and hooked her leg across his hip. She
bent her head and pressed her face into his chest, kissing the hair-roughened skin.

He slid his fingers into her hair and dragged her
face up to his, then he slid a hand between her legs, his
fingers moving through the light curls into her body.

Sabrina ached for his touch. There was nothing outside the ache; it consumed her totally, hit everywhere
she moved against his hand, her breath coming in a series of uneven, shallow little gasps as his fingers slid
along her delicate folds and deep into her.

Quite suddenly he rolled away and lay on his back,
gasping like a man coming up for air. He turned his
head and looked at her. 'I can't take much more of this.'

She gave a slow, slumberous smile, the primal need
pounding through her making her bold, as she placed
her hand in the middle of his chest, watching his face
as she moved her hand lower.

She watched him gasp as her fingers tightened slowly
around him.

He withstood the torture for a few seconds until his
control broke. With a low growl that rose up from some
place deep inside him, he tipped her onto her back and
parted her legs and positioned himself between them.
He watched her face as he thrust slowly, deeply into her.

Then deeper, as he begged her to take him all and she

wrapped her long legs around him and closed her eyes, whispering his name over and over like a litany as they moved together, breath mingled, touching everywhere, heartbeats in sync, as close as two people could be.

She felt it coming, she pushed towards it, every muscle in her body tensed and waiting, and when the white-hot rush came it was so strong it pushed her to the edge of consciousness.

When she fought her way back from the blissful place he had taken her to Sebastian was still lying across her, breathing hard, then with a groan he levered himself off her.

'I was rough... Should I say sorry?'

She touched a finger to his lips.

He looked into her lovely face and felt a swell of possessive tenderness.

'It was perfect, you were...' She caught his hand, her eyes flickering down his lean, muscled form, before lifting it to her lips. 'I suppose practice really does make perfect.'

It wasn't until Sabrina spoke that he realised tonight was not something he had ever *practised* for; what they had shared had been nothing like anything he had *ever* experienced before. He could not compare like with like because there was no like.

'Stay?' she slurred sleepily, her eyelids flickering but not opening. It was fine by him. Sebastian could barely keep his eyes open anyway.

He slid down and drew her into his body. She settled there with the trust of a kitten and gave a gentle sigh.

CHAPTER TEN

THE DAWN CHORUS was singing when he opened his eyes and Sabrina was still in his arms, her soft body warm, face pressed against his chest. Her hair, lying in a hon-eyed stream down her slender back, was tangled.

The corners of his mouth lifted in a smile as he ex-perienced a swelling surge of possessiveness that was outside his experience and a million miles from his ob-jectivity. His smile flattened and then reasserted itself as she gave a little sigh and burrowed deeper into his chest. He didn't want to recognise the tenderness that tightened in his chest as he thought about last night; the sex had been mind-blowing. His eyes darkened as he remembered the moment she had taken the initiative, tentative at first as she'd begun to explore his body with her hands and mouth, and then with more confidence as she'd learned to drive him to the brink and bring him back. Her instincts were incredible, her lack of inhibi-tions a delight.

It was just sex. So why, asked the voice in his head, had it felt like no sex he had ever known? Did a mar-riage licence really make such a difference? He had never been a woman's first before—maybe that was part of it. The fact that everything was new and fresh for her and her delight and wonder…her *hunger* made it new and fresh for him.

He lifted a strand of hair from her face and leaned in, breathing in the scent of her warm skin until the ringing phone in the other room reminded him that this respite had been temporary.

He eased his arm slowly from under her shoulders, and, pulling the sheet up over her naked body, he slipped from the bed. On his way to the door he grabbed one of the bathrobes that were hung up and closed the door quietly behind him. The phone had stopped ringing and it took him a couple of minutes to locate it to where it had slipped from his pocket. A glance at the screen revealed the identity of the person behind the five missed calls.

With a sigh he punched in the number. 'Hello, Father.'

Sabrina fought her way through several layers of wispy sleep before she surfaced, not quite sure where she was or why she ached in muscles that she didn't know she had.

She opened her eyes and encountered the cobalt-blue stare of the man who was standing at the foot of the bed sipping coffee.

Her husband!

Her lover!

She cut short her sinuous little stretch, sucked in a taut breath and sat up, dragging the sheet with her.

'What time is it?'

'Early.'

'You're…' *Not naked,* she thought, taking in his suit and feeling a little stab of disappointment.

'A meeting scheduled for tomorrow has been brought forward.'

'What meeting?'

He looked surprised by the question. 'The geological team who did the new survey are available to answer some questions. I have to fly back.'

She blinked, her brain still not working at full capacity. 'How long do I have to get ready?'

'No need for that. Take your time. I'm flying out.'

A cold, resentful feeling in the pit of her stomach expanded. She focused on that and not the hurt. 'Without me.'

'You are not missing much, I promise.' He put down his coffee cup and got to his feet. 'Depending on when the meeting ends, we will meet up tonight.'

Was that shorthand for *to have sex*? She didn't know, but she was concerned by how much she wanted it to be. Hell, one night and she was already an addict! It was no longer a surprise to her that her husband had left a swathe of broken hearts across Europe.

'Last night I…' She paused, unable to find the words to tell him how *right* it had felt without sounding…*besotted*.

'We are expected to make a baby or two. I think we might enjoy it.'

She brought her lashes down in a concealing sweep. It wasn't what he'd said, it was the realisation that she had wanted him to say something *more*, to *feel* something more.

Because she felt more, Sabrina realised, she *wanted* more, she…oh, hell, she had fallen in love with her Playboy Prince, but he was so much more. Pain and shock seeped through her, because for him she would always be a duty, even if it was one he enjoyed. At least when the lights were out and no others duties demanded his attention.

She was his wife but not his love.

'Are you all right?'

She dodged his eyes and pulled the sheet all the way up to her chin. Was this what being in love felt like? Nerve endings raw and exposed? The stomach churning? The need to cry until your eyes were red and puffy?

If so she was amazed it was so popular, that people actively looked for it. She'd had flu that felt better than being in love.

'Fine.'

Sabrina was a very bad liar, but, rather than challenge the very obvious untruth, Sebastian accepted the statement at face value with a shrug of his muscled shoulders because— *Because it's easier and you're a coward, Seb.*

'I'm not really human until I've had my first coffee.'

The brightness in her voice sent a knife surge of guilt through him as he lowered his lean frame onto the edge of the bed. 'I know.'

Eyes dark, wide and wary lifted very slowly to his face as she began to shake her head. 'No, it isn't...'

'You're dreading moving into your golden cage... I do understand.'

Her dark lashes came down in a fluttering curtain across her eyes; she gave something that sounded like a laugh before raising them again.

'Palace life is restricting, but...' He took a deep breath. It didn't matter how many times he told himself she knew what she was letting herself in for, that they were *both* victims of this situation, he still felt guilty as hell. 'Our apartments will be separate from my father and you...*we*...must...'

'Make the best of a bad job. Keep busy,' she quipped with a brittle smile as he danced around the message he was delivering: that their lives might collide and sometimes in the bedroom, but essentially they were to live their own lives. It was nothing more than she had ever expected from marriage, but that had been before she had been stupid enough to fall in love with her husband.

That changed everything!

'That wasn't what I was going to say. The next twelve months...the workload will be... I won't be there to—'

She lifted her chin, her pride coming to her rescue. 'I am not a child, Sebastian, so relax. I do not need entertaining.'

I just need loving!

'I do not need my hand held,' she continued, ignoring the ache in her chest. 'And I am not going to be a *needy* wife,' she promised, managing to inject a note of amusement into her voice. 'I'm not going to ask you for anything.'

She finished saying what he wanted to hear, getting a hard look for her efforts.

Sebastian knew he should be feeling relief; instead he felt an odd sense of dissatisfaction as he listened to her list the things she would *not* be asking of him. He knew that anger was an irrational response but struggled to put his finger on the exact cause.

'What if I need my hand holding?' From her expression the unplanned question appeared to surprise her almost as much as it had him. 'Not literally, just a figure of speech,' he said, responding to a need to clarify his comment. After all, he had never actually needed someone...anyone.

The addition made her wonder if she had imagined the hard-sounding question. Her eyes flickered from the brown hand he had moved across the counterpane until his splayed fingertips were a whisper away from her own, before shifting back to his face. A wave of sheer longing and lust pierced her like a knife blade, causing her chest to lift as she caught her breath.

'Oh, for one moment there I thought the story that you don't actually need more than one hour's sleep a night was more than an urban myth.'

He responded with a half-smile to her comeback, not seeming to notice her heightened colour. 'I have watched your parents. They work as a team.'

She nodded agreement. 'Yes, but that's different. They—'

'Love one another.'

It wasn't his assertion that sparked her angry response but the patronising little half-smile that accompanied it, though that faded as he continued. 'But leaving the emotional stuff to one side...'

Suddenly the anger blocked out everything. It was simply too extreme for her to navigate around. 'As far as I'm concerned marriage...a *real* marriage...is all about the *emotional stuff*! There,' she charged, discovering that it was possible to love someone and want to throw something at them at one and the same time. 'Is *that* emotional enough for you? Sorry if I lack your control!'

The mattress shifted, making her slide sideways as he got to his feet and turned, spreading his hands in a pacifying gesture as he looked down at her. 'I'm sorry if I'm throwing the cold water of realism on your dreams, but we have to be realistic. Palace life...marriage, if I can say the word without you throwing something at me? It will take some adjusting to but things might work better if we don't immediately form two opposing camps, if we are one...team.'

His logic was impeccable and deeply depressing, and the only thing, she reminded herself, on offer.

She lifted her brows before directing her retort at her pearly polished toenails. 'Who knows? Your robot logic might cancel out my silly, girly emotionalism.' As the last quivering resentful words left her lips her head lifted, but there was no answering anger in Sebastian's face as their eyes clashed. He looked...hell, he looked incredibly sexy and *exhausted*. Her anger was lost in a wave of protective empathy.

'For God's sake, Sabrina, I want you in my bed, not in my head!' he blasted, then saw her expression and stopped, a curse of frustration escaping his clenched teeth. 'Sorry, I didn't mean—'

'Yes, you did.' She sat there looking frozen, offended and so incredibly sexy with her honey tumbled hair and pink mouth still partly swollen from their kisses from the previous night that he experienced the tsunami of all hormone surges. It struck with no warning and the results on his brain function was devastating—a white-hot, brain-melting blast.

Endurance was the only response. Waiting for it to pass, Sebastian closed his eyes, the muscles of his throat working as he fought for control—this should not be happening. Sex should have smoothed the path; the absence of love should have meant this was easier, not more complicated...yet another occasion when theory fell well short of reality!

He took a deep breath and tried again to breach the chasm he could feel forming between them. 'Look...' Their eyes connected and the silence stretched, only interrupted by the discordant sounds of their individual jagged breathing.

'Marriage does not have to conform to any set pat-

tern. We need to set out our own rules, not conform…
and we must be flexible.' She had been beautifully flexible last night.

'What are you saying?' she whispered, unable to tear her eyes away from his hot, scorching stare. Her insides were melting.

Good question, he thought. 'I really don't know…' he said, because this was very much outside his experience. 'I can't promise anything, Sabrina. I know you have dreams and…' He gave a short laugh, hating himself and the system for all that she had been robbed of. 'Maybe you never had any, but anyway I'm sorry that this is your life, the politics, the scheming. I guess what I'm trying to say is that I don't want us to be warring factions, sending notes to one another through a third party. You deserve more than that.' *And more than me,* he thought.

His driven words penetrated the warm sexual whirlpool that was drawing her inside, a weird but oddly seductive experience. 'That won't happen,' she managed faintly.

'It could. I've seen it in action…my parents…no matter what, we will never be them.' *Kill me first,* he thought. 'I'd tell you about it but maybe in the long run it will just get easier when this chemistry wears off.'

Did the fact his deep voice was actually shaking with need make his prediction any the less painful? The rampant hunger glowing in his eyes made this a question for later; right now all she wanted to do was feel him inside her.

'But in the meantime let's enjoy it?' he growled.

The hungry intent stamped on his lean face made her insides quiver with helpless desire.

Sebastian was fighting his way out of his jacket as he levered his long length onto the bed beside her.

Sabrina helped him.

It was the following day before he saw her next.

In that time, he had been able to gain some perspective, and a little sympathy he had previously lacked for people who actually convinced themselves that a hormonal response was something spiritual and everlasting. It was an easy mistake to make, he now appreciated.

Of course, there was more involved with his situation with Sabrina. They were two people in a unique arrangement that very few would ever experience; the affinity, the sense of understanding, when combined with a physical attraction had, when you viewed the situation logically, been almost predictable.

Then he saw her, and the smug, comforting conclusions slipped through his fingers like sand.

'Hello, there.'

Sabrina started guiltily, looking from him to the heavy tome in her lap. She removed the rather sexy specs that had been balanced on the end of her nose.

'Sorry!' she said as she stood, clutching the heavy book to her chest. 'We weren't expecting you until later.'

'Is that a royal we?'

She tried to slide her foot back into a sandal. 'Hard to be royal when you're barefoot.' Hard to sound as if you had more than one brain cell when this man was standing so close. 'How did it go?'

Well done, Brina, you sounded almost sane and not sadly deluded and desperately in love.

He dragged a hand through his hair 'I have some sympathy with the idea of being a despot...'

'That's because you are incredibly impatient.' Gifted with a quick mind and an exceptional intellect, Sebastian struggled, she suspected, with the intellectual pace of a normal human being.

'So what are you reading?'

Heart beating fast, she hugged the book closer to her chest, knowing she looked guilty as she shrugged and took a step back. 'Just a thing...nothing really.'

He bent down to her level and read the spine, running a finger along it as he read out the title. '"*Dementia and the Socio-Economic Impact on Developing Nations...*" Wow, racy stuff! Don't look so worried—it can be our guilty secret.'

'Someone I know wrote it. They asked me for a review.'

'So they are getting paid to read it?'

She frowned, wondering if that was against the rules. 'Not exactly. I keep the book.'

His teasing smile faded as the full impact of what she had left behind, the expertise that she was never likely to use, hit home. In contrast to the knot of anger in his belly, his voice was gentle. 'This really is not your world, is it?'

'It is now.' She lifted her chin and along with it any wimpish impulses to throw herself at him and confess it had been awful: the arrival, tea with the Queen and being introduced to the women who she was expected to be friends with, *suitable* women.

She could deal with that, but she would be the wife he needed even if he didn't know he needed her yet... *Would he ever?* 'You never said—beyond discovering buried despotic tendencies you discovered, how was your day?'

Better since I saw you.

And the shocks just kept coming, he thought, pressing a hand to the region of his chest where the pleasurable warmth had ignited when he'd seen her sitting with her bare feet dangling in the historic fountain. He lowered his hand and focused instead on the lust that had come with it. There was something delightfully uncomplicated about lust. It was one of the basic needs in life, like hunger and sleep, and he was tired. It was a known fact that exhaustion could do weird things to a man's brain.

His glance slid to the inches of smooth calf revealed as she lifted her skirt to grimace at the inches of damp silk that clung to those smooth calves. As it lifted he saw there was still a question in her eyes.

'Long.' And so were her legs.

The signs of tiredness in his face intensified the ache inside her.

'And you?'

'I had tea with your…the Queen.'

'And you're not lying down in a darkened room? I'm impressed.'

'She was trying to be helpful.'

One dark brow elevated. 'That bad.'

'Apparently I am meeting a stylist tomorrow.'

'No!'

Her eyes flew up to his face. 'No what?'

'Just no, you do not need a *stylist*, and the last thing you need is to be turned into some sort of "ladies who lunch" clone, and the idea that you need a makeover is an insult.'

His indignation on her behalf made her lips twitch but also filled her with a deep sense of relief. She didn't want to emulate the women she had met today. 'Is that an executive decision?'

He arched a haughty brow. 'You have a problem with that?'

She gave a tiny smile. 'I'll let you know when I have a problem.' She responded to the touch of his hand on her elbow, skipping a little to keep up with his long-legged pace. 'Obviously I can't offend the Queen.'

He gave a laugh. 'She has the hide of a rhino.'

'I will see the stylist.'

He stopped and swung her around to face him.

'I'll just ignore what he says.'

The annoyance slowly faded from his face and he laughed.

'It's called diplomacy, Seb. You should try it.'

He placed his hands on her shoulders and leaned in closer, his breath warm on the cool skin of her face. 'You offering to give me lessons, *cara*?'

She shivered and raised herself onto her toes and his mouth brushed across her wavering lips. 'Sometimes,' she whispered, 'the direct approach is better.'

She went limp as the hunger in his kiss drove the breath from her body.

He stroked her face and felt the tensions of the day slip away. 'You really are a very beautiful woman, Sabrina.' She sighed and turned her face into his hand. 'I've never believed that it is possible to maintain any sort of friendship with a woman after an affair is over, but we just might.'

Her half-closed eyes snapped open and she stepped back abruptly, leaving him holding empty air. What the hell had just happened?

'What's wrong?'

She gave an inarticulate little growl of fury and stuck out her chin, glaring at him, dark eyes glowing with angry contempt as the words fell from her lips in an angry rush. His comment had pierced the protective shell of a core of pain she hadn't known was there until now.

'That you have to ask that says it all! I'm not a woman you're having an affair with. I'm your wife.' In the act of turning her back on him she swung back and shook her head. 'Has it ever occurred to you that you were never friends with those women afterwards because you were never friends before?'

An expression of seething frustration on his face, he watched her stalk away, her head high, her narrow back eloquently rigid. Any inclination he had to follow her faded when she stopped twenty feet or so away and paused to fling over her shoulder, 'And, for the record, neither are we!'

CHAPTER ELEVEN

UNREASONABLE DIDN'T EVEN begin to cover her attitude, he decided as he paced up and down his study, pausing only to take a mouthful of the brandy that he held.

He had held out hope for the future and she had thrown it back in his face; she had acted as though he had insulted her!

And hadn't he?

Pushing away the suggestion, he nursed his sense of injustice along with the brandy as the level of one rose higher, the other sank lower, until the glass was empty.

He stopped pacing and sat staring morosely at the wall; as the minutes ticked away his anger slipped away. When there was a knock on the door, it opened before he responded.

Sabrina took a deep breath. It had taken her half an hour to work up the courage to do this. Half an hour after a lot of angry tears to reach the point where she had asked herself *why* she was angry.

She was angry because the future he saw, even the best-scenario future, was not the one she dreamed of. She couldn't force him to love her and she couldn't punch him for not loving her.

Rather than be angry and bitter about what she

couldn't have, she should do what he had said and enjoy what they did have while it lasted.

'I overreacted. Sebastian, I don't want to sleep alone.'

She held her breath as he got to his feet. It seemed to take a long time and even longer for him to cross the room to her.

'Neither do I.' With a groan he dragged her to him, kissing her with a rough, hungry intensity that drove the breath from her lungs and the strength from her legs. As her knees sagged he picked her up and carried her over to the sofa.

She knew it was only sex he was giving her but when she closed her eyes his tender response felt like love. When he moved inside her it felt as though they were truly one, not just physically, but in every way.

He took her to a place within herself that she hadn't known existed; she lost a sense of where she began and he ended. The sadness, deep and profound, came afterwards, when he held her tenderly, because she knew that Sebastian was not feeling what she did. He gave her his body but she would never touch his soul.

'The ladies are in the Small Salon.'

Sabrina smiled in response to the gentle reminder from her assistant and thought, *I can't wait,* but carried on moving papers around her desk.

She stopped and asked herself for the first time that day—*what am I doing?*

Beyond the obvious, which was waiting for Sebastian to return. They had spent an entire week together before he had left for a week.

She had tried to fill the hours, telling herself that she had to build a life that didn't revolve around a husband who most likely forgot she existed the moment he walked out of the room, and one day in the future when she was in the room.

Live in the moment, Brina!

Great advice, but really tough to follow through with.

Work of a sort had saved her: the timing of the approach from the university hospital, asking her to help to fill the vacancy for a head of the new Alzheimer's research unit they were keen to establish, had been perfect.

As well as using her contacts in London to line up someone for the post, Sabrina had surreptitiously channelled some funding their way too and acted suitably surprised when the dean of the faculty had remarked on their good fortune.

'The ladies?'

Sabrina, who realised she had been sitting there with her eyes closed, opened them and looked from the pencil she had just snapped in half to her assistant. She painted on a smile.

'Oh, yes, the *ladies*. And I use the term loosely.'

Rachel struggled to hide her smile.

Sabrina paused outside the open door of the room where her new *friends* were gathered and glanced in the mirror, smoothing down her already smooth hair.

The half a dozen women inside apparently represented the cream of society. One lunch had conformed her suspicions that she had nothing whatever in common with them and she despised them almost as much as she knew they despised her.

'I heard that he was seen going into her hotel suite at one in the morning.'

The low murmur of laughter made Sabrina pause in the act of entering the salon.

'Do you suppose *she* knows?'

Sabrina pressed a hand to her stomach and told herself to breathe.

'Why would she care?'

She had no problem placing this speaker with a face. Sabrina could imagine the malice and contempt in the pale eyes as the woman gave a dramatic pause before concluding, 'She's got *exactly* what she wanted…a crown.'

A *crown*…the irony drew a tiny grunt of reaction from the listening Sabrina. She smoothed a hand across the fair hair twisted away from her face in a shiny chignon, almost feeling the symbolic weight.

'And I suppose all royals are trained from birth to turn a blind eye.'

'*Royal?* Have you seen where they live? Her mother wore the same outfit to three state events last year and her father sits in the public park playing chess with the…the peasants…'

Sabrina walked quietly into the room; unobserved, she stood in the doorway and made the decision not to waste another moment of her life playing nice with these spiteful women. It came as a relief.

'Well, I feel sorry for her. If my husband cheated on *me*—'

'You don't have a husband, and if you carry on stuffing your face with pastries you won't.'

Sabrina didn't slow or quicken her pace as she walked towards the group of expensively dressed, beautifully made up women sitting around a table set for tea.

They got to their feet almost as one when they saw her.

She ignored their furtive expressions—a couple even

had not lost the ability to blush—and kept her eyes fixed on the one woman who had remained seated.

Brought up in a much more relaxed atmosphere, Sabrina had always viewed the protocol that made everyone scramble to their feet when she walked into a room ludicrous, but on this occasion?

Sabrina's smile was practised and smooth when a few moments later the other woman got to her feet, her pouty mouth twisted into a forced, rigid smile.

Sabrina's eyes moved past her to the other women. 'Please, ladies, as you were. I'm so sorry to keep you waiting but something unexpected has come up, so I'll see you all on Thursday. No, actually, no, I don't think I will. Our little gatherings are cancelled for the foreseeable future.'

She took a step towards the door before pausing and twisting back. 'Actually, we don't have *peasants*. My father was a chess grand master at seventeen, and my mother always taught me to judge the person and not the clothes they wear. Oh, and by the way, the only woman sharing my husband's bed is *me*.'

Without waiting to observe the effect of her words she swept from the room.

Her painted-on smile faded the instant she stepped out of the room. She still felt dizzy with the anger that cooled slightly as she made her way back to her office.

'Rachel, would you cancel all the lunches with the—?' She stopped as she saw the personal items that her assistant was pushing into a large tote bag. 'What are you doing? Have you been crying?' She went over and put her arm around the girl's shoulder. 'What's wrong?'

'I… I'm leaving…'

Sabrina shook her head. 'I don't understand.'

The girl managed a watery smile. 'I have been—'

'Rachel has been reassigned, Highness.'

Sabrina turned and saw a tall woman whose presence she had not been aware of move away from the wall. She arched a brow and kept her arm around Rachel's shoulders. 'And you would be…?'

'I am Regina Cordoba, Highness—your new assistant.'

Sebastian's jaw clenched in frustration as his father's attack dog, Count Hugo, appeared from a doorway just as he was about to enter the private wing of the palace he shared with Sabrina. The man's ingratiating manner irritated him, as did his conspiracy theorist determination to blame everything that was wrong with the country on the republicans he saw lurking in every corner.

'Highness.'

Sebastian tipped his head, a glint of anger in his eyes as he responded smoothly, 'Count, lucky coincidence or—?'

'When he heard you had abandoned the meeting…?'

Sebastian arched a brow and let the silence stretch until the man, finally realising that the Prince was not about to issue an explanation, continued.

'The King hoped that you might be available, unless you are unwell?'

'Unwell?' He shook his head. The man would probably disagree if he told him why he had wound down the meeting. 'No, just…' He shook his head. 'Forget it—where is he?'

His father was in his study sitting behind his big desk that was raised on a dais. The tactic drew a wry smile from Sebastian as he walked past the chair meant for him on the lower level and straight up to the desk, where he remained standing.

'I understand you wanted to chat, Father?'

'*Chat?* I do not want to *chat*. I want an explanation as to why you saw fit to walk out of a meeting wasting the time of the people who had made the journey there.'

'Do you really want to know? Fine, well, apart from the fact that everyone was so busy protecting their own interests that we could have sat there until next week and been no further forward, I made a joke and no one laughed.'

His father stared at him.

'I know it sounds stupid but it was a very good joke and Sabrina would have got it, she would have laughed, so I came home to share it with her.' He did not add that during the absence of laughter he had strongly felt the absence of other things…or another person, and in the process had finally diagnosed the vague symptoms that had been plaguing him recently—*loneliness*… That shock had barely penetrated before he had realised that his exile from the one person who eased that ache was self-imposed.

His father, very red-faced, drew himself up in his seat. 'Well, if you are not going to do me the courtesy of being serious I can see there is no point… However, as you introduced the subject, there is something I must tell you concerning your wife.'

The faint air of humour in Sebastian's manner vanished as he laid his hand flat on the desk and leaned forward, looking at his father through narrowed eyes. 'Really?' he said with deceptive calm.

'I do not blame her—she doesn't know how we do things here—however, it has come to my attention that she has been getting involved with areas of life that are unsuitable. Like, for example, the university.'

'That well-known den of iniquity? What puzzles me is how you come to know what my wife does.'

'There are dangers, a very real threat from malcontents and terrorists. The surveillance is for protection.'

'I can and *will* protect my wife.' A smile curved his lips as he repeated the last two words 'My wife. And you will remove your spies from my meetings.'

The King blinked and looked horrified. 'I need to know—'

'And you will. I will keep you in the loop. That is the way it is and if you don't feel able to agree with my terms—'

'Terms!' The outraged King looked like a man who had just had the rug pulled out from under his feet.

'Crude, but accurate. I will do things my way or not at all and the next time I see that worm Hugo I will kick his bony butt...' His voice lowered another icy note as he straightened to his full imposing height and looked down at his father with icy contempt. 'I will do my duty by you but I will do it my way and with my wife by my side.'

'And if your wife found out about your Paris trip? There was no meeting, was there?'

'Is that a threat? Are you trying to blackmail me?'

The older man lowered his eyes. 'No, of course not, the idea is disgusting. I am your father!'

'Be careful, Father, the "how dare you?" attitude looks remarkably like guilt.'

'Me, guilty? I'm not the one spending time with—'

'My brother,' Sebastian cut in softly.

The words stopped the King dead.

Sebastian closed his eyes and cursed softly. 'I didn't mean to tell you like that. Are you all right?'

'You saw your brother?'

Sebastian nodded, feeling a spasm of pity for the old man.

'Yes, I have been in contact with Luis. We did meet up in Paris last weekend, where I met his wife, who is actually rather charming.'

'I told you I do not want that name mentioned!' the older man thundered.

'It's kind of hard to discuss the elephant in the room without saying the word elephant,' Sebastian observed. 'If you want to blank your son that is, of course, your choice—but Luis is my brother and I intend to carry on seeing him. I would like to invite him to the official reunification ceremony next year. I think he'd like to come but he has made it clear that it will only happen if the invitation comes with your blessing.'

'Never!'

Sympathy flickered into Sebastian's eyes as he got up and walked across to his father. 'You are the one who taught me the value of family.'

'He was the one who walked away. He betrayed us.'

'He fell in love.'

'Love!' his father pronounced with scorn.

'Yes, the thing that makes the world go around,' he said, picturing a pair of beautiful brown eyes. 'Luis is family, his wife is family—their child will be family.'

His father paled. 'She is pregnant?'

'It's a boy, apparently.'

He saw his father fight off a smile. 'A boy? I was beginning to think I'd never have a grandchild.'

'I am doing my best, Father.' The image of Sabrina with a child at her breast came into his head. Fatherhood was not something he had ever thought about before, except in the abstract. He was shocked by the wave of emotion that came with the image in his head.

The King cleared his throat. 'So when is this baby due?'

With a sigh Sebastian took a seat. He took a photo from his wallet and put it on the desk in front of his father. After a moment the older man took it, and when he eventually glanced down at it he stared, his eyes filling with tears.

'By the way, did I mention that the university have shown an interest in recruiting Sabrina?'

The monarch's eyes lifted. 'Just thought you'd slip that one in, did you? Raising money or even a place on the board is one thing, but your wife cannot work. That is preposterous.'

'What would be preposterous, Father, would be for a woman with Sabrina's qualifications to waste them—for her not to be an example to the young women of Vela and her own daughters.'

The old man shook his head. 'Never while I draw breath.'

The office was the second place Sebastian looked for her, and the sound of voices through the half-open door, or one voice in particular, told him he was in the right place.

He pushed open the door and was stopped in his tracks. On one side of the room his wife's PA stood weeping while Sabrina, her chin up, her eyes blazing, was facing a third woman he vaguely recognised—then he placed her. The tall brunette was Count Hugo's niece.

'What is happening?'

'Sebastian! This woman...' Teeth clenched, Sabrina looked at the tall brunette and took a deep breath. '*This* woman says she is my new assistant and I was telling her that I already have an assistant.'

'Highness, the workload has become too much for

Rachel, who is being reassigned to a less stressful position.' She held out a file she was holding and a memory stick. 'I have already made a start on the speech Her Highness is giving to the friends of the hospital. I have redrafted it into a more...acceptable form.'

Sabrina put her hands on her hips. 'What was wrong with it as it was?' she asked in a dangerous voice.

'It is a professional occasion. Certain things can be misinterpreted when taken out of context.'

While the other two women faced off, Sebastian went over to where the weeping girl stood and put his hand on her hunched, shaking shoulder. 'Do you find working for my wife stressful? You can be honest.' He exchanged a look with Sabrina. 'She can be difficult.'

The girl dashed a hand across her damp face and shook her head. 'No, I love working for the Princess. She is so kind and...' Her lips began to quiver again as she wailed, 'She's lovely.'

Sebastian nodded and turned back to Hugo's niece, who was regarding the weeping younger girl with distaste. 'It looks like there has been a mistake. As you see, my wife already has an assistant.'

'With the greatest of respect, Highness, the King himself has asked me to step in and, though I do not like to say it—'

'But you say it anyway—admirable. And I see a family trait.'

'Certain aspects of Rachel's work have been found unsatisfactory.'

'Not by me, they haven't!' Sabrina retorted.

'No, *cara*, what she means is that Rachel has not been passing on the information about you when requested.' He glanced towards Rachel, who sniffed and nodded. 'So,' he added, 'they decided to insert a more qualified spy.'

'I must protest…!'

Sebastian whipped around and fixed the woman with a stare of arctic contempt. 'Then do so out of my sight.'

Sabrina, whose inarticulate rage had been replaced by shock, watched, her mouth slightly open, as the woman, red-faced, walked from the room. 'What just happened?' she said faintly when the door closed.

Sebastian smiled at her and moved to where Rachel was drying her eyes.

'Does that mean I'm still working for Sa… the Princess?'

'It does.'

'But the King—'

'You work for Princess Sabrina, you answer to Princess Sabrina, and she is the *only* person who can dismiss you.'

Sabrina went across to where the girl stood. 'And I don't,' she said, giving the girl a hug.

'Now, Rachel, I will obviously defer to the boss here—' he glanced at Sabrina '—but I think you deserve the rest of the day off. Have a tissue, a box,' he added generously, handing the girl the box on the desk.

Rachel, receiving it, looked at Sabrina, who nodded. 'Yes, that will be fine, Rachel, thanks, and sorry.'

She waited until the door closed before turning to Sebastian.

'Thank you for that, but I could have handled it,' she added, just in case he thought she was pathetic.

'I never doubted it, but you shouldn't have needed to. I should have laid some ground rules with my father before I left…but I've done that now and I don't think there will be any more incidents like that.'

'You've spoken to him already…before…?' She stopped, lowering her eyes and thinking, *Of course he went to see his father first, Brina. You are not his first priority.*

'How was your trip?'He dragged a hand through his hair. 'It was pretty much like every other meeting I have attended—long…lots of time with nothing to do but think. I've been a fool.'

He took her face between his hands and paused, his eyes closing as he relived that moment of mind-numbing shock that had come after a week of denial and misery. A week spent wondering what she was doing, if she was all right, missing her voice, the smell of her skin, missing her! Fighting the knowledge that at some point Sabrina had crept into his heart, into his soul. Fighting because he was a coward, fighting what he ought to have been rejoicing, pushing her away when he ought to have been pulling her to him.

Sabrina saw the pain in his face and ached for him. It must have been a pretty catastrophic meeting to make him look like that. 'I'm sure you weren't.'

His soul-piercing blue eyes opened. 'I was… I am… I feel as though the earth has shifted beneath my feet. Nothing is… I used to be so *sure*…' Sure that love was a fool's game, sure that it was not for him and enjoying the smug sense of superiority and the false sense of security his tunnel vision had given him.

The fact that this mind-set might actually shut him off from one of life's greatest joys was not something he had ever considered.

'You remember something I said once? That it wouldn't happen to me…that I was not expecting to—?'

His words were like a blow she hadn't seen coming. They drained her face of colour, and she spoke quickly because she didn't want to hear him say it. 'You've met someone,' she said in a dead little voice.

It seemed ironic now that when she had overheard those gossiping bitches it had not even crossed her mind that they were telling the truth.

'I appreciate your honesty,' she lied, 'but I would prefer not to know her name.'

'What are you talking about?'

'You've fallen in love.' It was not a question; it explained the difference she sensed in him.

'Yes.'

She tried to pull away but the hands on her shoulders tightened. 'Look at me, Sabrina.'

'I can't. I hate you.'

'Has anyone ever told you you have the most incredible mouth?'

Her head slowly lifted; she looked up at him, tears trembling on her lashes. 'Why are you saying that?'

He stood there looking down at her feeling that he was standing on the brink of a precipice about to step out into the black unknown. It didn't make him the least bit fearful.

'And why are you looking at me like that?' She gasped, feeling her insides melt.

'Because you're incredible. Your skin is like cream.' He reached out, an expression of fascination stamped on his lean face as he let strands of caramel-streaked honey slip through his fingers. 'Have you any idea of how much of a turn-on it is to know that I can make you shake without even touching you?'

'But you are touching me.' Sabrina, her head spinning, let out a faint whimper as his hand moved to cup the soft curve of her cheek in his hand before rubbing his thumb across the plump lower lip of her Cupid's bow mouth. 'You love someone else.'

He shook his head. 'How could I when I can only see you? Your eyes are extraordinary.' He stood staring deep into the dark liquid depths framed by long curling lashes, waiting for them to darken with passion before he kissed her.

The kiss seemed to go on for ever, and when he lifted his head she felt as though she were floating.

'You are my life. I love you.'

'I love you, Sebastian…' Her whispered echo was barely audible above the clamouring beat of her heart.

CHAPTER TWELVE

THE KISS WAS deep and so tender that there were tears in her eyes when he finally lifted his head.

'The first thing I remember is your mouth and kissing you in the car.'

'You were cruel,' she remembered. 'And drunk.'

'Not really, but I do remember that you looked at me like I was the devil so I played it up a bit.' His eyes darkened as he curled his fingers round her chin and turned her face up to him. 'But all the time I was thinking about your mouth.'

She swallowed, feeling dizzy, happiness bubbling up inside her. Could this really be happening? 'Thinking what?'

'That it was a total miracle and many...so many things I wanted to do to and with it, and I thought of my brother having that mouth and I wanted to—' His hand fell away and he inhaled. 'I felt like hell.' He gave a twisted smile. 'Because as you probably realised the honourable stuff is not a natural fit for me. Every time I looked at you I wanted to taste you and every time I tasted you I wanted to do it again, but you belonged to Luis.

'When he dumped you at the altar I was furious with him—for about ten seconds. Then I was glad, because there was nothing stopping me from having you.'

She lifted a hand to his cheek. He turned his face into it and kissed her palm as she stood there, tears streaming down her face as the words poured out of him.

His blue eyes blazed fiercely, bathing her in the love that shone in them as he took both her hands in his and, bending forward, kissed her again. This time the tenderness tipped over into hunger that made her knees give way.

Sebastian reacted by picking her up and carrying her over to the sofa in the corner of the room, and after pulling her across his knees he carried on kissing her.

Then minutes later, breathing hard, several items of clothing on the floor, she pressed her hand on his chest and shook her head.

'Why...why now? I've been crazy about you for weeks and weeks and you...couldn't you see that I loved you?'

The breath caught in her throat at the look in his eyes. 'Say that again!' he demanded fiercely.

'I love you, Sebastian.'

He smiled, the fierce tenderness in his face making her head spin as he curved a hand around one side of her face, taking his time to taste every inch of her face before pausing, his nose pressed to the side of hers, their warm breath mingling.

'You were with me out of duty, not choice. I never forgot that, and I have gone through life telling myself that love was a mugs' game, I didn't believe in it, but the truth is,' he admitted heavily, clenching his teeth as the full level of his stupidity was laid bare for her, 'I was scared of feeling anything that much. I watched the person I cared for most in the world destroyed by love...'

'Your mother...' she breathed, her voice soft with sympathy.

He nodded. 'I judged her and I was helpless to help her. I never wanted to love anyone again and let them down.' He gave a hard laugh. 'I *really* thought that there was choice involved and then *you* happened. I have learnt so much being with you and I swear that I'll always be there—'

She pressed a finger to his lips. 'Don't swear—kiss.'

With a growl he responded to the imperious little command and, tipping her under him, he gathered her to him and proceeded to kiss her senseless in the process, losing his own sense also.

As she moved in his arms and almost fell off the narrow couch her eyes caught sight of the clock on the wall. 'Oh, my God, look at the time!' she exclaimed. 'There's no need to look so smug.'

'I feel smug.' He felt…*complete.*

'We've been here all afternoon, Seb. We need to get dressed for dinner.'

She was about to draw her legs up to her chin when his hand went to the smooth naked curve of her bottom. 'You look like a little cat when you stretch.'

'Seb!' she pleaded, struggling to inject some reproach and not only throaty appeal into her voice. 'Dinner…' She felt a little slug of disappointment when he reacted to the reminder and sat upright.

Sabrina followed suit, mentally calculating how quickly they could make themselves presentable for the formal dinner awaiting them and get back to their suite without anyone noticing how dishevelled they both looked.

'Should I ring down and tell them we'll be late dining?'

'Don't bother. I've already dealt with that.' He stretched

to ease the kinks out of his spine, drawing her eyes to the perfect muscular development of his lean torso. Everything about his body delighted her.

'You're totally...' Their eyes connected; emotion rose in her chest, consolidating into a knot of sheer longing. She had never in her life imagined that loving someone could feel like this, that it could be so all-consuming and the physical aspect so incredible.

And he loved her back...it still felt as though she were living a dream.

'Looking for these?' He picked a pair of lacy pants from the table on her side of the sofa and tossed them to her, feeling his libido kick in hard as she straightened and raised a hand, causing her firm breasts to jiggle and sway as she caught them.

'How organised—and when?'

'While you were snoring.'

'I do not snore!'

'I shall invest in a set of earplugs.' His eyes were warm as he levered himself lazily from the tumbled bed, reaching for his boxers.

Sabrina watched the play of muscle gliding and bunching under the golden skin of his back as he stood with his back to her pulling his jeans on over his narrow hips.

God, but he was beautiful!

Hand in hand, they walked up the rear staircase that led to their bedroom suite; the sitting-room door was not closed. Inside two maids bobbed curtsies as they entered before one pushed a trolley with a cloth thrown over up to one of the sofas in the room and the other plugged in the large flatscreen TV that rested on the second trolley.

'We'll serve ourselves, thank you.'

The maids nodded and vanished.

Sabrina watched as Sebastian lifted the cloth with a flourish to reveal silver domes, which he lifted to inspect the food underneath, filling the room with smells that made her realise how hungry she was.

'We are going to eat on trays and watch *television*?' she said, thinking, *How crazy is this?* She was feeling the sort of excited incredulity that most women would if their husband said that he'd arranged for them to eat food created by a Michelin-starred chef served on antique china sitting at a table loaded with silver and crystal.

But in her world this was a treat.

'Isn't it what people do?'

She nodded, thinking that Sebastian was a billion miles from other people; he was extraordinary!

'I thought you might like a night off.'

She nodded vigorously.

'Movie's your choice, so kick off your shoes—'

She looked down, a smile tugging at her lips as she realised she had walked barefoot down the corridor. 'I'm not wearing any.'

They had just sat down when the door opened; without warning a figure scanned the room before the King walked in.

When he saw the TV and the trays he could not have looked more shocked had he walked in and found them rolling around on the floor naked. Half an hour earlier and he might have, she thought, hiding a grin.

'Father.' Sebastian got to his feet slowly, his casual attitude thinly masking his anger. Seeing it there just below the surface, Sabrina felt her heart sink like a stone. 'Sorry, if we'd known you were coming we'd have saved you some.'

'You would possibly have dressed for dinner too?' The King took a deep breath and shook his head. 'No, it is none of my business. I accept that things change. I have come to apologise,' he said stiffly. 'Some...most of the things you said were right. You are doing a good job. I should have said it before but I... It is hard not to feel needed.

'Your brother—if he and his family wish to come to the reunification ceremony then I will be glad to see them as my guests. And, Sabrina, I have no objection to you working, and, yes, I agree it will be a good example to set to your daughters and the young women of our country.' He inclined his head. 'So I will say goodnight.'

'What,' Sabrina gasped as the door closed, 'was that?'

'That, my dearest darling, was hell freezing over—with style, to give the devil his due,' he added wryly. 'Now, where were we?'

Sabrina shook her head and pushed him away as he leaned in to kiss her. 'Luis? Me working? What was all that about?'

'When I went to Paris it wasn't for a meeting—I was seeing Luis.'

She drew back, startled. 'Luis?'

'Do you mind?'

'Why would I mind? I would actually love to thank him for dumping me at the altar considering how things have worked out.'

Sebastian grinned. 'So you'd have no problem with him coming to the reunification ceremony next year?'

'And your father agreed?'

'That was quite a climb-down. And quick,' he admitted. 'But I think it is the idea of a baby—'

'Luis is having a baby?' she exclaimed.

'Well, not Luis—but, yes, and I think that might be the swing vote. I'm starting to think that Father is getting a little soft in his old age.'

Sabrina gave a sceptical grunt. 'That is only one part of the mystery. What about me working?'

'I think he has decided that to have talent in the family firm and not utilise it is a waste—especially when the research is so important.'

'He has decided?' She shook her head. 'What have you been up to, Seb?'

'Me?' he said, looking innocent. 'I had nothing to do with it except to mention the need for further research into dementia and expertise right here.'

'Oh, my God—truly? Me, work?' She began to bounce excitedly.

'I expect you'll be running the university in a few years.'

'If having those daughters he was talking about doesn't get in the way.'

'What can I say? He's keen on grandchildren.'

She smiled and looked at him, eyes gleaming through her lashes as she straddled him.

'And how do you feel about children?'

'Pretty damn good so long as you're the mother.' He let out a low growl and tugged her down onto him. 'How do you feel about starting now? I've heard it can take a while.'

'In that case, less talk more action, hmm?'

'Shut up, woman, can't you see I'm dynasty-building?'

There was very little talking for some time, but a *lot* of communicating.

EPILOGUE

SEBASTIAN WAS THE last to speak. He kept it short.

'I feel that the people here today to celebrate the day our country becomes one have already said it.'

He gestured with a flourish towards his father and the Duke, who were seated on the stage, and there was a cheer from the crowds that filled the palace parkland as far as the eye could see.

'I have only one thing to add. A wise man once said...' he smiled at his father '...that it is all about family.' He moved to the edge of the stage and held out a hand to his brother, who sat with his wife and baby in the front row.

Luis jumped up on the stage to a loud cheer.

Sebastian put his arm around his brother.

'And today our family, our country, has expanded in a beautiful way, a little like my lovely wife.'

It was Luis, along with Chloe, who pulled Sabrina, heavily pregnant, to her feet and escorted her over to Sebastian before clapping his hands and backing away to leave them centre stage.

The applause was thunderous as Sebastian kissed his wife on the lips, his grin flashing.

'You promised you wouldn't do this.'

He shrugged. 'My memory, darling, it is not what it once was.'

She dabbed the emotional tears running down her cheeks and began to laugh while the crowds cheered on, but she had the last laugh.

'If my waters break right here and now it won't be pretty.'

He leaned in close and whispered, 'Everything you do, my love, is *beautiful*!'

The reunification of Vela was also the birthday of the future King—the people said it was a very good omen…

* * * * *

CROWNED FOR MY ROYAL BABY

MAISEY YATES

To the librarians.

And mine especially.

At school and at the public library.

You made sure I had books. Lots of books.
All the books.

If not for my love of reading, I'm sure I wouldn't
be writing.

Thank you.

CHAPTER ONE

Marissa

I'LL NEVER FORGET the first time I saw Prince Hercules. A ridiculous name, and one more suited to a bronzed god than a man. The kind of god my father would have called a false one and told me to steer clear of.

If he could only have known. He would have locked me in my room for the foreseeable future if he'd had any real idea of how fallible I was.

Something in me must have known.

Because Hercules immediately became a secret. Even when I watched him from a distance.

Secrets were not allowed in my family because a secret meant that someone was concealing a truth. And if you were concealing a truth, it had to be because it was a sin.

Hercules became sin for me very, very quickly.

It was after church that first time. I had gone down to the water, as I often did on the small island of Medland, Massachusetts.

It was summer, and the elite had already descended on the tiny town as they did every year. The influx of seasonal residents as welcome as they were over-whelming.

The island ran on summer business, the money made during those months often necessarily hoarded through the rest of the year.

The collection plates at my father's church were certainly fuller during those weeks.

And while I knew, even at sixteen, that the rush of people was necessary for the economy, I still found it overwhelming.

And so I retreated, not to the most heaving parts of the beaches, but to private paths that beat through tall seagrass and down to rocky but tranquil shores that were far too rustic to attract the volume of visitors the vast stretches of sand did.

On a Saturday it was difficult to find spaces that weren't overrun, but I'd lived there all my life and barely knew anywhere else. I knew where I could find solitude if I wanted it.

And that was where I first spotted him.

He was standing in the waves, the water lapping at his knees, his pants rolled up, his shirt off.

He was surrounded by people—women specifically—laughing and chatting, splashing each other. But he stood out, his face looking like it was carved from granite.

His eyes reminded me of obsidian. The black glossy rock that both gave off light and consumed it all at once. I thought I could get lost in those eyes.

In that darkness.

I'd been taught to run from darkness, but there was a

glow in his I couldn't turn away from. I felt like I'd just discovered a creature I wasn't allowed to know existed.

He seemed lost in whatever his darkness was.

Until one of the women touched his arm, and those features shifted into a smile that seemed to eclipse the sun. And I was suddenly overcome by a strange, bitter taste in my mouth that I'd never experienced before. It made my whole body feel tight and strange.

I ran away.

But the next day, I went back after church, and he was there. This time, not out in the water, but standing on the shore.

And he saw me.

"Are you going to stare all day?" he asked.

"I wasn't staring at you," I replied. "I was simply taking in the view behind you."

"I saw you yesterday," he said. "On the shore." The way he said it made it clear he didn't believe I was looking at anything but him. "You ran away."

"I knew my father would wonder where I was. You weren't in church today?" I asked him. An inane question. I knew he wasn't there. I would have noticed. Everyone would have.

"No," he said with a laugh. "I find my worship, such as it might be, is best conducted outside four walls. And you?"

"My father is the pastor. I'll get in trouble if I don't go."

"And would you get in trouble if he found out you were here?"

He was even more beautiful up close. His chest was covered then, thank God, or I probably would have expired on the spot. It was a weakness, I knew, the way that I looked at him. The way that I hungrily took in every inch of bronze skin that was on display. Just a wedge, where the fabric of his white shirt was separated.

I knew that I was wicked.

Like a sudden answer to my restlessness had locked into place and printed the definition in my brain.

Wicked.

It was evidenced in the way I feasted on every detail of his handsome, sculpted face. But I couldn't help it, and for the first time, I didn't want to.

He looked familiar, but I couldn't place him. That square, sharp jaw and compelling mouth, those dark, intense eyes.

"Possibly," I said. "I'm supposed to be careful about talking to… Well, most people who come here during the summer are very important. And also…of a certain sort of character."

"Whoremongers and the like?" he asked, a glint of humor in his eyes.

I felt my cheeks heat. "I suppose so."

"Sadly, I'm both," he said. "You should probably run away."

"Okay," I said and instantly turned to flee, doing exactly as I was told, because I didn't know another way to be.

"Do you always do what people tell you to?" he asked me, stopping me in my tracks.

"I… Yes."

"You should stop that. Figure out what you want."

"I'll probably just get a job here. Get married." Just

mentioning that word in front of him made my insides feel jittery.

He arched a brow. "But is it what you want?"

He was looking at me so intently, and I couldn't for the life of me figure out why a man such as him would look at a girl like me the way that he was.

Of course, I didn't exactly know what the look was. I had never spoken to a man I didn't know from church. Not outside of exchanged pleasantries on a street. We didn't even know each other.

I didn't know his name, and he didn't know mine.

He was an admitted whoremonger, and someone very important. And there I was, talking to him anyway. Feeling pinned to the spot by all that intensity.

"I've never thought about it," I finally admitted.

"Do," he said. "And get back to me."

I didn't see him for the next few days, but I was consumed by schoolwork anyway. It was summer, but as I was homeschooled, my parents didn't much acknowledge breaks. It was fine, because I was on the verge of graduating at sixteen, though to what end, I didn't know. I had considered going away for a while on a mission, which was something that my parents heartily approved of.

I went back to check on Saturday again to see if I could find the mystery man.

I didn't.

But I did again, that next Sunday.

"Have you thought about what you want?" he asked.

I just stared at him blankly, because no, I hadn't. I had thought about him. And that was it.

That began a strange sort of friendship. We would

talk by the seashore when he was alone. About everything and nothing. Not about ourselves, but the world.

He'd been everywhere, and I'd been nowhere. We
both found that fascinating.

We didn't exchange names. He gave me a seashell,
and he told me that the way it swirled at the center reminded him of the way my hair curled. I put it in a box
and hid it under my bed.

When the summer ended, I couldn't breathe.

He was gone and the world was gray. It was silly to
grieve over a man who was alive, but not with me. A
man whose name I didn't know.

But I grieved all the same.

Sometime in the middle of winter a photograph on
the front page of a tabloid in the grocery store caught
my eye—it was him. It was him with a beautiful woman
on his arm and his name plastered right there on the
newsprint, and I had to ask myself how I could be so
stupid.

I wasn't one to pay attention to popular culture—in
fact, my father expressly forbade it—and often I averted
my eyes even when waiting in the checkout line, so
there was a certain sort of sense in the fact that I hadn't
realized immediately who my seaside friend was.

Not just someone important.

A *prince*.

Prince Hercules Xenakis of Pelion, one of the most
renowned playboys in the entire world.

That night I took the box out from under my bed
and stared at the seashell, and I told myself I should
get rid of it.

He wouldn't be coming back to the island—I was certain of it.

I would never see him again. Our meeting—our friendship—had been a fluke, and what was more, I was sure that I meant nothing to him. I was a schoolgirl, a common one at that, and he was one of the most wealthy, desirable men on the planet.

I couldn't bring myself to throw it away.

Summer rolled around, marking my birthday and marking the return of the seasonal residents.

And there he was.

Sunday afternoon.

I told myself not to smile like a giddy fool when I saw him, but I did. And he smiled at me.

"You're still here," he said, shoving his hands in his pockets.

"I live here. So it's not truly that surprising. You came back," I said. I looked away from him. "You're a prince."

"Ah," he said. "So you've discovered my secret." He sounded regretful.

I peered at him while still trying to keep my head tilted down. "I'm not sure how it can be a secret, given you are frequently on the cover of newspapers."

He touched me then. His fingertips brushed my chin, and I lifted my head, my eyes meeting his. The impact left me breathless. "Does that change things?"

I was stunned. "Doesn't it have to?"

"I don't think so," he said. "I knew I was a prince this whole time. And anyway, that you didn't is part of why I liked spending time with you."

I held that close for the rest of the week.

He liked me. He liked me because I didn't know he was a prince, and he didn't think I was a fool.

That next week I told him my name. "Marissa," I said. "Since I know yours."

"Yes, it's quite a difficult name to use in conversation, don't you think?"

"I assume that's helped by the fact that most people probably call you by an honorific."

"Indeed. But I would rather you did not."

"Hercules?" His name tasted strange on my lips, and not just because it was foreign.

"Yes," he said, smiling at me.

"Then I will."

I knew he was older than me, richer than me, more experienced than me, impossible in every way. But in that moment, as his smile lit his face, I fell in love with him.

He gave me another seashell, and I thought maybe he might feel something for me.

When he went away that summer, I couldn't help but follow the headlines about him. I made myself sick with them.

Because there he was, with beautiful women on his arm, and if he felt for me even a fraction of what I did for him, there was no way that he would be with them. I bought an entertainment magazine with his picture on it, and I knew that if my father found it, I would be in trouble. I put it in the box with the seashells. I felt guilty, because now I had secrets.

Now I didn't do what I was told.

I seemed to do things because of Hercules instead, and that was something entirely different.

I finished school, but I didn't want to go away on a mission trip, because he would be coming back. So I made an excuse about wanting a job, got one at a local coffeehouse called the Snowy Owl.

And mostly, I lived for Sundays.

Of course, nobody scheduled me to work on a Sunday, because my father would forbid that I do anything on the Sabbath.

I didn't care about that. I cared about him.

"You're back," I said to him. First thing, just as I had done the year before.

I was eighteen, and I burned with a strange kind of conviction in my chest, because I didn't feel quite so helpless. Quite like there was such a barrier between us.

Oh sure, there was the Prince thing. The fact that he spent the year dating supermodels and traveling around on private jets. But I was a woman now. And I felt like that had to mean something.

"Of course."

"I'm glad," I said.

"So am I."

Then he reached out his hand and took hold of mine. "Shall we go for a walk?"

"Yes," I said.

And for the first time, I held a man's hand. His fingers were so warm, and it made my stomach turn over, made my heart feel like it was going to race right out of my chest. I looked at him, and he looked completely unaffected, but he still held on to me, and so I held on to that.

He kissed me on one of those Sunday afternoons.

My whole body felt like it would burst into flame.

His lips were firm and sure on mine, and he was so impossibly beautiful.

Every feeling he called up in me I had been taught to identify as a sin, but it was so beautiful, and part of him, and I couldn't bring myself to turn away from it.

So instead, I wrapped my arms around him and kissed him back. Parted my lips for him and allowed him to brush his tongue against mine.

I allowed all kinds of things on those Sunday afternoons. For his touch to become more familiar. For the feeling of his body against mine to become the dearest and most precious thing in the world. All that hard, powerful muscle, gentled as he held me.

I wanted to tell him he didn't have to leash that strength. But I didn't have the words for it. I didn't have the vocabulary for what I wanted at all.

"Can you meet me tonight?"

It was near the end of summer when he asked me that, and I wanted to. Desperately. But I knew that I would get in so much trouble if I were caught.

Do you always do what you're told?

That earlier question came back to haunt me. And no, I didn't do what I was told. Not anymore. Not now.

I lived for Hercules.

It wasn't about whether I might marry him and become a princess. I never thought about the future. I only thought about us, as we were, there on the beach. His life outside of that didn't matter, and neither did mine.

And so I made the decision to expand it. To push outside those isolated Sunday afternoons and see something more.

"Yes."

I climbed out my window that night and met him there at our spot, in the darkness. He had a blanket and a bottle of wine, and I had never tried alcohol before. I declined the wine, but I got drunk on his mouth, on his touch. And before I knew it, things had gone much further than I had intended.

It went on like that over the weeks, until I didn't care anymore what was supposed to be right. The only thing that felt right was being in his arms. And when I gave him my virginity, I gave it easily, joyously. And he showed me what pleasure meant, and why people jumped into ruin with careless abandon and joy in their hearts.

It was the night he left that it happened.

He had to go. He couldn't stay away from home any longer.

He didn't ask me to go with him.

I told myself he couldn't.

He and I forgot everything. We made love on a blanket in the sand until neither of us could breathe, and it wasn't until later that I realized he'd forgotten protection of any kind.

He was gone the next day.

And three weeks later I knew my life had changed forever.

I had no idea how to begin contacting the palace.

But that wasn't even what worried me, not right at first. It was telling my parents. But I knew that I had to call Hercules first.

I knew you couldn't just call up a palace. Still, I had to try.

I called the palace directory. I left a message. I heard nothing.

I called again. Again and again.

Finally, in my desperation I told the person on the other end of the line that I had to get in touch with Prince Hercules, since I was having his baby.

The next day, men in suits came to the coffeehouse.

They whisked me into the manager's office, and they told me that I was never to reach out to Hercules again. And that if I agreed to sign stacks of thick legal documents and never reveal the paternity of my child, I would be given enough money to live more than comfortably forever.

My heart shattered into pieces. Desperate, enraged, I threw the papers and ran. I ran all the way back home.

My secret burst out of me. Flowing like the tears that were pouring down my face. I admitted to my parents that I was pregnant.

My father's face turned to stone. He asked if I intended to marry the father of my child, and quickly. I told him I could not, because he had abandoned me.

He didn't have to say anything. His face said it all. He had warned me. He had told me. And I had failed. I was wicked, just like the rest of them. And that was when he told me he would have to wash his hands of me. Because there was no way that he could have his daughter wandering into Sunday service visibly fallen as I was.

I stumbled out of the house on numb feet, trembling.

And the men in suits were there.

They opened the door to the limousine and bade me to get inside. I obeyed, because I had reverted to being obedient again, there at the center of my grand demolition.

"What does the paperwork demand of me?" I asked.

The men looked at me, hard, neither of them sympathetic at all. "You must stay away from here for a period of five years at least. You must never attempt to contact Prince Hercules. You must never come to the country. If you do that, the sum of money will be yours."

He pointed to a figure outlined on the contract, and my vision blurred. I would never have to work again. My child would want for nothing. And given that I was currently homeless, that was important.

But I could only think of one thing.

"How many times have you had to do this for him?"

"All these things are a matter of private palace business. Will you sign or not?"

And I knew that I'd been had. My virginity taken by a careless seducer of women. He hadn't waited for me because he cared; he had simply waited until it was legal. And then he had sent strangers to do this to me. To dehumanize me, to take what had been a beautiful gift on my part and turn it into something tawdry and worse than common.

"I'll sign."

And so I had. Because what other choice did I have?

Yes, I remembered the first time I saw Hercules Xenakis.

It had been the beginning of the utter destruction of my life as I knew it.

But I rebuilt it into something beautiful. Something that centered around our daughter. *My* daughter.

And I did not violate that agreement. Not in that whole time. Except…

Except I had come back to Medland for the first time, at the end of my five-year exile. And there had been rumors he would be here in the lead-up to his wedding.

I'd told myself I was going for a walk.

But that walk ended at a place I knew I was likely to find him.

There he was on a balcony at the country club, over-looking the ocean below. With a woman standing next to him, a giant ring glittering on her fourth finger. I knew who she was—I wasn't a fool. I didn't avoid head-lines about him. I didn't seek them out either. I refused to let him become a sickness for me, ever again.

But I knew he was getting married.

A part of me had to wonder if I was here out of a true desire to reconcile with my mother, now that my father was gone, or if I had really come in the hope of this.

Because of course he still came here. This site of my ruin. The site of his betrayal.

And he was with her.

There had been many *hers* over the years.

I'd forced myself to look at them all and imagine what lies he told them.

But seeing them in person…

It made my whole body ache. I suddenly wished that I had Lily with me. Because at least then I could've turned to her, used her as some sort of distraction.

No.

I would never, ever allow Lily to be exposed to him.

He didn't want her. He didn't want her, and he didn't deserve to see her. Did not deserve to set eyes on the miracle that we had created. The only good and beautiful thing that I had in my life. He had rejected her, and he never, ever deserved to have even a moment of that pure love that she possessed.

But then he turned, as if an invisible force had tapped him on the shoulder. And his eyes caught mine.

And the expression I saw there was one of pure hatred.

CHAPTER TWO

Hercules

MARISSA. HER NAME echoed inside me, as it always had. And for one moment I was stopped utterly and completely. For one moment I was transported back in time. To the strangest, most unaccountable three years of my life.

Three summers spent obsessed with a dowdy brunette who hadn't even known who I was upon our first meeting.

That was what had intrigued me at first. Women tried all kinds of things to get close to me. To get into my sphere and seize whatever power they thought they might have. But not her.

Oh, I hadn't believed her doe-eyed innocence at first. I had been waiting for her to show her hand at some point, the whole summer that first time we met. But there was never a hand to show.

We never exchanged names, and if she knew that I was Hercules Xenakis, Prince of Pelion, she did not let on.

I talked to her. And I could not remember a time

when I had ever talked to another person the way that I did her. And even now, years later, I could not quite account for why.

At first, it had felt like a game. I was one of the most recognizable men in the world and had been from the day of my birth, so the novelty of being anonymous was one that amused me greatly.

But there came a point where I began avoiding any and all others on Sunday afternoons so that I could go and meet the pastor's daughter, who had somehow captured my attention.

She became a sickness.

I was obsessed with her smile. Her eyes. The way the sunlight caught her hair and created a halo of gold around her. Like she was an angel. The kind who shouldn't associate with a devil like me.

It has never been my habit to question my motivations. An entire staff of hundreds exists, and always has, to see to my every whim. I've never had to put much thought into why I do anything. If I want something, it appears.

And so I didn't put any thought into why my little fascination had a hold of me the way that she did. It was innocent, that first summer.

But things changed.

The way that she looked at me, with that hunger in her eyes. And I knew that she didn't understand what was burning between us, which should have been my first warning to stay away.

But as the Prince of Pelion, I did not have to heed warnings. The world rearranged itself around my desires, so denying myself the diversion never crossed my mind.

My first mistake, and one that I would come to understand as a weakness.

The kind of weakness that my father worked to train out of me from the time I was a boy.

A man, in my father's opinion, had to be able to withstand anything. Any pain, any betrayal, without a hint of emotion. If his child was to be tortured in order for an enemy to gain secrets, the man must not bend then.

He had done his best to ensure that I could withstand any physical torture.

Even if he'd had to be the one to test me.

And he had.

But in my father's view of the world, that same man could not put shackles on his excess. It was balance, he had told me, that a man be the hardest, cruelest of weapons when the time came, and that he indulged his baser urges when it was not a time of war.

Well-fed appetites for drink and women contributed to strength in lean times, or so he'd said.

Weakness in himself was the only thing that a ruler need fear. My father ruled Pelion with an iron fist, and he ruled his life the same way.

He ruled his children in that manner as well. Making sure that from infancy I was fit to take the throne when he passed on. If he could have taken on the Roman practice of leaving his issue out in the dirt overnight to see if it was strong enough to survive, I knew he would have done so.

Being the son of King Xerxes was not for the faint of heart. Or mind or body.

But one petite brunette that I met on the shores of a deserted ocean could hardly be a threat. That was what I told myself.

My heart had been forged in fire, covered in iron from the time I was a child. I excelled at playing a part. The international playboy who cared for nothing.

But in truth, behind the scenes, I was always ensuring that my father did no damage to the country. Did no damage to my mother.

For her part, she removed herself from the palace whenever she could.

I had been hurt by that, as a boy. Left to my father's particular brand of care, which included torture and time spent in solitary confinement.

I'd ached for my mother then.

But there was no point in regretting anything.

My father had made me a weapon. One intent on being turned around on him.

And I would have engaged in a more open rebellion in the beginning if I had not known it would come back tenfold on my much younger sister and the Queen.

There was no place in my life for softness, nor any place for a commoner who would endanger the plans that I had carefully put in place.

The Council of Pelion and I worked together to find an existing precedent for change of leadership. Once the current ruler surpassed his seventieth birthday, if the successor had produced an heir, he could take control.

It was a complicated process, and as I did not want to create a Civil War, I knew I had to play my cards right.

My father was nothing if not a self-preservationist. And I knew that I would have to do everything in my power to have the full favor of the people. And that meant, of course, marrying a woman from Pelion, one who came from the high echelons of society and who was well loved by many.

And I had done my part. I had managed to gain an agreement from my father that he would allow this, once his birthday passed and I had fulfilled my obligations.

One of which was marrying a woman he found suitable.

But in my foolishness, I had begun to negotiate in my own mind, as one summer with Marissa turned to two. And then it became three, and the heat of passion had burned between us, so hot and bright it obliterated the memory of any woman who had come before her.

I had to leave, had to return to Pelion to make a case for why this woman was worth upending the existing agreement that I had with the daughter of a politician.

But when I returned to Medland she was gone. Nowhere to be found at all. Her father simply opened the door with a stony face and said she had gone.

And I wondered if she had gone off on the mission trip she had spoken of all that time ago, but it had seemed to me that her devotion had rather turned to the worship of me and my body rather than a deity.

I was not content with that. I sent my security detail out on a search for her, engaged the resources of the palace, and still, it turned up nothing.

She had abandoned me.

The woman that I had been willing to risk an agreement over was gone.

No one had ever dared to defy me before.

That she would felt like a near unendurable blow, one that had left a great crack inside my chest.

But I had repaired that. Let it go.

Still, as I stood there, looking at her and her shocked face, I knew that it wasn't fully repaired. No. But it had changed.

It had been pain at first—a shock to me, as I had no idea I was capable of such fine feelings. But then it had changed, shifted into a deep, raging fury that had propelled me on. Had cemented my motives.

I had allowed myself to become distracted, and that was unacceptable.

I had gone back to Pelion, reaffirmed my commitment to my future marriage.

And now, five years on, it was set to take place. It had all been put on hold until my fiancée, Vanessa, was ready, and I had been happy enough to wait, as I knew that I could not rush something like this, so poised on the knife's edge.

Once, once I had been impatient. Once I had nearly ruined everything. It would not happen again.

Except, I forgot why in the moment that I stared at Marissa.

But there came a point where I began avoiding any and all others. And then she did what she had done that first day, the very first time I saw her.

She turned and she ran away.

I spared a glance at the woman by my side. "I have business to attend to."

"What is it?" she asked, only half-interested.

She was more interested in taking in the surroundings at the country club's deck. And the people who were there. Not so she could see them so much as she could know who had seen her. Vanessa was accustomed to status and luxury. It was one thing I valued in her.

Vanessa and I had an arrangement that centered squarely on politics and personal gain. She was not interested in my comings and goings, not any more than I was interested in hers.

She tucked her blond hair behind her ear, and her ring glittered in the light. "If I don't return soon, have security detail escort you back to the house."

"Very thoughtful of you," she responded, smiling at me, ever conscious of the fact that we might be photographed at a given moment.

A good thing she remembered, because I could not spare a thought for it. I charged away from the deck, going back the way that Marissa had gone. And I saw just enough to see which direction she fled, rounding a corner down one of the quaint streets.

I wondered if she was going to her parents' house, though I had checked periodically for months with palace security, and they swore she had not gone to her parents' home.

But she was here, so clearly something had changed.

It occurred to me suddenly that I should perhaps feel like a fool, chasing down the footsteps of a ghost from my past wearing a custom-made suit on the night of my engagement party. But I was a man who was accustomed to his word being law, and the matter felt as if it bore more importance than it did.

So I felt it. So it was.

And I ignored the slight kick in my gut that told

me it was a shade too close to something my father might think.

I didn't know why I was going after her. I'd had countless lovers before her, and countless sins stained my soul.

I didn't know why she mattered.

Because she got beneath the armor. That was why. Because she had done something to me that no one else had ever done. Not before, not since. Because she had made me question my primary goal in life. Had made me question the very foundation that it had been built upon.

Because of her, I nearly put the plan to rescue my nation in jeopardy.

I would have chanced marrying a commoner, a woman unapproved, who could add nothing to the throne, ensuring that my father stayed seated for years longer than he might have otherwise.

My father was too mean to die. Far too cruel to do anything quite so prosaic as give up the ghost.

And she had walked away from me. It was not I who had come to my good senses, no.

It both incensed and fascinated me even still, and that was why—I told myself—I was now chasing after her through the streets of Medland.

Her family home was small, a classic saltbox house with shingled siding like every other house on the street. I crossed the lawn, prepared to walk in without knocking, because princes did not knock, when I realized that it was probably for the best if I attempted to open with a small modicum of courtesy, as I had no idea if her parents still lived there, or if it was the home she had in fact gone into.

I rapped on the door and waited.

It opened wide, to reveal an older woman with the same color eyes as Marissa. She swung the door just wide enough that I caught sight of Marissa standing behind her. Marissa quickly retreated into the kitchen. The older woman looked behind her. "Can I help you?"

"I think we both know why I'm here."

"I don't, I'm afraid. I'm the only one here."

I admired how brazen she was. But that didn't mean that I was going to allow her to get away with it.

"I'm here for your daughter."

"She is not here for you," the woman said. "How dare you show your face?"

No one save my father had ever spoken to me with that tone of voice. This woman, who only came to the middle of my chest, spoke as if she would cheerfully remove my head from my shoulders. "Go off and have your wedding. Leave us in peace."

"I have questions for Marissa."

"And she has none for you. If she did, she would be out here. My daughter is strong. Made stronger because of you. We don't need you here."

"I am very sorry," I said, feeling nothing of the kind. "But I can't take no for an answer."

I stepped inside, and she moved back, allowing the entry. My footsteps fell heavy on the wood floor, and I knew that was what signaled Marissa, who came charging in from the next room.

Damn, she was beautiful.

Even more than the last time I'd seen her. She'd been

a woman then, but she… She had blossomed in the years since.

Her curves were more exaggerated, hollows in her cheekbones, rather than the pleasant roundness that had been there before. Her dark hair was long, curling at the ends, and there was a wildness to it now. I had thought, the first time I'd seen her, that she did look every inch the church secretary.

She did not now.

There was an edge of sophistication to the way she was dressed, even though it was simple and not designed to draw attention to her. She was wearing makeup, which I had never known her to do before.

I resented it. I wanted to wipe it away, just like I wanted to wipe away the years. Wanted to go back to a time when things had made sense to me in a way that they never had before.

When my world had been contained in an empty stretch of shore and this woman.

But I had been wrong then. Wrong about what mattered. Wrong about everything. So there was no point going back.

And there was no point mourning the passing of the years.

"How dare you?" she asked. "My mother told you to leave."

"And I said no." I took a step forward. "Have you forgotten who I am, Marissa?"

"In the five years since I've seen you? Almost. Your name has not crossed my lips once, Hercules. This is the first time in all that time. I swear it."

Her expression was guarded, the words hard, and

she was nothing like the girl I had once known. And I believed her.

"I want to know where you went."

"You want to know where I went?" Confusion and anger contorted her beautiful features.

And it hit me then that however much Marissa had changed, it was strange that she was angry at me.

She was the one who had left. And I had racked my brain over the years to try to think of reasons why. But I had been faithful to her. And yes, I had gone back to Pelion and left her in Medland, but I had assumed she would understand I would be back. And I had been.

She was the one who had abandoned us. A good thing, I could see now. But that made me question why rage still burned in my chest.

I heard the clatter of footsteps on the stairs, but they did not sound heavy or even enough to be an adult's. I looked and saw a little girl leaping down the steep staircase, her dark curls bouncing with the motion. And everything in me went still. I'm not a man who believes in premonitions. I believe in what can be seen, felt and touched, but in that moment, I felt something supernatural steal over me.

And when that child looked up at me, her chocolate eyes connecting with mine, I felt a stirring of recognition down in my soul.

I knew this girl. I, who had never had exposure to any child and who had never had a strong feeling about one, was suddenly overcome, immobilized by the strength of the connection that I felt to this one.

Because looking in her eyes was like looking into a mirror. I recognized her face, because it was mine, but smaller, rounder, cherubic in a way I was certain I had never been. I looked up at Marissa and saw she had gone pale.

"What the hell game are you playing?"

CHAPTER THREE

Marissa

IT WAS THE shock on his face that confused me. I don't know what I had been prepared for. But I had always rejected the idea that he might lay eyes on Lily, because he didn't deserve to. Because he had rejected her. I had thought in terms of protecting my daughter, because what mother wouldn't? He didn't deserve to see what a wonderful child we created, because he had rejected her. Because he had sold her when he bought my silence.

But the look on his face was not that of a man who saw this child as being inconsequential. No. The look that he had on his face was that of a man who was… shocked. As though he had been struck by lightning. Of all the things I had expected, I had not expected this. I had done my best never to think about it, of course. But…

No, something was wrong about the way he was looking at her, and I knew it. Deep down I knew. I had seen his face when he thought no one was looking. That sort of blank hardness that I'd witnessed on his features the first day I'd seen him all those years ago.

I'd seen him smile. Laugh.

I'd watched as his guard dropped completely and he'd given himself over to pleasure.

But I had never seen him look like this.

It was not rage; it was something beyond that. His skin had taken on a waxen pallor, and for the first time he seemed...

Well, human, and not so like a god.

"Explain this," he said, his voice hard.

My mother looked at him and then at me, her expression helpless.

My mother had worked hard to repair the relationship that had been severed by my father. She had secretly traveled to visit me and Lily a few times over the years. And I hated that my father's death had brought me a sense of relief, but it had. Because it had returned my childhood home to me, and my mother and I no longer had to stoop to subterfuge to see one another.

She felt nothing but sympathy for me, and I wondered if sometimes she felt a bit of envy.

Because I'd found a sort of passion that had made me behave the way that I had.

Because I had then gone out and raised a child on my own, which she'd not had the courage to do.

In spite of how unhappy she had been.

And now I could see that she was prepared to fight for Lily and me if need be.

"What do you mean what is this?" I asked. "You know perfectly well."

"I don't know anything," he said, his eyes never leaving Lily.

"We cannot have this conversation in front of her," I said.

Lily, being four and full of inquisitiveness without an ounce of perception, tilted her head back and stared up at the man I knew to be her father.

"Who are you?" she asked him.

"I was going to ask you the same thing," he responded, his voice far too hard to speak to a child.

"I'm Lily Rivero," she said. "It's nice to meet you."

Lily was precocious and polite, and I was happy that I had been able to stay home and take care of her. That we'd been able to afford to buy a wonderful house in a beautiful neighborhood. I had made the absolute most of all that I had been given, if for no other reason than to throw it in the face of Hercules, whether he could see it or not.

When he looked at me, the fury in his eyes was terrifying. It wasn't fire. It was like ice. And I sensed that it had the power to utterly destroy me.

But then, he always had. He was my weakness. My undoing.

My brightest and most beautiful sin.

My father had repeated the quote that the wages of sin was death.

Looking at Hercules now, I was beginning to wonder.

The words were quite literal and not spiritual as I had originally taken them to mean.

"Perhaps there is a place where we can talk," he said.

And I feared slightly for my own safety and health. It was like staring at a stranger. A large, incredibly muscular stranger, who bore no small amount of anger inside him.

But then…

The light hit him, just so, a shaft of sun coming through the window. And I knew him.

It was like being cast back to those sunny days on the beach.

When I had trusted him. When I had given myself to him.

When I had known him, better than I had ever known anyone.

It was still true.

That this man would always have a piece of me that no one else would. What we had shared, my father had called a *sin*. The result of which he had called the *consequence*.

But it had been *intimacy*.

And it had been real.

Whatever had happened after, it had been real for me.

And that was why I found myself unable to deny him. That was why, in spite of the years of pain, anger and anguish, I could not deny this man now when he asked for an audience with me.

Or maybe I was weak.

I would have to allow for that, I knew. I had always been weak for Hercules.

But strong for Lily.

Strong for Lily from the very beginning.

I would be strong for her now.

I followed him into the kitchen, and then I gestured to the back door. It was his turn to follow me, out to the backyard with a scant covering of crabgrass, peppered down a rolling slope.

You could just barely see the ocean through the trees,

the most beautiful views on the island not afforded to a family like mine.

I had always found that unfair when I was a child. That the bright, brilliant ocean views were granted to those who only lived here a few months out of the year.

As an adult, of course, I understood. The cost of such beauty.

I looked back at Hercules, and my previous thought echoed in my head.

The cost of such beauty.

I knew the cost of touching beauty like his.

Or so I'd thought.

I had not realized a further payment might be required.

"Is she mine?" The question was a growl.

It took me a full minute to process those words. Because it was not the question I had expected him to ask.

There had been papers. Demands. He had never wanted her. He didn't want me.

"How can you ask me that?" I sputtered.

"What else could I ask? Is that child mine?"

"You know she is," I said. "You know. You sent men. You made me sign papers. I was never supposed to come and see you, and here you are at my parents' house…"

"What men? What papers?"

"They were your men," I said. "Men from the palace. I called, Hercules. So many times. I was pregnant, and I was terrified. And do you have any idea what my father…? I needed you. I needed you, and you sent a nondisclosure agreement."

"I did no such thing," he said.

The light in his eyes had gone obsidian, and for the first time I was staring full in the face of the blackness I had witnessed in that unguarded moment when he thought no one had been looking at him that first day I'd seen him.

There was something beneath that careless playboy facade that the paper saw, something beneath the caring lover that I had spent time with years ago.

It was something I had not touched. Had not tasted. Until now.

"I don't know what to tell you," I said. "I called the palace and left messages, and no one returned them. Finally, I said… I told them that I was pregnant with your baby."

"You told someone at the palace?"

"Yes. There was nothing else I could do."

"You told someone at the palace and then men arrived." It wasn't a question, more grim statement.

"Yes. Men came, and they offered me a sum of money if I never spoke to you again. If I never contacted you again."

"You took a payoff in order to avoid telling me about my child?"

"I thought you were the one offering the payoff," I said, my heart fluttering in my chest like a trapped bird. I was beginning to feel sick, because the implications of the words being spoken between us were starting to turn over inside of me, revealing facets that I had not immediately understood or seen. "I didn't choose money over you. I thought you were demanding that I never see you…"

"This child is my heir," he said.

"She's a girl," I said, defensively.

"That doesn't matter. A law as old as time in my country, which my father would have changed if he could have, believe me. But he could not, alas for him. And so it remains. Any child of mine—as long as she is legitimate—can take the throne."

"Well," I said, drawing myself up as tall as I possibly could. I still fell laughably short of the top of his shoulder. "She's not legitimate. She won't be. She can't be. Surely you know that already."

"That isn't how it works. If I choose to recognize her by marrying you, then she will be legitimate."

"I don't… I don't understand any of this," I said, panic rising up inside of me.

How was I supposed to make sense of it? I had thought all these years that he never wanted to see her. That he would rather pay exorbitant sums to keep Lily and myself as his dirty secret. Making sense of the fact that he seemed to want Lily was almost impossible.

It was untangling a web that had been stretched across my life five years ago. One that I had built myself with the remnants I'd had left.

I'd lost him.

I'd lost my parents.

And now here he was, larger than life and every inch as heartbreakingly beautiful as he'd been at the first, and he was telling me that he wanted Lily.

"This is my father's doing," he said, reiterating what he'd said before. "He and I have an agreement. I don't know if you know much about the history of my country."

"I steer clear of everything concerning you to the best of my ability."

His lip lifted into a curl. "Except for my money."

Anger sizzled through my veins. "I'm sorry. Should I have sat in poverty and virtue with your child after being rejected by you and by my parents? Would that have made a more beautiful and sympathetic picture of maternal suffering for you? When I had an offer of comfort and riches on the table, should I have opted to take something else? There is no shame in poverty, not when life has given you no choice. But I was given a choice. A choice to make sure that no matter what happened, my child would have food. Would have shelter. That I would be able to be home to take care of her. I have been all she's had. Her only parent. It is my job, and mine alone, to care for her. There has been no one else. If you would have preferred to come back to a life in ruin so that you could rebuild it again, I am sorry to disappoint you. When you left, my life *was* ruin. My father looked at me and called me a whore. I had nowhere and nothing, and I rebuilt it with what I was given. I will not feel shame for that."

"Do you know what I think?"

I crossed my arms and took a step toward him, and I could see shock flickered behind his dark eyes. If he thought that I was still the young girl in love that he had met back then, then he was to be reeducated, and quickly.

Five years I had been without him. Five years I had been on my own in the world. Learning what it meant to live beneath the judgment of others, sleepless nights spent caring for my daughter, without any help when I found myself in a state of utter exhaustion.

And I had become strong.

Arguments in doctors' offices when I knew my child had pneumonia and they simply wanted to send me home. Standing up for Lily when she had pushed someone to the ground in her preschool class because they had said her mother was bad since Lily didn't have a father.

Standing up for myself when people sometimes didn't let their children associate with mine for those same reasons.

Years alone and motherhood had sharpened me, and sometimes I resented it.

Because I had been soft once, and I had believed in love.

The only kind of love left that I believed in was the kind between a mother and daughter, strengthened when my own had attempted to mend the bridge that had been broken between us by my father.

Fathers I could do without, thank you.

Mothers I had found strength in.

But like a stone battered about, my smooth edges had been cracked against the hardships of life, creating hard, sharp edges.

And he was about to understand just how much I'd changed.

"I'm sure you're going to tell me what you think," I said, "because you think the world stops and starts on your word. Because once you were able to make my world stop and start at your word. But I made a life without you in it. And I will tell you gladly that there is nothing for you here. So whatever you say, it better be compelling, and not predictable as I suspect it will be."

"I think that you didn't want to hassle with me, and when you were offered a payoff, you took it rather than making sure you did the right thing."

I scoffed. "The right thing? The right thing. To ensure that a man who goes about the world spreading his seed whenever he feels the urge knows about a child he didn't even want? How many other women are like me, do you think?"

He drew back. "None."

"You don't know that."

"I have always used condoms," he said ferociously. "With every other woman."

"Oh," I said. "So I'm special. The woman who had never even touched a man's hand before you is the one that you couldn't be bothered to protect? I'm glad that our dalliance meant so much to you."

"Say what you want, Marissa, but I came back for you. I came back for you, and you were not here. And a damn good thing, I have told myself over the years, because I had a responsibility to my country and to my people, and you did not fit anywhere into that responsibility. But now there is her. Lily. And I cannot ignore the implications of her existence. My father has ruled Pelion with an iron fist for generations. And the only reason that I have not overthrown him in some kind of civil war is that the casualties would be too great, and there is a law that states the current leader is to step aside at seventy if the successor has married and produces an heir. I found that suitable woman some time ago."

"Yes. I know. I've seen photos of you with her."

"But Lily is my heir. And my father has had a significant birthday. That ushers in a new order in my country immediately. And that must be fulfilled. Because over the years my father's tyrannical tendencies have gotten worse. He is beginning to crack down on even the most basic of freedoms people in my country used to experience. And while there is breath in my body and power to do so, I cannot allow it. But the consideration of the cost to civilian life and the danger to my mother and sister has weighed heavily on me. But this… We have a binding document."

"Your father is a tyrant—do you think he would honor it?"

"It is not him that I need to honor it. It is the military. They serve the King. Not only that, it's whether or not I am King in the eyes of allies."

"It all seems trivial to me."

"It is the nature of being royal. Tradition is what it is."

"But will I be deemed acceptable?"

"That is for the Council to decide, but I suspect that the existence of an heir and the law as it is written will trump any concerns about your suitability."

"I have a life. I have built a life for Lily and myself in Boston. I am terribly sorry about your country. Not for your sake, but for the sake of your people.But I fail to see how it's my problem."

"It is your problem because you had my child."

I stepped forward, rage simmering in my blood, boiling over. "She is my child. Your contribution to her genetics does not make you a father. It does not make her yours. I gave birth alone. The pain and fear that I felt in that moment was horrible, and if not for a nurse who felt sorry for me and sat there and held my hand the entire time, there would've been no one there for me. I took an infant back to my home by myself, and I'm the one who didn't sleep for months. I'm the one who paced the halls rocking a crying baby."

I took a jagged breath and continued, all my anger— at him, my parents, the world—spilling out now. "And you... You were at parties. You had a new lover that same week that I gave birth, and she was on the cover of magazines with you, all slim and beautiful and perfectly made up, and my hair was in one giant mat, my pajama pants were too tight and I wanted to weep from lack of sleep. Lily is *mine*. She is mine by rights. You have parties. And endless photos to document the way that you enjoy spending your time, and all the glittering, sparkling objects you can lay claim to. But I am not one of them, and neither is she. Your father might be a bastard, but it's his money that kept us off the streets, if I'm understanding this correctly."

His face went grim, the light behind his eyes unreadable, opaque.

"I don't have room for emotion in this," he said. "There is a means here to liberate my country, and it will be done. Lily is coming with me whether or not you like it."

"What are you going to do?"

"Take her from you forcibly if I must, and deal with whatever fallout results. But I would rather that you came with me, as it would make things easier for the child."

Horror stole through me, and I could see that he

wasn't kidding. I could see the hardness in him. And I wondered how in the world I had ever thought this man to be a creature of pleasure and lightness, when I could see now that he was all rock and cold.

"You can't do this."

"I can. Even legally. I have diplomatic immunity, first of all. Second of all, Lily is a citizen of Pelion. And I am her father."

"Your name isn't on the birth certificate."

"It doesn't matter. Or have you not been listening? I am a prince in line to be a king and my word is law, even here."

I felt some of the fight begin to drain out of me, but then I steeled myself, took a breath and did my best to renew it. "I will not go easily. I will not uproot my child from everything that she knows, everything that she is, because you have decided that it's time to take responsibility."

"I didn't know. And if you want to make it about Lily, then you have to ask yourself what the ramifications of your decision are. She could be Queen."

The words shocked me, because it had honestly never occurred to me. That Lily was royal. That she was a princess. One that was in line for the throne of Pelion, but only if Hercules and I married.

"Would you rob your child of her rightful place in this world?"

I didn't want my child to be a queen. That was my very first thought. Because the very idea of her being a world leader, of her having such scrutiny placed on her, such a broad target painted on her back... It filled me with dread. I couldn't stand it when children made fun

of her parentage. The very idea of her being a leader—
a woman leader in this world—and the kinds of things
that would be said about her... It scared me to my bones.

But on the other hand, there was a truth to what he
said that I found difficult to deny.

But the idea of being married to this man that I had
hated for so long, who had hurt me so much...

A little bubble welled up inside my chest, and I despised it. Because I recognized it for what it was.

Joy.

That I could feel joy in some part of myself that
Hercules was back, that he was proposing marriage...

Well, it made me feel like the foolish idiot my father thought I was. The immoral fool who would throw
over all scruples and morality for the touch of a good-
looking man.

This wasn't about me. And if I was to claim truth for
all the things that I'd said to him in the past few minutes, I had to take myself out of the equation.

I had to think of Lily. Only of Lily.

"It's not my permission you need," I said. "But you
will ask my daughter's."

"I'm sorry," he responded, arching a black brow.
"You expect me to go to a child and explain all of this."

"She has friends," I said. "She's just now reconnect-
ing with her grandmother. It is her future you're talking
about, and yes, I know she's four. And I know that..." I
blinked back tears, because I knew that what my daughter would see was this tall, beautiful man telling her that
he was her father. And that she was a princess. And I
already knew what Lily would say.

But it was that vision in my mind that made me so resolute.

That Lily would be a princess. That she would have a father.

Whatever my feelings about him were...

He hadn't known.

He hadn't rejected me. He hadn't rejected her. And I couldn't shrug off the layers of armor that I had put on over the years with the ease of that revelation, but it was what made me give him time to speak, rather than simply attempting to run him through with a kebab skewer that I might have found in my mother's kitchen drawer.

"It's her life," I said. "And so, yes. I expect you to speak to her." I sighed heavily. "If she says no...you'll have to kidnap us both, I guess."

CHAPTER FOUR

Hercules

UTTER DISBELIEF FIRED through me as I stared down at Marissa. I hardly recognized the woman who stood before me, and I had known her intimately five years ago. But she was not the scared creature who had fled, no matter that I had thought she might be, given the way she had run from me back at the restaurant.

She had not been running to protect herself, but to protect Lily.

Lily.

Who was undeniably mine.

But I could not afford to falter, could not afford to allow emotion to have any purchase on this moment, because I had a responsibility.

First and foremost, Lily was the heir to the throne of Pelion. Lily was the key to ousting my father from power, and she would have to be treated as such.

But somehow I had been thrust into a position where I was going to have to make political negotiations with a child.

Marissa was staring me down, her dark eyes never

wavering from mine, and I had no doubt that everything she said was true.

I would have to bundle them up and carry them out of the house, forcing them onto a plane, if I did not do this.

Now, whatever Marissa thought, I was not ashamed at the thought that I might take that action. I would do what I had to do.

But I was also happy to avoid it, given it was an action that was guaranteed to draw press.

It was a tangled mess. I was set to marry Vanessa in just two weeks' time, and now there was no question of that happening.

I didn't need allegations of me being a kidnapper to come out on top of it.

I was not a man who dealt in uncertainty—a man in my position could not afford to be. But as I followed Marissa up the stairs, I felt a shadow of it. And I realized that the only reason I even knew what I could be feeling was because of her. Because Marissa had, all those years ago, taken that bedrock certainty of who I was—and my confidence that I could make whatever life I chose to arrange for myself—and dashed it against the rocks, as if she were the siren to my wayward sailor.

She pushed the door open at the top of the stairs, and I followed her in. "Lily," she said, "Hercules would like to speak to you." There was a tremor in her voice for the first time. And if I had been a different man, I might have felt some uncertainty along with it.

But I could not afford to waver. Not ever. And I could not afford sympathy in any measure.

Lily looked confused. Curious. Her dark eyes swept over me, and even amid the confusion, even in her youth, I could see an imperiousness there. Inherited, I knew.

Lily.

What would her name have been if I had been there? Her name would have been a family name. Aphrodite or Apollonia, perhaps.

Lily was so simple.

It sounded like something that could be easily crushed, and everything inside of me rebelled at that. But when I looked back down at the child and her steady expression as she looked me full in the face with an ease that men found next to impossible at times, I knew the name suited her well.

Because her enemies would never know that she was made of steel at her core. They would be distracted and confused by her apparent softness, and they would never see her hit coming.

I would teach her to hone that. I would teach her all she needed in order to ascend the throne of Pelion. She was young enough that it was not too late, and I might have missed her earliest years, but I would not miss anymore. I kept my gaze on Lily, because this discussion was between us, and only us.

"I have something I wish to speak to you about," I said, trying to decide if I should loom over the child or crouch down and meet her eyes.

I was a prince. I did not crouch. It was near to a bow, and I wasn't entirely sure my body could form such a submissive posture.

But speaking over her as I was didn't seem right either.

And so for the first time I could remember, I bent a knee.

"Your mother and I were..." How the hell did you explain such a thing to a child? I had no idea. Did she even know a man and woman had to *know* each other in order to reproduce? And I could not say something that would cast her mother in a negative light. That was just diplomacy. She was on her mother's side. Clearly, she would not take kindly to an interloper telling her that her mother was anything less than perfect. So I would have to select my wording carefully. Not out of deference to Marissa, but out of care for my particular political mission.

With a four-year-old.

My child. My *daughter*.

It was something I could not fathom still. It settled on my skin like a crackle of electricity, rather than sinking in.

"We knew each other for a time," I continued. "And we were...separated. I had to go back to my country, and you moved away from here."

She scrunched up her face. "You talk funny. Is it because you're from another country?"

It was not a question I expected, and one that came in slightly from left field, given the direction my line of speaking was headed.

"Yes," I said. "I imagine so." Though, I did not think I had a very marked accent. I've been told my English was nothing short of excellent.

"Okay," she said, apparently satisfied by my admission.

"I am from a country far away," I continued. "Across

the ocean. An island in the middle of the Mediterranean Sea. It's beautiful. You see, I had to return there to see to business because I am a prince."

"A prince?" Her eyes got round.

"Yes," I said, satisfied that that statement had landed anyway. "And I have just discovered something, Lily. You are my Princess. You're my daughter. I... I'm your father."

And then she did something I couldn't have anticipated.

I didn't realize that children felt emotion in that way, but she demonstrated to me that I knew nothing. Her face crumpled, almost immediately, and the sound that came out of her tiny body was almost inhuman. A high-pitched wail that pierced my heart, pierced any defense I thought I might have had. And then she wrapped her arms around my neck and held me, as if I weren't a stranger. As if I weren't a man who had stormed into her grandmother's house and made all manner of threats to her mother.

I went stiff, completely uncertain of what to do. And for the first time, I looked to Marissa. Her expression was neutral, but there were tears in her eyes. I tried to straighten, but Lily would not let me go. So I wrapped an arm around her and stood, holding her against me as she wept. "Your mother told me that I had to ask you," I continued, "if you want to come with your mother and live with me in my castle."

I realized how truly unfair a line of questioning that was, and also realized that by asking me to go and speak to Lily, Marissa had not set me up for failure. Her motive had not been selfish, not at all. Because anyone would know that a four-year-old would not have the willpower to turn down such an offer.

She lifted her head, wiping at her eyes with closed fists. "What about my nana?"

"Your nana can come too," I said. "It's a very big castle."

I didn't know how I'd come into the position of negotiating details of something so delicate with a preschooler, but there I was.

"Mommy," Lily said, her voice plaintive. She reached for Marissa.

Marissa stepped forward, and I transferred the warm weight of the child to her.

It was a strange thing, one that I imagined normal parents did.

Mine certainly never had. There had been no affection spared for me in my youth. I imagine my mother had felt inclined to give it to me, but my father had not allowed it.

And I...

I had spent so much time planning for what it would be like politically when I had an heir that I had never once spared a thought to what kind of father I would be.

Only what kind of king I might be.

But Lily was not a hypothetical—she was very real, and seemed to need something from me that I could not quite fathom, but knew I had to find it in myself to give.

"It's true," Marissa said, brushing Lily's hair back from her face. "Everything he said is true. You're a princess. If you want to be a princess, it means moving away from here. Away from our home in Boston. Away from what we know. But I'll be with you. And...

you were born a princess, Lily." Her voice broke. "You were born a princess, and whether you go to Pelion or not, you're still a princess. But everything that your father has belongs to you too. And it wouldn't be right for me to ask you not to have it."

It was clear to me that Lily didn't understand Marissa's impassioned speech. But I did. I appreciated how difficult this was for her, even though it couldn't affect my ultimate action.

Lily's expression was serious, and she looked at me with luminous eyes. "Daddy?"

The word hit like a bullet. I felt as though it had ripped its way through my chest and torn my heart utterly into pieces.

The heart that I didn't realize had been quite so vulnerable, or quite so...

Quite so able to feel.

This child was innocent. Of everything.

Of what had happened between her mother and me, whether it was subterfuge on the part of Marissa or not. Of the royal lineage she had been born into.

She had no control over any of it, and I knew exactly what that felt like.

Except when my father had taken me in hand, they had been the hands of a monster, and there had never been any question that I call him something so affectionate as Daddy.

But this child was handing me trust. A moniker of affection that I had done nothing to earn, and I feared might never.

I felt utterly and wildly adrift in that moment, in a way that I had only ever done two other times in my life.

The first time I had seen Marissa—when it hadn't even been sexual in nature—and when I had come back to discover she was gone.

"Yes," I said, my voice less than steady, which was unacceptable.

And yet we were not in the throne room. Not before the press.

It was just me and this child. My child.

And Marissa.

"I want to go with you," the little girl said, while simultaneously tightening her hold on her mother.

"Then we will go together," Marissa said, holding even more tightly to Lily. "We will go together."

"And you will be my wife," I returned. "My Princess. Both of you."

I was resolved. And it was done.

"My mother?"

"Is welcome to come."

Marissa nodded slowly. "Okay. I'll… I'll talk to her."

"We must leave tonight," I said, decisively. "I will send men to handle my things, and to handle Vanessa as well."

"Oh…" Marissa looked crestfallen. "Vanessa. What are you going to do about Vanessa? You're engaged to her. You're supposed to get married in two weeks. How are you going to…?"

"I just told you," I replied. "I will send men to handle her. And to help mitigate any disappointment that she might feel. I'm not a monster. Whatever you might think."

"You're breaking up with your fiancée via your goon squad. Who, by the way, are likely the very same men who told me that you wanted—"

She cut herself off, and I saw her flick a glance at Lily. "You and I will have to discuss this at another time."

"We will."

I picked up my phone. "Have my private jet ready to go in one hour. Please arrange alternative transport for Ms. Carlson."

And with that I hung up, not cowed by Marissa's disapproving gaze. She could disapprove all she wanted. We were in a mess that I suspected had been made by my father, and I refused to let him win. Absolutely and utterly refused. Marissa may not have liked my methods, but I knew that in the end my way would be the best way.

"An hour? That's not enough time to pack. What about all our things? Lily and I don't live here. We have a house in Boston. All of her toys..."

"Someone will be sent to retrieve them," I replied. "But I will not delay taking the two of you back to your rightful place."

"My mother..."

"I suggest you speak to her quickly."

"So all of this will be your way?" Marissa asked.

"I did this part your way," I said, nodding toward Lily, indicating the fact that I had asked her permission. "Yes. The rest will be done mine. I regret to tell you that there is no other option."

"Somehow, I very much doubt that you're filled with regret of any kind."

But she was wrong. Because what I felt swirling in my chest right now as I looked at my child, as I looked at the way she fitted in Marissa's arms, was a tangle of regret that I had not felt before in my entire life.

I did not like it. And so I did what I must do. I took action.

"We are going. Now. Don't tempt me to change the deadline."

Marissa turned away from me and bumped against a box on the edge of the dresser. She cursed—which surprised me—as the box hit the ground. The lid fell open and out spilled two shells. A larger one and a smaller one.

She looked at me, and my eyes went to her hair. The way it curled.

And then I looked back at the shells.

I'd given those to her. Because in my madness I'd seen her in everything, even in nature.

And she'd kept them. Even while claiming to hate me.

She bent down and picked up the box, put the shells back in and cradled the box to her chest. She stared me down for a moment, as if daring me to say something.

I didn't.

Then, without a word, Marissa nodded and swept from the room, leaving me standing there.

Something no one would typically dare to do.

But Marissa had never been typical. She hated me, and yet she had my shells. And I was fascinated all over again in spite of myself.

But Marissa had nothing to do with the decision that I had made.

This was about Lily. This was about the throne.

This was about making sure my father knew he would never win against me.

Of that I would be certain.

CHAPTER FIVE

Marissa

I HAD KNOWN that he was a prince. I had followed news stories about him over the years and seen the lavish way he lived his life in stunning photographs splashed across search engines and tabloid newspapers.

But it hadn't really taken hold of me just what that meant until we boarded his private plane.

Luxury on that scale was something so theoretical to me that I could only imagine it, and even then, I could only imagine it at a reduced scale.

My brain hadn't had the textural vocabulary for leather as soft as what was found on the plush couch in the seating area of the plane. It didn't have the concept of the scale that something like a prince's private plane might have. I had imagined something like I had seen in movies, where one still had to duck down when they stood, and there were a few seats with ample legroom, and glasses of champagne.

No.

This plane was mammoth. One that could easily fit the same number of people as commercial planes that did domestic flights. And there were rooms. Multiple rooms, though I didn't know what they all were.

The stewardess quickly ushered Lily to a beautifully appointed bedroom and did the same for my mother. Then she made herself vanish, and I knew that everyone had been carefully dealt with so that Hercules and I could talk.

My mother had of course decided to come with us. There was nothing left for her in Medland, except the beautiful house that she had once shared unhappily with my father.

I could tell that my mother was hesitant to leave me, but it was also clear to an extent that pushing back against Hercules was futile. Far better to try to negotiate with him and get a handle on what this new reality was. And what it would be in the future.

"This is…nice," I said, taking a seat on the couch and sinking into the buttery softness. But I refused to show him that I took pleasure in it.

"Champagne?" he asked.

"A toast to our upcoming union?" I asked. And I immediately regretted making the dry comment, because I was in no place where I could joke about such things.

I couldn't take it lightly.

It made my insides twist into a knot.

And that hope bubble in my chest became more pronounced.

I wanted to pop it.

I felt so foolish, revealing to him that I'd kept those shells. And even more foolish that I hadn't dumped them straight in the trash but had packed them instead.

"If you like."

"I don't drink," I said.

"Do you still not drink? I thought that you also didn't have premarital sex. And yet…"

I didn't tell him that I hadn't had sex since. That he was the only person I'd ever made the exception for.

I didn't tell him that I didn't drink because holdovers from my childhood were still hard to shake, and sometimes I worried a little bit about hellfire being in every breath I took wrong.

"Well, when do you suggest I might have started? During my pregnancy? After? When I was single parenting a young child? There never seemed a good time. And at the moments when I thought I might need a drink most, it occurred to me that perhaps it wasn't healthy to be thinking of it as a crutch."

"Fair enough."

He put the bottle of champagne back and then to my surprise opened a cooler and took out a bottle of sparkling cider.

"You can have champagne," I said.

"I don't need it," he said. "And, as you pointed out, perhaps if one is using it as a crutch, it's not a very good thing."

"I wouldn't think that Your Royal Highness needed crutches."

"In this current situation, I'm finding that I might need more than I think."

I didn't know what to say to that. The admission of weakness was so unexpected that it momentarily silenced me.

"Well, I find that I'm in want of some as well. But… but again, it seems an inadvisable reason to start."

"I don't disagree with you," he said. "And so, in the interest of fending off addictions, we can have this together."

"I did try to contact you," I said. "Whatever you think of me… I could have had much more if you would have known. Surely you must see that. If you can't believe in who I am as a person, if you can't believe that maybe what we had for a while was real, then believe that, even if I'm grasping, I'm not stupid. Believe that if I really wanted to take you for your money, I would have done so in a spectacular fashion. I would have shamed you publicly, but I had no interest in that. All I wanted was what was best for Lily. When those men came… Hercules, I thought I was nothing to you. Nothing more than one of the many women that you seduce and leave behind. I had no reason to believe that I was anything else. And I had no reason to believe those men were not sent by you."

He began to pour a glass of cider, and then he paused. Suddenly, the look on his face became one of stone. "It's why they couldn't find you," he said. "They didn't look. They were working for him, not for me. They had orders not to find you."

"What?"

"I searched for you," he said. "Your father said you were gone, and I didn't accept it. I had my men go after you. I had them search. I have resources that stretch far beyond that of a normal man. I should have been able to find you. They should have been able to find you. The fact that they did not…" He shook his head. "Why did I not realize it before now?"

"He wanted to keep you from her," I said.

"He did. Because he knew that when his birthday passed, I would succeed him. As is the law in Pelion. He wanted to delay my heir, wanted to set up hoops for me to jump through. Vanessa was a hoop. A suitable bride that was not ready to marry and reproduce immediately when my father passed his deadline."

"We don't need to punish each other," I said softly.

For the first time, I honestly felt some sympathy for him. He didn't know.

But I couldn't just turn my whole sense of the last five years on its head.

"I… I felt so utterly abandoned, Hercules. I betrayed who I thought I was for you."

He shook his head. "No. Don't tell me that. You are a strong woman, Marissa. If you did not want to have sex you wouldn't have."

The truth in those words set me back on my heels. He was right. I hadn't been seduced. Not in the way that I often let myself think of it. Yes, he was new and exciting, a window into sensations that I hadn't even known I wanted. But I had wanted him. I had wanted him deep in my soul. Wanted him with a desperation that defied sanity.

It reminded me of when he had asked me if I always did as I was told.

I had, because it had never occurred to me to do things a different way.

And when I stopped doing as I was told, it wasn't because I had simply replaced one set of commands with another.

It was because I had realized what I was. Who I was. And that I wanted it to be something different than I had been fashioned into.

It had nothing to do with faith, for mine had remained intact all these years. But it had become something deeper in many ways, something more personal, because I wasn't following commandments and dictates because my father said so, but because of what rang true in my own soul.

And perhaps I didn't have a life that looked perfect to everyone from the outside, but something in my heart felt healed.

No, it had never been about rebellion. It had never been about burning down what I believed in and starting from scratch.

It had been about finding me.

In the midst of everything that I had been taught to be, I found the person I was born to be.

I didn't have to hide. Not now. Not behind excuses, and not behind the idea that I had somehow succumbed to the temptation only because of his wickedness. Or even my own.

"It doesn't matter. Not now. I've changed. I assume you have too."

"No," he said, his expression opaque. "I have not changed. I am as I ever was. I'm a man who has the responsibility and the weight of an entire nation on his shoulders. And I never forget it. It doesn't matter what you see in the media. If you see photos of me looking carefree. All that time we spent together on the beach. I am never carefree."

I looked him right in the eyes. "I know that."

He appeared shocked by that. "What is it you think you know?"

"The first time that I saw you, standing there on the

shore. None of your friends had caught up to you yet, and you were standing there with your hands shoved into your pockets and a grim look on your face. You were clearly a man with a great weight on you. I could see it. A man who carried darkness around inside of him and understood that there might be a cost to that. I knew it. I did. I knew it then, and I know it now. All of what you show the world is... It's an oversimplification. And even what you showed me, back when we were together."

"Well, isn't that a neat trick that you managed to speak of it now, and yet you didn't say anything then."

"I always felt like there was a timer ticking down on what we had. I didn't want to clutter it up with unpleasant topics. And I never wanted to betray how much I cared. But I'm not a girl now. And while you may carry the weight of the fate of your nation on your shoulders, I carry the responsibility of taking care of our daughter. She is my primary concern, and she always will be. Lily is the most important thing in my universe. You must worry for millions. I worry for only one. And that means my focus is not split. I will defend her and her interest with all of me. Forever."

"And what about your own?"

"I am second. And I chose to be second when I committed to being her mother. When I knew that I wouldn't give her up. My father threw me out. He said I was an embarrassment. But it didn't matter. Because at that moment it ceased to be about me. It was about Lily, and me doing the best that I could for her. It was a free and wonderful realization, and it has been a free and wonderful way to live. And maybe...maybe this isn't what I want. I didn't sign on for this. For the life of public scrutiny, or to be…at the center of your engagement falling apart, which I can only imagine is going to make headlines everywhere."

"Yes. We are about to create something of an incident. I won't lie to you."

"I'm doing it for her."

Suddenly, he closed the distance between us, reaching out, his large hand cupping my cheek. He was like fire. His touch was a flame. And I had not expected that. I had thought that all those years would have given me a sort of immunity to the man, and yet there was none. "Is it?"

The words were husky, and his breath was warm and I could feel it across my lips.

It made me ache. Everywhere.

"Is it just for her?" he pressed. "You do not think that even a small part of yourself is going to find some enjoyment in this?"

My heart was thundering hard, so hard that I was convinced he could hear it. I swallowed.

I would not give him the satisfaction of seeing that he had shaken me. I would not let him come in and simply think that he could assume control of not only everything outside, but all the things inside me too. I had raised my daughter on my own for years. And yes, I was affected by him, but I would not simply give him the satisfaction of knowing that.

"Are you sure that this is entirely for your country?" I shot back. "And not you satisfying your thwarted hunter's instinct? You've caught me. And wasn't that what you wanted all those years ago?"

He growled and closed the distance almost entirely between us. And I faced the black fire, so close that I thought it might reduce me to ash. "No one leaves me," he gritted out. "No one abandons me."

"Don't they?"

I didn't know why I asked the question, or if it would have a particular sort of significance to him, but he released his hold on me, dropping his hand and turning away.

He raked his fingers through his black hair and then moved to face me again.

"Rearranging a wedding should not be too difficult. We have the venue. Guess all we need to do is change out the bride."

I gritted my teeth. "Just as I dreamed. From the time I was a little girl. That I might be a replacement bride for the Prince."

"She was your replacement."

The words were stunning. Rough, and for a moment I was certain that he had actually been speaking in a foreign language and my brain had translated them incorrectly. It took me a moment to realize that I hadn't been insulted in some way. Quite the contrary. He had admitted something to me that I didn't think he was happy to have spoken into existence.

"Well, then isn't it good that we put things to rights," I said. The words were barely above a whisper.

The problem was nothing felt put to rights at all. It all felt wrong and strange, deeply disconcerting.

And yet…

When he touched me, there was still heat. When he was near me, I still felt a kick of desire.

And if I was perfectly honest with myself, I would have been unhappy to go back home now.

No. That could not be. He could not have that kind of power over me. Never again.

I was not so weak that my attraction to Hercules could cause me to abandon reason.

"Perhaps we should toast," he said, lifting his glass. "To our union."

I raised my glass, my eyes never leaving his. It was a challenge, and I was not going to back down. Because I had changed. I had become someone different, forged in steel, in the fires of the conflagration that had occurred between us.

I had been a fool then. A girl easily wounded.

"This is for Lily," I said, more for myself than for him. "And our marriage is for Lily. It is not for us."

"Is that so?" he asked, his voice rough.

"Yes," I responded, pleased that I managed to keep my voice steady then.

It was the fire that terrified me. But more than that… it was the hope.

Because I could not seem to banish it no matter how much I tried.

"I don't care who you sleep with," I continued, the words catching in my throat. "But it won't be me."

"Excuse me?" The cold, dark ice in his tone sent a chill through me.

"We must be good parents to our daughter," I said. "Unless you're willing to drop down on your knees now and profess undying love, it won't work. We must be able to parent together, to exist together. To attend functions together and present a united front."

"My parents managed to do it for years. And trust me when I tell you they do not care much for each other."

"I am not your mother," I said. "And you are not your father. I'm confident of that, without ever having met either of them."

He stiffened. "Have it your way, Marissa. But I have to tell you I think your goals might be unrealistic here."

"Why?"

He smiled at me, and he didn't have to say a word, because electricity passed between us in that space, a switch flipped by the crook of his lips. And he knew it.

"We are not animals. We managed to go five years without touching one another, after all."

"True," he said, leaning in. "But that was when we were nowhere near each other. With an ocean between us it's quite easy to resist, is it not?" He reached out, the rough edge of his thumb resting against my upper lip. "But is it so easy to resist now? When I am here. And you still want me, so very much." My heart was tripping over itself, like the fool that I was, giddy and excited over the touch of this man.

"There is unfinished business between us," he continued.

"No," I whispered, calling on all of my strength and taking a step away from him. A step toward sanity.

"The business between us is Lily. And when she is finished, when she is grown, we will be too."

"Divorce then?" he asked. "How dull."

"It doesn't have to be divorce. We can simply separate. Whatever you need for your perfect royal image."

"You will not shame me by going out with other men," he said, the words shot through with iron.

I might have taken pleasure in the thought that he was jealous if I wasn't so desperate to release my hold on any sort of feelings for him. "I have no problem with that. I've managed just fine on my own this whole time."

"Have it your way, then." He downed the rest of the contents of his glass and took a step away from me, and I felt unaccountably cold when he did.

Then he removed his presence entirely from beside me.

"You might want to get some sleep. When we land, it will be morning in Pelion. And there will be much to attend to."

CHAPTER SIX

Hercules

OF THE MANY rebellions I had expected of Marissa, this refusal to be my wife in anything beyond name had thrown me off entirely.

It was one thing that I knew we could count on between us. Our passion.

Yes, we'd had an innocent relationship at first, but when passion had ignited between us it had been undeniable, unstoppable. We had traded in words for sighs of pleasure, and I had never regretted it. But this... This could not be endured.

I gritted my teeth. What man was this inside of me who could not handle being absent the touch of a particular woman? Since when had it ever mattered to me? I had more pressing matters to deal with than Marissa and her reluctance to be my bride in any real sense.

I had my father to deal with.

There was no question of having Marissa and Lily or Marissa's mother come to the palace.

Instead, I had them driven to my home that was nestled in the mountains of Pelion, on the opposite side of our major city from the palace.

My home was not a castle, but in many ways my father's home and mine had been set up like two warring palaces on opposing hills, facing each other down.

But now I was ready.

Ready to cross the gulf, ready to go to war.

I had steadied my hand; I had played at diplomacy. And I had done so in order to keep my father's wrath away from my mother and sister.

Though I knew at the moment neither of them were in residence in Pelion. They were in the French Riviera, as both of them preferred.

Even if not...

My father had already done the unforgivable.

He had kept me from my child.

I would not be civil.

I was given admittance into the palace immediately, and I walked directly through the glimmering obsidian halls down to the throne room.

It was Gothic, this palace. It always had been. As if the black heart of the Xenakis family resided at the center of this gilded mausoleum.

But then, I supposed it was true.

Whoever sat on the throne was the heart.

And my father had been up there spreading poison for far too long.

I would be better than the heart of this palace, than the heart of this nation.

I would be the brain.

That at least had a basis for reason. That at least had a code.

There were so many people who thought that the heart deserved to be followed. That the heart was the core of our humanity, but I knew the truth.

The heart could produce both humanity and unspeakable horror.

The heart was wicked. And it was deceptive. If you could find justification for your behavior deep in your heart, then a man could do anything.

However, reason would win out. I was confident in that. Reason I trusted in.

Reason I had violated only once.

With Marissa.

But it was funny how in the end she was the key to Pelion salvation. She had caused a shift in what was possible, and therefore a shift in my reasoning.

Something fascinating to be explored later, perhaps, but not when I was about to cross swords with my father.

I pushed the double doors of the throne room open without signaling my arrival.

The two Secret Service agents standing next to my father reached for their weapons, and I held up my hand. "Prince Hercules," I said.

"Prince Hercules," the other men repeated, nodding once.

"To what do I owe the pleasure?"

I had not been home in some time, and I was surprised by how diminished my father looked.

It was not just aging, for the Xenakis family tended to remain strong like oxen until the end. He looked weathered, and he looked weak, and my father was many things, but he had never been that.

"Have you climbed off of your latest whore long enough to see to issues of state?"

His voice was not frail, and apparently the meanness that coursed through his veins was well intact.

"I have been on a fact-finding mission," I said. "And I am not certain you will like what I uncovered."

"Is that so?"

The gleam in his eye seemed to swallow the light rather than give it off. Like the obsidian walls all around us.

That darkness was my legacy. And I would wield it against him happily now.

"Yes. Perhaps there is a secret that you forgot to tell me."

He did not look cowed by this; instead, he looked smug. "Oh, there are many, Hercules. Did you imagine all this time that you were sitting back pulling my strings and I never pulled yours? A common error of the youth. You think you know more. You think you know better. And because of that, you never take a moment to consider that I might be an opponent that is equal to you."

My lip curled. "I am not you," I said.

"That may be. But whether or not we are the same, we are an equal match."

"You're a monster."

"There are reasons that monsters live in caves for hundreds of years terrorizing the townspeople, and it isn't because they are stupid. You don't have to be good to win, Hercules. Perhaps you should remember that. If you're looking at your victory as an opportunity to measure the purity of your morality, I feel that might come to a disappointing end."

"Moral absolutism is not exactly at the core of what I've come to talk to you about. I found my child."

That I could see impacted him. "Have you?"

"Yes."

"Her mother was happy enough to sign away your rights for a payout."

"Because you made her think it was what I wanted. Marissa is a proud woman and she would no more beg me for anything, for my attention, than she would submit her child to a life on the streets."

Marissa's own words filled me, and I found I believed them with a great conviction in that moment.

"She is a woman of absolute strength and dignity, and she has done what we all should have done for the past years. She has raised Lily. Lily is the heir to the throne of Pelion. We owe her the same that we have owed every ruler that has come before her."

"A girl," my father sneered. "Of course you would produce a girl."

"She will be Queen. She will be Queen after me, and I daresay that whatever I don't manage to blot out that you brought on this country, she will erase entirely."

"Do you imagine I will step aside for you? For her?"

"You have to. Your birthday has passed. And I can see that age has begun to eat away at you."

He chuckled. "It is not age. But illness. It has long been said that I am too mean to die. I suspect soon we will see whether or not that is true."

"Step aside now."

"Have you not even a flicker of emotion for your father?"

"No," I said, "and you are not shocked. You concealed my child from me, and I have told you that I brought your granddaughter back to the country and you have no emotion to spare for that except disdain over her gender. No, I have no emotion to spare for you. None at all. You had none to spare for me. You had none to spare for her. I will stage a coup. We can end this in blood if you like."

"What if you didn't like the blood that was spilled?"

"If that is a threat against my family, I will end you now with my own hand."

"Do not speak of threats, Hercules, for we are more civilized than that, are we not? Political warfare is best waged with words and bureaucracy, don't you think?"

"The war is won. Engaging in a battle with you is a pointless waste of time. I marry Marissa in less than two weeks' time. The original wedding date stands. And upon that wedding you will abdicate."

"Will I?"

"Yes. Because if you don't, trust that I will make public what has occurred with Lily. Trust that I will destroy whatever fragment of a reputation you have left in this world. What do you want in the history books, Father? That in your current state is your primary concern anyway."

"I will require medical staff," he said. "I will require a residence."

"All to be provided," I said. "I will send you off with the most lavish of severance packages. You will want for nothing, and to all the world it will look as if the

Xenakis line has continued as it should. No one need know that I had to wrest it from you."

"If I resisted, what would you do?"

"I would have the military on my side, Father, and I think we both know it. No matter your threats, the blood that spilled would be yours."

My father was dying, and I knew that he was not fighting me because he wanted to extend his time as ruler, not when the tasks were clearly going to be too much for him and soon.

No, my father was fighting to avoid losing to me.

And that was why, whatever he said, I always would find victory.

Because I was not fighting a war of pettiness, but one for the people of my country.

"You have until the wedding to vacate this place. We will notify the Council that power is changing hands, and we will notify the press that my bride has changed. And we will come up with a suitable story for how I have only just now discovered my heir. And if you do anything that I do not care for in the meantime, that story will become more fact than fiction, and you will not like the results."

I considered how much I was counting on my father's ego to remain predictable as I made my way back to my home across the city.

He was a dying man, and many could argue he had nothing to lose. It was true enough. But for my father, legacy would always count in the end.

I wondered if it occurred to him that I had control of that legacy. Because whatever I told him while he drew breath I could change once he was gone.

The ultimate tragedy for a man who sought to control everything in his life, I supposed. A man who did not think he had to give deference to a son who was beneath him.

Not even my father could manipulate death. And once he was gone, he would have power over nothing.

The house on the hill was not my home.

I had never given much thought to homes.

The castle had always felt very much like my father's domain, and like it was sadly tainted by the sins of the previous generations.

One thing my father would get to live to see, and it gave me an extreme amount of pleasure, was the joy that our people would feel when he was finally removed from the throne.

My wedding would be a cause for celebration in a way no one had anticipated.

And—something I had not thought of—Marissa would be a welcome bride, even though she was not from Pelion, by sheer virtue of the fact that she was the method by which my father was uninstalled.

In contrast to the darkness of the palace, my home was made of light. Windows and stark walls, and white marble on the floors.

Not because I was a creature of virtue so much as even devils got tired of hell.

I was so used to my staff being invisible and everything being in a certain order that the disruption in the white—Marissa's figure and Lily's small one—gave me pause.

"You're back," she said.

"Yes," I said, battling against the warring responses

to the sight of both of them that were occurring in my body. There was an ache when I looked at Lily and I did not know what to call it.

I *knew* what I felt for Marissa.

And I disliked very much the sensation that she was holding the most vulnerable part of me in her hand and guiding me around by it.

If she wanted to do that, she had to give me pleasure, rather than just attempts to manipulate.

"Have you not found everything to your liking?"

"Lily wanted to see more of the house," Marissa said.

"It's the biggest house I've ever seen. Is it the castle?" Lily asked.

"No," I said, working to gentle my tone. "We will move into the castle after the…after the wedding."

Lily's eyes were shining. "You're going to marry my mom."

"Yes," I said. "And she will be a princess too."

Lily was enraptured, clearly captured by what to her felt like a real-life fairy tale. She wrapped her arms around her mother's leg. "We'll be princesses together," she said.

Marissa, for her part, tried to force a smile and patted Lily on the back. "Yes. We will."

"Can I go and get Nana?"

"Sure," Marissa responded.

Lily bounded up the stairs, her dark curls bouncing behind her.

"What were you doing?" Marissa asked.

"You don't care what I was doing," I said. "Remember, I have permission to be with anyone I choose at any time I choose. Your edict, Marissa, not mine."

"It was not a question of where your private parts were, Hercules, but your person."

"I was speaking to my father," I said. "And somehow I managed not to kill him." I made my way over to the bar that sat in the corner of the living area and I poured myself some scotch. Crutches be damned, some things were better done with alcohol.

"I see."

"It has never been a secret to me that he was a monster. But he kept my child from me, Marissa, and I cannot forgive that. I will not."

"Why should you? If you had come back into my life simply telling me you had changed your mind… If you had known about Lily all this time, I would not have forgiven you. There are some things that are simply unforgivable."

I thought of her, as she had been. Young and pregnant and alone. And for the first time, I could see clearly enough through my rage to truly think of her as a victim.

I had cast her in the role of defector for so many years. And then the shock of discovering that I had a child had…

It had undone my world.

And then it had put it back together with strange and new possibilities, and I had not been able to ignore the political implications.

"I'm going to need you," I said.

Because it did no good for me to dwell on the past. On what might have been, and who she was to me. On how terrified she must have been. Alone and…heartbroken.

It didn't sit well with me.

When I had touched her, I had known that I had crossed a boundary I normally would not.

Virgins were not something I had ever cared to trifle with before. There were too many unintended consequences.

But I had decided on some level that I would make Marissa mine, and so I had justified it.

And then, when she abandoned me, I had recast her in my mind in the role of scarlet woman somehow, even though I knew full well that she had never known the touch of a man before me.

Marissa.

No, there was no point in thinking of her that way. It was better to focus on now.

"Need me for what?"

"We have to speak to the press."

"Why do you need me for that?"

"Because. Because I need to put a face to my new bride, for all the world to see. Because there is going to be an interest."

"I'm exhausted," she said.

"And we are getting married in two weeks' time. Sleep now if you can. Try to catch up. Tomorrow, they will be here."

"In the house? I don't want Lily on camera."

"You understand that is impractical. Lily will be on camera from now on to the rest of her life. She is going to be a public figure. An object of interest and curiosity. It is far better that we have Lily on camera when we decide. Far better that we have official photographers taking her photos. It will be better, trust me."

"I… But she's very little. And this is all very new."

"Tomorrow I will only need you. But you will have to look the part. And whatever your personal feelings on me or the subject…you will have to look as if you can bear my touch."

The air went thick between us, and she captured her lower lip between her teeth. Worrying it.

I reached out and then dropped my hand quickly. I had been about to touch her. But I refused.

I would not allow her that kind of power. I would not allow her that kind of control.

Everything had been put in motion. By my hand.

I had the power here, not her.

We would both do well to remember it.

CHAPTER SEVEN

Marissa

I SLEPT TERRIBLY. I kept waiting for Lily to crawl into my bed, because I was certain that the new environment would be uncomfortable for her, but she didn't come.

And when I woke up early in the morning, unable to stand staying in bed any longer, I tiptoed down the hall to her room and found her sleeping like the little princess she was in the middle of a giant king-size bed. She barely made a dent in the feather mattress; her dark hair spilled over the pillow.

She felt happy here. She felt safe. I was the one with the issue.

But then, I was the one who had a history with Hercules.

I sighed heavily and padded down the stairs, searching for coffee. I kept waiting to see Hercules. But he didn't materialize.

And when the sun finally came up, I could see the breathtaking view out the window. The craggy, glorious mountains all around limned with gold. And below...

The sea. The glorious Mediterranean burning like a jewel in the early morning.

This place was beautiful.

It would be my home.

I could see the ocean.

The wave of relief I felt at that realization surprised me.

Lily and I were near enough to the water in Boston. We didn't have a view, but we could easily walk down to the harbor.

Even so, sometimes I ached for the beautiful simplicity of the shorelines in Medland. The bristling seagrass that grew from the soft sand hills and the rich blue water.

This was different. But it was so close. The sea as if it was illuminated from its center.

My heart felt inexplicably tied to the ocean.

And it made sense suddenly that it was by the ocean I had first seen Hercules.

I stood out on the balcony, looking down over the water for an untold amount of time, until I heard the sound of footsteps behind me.

It still wasn't Hercules.

It was a woman, immaculately dressed, her hair and makeup flawless.

"You must be Marissa?" She spoke with faintly accented English, her voice gloriously cultured. "I am Isabella. I'm here to help you get dressed for the press conference."

It turned out that Isabella's statement was an understatement. She was not there simply to help me get dressed, but to acquaint me with an entirely new wardrobe that she had selected sometime between the moment I had been whisked away from Medland and when we landed in Pelion.

We set aside multiple items to be altered and chose one formfitting red dress that fell past my knees and was cut classically, that needed only a bare minimum of sewing sorcery. Isabella accomplished it in moments. Then she did some expert styling on my hair, promising that I needed a bit of salon time and would get it later on.

She also did makeup, miraculous things with it—things that I hadn't known were possible.

With a bit of shading, she made my face look narrower, more sharply defined, and with some glue and fake lashes made my eyes look stunningly wide.

"Camera ready," she said.

I turned and looked in the mirror, feeling shocked by what I saw. "That doesn't look like me."

"It doesn't have to. It has to look like a princess."

I recognized the truth of that. It wasn't meant to be insulting, not in any way. It was simply the truth.

Hercules needed to present a woman to the country—to the world—who was believable. Who could be likable enough to smooth over the narrative that was going to have to be spun about the existence of Lily.

Come to think of it, I didn't even know what that narrative was going to be. And I still hadn't seen Hercules. So we had not had a chance to talk about it.

As soon as Isabella was finished, she whisked me out of my bedroom and down the stairs. And then suddenly she was gone, and Hercules was there.

"We will be meeting the members of the press out in the courtyard."

His eyes flicked over me, and I saw heat there that made my skin feel like it was prickling.

"She's done a good job."

"Yes," I responded.

"We will tell them you did not know my identity, and I didn't know about Lily, and it was only recently when headlines of my engagement hit the news that you realized who I was. You came to me, not to destroy my wedding, but to make sure that I knew about my daughter. And that was when we decided it would be best if we were together."

It was so close to the truth, and it made my heart twist. I should be happy with that. That it wasn't an outright lie. But…

"It's not exactly a story that will sweep people away."

"What do you want?"

"It's not about what I want," I said. "But…people want to know. They'll want to dig in deep. And I… It all sounds so practical, and there's nothing beautiful to weave from it. People want to weave a story."

"We are marrying for practical reasons."

"Yes," I said softly. "But don't you think it would be more impacting if you said that when I came to find you, you realized that… I was what you had been missing all along?"

The words tasted so strange on my lips, almost like honey, and a surge of longing welled up inside of me, and worse, hope.

Hope was a beast inside me I could not seem to banish.

"I like that," he said. "I'll use it. You're right. It is

much more compelling. Unfortunately, not much can be done for Vanessa's feelings."

"Did she love you?"

He shook his head. "No. I don't believe so. She will be angry that she isn't going to be Queen. On that you can trust me. It has been a goal of hers most of her life. She has always known that she was the most suitable woman in all the land for the heir apparent."

"Bloodlines."

"Bloodlines," he said. "They are all important when you are royal."

"For all that my father was difficult, and there were things that he…that he did and said that I feel were wrong… I was taught that people were more than blood. That we are spiritual. That our souls are what truly matter. This idea of blood overshadowing everything is so foreign to me."

"It's a lovely concept," he said. "That a human being's spiritual self might matter more than, say, who his father was. But in my experience that is simply not the case. Man is a physical being. He wants power. Above all else. And the best way to consolidate that is with money. And then you can make rules. Any rules you like. About how the power can only be passed down through blood. When a man is hungry, he eats. When he desires a woman, he finds physical release with her. When he is tired, he sleeps."

"And what does he do when he is sad? What does he do when he's lonely? When he has a fear, or a hope or a dream, who does he confide in? And when he finds satisfaction for those things, what does it feed? His body? Or his soul?"

"I don't believe in what I can't see. What I cannot touch."

"That's very sad."

"Everything else is simply the way man builds justification for things. All manner of things. We dress our selfish desires up as matters of the heart, as dreams and callings... Morality can be lost much easier than when we view the world through black-and-white terms."

"Well, for the purposes of the press conference, perhaps we should borrow from my philosophy more than yours."

"I believe it likely we should."

I didn't know why the conversation with him made me sad and happy all at the same time. It reminded me a bit of the kinds of talks we used to have down by the shore. All kinds of things.

Ideas that challenged my view on the world and on myself.

But there hadn't been an edge to him then, not like this. It was as if he'd let his guard down with me then, rather than wrapping his every word in hardened cynicism.

I studied his face. There were new lines there. Grooves that had settled in by his mouth, by his eyes, just in the years since I had seen him.

I wanted to will them away. To will him back in time.

But I couldn't. And I knew it.

But we were in the here and now, and he was propelling me out the door and toward the courtyard. It was beautiful, flagstone and vivid green grass, surrounded by glorious flowering bushes.

The security detail was there, and a limited number of press members had arrived as well.

"We will stand in the front. You will stand beside me. You do not need to speak. I will do the talking."

And then I was following him, right into the public eye. I stood beside him, my hands clasped in front of me as I had seen any number of political wives do at press conferences over the years. I did my best to mimic that pose. That smile, and those rigid, resolute shoulders that they seemed required to possess, whatever their husband might be confessing to.

"I thank you for coming today for this announcement. I appreciate that it is a bit unorthodox. But it seemed the best way to proceed. After I am done speaking, I will give the opportunity for three members of the press to ask a question. And only one question. Then we will be done, and you will be escorted from the premises."

I could feel the need to ask questions radiating from the people in the audience, but they all seemed too afraid to do anything out of turn.

"To begin with, my marriage will still proceed on the appointed date. But I have an important announcement regarding the bride. Vanessa and I will no longer be getting married. Instead, I am marrying Ms. Marissa Rivero of Medland, Massachusetts."

To those who didn't know, that might make it sound as if I had a pedigree. Medland was known for being the preferred second, third or fourth home location of the rich, connected and political. But anyone who truly understood would know that if I was from Medland, I was not one of those people.

If you were well-off, you spent summers there. You didn't live there.

You certainly weren't from there.

"I knew Marissa years ago, and we had a romance," he continued, yet again being very careful with his wording. "Due to the delicate nature of my position, I did not reveal to her who I was, and she was not aware. When our relationship was cut short during a time when I had to return to Pelion, she could not locate me, and when I returned to find her, I could not locate her. Over the course of years, she discovered who I was, and was only recently able to establish contact. When she did, I discovered that she'd had my child."

The members of the press couldn't help it—a wave of shock went through them, and chatter rose up in the serene garden.

Hercules held his hand up. And as if he'd roared, they silenced. "I'm not finished. When she found me, not only was I overjoyed to discover that I was a father, but I also found I was overjoyed to be reconnected with her. It was a relationship that I…was never ready to let go of. And I knew that I could not let her get away from me again. It is with great regret that I broke my engagement to Vanessa off, but she understands the extraordinary circumstances that were at play."

The crowd shifted, and scattered observers began to stand, lurching forward, questions competing with each other to exit their mouths first.

"I'm not finished," he said again, and again, the crowd stilled. "Further, on the date of our marriage, I will be crowned King of Pelion. Marissa will be my consort, and that is the final word on it."

They all stood frozen, like dogs on the hunt waiting to be given the command. They didn't want to incur a scolding from him yet again, Marissa assumed. The disapproval of Hercules Xenakis was a powerful thing.

He inclined his head. "Now you may speak."

They all jostled for position, raising their hands and hurling out queries. But Hercules pointed to one.

"This question is for Ms. Rivero," the first man said.

I didn't know that I would be asked questions, and I wasn't certain if it was allowed, but Hercules did not deny them, so I turned my focus to the reporter. "Did you track him down finally solely because he was getting married?"

My tongue felt thick and my heart was pounding hard. I didn't have experience speaking in front of people. I'd even avoided it in church, during prayer or when we'd been asked to share good news in our lives.

But this was for Lily.

I would be a reflection on her, and I had to deal with my nerves, I had to deal with my reservations, my issues, because they would rebound onto her. It couldn't be helped.

"Yes and no," I said. Which was true enough. "I had no other way of getting in contact with him. But his location for his celebration before the wedding was revealed. And so I was able to approach him. And I was able to tell him…to tell him about our daughter. The timing is unfortunate, I know, but believe me, if I had been able to tell him sooner, I would have done."

Hercules looked at me, the expression in his dark eyes unreadable. Unknowable. I would have given much to be able to see into his mind. "There is a duty that a man in my position must assume for his country. A responsibility. Making Lily legitimate is part of that responsibility. She is my heir, and the future ruler of this country. Therefore, whatever speculation you might want to apply to Marissa's motives, you should know that the right thing was done here. What sort of man would I be, what sort of King would I be, if I ignored my child? If I refused to recognize her, to grant her the legitimacy that she requires. What sort of man would I be if I replaced my heir with another simply to avoid making waves? What would that mean for her? Indeed, for the fate of a nation. But quite beyond that… A man might have responsibilities, but a man has a heart as well. And when I saw Marissa again, I knew that I could not ignore mine."

I was shocked by the words that had come out of his mouth, for they were in direct opposition to the sort of thing that he had said to me just before we came out here. He wrapped his arm around my waist and then he was pulling me to him. And I couldn't breathe. I couldn't think. All I could do was feel. All I could do was breathe him in. Him. Hercules.

My greatest triumph and my greatest sin.

The man who had made me a woman. In so many different ways. More ways than just the simple euphemism that was often used for that phrase. No. It was his attention that had given me strength. His touch that had made me wild, and his betrayal that had made me fearless.

And now it was his hand on my chin making my heart beat so fast that I thought I might fall over.

When he claimed my mouth with his, it was like the

world exploded. Brilliant bursts of light behind my eyes that left me trembling, shaking.

His mouth was like I remembered it. Warm and firm, but so much better now for all the years of separation.

Like going home.

I had just returned home after a five-year absence, and it had not been like this.

It was as if I'd been struggling with a door for years, and he'd handed me the key to the lock, only to have it click in place and turn easily.

I felt walls collapse inside of me. Walls that had been protecting me. That had been closing off so much in the way of feeling.

Of being a woman.

I had become Lily's mother. And when I had taken that role on, I had assumed it entirely. I had made myself forget. I had made myself forget the rude insanity of what had caused my change in identity in the first place.

I had done it deliberately. And I had done it well.

But it had only been sleeping. It had not been banished.

That mouth.

He parted my lips with his, sliding his tongue against mine, and that was not for the press, I knew. Because a kiss to the mouth would've been just fine without increasing the intimacy.

He had done that for me.

To show me. To show me that no matter what I said I still wanted him.

Of course, I had known that already. I didn't need his games as a reminder.

It was why I had told him that we would not be having a physical relationship in the first place.

Because I understood that in that equation I was the one who was vulnerable. I was the one who would be wounded.

But right now, I was just the one on fire.

And I was gladly allowing myself to burn.

His hands were large and warm, pressed in the space between my shoulder blades, holding me firmly. He was such a breathless temptation. And I wanted to give in. I remembered all too well how it felt. To leap off the edge of reason and into his beautiful obsidian abyss.

It took me minutes—at least it seemed so to me—to realize that I was making a fool of myself on a public stage. I was melting in the arms of this man for all the world to see.

But I couldn't pull away, because we were being watched. Because this was the moment he'd warned me about.

It was for show.

It was for show.

That doused some of that fire in me.

It wasn't that Hercules wanted me so. He wanted to drive the point home to the press that what he'd done he did out of duty and love, to instill in his people a sense of confidence that he was a ruler who would do things in a much more measured way than his father.

When we parted, he still held me, his arm around my waist.

And he took a breath. Just one, but it was ragged at the edges, and it gave me the hope that he had not been unaffected by what had passed between us.

I shouldn't care.

I truly shouldn't care.

"So you see," he said, his voice slightly lower. Slightly rougher. "There is duty, and then there is something that goes beyond it. It would've been a grave misstep for me to carry on with my engagement to Vanessa, even though it would have been the path of least resistance. But I'm not a man who takes the path of least resistance. I'm a man who acts for the best interests of all those involved. And I am a man who will do more than simply lead clinically, as has been done before me.

"And I will make change where change must be made. To ensure that the citizens of Pelion are living with freedom and are not being shut out of the comforts which the royal family has enjoyed without them for far too long. I hope, if you can, that you will see these actions I've taken now as an indicator of who I am, and that you will find it to be positive."

Another reporter stood up.

"No further questions," Hercules said.

"You said we got three," the man said.

"I did," Hercules confirmed. "I have changed my mind. And as I told you, I reserve the right to do so."

And then he whisked me away from the reporters, and from the clamor behind us, ushering me back into the house.

I had to lean against the wall for strength, my energy suddenly draining out of me as if those questions had punctured a hole in me. And I told myself it was because all of this was overwhelming. Not because Hercules himself was overwhelming.

"You did well," he said, his dark eyes appraising me,

but I saw it there. That he wasn't unaffected. And my own heart tripped over in response.

"The wedding is in two weeks' time," he said. "I have no doubt you'll be prepared for it."

"I'm glad you don't have any doubt, because I… We don't really know each other, Hercules. We had stolen time together away from both of our real lives. I'm a pastor's daughter who never left the island the whole time I was growing up. I wasn't thrust into the real world until after I had Lily… And I had to become so…so hard to protect myself. To protect her. To stop myself from missing what I'd left behind so much that I ached. All the time. And you… All of this is yours. It's your legacy. But it isn't mine."

"But it is Lily's," he said, his voice firm. "And that you are bringing yourself into it so she can have it is a great thing you've done."

I was floored by the compliment. "That might be the first nice thing you've said about my parenting."

"I've had time to accept that what you did… You had no other choice. That it was my father who did this to us. Not you."

"It's forced you to have empathy."

"I wouldn't call it that. I would simply say that there is no logical way to look at it that casts you as a villain, Marissa, and I am a man of logic, always willing to be corrected if a more reasonable scenario presents itself."

"Well, I'm happy that my villain status seemed unreasonable to you."

"There is much to be done in the lead-up to the wedding. Much diplomacy to be handled, seeing as I am assuming the throne the day of the wedding, and there will be policy ready to be enacted upon the exact hour. I will not see much of you over this time."

It was a relief, though I didn't tell him that. "Okay. I think I can handle that. Since I haven't seen much of you over the past five years."

"Lily will be the flower girl for the wedding."

My heart squeezed tight. Because somewhere in all this was a mixed-up fantasy of what I had dreamed would happen all this time, even if it hadn't been a conscious dream. That my Prince had come, even if he was late. That our daughter would share in our special day.

Except, it was not our special day. It was Lily's, perhaps. It was the kingdom of Pelion's. And those were good things. But the last thing it was about was myself and Hercules. And, no matter how incendiary a kiss between us might be, I had to remember that.

If I didn't, I was in danger of breaking all over again.

And I wasn't sure that I had it in me to emerge stronger the second time. I didn't know if I would be able to emerge at all.

"In two weeks," I said, nodding my head purposefully and turning away from him.

Because I had to turn away. Because I had to be strong.

Because none of this was for me.

And it never would be.

CHAPTER EIGHT

Hercules

THE DAY OF the wedding, of the coronation, dawned bright and clear. My father was nowhere to be seen, and I was not unhappy with that. I was told by members of staff that he had gone up to his new home—a lavish keep nestled in the mountains—and would likely not be coming down.

It was fine by me, and I would be making an announcement regarding the King's health for the benefit of the media.

I was ready.

Ready for all of this to be cemented. Ready for it to be over.

We had settled into a pattern at my home, the four of us. Lily chattered and filled the awkward spaces that existed between the adults, and Marissa's mother had assumed an easy and content position nannying the child. Marissa had been undergoing a crash course in the customs and laws of the country, and what duties were required of a royal spouse.

Meanwhile I had made sure that every piece was in

place for an easy transition of power and that I could swiftly repudiate the prohibitive laws my father had placed that kept the people in poverty.

Change what happened. And I knew that change would not be instantaneous, but it would be as close to it as possible under my watch.

And Lily would bear witness to it. To the changes that a good ruler would make, and I had confidence that she would make changes of her own. Her sweet nature—which seemed natural to her—surprised me at every turn.

And it made me wonder if she would have turned out half so well at this point in time if she had been raised with me.

There was something in that child—a lightness—that was not in me. And I knew that it could have only come from Marissa.

I wouldn't see Marissa until she actually began to walk down the aisle, but I did see Lily, dressed all in white, with ribbons woven through her dark hair and a basket of flowers in her hand. She lit up, and she ran to me, opening her arms.

And the sight was enough to bring me to my knees.

I did not understand how this worked. I had never cared for children much at all. I didn't dislike them, but they weren't often in my presence. My sister had been born when I was fifteen, but my father had never allowed me much interaction with her.

But every fiber of my being responded to this child, and I knew beyond a shadow of a doubt that I would wage war for her.

Essentially, I had. And it had nothing to do really

with fairness to her. Everything to do with the fact that I wanted her. She was my child, and I wanted her as mine. I could not go on in a world where I knew she existed and pretended that she did not. An emotional revelation for a man like me, especially one who had a father such as mine.

Every so often that terrified me.

Because wanting just for the sake of it was a dangerous sort of drug. The beginning of all those outrageous justifications that my father himself engaged in.

A man had to act from a more morally superior place than his own soul. And I knew that well.

My father acted from a place of using his own desires as guidance, and he had not been a good father.

I might not know how to be one either, but one thing I knew for sure: I did not want to be like him.

"Daddy," Lily said, "do you like my dress?"

I was frozen. I didn't know quite what to do or say. "Yes," I said, the word sticking in my throat.

"It's good for twirling." She spun in a circle happily, and the freedom and simplicity with which she did things struck me. Because while I was contemplating the future of the country, of my humanity, just before my wedding to Marissa, Lily was spinning circles.

I had never been a carefree child. I had not been allowed. I wondered how different I might have been…

But then, there was no point mourning the loss of childlike joy.

What I had become was what was needed for Pelion, for my people, my country. And I would honor my responsibilities.

Right now, that responsibility included seeing to Lily's happiness.

That was a logical choice.

I liked what Marissa had built in her. And I could see how she was the future of Pelion.

I could see that I would have to work at being a softer parent than my own had been.

That satisfied me because it was a logical conclusion that would put me in a position where I would not crush my daughter's spirit. The very thought of crushing my Lily made my chest feel like it was so tight I couldn't breathe.

I moved to my position at the front of the church, and I looked around. It was amazing, the number of people that had come for this. Who were looking to the future of Pelion. We were all done with business as it had been conducted under my father's reign. So many of the people in my country didn't even know life out from under his thumb. But it would change.

It was all changing today.

And I kept my thoughts on the state of the country as music began to play. As my daughter came down the aisle with her flower petals and a grin on her face to light up the entire church.

And then the music changed, and the spectators stood. And I knew beyond a shadow of a doubt that if it had been Vanessa I was waiting for, if it had been Vanessa concealed by those double doors, my chest would not be locked up like there was a rock directly in the center of it. I knew. I knew. I knew.

But as it was, I found that I could not breathe.

That kiss...

Two weeks ago, my lips had touched Marissa's for the first time in years. And I remembered.

Remembered why that particular spark was an insanity that transcended all else. I remembered why I had been willing to overturn cars, my life, anything in order to get another taste of the passion that was between us. A passion that was unlike anything else I had ever experienced. Marissa. An intoxicating flavor unlike any other. I needed it like none I had ever known before.

And then those doors parted, and it was like the sun had been let into that old stone building.

She was an angel. An angel of light come down into hell with me.

I was going to take her back to that glittering obsidian palace, full of darkness and soaked in centuries of despair.

And I did not even regret it. How could I? How could I win this vision of beauty that was mine to capture? Mine to hold an ethereality just short of heaven that had fallen down to earth so that I might pick her up and conceal her in all that darkness.

The dress was a cloud, falling effortlessly over her body, swirling around her legs with each step she took. The neck was square and low, revealing a tantalizing amount of her beautiful curves.

Her dark hair was pulled back, wisps of curls cascading around her face.

I was thankful that the makeup for the wedding day was more natural than what she'd had the day of the press conference. She had been beautiful—she was always beautiful—but I had missed that familiar beauty.

As she drew closer, she filled my vision, made the edges of the view before me go fuzzy, until it was only her I saw.

For three years I had seen only Marissa.

So this was a familiar state for me.

But not a comfortable one.

And she thought that we would not consummate this marriage.

I reached out, and she took my hand.

It was trembling.

I was cast back to that first time we'd been together on the beach in Medland.

She'd been a virgin, and I had ached with a strange sense of humility.

That she had given her body to me. That she had done so with joy, in spite of her nerves.

I had never known such a feeling. I had never been given such a gift.

I was struck with the parallels between that moment and this. This vision in white walking toward me like a virgin sacrifice.

But she was not a virgin.

And she was not giving herself as a gift.

I had to remember that.

I had not told her about what was to happen after the wedding. She would not be happy.

But the decision had been made, and I had not consulted her. She would have to get used to such things.

The vows felt like they had an especially heavy weight to them. Perhaps because I was promising myself to her for the sake of a nation and promising myself to the nation as well. And to Lily. Because the vows were a tangle of vines around the both of us, and so many other things.

But then, nothing else mattered. Because then it was time for me to kiss her again. And it consumed me.

When the minister gave the command, I was more than ready. And it didn't matter to me that we were in a church, or that we had onlookers. All that mattered was her.

I cupped her face with my hands, and the silk of her skin made me shudder. I leaned in, inhaling the scent of her. Her beauty. Her perfection.

Her.

And then I tasted her.

Slowly at first, encouraging her to part her lips for me that I might taste her even deeper.

And she obeyed.

I would feast on her, except that I knew I would not be able to gorge myself entirely on her beauty because there were limits to what could be expressed here and now. So I ended the kiss, with much more regret than I care to admit.

We were then pronounced man and wife, and immediately after I took bonding vows to become the King, as she vowed to be consort and, like myself, put the kingdom of Pelion before all else.

It was a funny thing, but as she took the vows, I knew that they were a lie. She would not put the kingdom above all else, because she would always place Lily above anything else in the world. And I found a measure of satisfaction in that. Because whatever my feelings, they would not be hers. She would be the one who compensated for all my shortcomings. And I would rule. As I should. As I must.

When it was done, I bent down and picked Lily up from the ground, holding her, and she clung to me as if it were the most natural thing in the world.

It was not. Not for me, still not. But that it was for her was one of the more revelatory things I had ever experienced.

We would do official portraits later, but for now, these would be the first photographs together of us as the royal family.

Family.

It was one of those words that was thrown around often enough, though in my family, it was more likely that you would hear about blood. Blood, that most important of connectors, that essential component that made a person, and/or Royal, worthy or not in the eyes of my father.

It meant something different to me in that moment, and I could not credit why, which was added to the list of unsettling things I'd been grappling with for the past two weeks.

There were postwedding celebrations planned, but we would not attend them. It was not customary for a royal couple to do so. They would either retire to small, private parties, or they would do as we were about to do.

I set Lily down, taking hold of her hand, and we walked down the aisle together.

Marissa's mother, who had been seated in the front row, joined us, and when we were in a private room at the back of the church, I knelt down in front of my daughter. "Will you be all right staying with Nana for the next week?"

Lily frowned. "What?"

"We are going to move from the big house into the palace," I said. "But it will take some time." Some of that to do with the fact that I was having every piece of my father's legacy removed from the place.

"And your mother and I are going on a honeymoon."

Marissa sputtered, "You didn't say anything about a honeymoon."

"I know I didn't, because I suspected you would fight me. But this is not something worth having a fight over, my Queen. It is a tradition among royal families that we retreat to the private island for this period of time away from the spotlight, away from all others. It has been prepared for our arrival, and there is no question of whether or not we will go."

"You would have gone with Vanessa?" she asked, and I was surprised at how quickly she reversed the immediate spark of rage in her eye.

"Yes," I responded. "I would have. As tradition dictates."

"Our agreement stands."

I cast a glance at my new mother-in-law. "Our agreement stands," I said, and I wonder if her mother had any idea what that agreement was.

I gritted my teeth, because of course I could not help but imagine demolishing that resolve of hers.

"You might have asked me," she said.

"Did you have other plans?" I asked.

Perhaps not the best tone to take immediately with one's mother-in-law looking on, but I was King, after all.

"You know I didn't," she said.

"You and Lily will have free run of the house while the palace is being prepared," I said to her mother. "When Marissa and I return, we will all go together."

"Are you all right?" her mother asked.

"I'm fine," Marissa responded. "If not blissfully happy."

It was all quite a bit much in the way of family connection for me. Given that I had been raised by wolves essentially. Blue blood notwithstanding.

"We must go," I said.

"Now?"

Marissa suddenly looked terrified.

"Is that a problem?"

"I've never left Lily."

Lily patted her mother's arm pragmatically. "You'll be back," she said.

Marissa looked stunned.

"Yes," she responded, looking down at her daughter with wide eyes.

"And I'll be with Nana," Lily said.

"Yes again," came Marissa's reply.

"Then it's settled," I said.

"Do I have to go in this dress?"

"No, don't be silly. I've had your going-away outfit selected for you."

"What is it?"

"Something befitting a honeymoon on a private island."

CHAPTER NINE

Marissa

I WAS MARRIED, and I was a queen.

And still, my predominant concern was the fact that I was going to a private island dressed in a very brief gold dress that left little to the imagination with a man who I was going to have a very hard time resisting if he put his mind to doing any sort of seducing.

I felt the strangest things in that moment, and I had no idea what to do with them. I was…sad and terrified and filled with guilt at leaving Lily, but there was also a strange sense of exhilaration inside of me.

I hadn't spent even one night apart from Lily since I'd given birth four years earlier. I didn't know what it meant to be away from her. And now I was going to a private island for a week with only this man for company. No responsibilities. Nothing.

It was an invitation to the kind of sin that I had only gotten a taste of all that time ago. If only things weren't so complicated.

Being pampered the last couple of weeks had reminded me…that I was a woman.

Kissing Hercules twice in the last couple of weeks had reminded me that I was a woman.

Not just a mother. Not just a caregiver. But a woman. One who was sensual, and who had…needs, whether or not I had tried to suppress them. And I had tried.

Lily was well cared for, and the island was certain to be beautiful, and if it wasn't for the fact that I didn't trust myself, everything would be fine.

But Hercules was so big, so hot and hard and beautiful, and I had been reminded yet again today when he had kissed me at the wedding. But at least then I'd had layers of wedding gown in between our bodies, and now I had been reduced to the flimsy article made of netting and gems, and it felt like his heat, his body, was that much closer to mine.

"How come you stayed in a tux?" I asked as our plane touched the ground.

"Because you didn't choose anything for me."

The grin that he treated me to was wicked, almost light, and it made my heart lift, because I had not seen him look like that in…

A long time.

"Can you really leave for a week after being crowned King?"

"Yes. Everything necessary to create a smooth transition was put into place some time ago. And I knew that I would be away. Everything is set in motion. And we are a twenty-minute plane ride away. It's not as if we can't return home quickly if need be."

Considering that Lily was on another island, it was a comforting thought. "There was no one else here," he said, as the door to the plane opened.

"Well," I said, "the pilot is here for now."

"He will be leaving with the plane."

He stepped out of the door and held his hand out toward me, his right foot on the second stair. "Come with me."

I had taken his hand once before, and I had followed him wherever it led. I would be foolish to do it again, and yet I found myself grasping on to him, allowing him to usher me down the steps.

The surroundings were beautiful. Breathlessly so. This island was a rough-cut gem in the middle of the Mediterranean, without another soul or another building in sight. I hadn't realized that a place like this might exist. Or that it would be part of Hercules's legacy. He was so urbane, so very smooth, that I had imagined him out of place on the small island of Medland. Even though it was a sophisticated old-world form of rural living, he had seemed like a fish out of water there. But now I wondered.

There was a car parked partway across the runway, and he led us toward it.

"We will take this," he said. "The house is across the island."

"On a mountain?"

"Naturally," he responded.

"Do rich people live on mountains just for the views?"

"Well, yes, and to remind others of their place in the world. How will people get the full sense of how above them we are if we don't place our houses up off the ground?"

"Good point," I said. "But there are other ways to

lord superiority over people. To make them feel small. My father was an expert at doing it through religion."

"Your father threw you out," he said.

"Yes. When he found out about Lily."

We got into the car and he began to drive.

The scenery outside the window was stunning, lush trees and bright pink flowers with the clear breathtaking sea beyond.

"Your father died," he said, clearly intent on pushing this line of personal conversation.

"Yes," I responded.

"And that's why you were able to reconnect with your mother."

"Yes. She sneaked away to see us sometimes. She lied to him. He controlled her, but...not in the way he thought he did. He...he was terrible. He was a man who liked power more than he loved God. Believe me when I tell you that. And people trusted him... They... I did too. I trusted what he had to say because I didn't know any better. I believed that I had no other choice but to feel guilty all of my life because there was something wrong with me. You don't need money to make people feel small. But in the end... In the end, when you live a life like my father did, I don't know that you leave a lot of people behind to mourn you. More than anything, I mourn what could have been."

"Do you?"

"I mean, I try not to. But sometimes I wonder what it might have been like if we had a different relationship. But then I realize he would've had to be a different man altogether. And that's impossible. I had the relationship with my father he was capable of having. It's sad, but it's true. And there's ultimately nothing that can be done."

"As long as my father is in the history books in the way that he wants to be, he will be happy." He laughed. "I'm not sure how he'll know, but…maybe the view from hell is clear."

I rubbed my chest, but didn't say anything more. After that I didn't need to anyway, because the house came into view. I had thought I was quite past having my breath taken away, but apparently I wasn't.

Apparently, there were still levels of luxury that could shock me.

This house seemed to be made entirely of glass, set into the mountain, facing the sea. If his home in Pelion was beautiful, then this was otherworldly.

The inside was even more amazing, the pale coastal light bathing everything in a glow. Everything was white, as it was in his home.

"You know, this really is an impractical color scheme for children."

"Children?" He arched a dark brow and looked at me.

And for the first time, I saw the future. A possible future, anyway, one that wounded me and lifted me in ways that I could not begin to describe.

Children. Plural. I had not meant to say that, but it was all too easy to imagine.

The two of us having more children, together. Having him with me while I felt sick, while I grew round and while the baby stayed up all night. Seeing him hold a tiny new life that we had created together.

My heart stuttered. "I misspoke. Or rather, I meant children in general."

"Of course," he said.

"Lily could easily turn this room into a Pollock painting in ten minutes."

"I have no doubt. Although, I must tell you, this hideaway was not designed for children."

"I don't doubt it."

"It has always been the place where the Royals could escape to engage in fun. Obviously the house has been updated."

"Your parents came here together?"

"No. My father took lovers here. But I have had the house that he used razed to the ground. It has been under refurbishment for the past five years. This is the first time I have been here since."

"I find that all comforting."

"I thought you might. There is something quite distasteful about bringing your new bride into your father's former den of sin." His lip curled upward. "I find something distasteful about being in it myself. But as I said, none of that original structure remains."

His words seemed oddly symbolic, and I let them settle there for a while, but he didn't continue. Didn't elaborate on it all.

"So here we are, on our honeymoon," he said.

I shifted. "Yes. Here we are."

"You are welcome to change your mind about your rules."

Suddenly, my throat was dry. I felt parched, down to my soul, and he looked... Well, he looked like water. Like the only thing that might make me feel right.

"No," I said, stumbling backward. The moment brought to mind the story of Joseph in the Bible. When his master's wife had tried to seduce him, and he had run away, leaving his jacket behind.

I could imagine doing such a thing now. Running away and, if he grabbed hold of me, slipping out of my dress if I needed to.

But that only put me in mind of being naked with him, and that destroyed the point of the image in the first place. Which was to remind myself that sometimes the better part of valor was absolutely fleeing temptation.

"Then you will find your room at the end of the hall. Upstairs. You will not be bothered. It is perfectly fine for us to spend a week in solitude, I suppose."

"We don't have to be in solitude," I said.

He looked at me, and the expression in his eyes left the soles of my feet scorched. "Believe me," he said. "We do."

Isolation was easy in theory, but not so much in practice. My room was beautiful, my view of the beach, the white sand stretching out empty and pristine as far as my eye could see. And the ocean beyond might have kept me mesmerized for days on end, but I itched to be out in it.

The fact was, we were the only two people on the island, and even given all the space, we couldn't seem to stay away from each other.

Not quite.

We would pass each other on the stairs, down in the kitchen. The kitchen was the worst. Because there was something so unaccountably domestic about those familiar, everyday movements in a kitchen.

The opening and shutting of drawers, the clanging of

silverware, and there was no way that familiarity and domesticity should be attached to a king, especially not a king like Hercules, and yet it was even more impacting than those moments when I had stood in awe of him and his power.

He was a human. He drank coffee.

He walked around in bare feet.

And I was fascinated by him even more than when he had been a man of my fantasies. Something immortal and untouchable. A god from Mount Olympus.

I was fascinated by the way he ate fruit in the morning, by the way he took his coffee.

But I was also afraid to let him know that.

I would look at him out of the corner of my eye and then I would scurry back to safety, to isolation.

I would call Lily and then take a walk on the beach.

On the third day, he found me down there, by the water.

"You do love the beach, don't you?"

"I didn't know anything else for years. And it was always where I would go to be by myself."

"Until you met me."

I took a breath to say something to set him back, but…it left me. Because he was right. Until him. Solitude had been my escape, and then I had met him down by the water, and he had become my escape instead.

"All right. Until you."

"Tell me about Medland. Living on it."

"Why?"

He looked at me as though he was helpless to come up with the answer. "You're the mother of my child, and while we talked about a great many things, we avoided personal details. Someday it might come up in an interview."

But I didn't believe the answer.

"So quiet when no one was around. The people on the islands year-round don't have stacks of money. Or status. It's almost like a place set forty years back in time. Until the seasonal people come. And you know Medland is a high-end escape, for royalty such as yourself. Politicians. Actors. It moves from being the sleepiest, most down-to-earth little community you could possibly imagine into a strange collection of the world's elite, if only for a couple of months at a time. It was a wonderful and strange place to grow up. And being my father's daughter was… Well, I was homeschooled. I didn't attend school with any of the other kids. And no one would have wanted to be my friend anyway, because… Well, no one wanted my father getting wind of anyone's sins."

"I did whatever I wanted," he said. "Always. My father didn't care about debauchery, but he did care that I was strong. He wanted to turn me into a weapon. Strong for him and…callous, I think. And he wanted me to be like him. To care about the quest for power more than anything else, to consolidate our bloodline. To make us richer while the people continued to get poorer. But that is not me. I knew at a young age that I had to defeat him. Not join him."

"I don't know very many boys who would have come to that conclusion on their own."

"Surely it can't be that uncommon."

"I had to meet you to know that I could make another choice. That you discovered that on your own is… Well, it's truly wonderful."

I wanted to close the distance between us, because it felt right, out here on the sand with the ocean bearing witness, because it was something we'd done any number of times before. But not now. Not in this part of the lifetime.

"How did he try to make you tough?" I almost didn't want to know, but I felt that I had to ask. I was so curious about this man. This man that I'd only gotten a piece of all those years ago. But it had felt like everything to me. Only now was I realizing that physical nudity just scratched the surface of intimacy.

And did I really want to court intimacy with him? After all my talk of keeping things simple between us…

It wasn't sex. It was just talking.

"It doesn't matter," he said.

"Yes," I said. "It does."

"No," he said, his tone decisive. "It doesn't matter. Leave it alone."

And then he turned and left me alone, which was what I had said that I wanted.

And now I found I bitterly regretted it.

CHAPTER TEN

Hercules

SHE WAS TEMPTATION. Temptation in a way I was not inured to. In truth, I had never much tested myself when it came to resisting what I might want.

My childhood had been a harsh landscape. My father had taught me to withstand torture. Starvation. Isolation.

And then he had told me that as a man I was free to indulge my appetites as long as I knew how to go without them.

It was a strange life. A firm, iron hand, combined with no discipline at all.

I knew how to go without certain things. Affection, food, water.

Apparently, I did not know how to go without Marissa when she was near.

She fascinated me. And I could tell that I fascinated her. When she approached me, it was often with the trepidation of a small mouse approaching a predator. Her hands were often clasped, just below her chest, her eyes bright as she would speak to me about something she liked—the food, the view, the way that the sun painted the sea with gold before it sank behind the horizon—and then she would scamper off as if she was afraid I might pounce on her at any moment.

She was not entirely wrong to be afraid.

I could not understand the point of resisting the thing between us, and yet she seemed to find it a moral necessity.

Except... I did understand. Why would she take a chance on a man like me?

I was not in the habit of talking to myself, but that had been happening more and more lately. As I questioned her, only to end up questioning myself.

All was running smoothly back in Pelion, at least as it had been reported to me. I received calls every day letting me know of the state of the nation. And I would take any necessary action that was required before going out of my office and into the rest of the house.

Going to Marissa.

To torture.

In many ways, Marissa was the perfect realization of what my father had raised me to endure. Indulgence and torture all rolled into one.

For I looked at her, and I was filled with desire, filled with lust, and I wanted her more than I had ever wanted anyone or anything.

And I constantly made sure that I was in her orbit, just to test my resolve. To test my strength. I wanted her.

I could not figure out why. I had never been able to.

It always came back to the way she had looked at me.

To the fact she wanted to talk to me. Didn't assume she knew what I thought about anything, but rather asked with an openness and innocence that shocked me.

I was distracted, thinking about Marissa when I should be thinking of the tasks ahead of me for the day, when the phone rang.

I answered, and the revelation on the other line turned the blood in my veins to ice as surely as Marissa turned it molten.

"Your father is dead." The palace official went on to tell me that my father had been found dead of an apparent suicide.

I could not fathom it. My father, the most self-interested man in the entire world, had ended his own life. He had never been anything but a master of his own self-preservation.

But then it suddenly made sense to me as I sat there in my office, my head reeling in darkness even as the sun rose high over the ocean.

He had chosen how it ended.

He had chosen it in a way that would make things the hardest for me. Because he knew that it would leave me with guilt, and if he left me with guilt, then how could I go on to sabotage his entire reputation? It was his final manipulation.

His final bit of torture. Rage tore me up inside as I tried to put the thoughts in my head in order.

Should I feel grief? Because he was dead, and there was no coming back from it. His revenge was hollow whether or not that was his intent.

Anger?

I did not want to bargain. Unless…

If I could only have had a few more words with him. He would never know now. He thought he had won.

He would never see that he was the one in the wrong.

Because I could not believe that he had taken his own life in a moment of despair. No. My father didn't have it in him to feel despair.

He would never see. Now he never would.

There was something so desperately hollow in that. Something appalling and vastly terrible in its scope.

Suddenly, I couldn't breathe. It reminded me of when I had been a boy and he had put me inside of a box. The kind of training that the military went through, he had told me. And the leader of Pelion could not afford to be any less stalwart than the military that protected it, because they would go for the King first. My father had told me that.

Isolation for hours, trapped inside of a box where I couldn't even stand up.

That was how I felt now. Unable to breathe. Unable to move. And I had to get out, because the walls of my office were closing in around me in spite of the fact that there were windows on all sides.

I did not know this feeling. I did not know helplessness. I did not know weakness.

Those things had been banished from me when I was a boy. Banished at the hand of the man who put me in that state now, and I hated him. Never had I hated him more in life than I did now in death.

I stormed downstairs, the blackness inside of me an entity that was beginning to escape. It had always been there. It was not new. I knew that. I had always known it was there. But I had always kept it locked behind a wall. Only allowing glimpses out. Reminded when I walked through the obsidian halls of the palace and had it reflected back at me.

But I did not let it out.

But now it was as a torrent of living water. Destroying all that might come into its path.

But I was on an island where there were so few other souls.

But there was one.

And I knew… I knew that if she came near me now I would only destroy her.

I stumbled out of the house, down the path that led to the beach. And she was there. I had gone to find her. I had gone to find her because I no longer had it in me to fight. Not myself, not the beast inside of me and not the desire that I felt for her. Why had I resisted? All this time, why had I resisted?

Why had I allowed her these proclamations?

I was the King.

I was her husband.

She looked up at me, the wind whipping her dark hair around, those eyes bright as that little creature I had only just imagined her to be.

"We are through playing games." I stopped with just a foot between us. "I want you. Do not deny me."

"What has happened to you?"

But any words she might have intended to say next I cut off. I pulled her up against my body, and a muffled squeak rose from her mouth.

"You're mine," I said. "You have been mine for eight years. Since that first moment that I saw you on the beach. Do you not understand that every woman I took into my bed after you was a paltry imitation? Do you not understand that you took me and you turned me into a creature of longing, when I have never had to want for anything in my entire life? If I demanded it, it was mine. But not you. You ran from me. No one runs from me."

And I remembered her questioning that proclamation I had made when we had first reunited. I remembered her asking me if that was true.

And I pushed away the disquiet in my soul. I pushed away the answer.

And I held on to the lie.

And I held on to her.

"There you are," she whispered. And she did not look at me like she was terrified. Those bright eyes examined me, and she lifted her hand, brushing her fingertips against my mouth. "I've seen you like this before."

"You have not," I said. "You don't know who I am. No one does."

"I do," she said. "I saw it. That first day. It might not have been this close to the surface, but I saw it. You hide it from the world. You hide from yourself, but it's there, Hercules. I know it is."

"Is it why you ran away from me?"

"No. I ran away from you that first time because of how badly I wanted to run to you. And I was taught. I knew better. To want something the way that I want you... To feel that sickness inside of me... It could only be wickedness on my part, and so I ran from temptation. And I have run from temptation. Every moment since you have been back in my company, but it was not to please my father, and it was not to save my soul. It was just to save… I am in your world. There must be something of mine that remains."

"I need you," I said. And it galled me to say it. It was why I did not press the issue before, because I had been unwilling to show her how much I needed her. Unwilling to show her what her denial of her body to me cost me.

But I had no pride left.

My father was dead, and for the first time in my life, I had no idea what to do.

And I had run to her.

I was not a man who ran, and yet I had.

But not away from anything.

Just to her.

And I wondered if she would deny me, or if she would demand conversation first.

But instead, she stretched up on her toes and pressed her mouth to mine.

Marissa

He was falling apart inside, and I could see it. And I knew that there was every chance that touching him would pull me into the darkness right along with him. That I would not be able to protect myself once I'd allowed myself to be stripped bare with him. Especially when he was like this.

But this—as little as it made sense—was the part of him that I had always craved. And it was the part of him I had always been denied.

He had been the smooth playboy around me. He had

found something a little bit deeper, and a little bit more authentic, conversations with me that weren't about trading innuendo, but were about the things that we believed in our hearts.

But he had not shown me this.

I had witnessed it, like a voyeur staring through a window, that first time I had seen him when he had thought that no one was watching.

And that was what had ensnared me. I realized the truth of it now.

The whole truth.

For I had not known who he was.

It was not his wealth, his title, his reputation that had fascinated.

It was not the way he teased me. Not the way he laughed. Not the way he touched me or made me call his name.

It was knowing that there was more to him. That he had shown me something just a little more than he had shown anyone else. And that there was yet another secret I might reach.

And he was giving it to me now.

I didn't know why. And in the moment, I didn't want to ask. I didn't feel that I should.

Because he didn't want me to know. And if I asked him now it would break the spell. He might be able to gain his composure. And I did not want that. I wanted him like this.

And later, much later, perhaps I would ask myself where my sense of preservation had gone.

But I already knew the answer.

It went where it always had when it came to Hercules.

And here on this island, we were man and wife. King and Queen of each other and nothing more.

Lily wasn't here.

Here on this island, we were not parents who had been thrown together by our compatible fertility. We were not essential strangers who'd had to marry for a bloodline, for the throne.

We were not those who had taken vows in front of the church only days ago, to each other, to a nation.

We were just Hercules and Marissa.

Even our names seemed at odds, mine so typical.

His, that of a god.

But in this moment my god had fallen, and he needed me to hold him. He needed me to be there for him. To bear witness to this brokenness.

I would ask later why.

Later, we would talk.

But now…

Now I wanted only this. Only him.

I was not a saint, and I had given up the idea that I might be long ago.

In his arms, I was just a woman. And I needed him to satisfy me as only a man could. "If you want me, then take me," I said.

"Give yourself," he said, his voice rough. "Give yourself to me because you have to be in this. All of you. Because if you are not I might hurt you. I might do something you don't like. I need to know that this is not me taking with my darkness but you giving in to it. Step into it, Marissa, but do so of your own free will, because I do not trust myself. Not now."

Perhaps that should scare me.

But nothing about him had ever scared me. Not really. It had been my own self that I was always the most afraid of. The feelings that he called up inside of me, and the way that he made me act in a way that I thought was out of character. A way that I had discovered was my character, at least with him.

He had put me in touch with places and pieces and feelings inside of myself that I had not known existed. And he had made me like them.

Then he had taken himself away from me, and I had been left sitting in charred ruin. Not knowing what to do with this new version of myself, unable to go back to who I had been, unwilling to.

And cut off from the joy that I had found in being new at the same time.

He had taken my journey of discovery and made it a hard climb.

And yes, there was joy in being at the summit, joy in holding my daughter in my arms. Joy in who I had become after that long, hard slog.

But I wanted to return to that spark of joy.

I wanted to go back in time to the first moment I'd seen him and be woman enough to handle the bleakness that I had seen there.

But the good news was I could handle it now.

I had been given a gift. A gift of time. A gift of being able to be with him in the way that we both needed.

Desperately.

And so I did as he asked. So I stepped in with both feet.

I pressed my hands to his face and stretched up on my toes, and I claimed his mouth.

Doing that was exhilarating. Being the one to lean in. To take responsibility for all that we were, rather than being the helpless, innocent virgin. The seducer rather than the seduced.

Oh, I knew enough to know that we were both, he and I, wrapped up in this thing that we could not control. That we didn't want to—not anymore.

A bubble of laughter rose up in my throat, even as I kissed him.

"Something is funny?" he asked, his voice rough, and I knew that I was on dangerous ground.

"It's not really funny," I said. I pressed my hand to his chest. "I always imagined parents as some other *thing*. Off in the distance, remote and mature, and in possession of every answer to the universe. In my father's case, I imagined that he was basically omniscient. And here we are. Parents. And yet the same as we ever were. Still…with this. Between us."

"Because children make the mistake of believing that parents are something different entirely," he said, something dangerous and sharp on the edge of his voice. "That they are not human. When, in fact, that is all they are. And as fallible as any other."

"Yes," I agreed. "Yes." But I didn't say anything more. I simply kissed him again, my lips on his, moving, desperate for access so that I could go deeper. So that we could be consumed in this.

And he gave in, growling and wrapping his arms around me, folding me into the strength of his embrace. I had never felt so safe, so protected and yet so perilously close to danger as I did in that moment.

This was not the sweet touch of a man having deference for his much younger, less experienced lover.

This was a desperation between equals.

And nothing had ever made me more certain of the fact that this had to happen than realizing that.

That this King was standing with me, not above me.

I stripped his T-shirt from his body, marveling at all that golden skin. At the way the years had only improved him. Made his chest deeper, his waist slimmer and more defined. He had more hair on his body, and I found that I liked it. The touch of it. The way that it reminded me he was a man, and so very different from me.

He pulled my dress away, leaving me standing there in nothing but the brief bathing suit that had been provided for me on the island. But I wasn't embarrassed. Then he stood and began to examine me, and suddenly each and every difference in my body felt large and highlighted to me.

My curves were fuller, my stomach softer. White lines marred the place beneath my belly button and my thighs.

I'd had his child, and I bore the evidence of that.

And I wondered what he would say. What he would think.

There was nothing but that endless black fire in his eyes, and he said nothing. Then he reached behind me and untied the top on my bikini, sending it to the sand. He knelt before me and undid the ties on the bottoms. He looked up at me and I was engulfed in the black fire. But I didn't burn away. No, if anything, I only became stronger.

He leaned in, and he pressed his mouth to my stomach. Right to the spot where my skin had stretched, where it was looser now and nothing like how it had been the first time he'd been with me.

I closed my eyes tight, fighting back against tears. I didn't want to cry. I wanted to seize this moment with both hands, to dive into the debauchery of it. To be consumed in the intensity. I wanted to have this. With no thought for the future. No thought for consequences.

For the first time in my life, that was what I wanted.

But I couldn't banish the feeling. The deep, heavy emotion that wound itself around my heart, around my soul.

Because this wasn't just sex, and he wasn't just a man.

And we might not primarily be parents here on this island, but we made a life together.

And there was a heaviness to what we were.

Marissa and Hercules.

We couldn't erase the history between us. And in that moment I didn't even want to. Because it made it all that much more.

The weight was a blessing. The weight was a curse.

The tears spoke of the beauty as much as the sadness, and I wanted to embrace both.

And he was embracing me. The changes in my body. He took a tour of the map that spoke of the years we'd been apart. Of those nine months when I'd carried his daughter inside me.

He kissed every single one of those marks. His big hands explored my thighs, around to my bottom. And he ignited me.

More than just my skin, more than just desire, it was a feeling that was almost too big to be contained inside of my body.

An ache welled up between my legs, my breasts heavy, my nipples aching for his touch.

But if it had been only that, I could have walked away.

He had captured me somewhere deeper. Had made me want in a way that only he could satisfy.

And when I opened my eyes, when I looked at him again, the bleakness there terrified and compelled me.

Hercules.

My only lover. My only love.

My husband.

The list of all the things he was to me was long, and I wondered if it could ever be true for him.

Oh yes, I was his wife. The mother of his daughter.

But did that mean something to him? Did it mean anything beyond the legality?

It didn't matter. Not now.

Because now there were no barriers between us. Now he was taking his jeans off for me. Showing me that body that haunted my dreams.

His powerful thighs, his very powerful... The rest of him.

And when he came back to me, his naked body pressed against mine, he kissed me.

And every hot, hard inch of him was against every pliant, willing inch of me. It was right that it was here on the beach. Because it had always been the beach for us. Always the ocean.

As if we were ready to sail away at any moment, he and I.

But it had always been an illusion. There had always been a duty for him to return to, and there had always been reality to return to for me.

But not now.

Not now.

We were enfolded in his darkness, and I welcomed it. His hands were rough on my body, his whiskers a hard scrape against the tender skin of my breasts as he took my nipple into his mouth and sucked it deep.

The sharp sensation it created between my legs a glorious and honeyed pleasure that I craved. More.

More.

That was what my father had said about the road to ruin.

One step.

One step on the wide path.

The easy path.

You would keep going that way.

But nothing about this felt easy. It was hard in the most beautiful way. Too much and not enough all at the same time.

Heaven and hell converging on a beach.

As we had always been.

He slid his hands down my back, gripped my hips and pulled me up against him, urged me to stand on my toes, and then he lifted me up off of the sand by my thighs, wrapping my legs around his back as he took advantage of the fact that he now opened me to him. He braced me with one arm and put his hand between my legs, stroking me, stroking me until I cried out.

Until I thought I might cry.

He was brilliant. And we were brilliant together.

I had missed this.

As if a part of myself had been revived and I was now whole.

Then he laid me down on the sand, his hardness pressed against my center, and I arched against him, seeking to find the thing that I knew only he could give.

He had ruined even that for me.

Because the pursuit of my own pleasure, when I ached in the middle of the night and couldn't sleep, always took the shape of him.

He was a fantasy I could not banish.

I could want nothing and no one else.

So I had forgone even the pleasure of release on my own, because I couldn't bear to fantasize about the man who had abandoned me and my daughter.

But he hadn't.

And he was here. And he was mine.

And I was his.

"Give it to me," I whispered. "Give me your darkness."

And I did not have to ask him twice.

He wrapped his hand around my head, burying his fingers in my hair, lifting my head from the sand and kissing me with a punishing strength that took my breath away.

He shifted between my legs and surged inside of me, his strength, thickness and power causing me to gasp.

I was unused to this kind of penetration, and it hurt just a little bit.

And somehow that felt all right.

Somehow it felt fitting.

That this was like the first time.

He was in me. All around me.

We were one again, and that was the most right thing in the world even if I couldn't explain it. Even if I couldn't understand it.

His touch left trails of heat across my skin, and as he surged inside of me, over and over again, I was close to completion.

Not just in the sense of pleasure, but in the sense of a wholeness, a fullness and realness that I hadn't known had been absent from me.

The sun was behind his head, and each time he moved, a flash of light would blind my eyes and then it was him. Hercules.

And even when I closed my eyes, he filled my vision, the light from the sun painting ghosts behind my lids.

Hercules.

It had always been him.

He had always been my sanity and insanity. My joy and my sadness. My ruin and my triumph.

He had always been.

He always would be.

And I realized in that moment, as I opened my eyes again and stared at that dear, beautiful face carved from rock, at those eyes that were capable of making me feel desired and making me feel destroyed. That mouth that I knew could deliver the most beautiful of compliments and the most cutting of cruelties, that this was what I had avoided.

Because I knew that once he touched me, it would be undeniable.

And I had thought that perhaps we could parent side by side and have some sort of sweet, amicable relationship. A marriage that was in a marriage. A life together that wasn't together. Hercules and Marissa with a space between them rather than wrapped around each other, but that had never been possible. And it never would be.

Because he was my other piece, whether or not I was ever his.

He had been the path to myself, and I had spent years living away from him, and I had not lost that.

My strength. The fortitude to stand on my own feet.

Even when I thought he had caused my diminishment, I had known that he had also created in me the strength to endure it.

The strength to go against my father, the confidence that what I felt and what I wanted was right.

A whole woman. Not a girl who was under the oppressive thumb of her father, who knew nothing of the real world or what she could be.

Hercules's woman. And that was when I shattered. Not slowly as he was doing, but one moment I was whole, come together completely, and then I was shattered, tossed into the wind like a billion stars in the sky.

And being broken with him was better than being whole had ever been.

Because he was the one who had made me.

And he was the one who had broken me.

I cried out his name as reality shattered through me, digging my fingernails into his shoulders. I had never done that before. I had never left a mark on him. But I would now. The joy that I took in our union would stay on his skin.

And I was proud of that.

With a growl, he froze, finding his own release that left him panting and spent just as I was, his forehead pressed against mine.

We shared the same air. Shared the same breath.

And for a moment we even seemed to share the same heartbeat.

But then that moment was over, and I remembered.

I remembered that he was bleeding something black and ugly from his soul, and I had managed to put a tourniquet on the wound, but I had not healed it.

I looked up at him, and I pressed my hand against his chest. "Tell me."

And on a ragged curse, still buried deep inside of me, he pressed his head against my neck and groaned. "My father is dead."

CHAPTER ELEVEN

Hercules

I DID NOT know what had possessed me to make that confession, still inside of her, still in reach of heaven.

I should not have done what I did. I should not have gone to her as I was. More beast than man, jagged and sharp and unable to control the rage that was coursing through me.

And Marissa did not deserve that.

Whatever I might have thought about her, she did not deserve that.

But she had said yes, and more than yes, she had taken the step toward me as I had demanded.

As if that had somehow taken the blame away from me. To put that squarely on her shoulders as I had done.

Take me.

She had commanded that I take her.

But she had taken me, and thoroughly at that.

In the sand, yet again.

Would I ever have this woman in a bed?

It was a question that I wanted an answer to.

But she had asked me a question, and it had nothing to do with when we might come together again.

I had answered.

And now there was a deathly, still silence between us.

She shifted beneath me. "I'm sorry," she said.

Two words. So quiet. Infused with sympathy.

Empathy.

She knew. She understood. That a horrible father could still be mourned, that the grief for someone such as him could be complicated and double-edged.

I barely understood it myself, but she did. Because she had been through it before. "It means it's over," she said softly. "And that is a terrible blessing."

Terrible blessing. A strange pairing of words, but she was right. It was a wholly terrible sort of blessing. To never have to deal with my father again, but also to never be able to experience the satisfaction of him being forced to change.

"For all I know," she said softly, "my father died believing that he did what's right where I was concerned."

I shifted, moving to lie beside her on the sand.

"Believing that ostracizing me, disowning his granddaughter... That it was the height of his piety. We never got to reconcile. Our final words were... Well, I didn't even speak. It was just him, telling me that I had to leave. Telling me it was the punishment for my sin. That Lily was a punishment. Perhaps it was something too large to repair. I don't know. But I would have very much liked for him to say he was sorry. To know that he knew he was wrong. Even if we could never have a relationship again, I would've wanted that."

"My father was a man beyond redemption," I said. "But I think I was waiting for that as well. For him to understand that he was the villain. But I believe that he died under the illusion that he was going to defeat me in his way. That he was the center of the story. And that he was the one who deserved triumph in the end. And that is…"

"It's not a good story," she said. "It's a terrible story. No one would want to read it, unless they were looking to feel sort of self-important. Unless they were looking to marinate in the gray areas of life, in which case I can only assume they don't have much experience with them. It's only a good story if it's not your reality. And for us…"

"It's uninteresting to watch them continue to be the heroes in their own worlds," I said.

"Very," she agreed.

"He was not a good man." I repeated it, mostly to myself.

She sat up, sand covering her bare body.

She looked so beautiful. She was different now, fuller breasts, fuller curves. She had a dusting of sand over her breasts, and I wanted to brush them off. And then put them in my hands. I was fascinated by her stretch marks. It made her pregnancy with Lily more real to me.

I wanted to focus on that, and not on the situation with my father. Not on the truth of him. Of my childhood.

But that darkness… I could not control it.

And everything was about to come spilling out.

"Do you know how elite military soldiers are trained?"

"No," Marissa said. "I can't say that I do."

She was clearly confused by the direction the conversation was going.

"In almost every country, a variant of these methods is used. But it is not just physical strength they must learn to withstand. They must learn to withstand physical torture. Because they are at risk for being tortured in order for the enemy to gain information. Torture is not simply shoving bamboo under people's fingernails. It is psychological as well. And the military in Pelion is well trained to withstand many forms of torture." I gritted my teeth. "My father believed that the ruler of Pelion must be trained to withstand it as well. He believed that I must be no less trained than our military. He started my training when I was a boy."

"When you were a boy?" She looked so horrified and I had regret that I was bringing my ugliness into her world. But we were the only people here. And she was the only one who had ever listened.

And for the first time in my life, I wanted to talk. Really talk. About what had created me. And what I really was.

"Yes. It was his belief that you created strength in a man early, or he would be compromised at the foundation. He approached me that way. As if I was something he was building. And I… I knew no different."

"Your mother…"

My heart felt like it was being squeezed. "Much like your mother, she did not have a say in most of her life."

She didn't try.

I clenched my jaw tight. There was no opposing the King. I'd had to go to great lengths in order to maneuver into a position where I might oppose my father. What hope would she have had?

Marissa looked away. "I think she would have put a stop to physically harming me."

"But you don't know. When powerful men with dangerous ideals ensnare those around them, when they feel powerless, what are they to do?"

I had repeated the same mantra to myself countless times over the years.

I ignored the hollow ache in my chest.

Like always.

"There were beatings, to be sure. Administered by some of his most elite soldiers. They knew how to make it hurt, but to avoid killing me. Very important, as killing me would defeat the purpose. But the beatings were easier to withstand than the other things. Being locked in a box with sound playing on a loop. Babies crying. Endlessly. I couldn't escape the noise. Sometimes they would strip me bare and hose me off with water as I lay on the cold ground. Shouting at me... Things I couldn't even understand.

"And they would demand that I denounce my father, and I would refuse. And that was how I won. Every time. That was how I proved my loyalty to the throne."

"Hercules..."

"No one has ever pitied me before," I said, marveling at her. "It is something of a novelty."

"Because everyone sees one piece of you. Everyone sees the money. Everyone sees the power, the money, the prestige. They don't know this."

"My upbringing was strict. Isolated. And then I was turned loose when I was fifteen. My father was confident that I had been trained, and he sent me out into the world and told me it was my buffet. I had the foundation I required."

"Why do you suppose he did that?"

"Truthfully? I think because he wanted to have it confirmed that his own debaucher nature was somehow ingrained in his blood. He wanted to watch me go out and do the very same. Have any woman that I pleased, buy expensive yachts and jets and go to the most exclusive parties and indulge myself in drinks and mood-altering substances. He wanted to believe that was the best a man could be, even when he was the very best man. He used me in a variety of ways, and that was just one of them. He created with me a perfect soldier—so he thought—and he created a mirror that showed him what he wanted. But inside I have always been different. I have always known that he was wrong. And when those men told me to denounce my father, I did it a thousand times inside. I didn't speak, not because I was afraid, but because I knew that my father could not see into my mind. Because I knew that I had to stage my coup in the neatest way possible. I feared, always, that any bad behavior would blow back on my mother, and later my sister."

"You feared for your mother's safety?" Marissa asked.

"Yes, of course."

"But she did not fear for yours. Or she was too afraid to act out and protect you. How can you worry for her?"

I shifted, and so did something in my chest. "She was not created to be strong. I was. I was not going to allow what he did to me to break me, Marissa. You must understand that. I had no control over it. No control over what happened to me. But I could allow it to forge me into the blade that would eventually kill my father. I didn't know that it would be quite so literal. I had imagined that it would be political in nature, and it very nearly was. I suspect... I suspect in essence he wanted me to feel that it was me who made that fatal blow."

"Because he knew that it would hurt you."

"Perhaps. Though, I think *hurt* is too strong a word. I'm not sure that he believes I possess the ability to be hurt. I'm not sure if I do either."

"You are hurt. I saw you when you came down from the house. This hurts you terribly."

I shook my head. "Animals feel pain. It's not the same."

"You think you're more like an animal?"

"Elemental. As I was trained to be. I do not feel far beyond what the basest creatures do. I do not have the ability."

"I think you do. I've watched you with Lily."

"It is beneficial for me to be kind to Lily."

I felt nothing when I spoke her name, and I was glad of it. I suddenly felt hollow, and I was glad of that as well.

"That's not the only reason," she said.

"Don't make the mistake of thinking that you know me," I said to her. But I was saying it to my own self as well. For it was easy to lie here with her in the sand, a moment out of time. Which was what we had always had. But when we returned, we would be returning to the palace, and I would be King. I could not afford to take that lightly, nor could I afford to assume that I knew everything about myself or what I was capable of.

I had been created by the hand of a monster, after all.

And the real danger was assuming that I could control the matching creature that lived inside myself.

That darkness.

She said nothing, but the way she looked at me clearly spoke the words for her.

She was intent on seeing the best in me. And I wondered if it was because she had consented to be mine again.

If she had to tell herself that on some level I was a good man or feel sullied by what had happened between us.

Marissa was a good woman.

Of that I was confident.

If anything had changed over the course of the week at the island, it was my certainty of that.

I had spent five years thinking of her as a defector. As one who had betrayed me in a way that no other woman had—because no other woman abandoning me would have felt like a betrayal.

But I had relearned her.

And perhaps the best thing was having confirmed that I had been right about one thing at least.

She was exceptional. She was like no one else. And that meant that I would have to be careful.

She was the one who would have to take the largest part in raising Lily. Because she was the one who would shape the best ruler, one who had not been touched by my father at all. I would make a conscious decision to correct what I could, but Lily would be unspoiled.

Of that, I was certain. Of that, I was resolved.

"Let us go back to the house," I said.

"Will we need to return for your father's funeral?"

I leaned in, and I kissed her, fiercely. "That man has stolen enough from me. He will not steal this too."

That seemed to soothe her, and she leaned against me. Trust. She should trust in me, as did Lily.

I would do my utmost not to disappoint them.

But that would mean keeping my distance.

But we had until the end of this week.

And I would take that with both hands, and her as well.

For when we returned to Pelion, things would have to change.

CHAPTER TWELVE

Marissa

THE TIME ON the island slipped away too quickly. I was angry at myself for spending a week avoiding him, when we could have been together. I was blissfully happy, but I missed Lily.

Of course, when we left here, I would miss being with him as we were now. I knew that. I somehow sensed that things were going to change.

Of course they would.

We would be back in a world that was completely foreign to me. I didn't know how to be a queen.

I didn't know how to live in this country; I didn't know the customs; I didn't know the way of it. Much less how to be royalty within it.

And so, I decided to ask him.

I felt raw, wounded by our coming together down at the beach, but more than that, the conversation we had after.

Thinking of what his father had done to him…

It tore me to pieces inside.

To think that a parent could do such a thing to their child… It was beyond imagining.

And he seemed to think…that he was fine. But I could see that he was not.

Or if not fine, he seemed to think that whatever remained in him was for the best, something that made him the sort of opponent that his father had required.

When I looked at him, I saw a wounded boy. And I knew he would not like that. Not at all.

So I didn't say that to him. Instead, I would touch him whenever I could, not just to solidify the sexual connection, but to find closeness. To offer comfort. I found myself wondering if anyone had ever touched him kindly when he was a child.

Or if all he had known was abuse and negligence. In some ways, he was right. And my mother could easily be accused of actions similar to his own. She had certainly been unable to act against my father in a meaningful way in those years when I had been banished from the home.

But I had read about his mother. About all the traveling she did, the way that she flitted off to tropical islands at her leisure. The rumors that the young Princess was not the daughter of the King.

And I did not doubt that Hercules had believed he needed to protect them. I could see it in the way that he spoke. In every line of his body. He was protective of them.

And from what I had heard about his father, possibly rightly so.

But I had a suspicion that his father more or less

ignored his wife and daughter, and did as he pleased with other women, and did as he saw fit to Hercules.

I wondered how much of the threat directed at Hercules's mother and sister was simply a smoke screen set up by his father. A way to take advantage of the good nature that his son had. Because of course the King possessed none of his own.

I knew that Hercules mourned him in a strange way. But I would not mourn King Xerxes. Not for a moment. Not after the way I had learned he had harmed Hercules.

The physical scars might have long healed, but his emotional scars were deep.

I thought about Lily and the way he seemed afraid to connect with her. Though, he seemed to try at that more than he did anything else. He was a good man, of that I was convinced.

It wasn't that he was incapable of connecting with Lily, or that he didn't want to. To me it seemed as if he was truly frightened.

Of her, of something in himself, I didn't know.

I wanted to fix it.

But I knew that I couldn't.

So instead, I decided to give him a chance to fix me, because that might give him something to tether him to the earth.

"I don't know how to be a queen," I said to him over coffee the morning before our last here on the island.

"Come to think of it," he said, his tone dry, "I'm not sure there is a very decent precedent set for a queen in Pelion."

It was the first time I had ever heard him come remotely close to insulting his mother.

"In what way?"

"You may have noticed that my mother is absent from the country most of the time."

"Yes. Will she return for your father's funeral?"

"Oh, I suppose. They were still married, whether or not they had a relationship."

"And you are not concerned about the rumors that will come from you not going?"

"There will be rumors, of course. But I stand ready to repudiate nearly everything about my father's rule. I will lead with this. And I will make a statement."

I was struck by his strength. By the way his face seemed almost carved from granite.

He was truly an incredible man.

"You're not afraid of scandal, then," I said.

"The only reason that I cared about marrying a suitable woman was that was part of the rules set for my father's early abdication. Once I found out about Lily, I was able to institute a bit of blackmail to ask him to step aside. But then he did the most convenient thing I could imagine and died."

"Well," I said, laughing reluctantly at his dark comment. "I suppose."

"I have never cared anything for convention. For in my eyes, the conventions established in my country were little more than a joke. Ways to keep pompous men like my father in power."

"Has there ever been a queen? I mean…a queen like Lily."

"No," he said. "In fact, that makes me suspicious that they might have…" He grimaced. "I don't even want to think about it. Hopefully no one made a practice of eliminating heirs to the throne based on their gender. Though, they might have just made them go away, the way that he did with Lily."

"He didn't know her gender when he did that."

"No, indeed. But that had everything to do with keeping me from taking power any sooner than I might have." He shook his head. "No. I don't care one bit for the pomp and circumstance of the Xenakis family. We are making a new country. And so you will be the Queen that you decide to be."

"I'm just a girl from an island who happened to meet a prince."

"A prince with very poor self-control," he said.

"That's not true. I think you have amazing self-control, and any indication to the contrary is a little bit of a put-on."

"I didn't have self-control with you."

I took that and held it close to my chest. "Well, I suppose that makes me special."

"There is no *suppose* about it. You are unlike anyone else I have ever known."

The admission seemed uncomfortable for him. Seemed torn from him.

"Then I suppose I will keep aiming for that as Queen."

"Do you have any special interests?"

"The care of single mothers," I said instantly. "Believe me when I tell you we face an inordinate amount of judgment while the men often responsible walk around without any."

"Perfect," he said.

"Perfect?" I repeated.

"Not perfect that they face judgment. But perfect that

you have such a strong and clear interest. That will be your vocation, if you would like."

"I would," I said. "You know, I was so focused on taking care of Lily that I never truly thought about having work. Or…a calling, I suppose. I was given so much money by…well, your father…that I was able to buy a house, and we were able to live quite comfortably. When she was older, I would have had to find something to do, but that wasn't encouraged in my home either. Women working. Having aspirations. So I just didn't. But I like the idea of this."

"Being Queen can be a vocation. A calling. No one else has taken it that way for my country in the past, but you could be the first."

"I imagine I'd also be the first to marry the King after our child is born?"

"Likely. Unless, again, there has been some revision in the history books."

"Well, we can always assume there might be. I don't mind being the first. Just another way that we are an oddity. Just another way that we will help change the country. I mean, not to co-opt your revolution."

He laughed. "No, it's perfectly fine if you want to join the revolution with me. You're free to pick up a sword."

"I hadn't realized that swords would be part of the job description."

"I can get you one."

"I don't think that's necessary." Our eyes caught and held, and heat spiked between us.

What a strange and wonderful thing to have both, this ability to laugh with him and want him all at the same time.

"I have some things to see to," he said. "I will… I'll find you."

There was something deep in that. Enduring. A promise that echoed in my soul. At least, I chose to let it.

"Okay," I said.

I chose not to dwell on the end of our time here.

I had to start thinking of it as a beginning. No matter how difficult it was. When we returned to the palace, we settled into a pattern. But it was one I didn't expect. It was reminiscent of our first days on the island. Hercules avoided me. At least, that was what it felt like. Perhaps that wasn't what was happening.

He was wrapped up in affairs of state. I discovered quickly that life as royalty did not simply mean a life doing whatever you wanted.

Not that I didn't have a sense of that before—I had seen news stories about royals all my life, but it wasn't as if I had paid close attention to them, and I definitely hadn't considered it some kind of guide for my potential later life.

I had never imagined that I might become a queen.

But here I was.

I spent a few hours a day working on ideas for outreach to single mothers in the community. I looked at budgets and talked to palace officials about things like free day-care centers and maternity leave.

It was fulfilling work. And when I wasn't doing that, I was taking care of Lily. Lily made me happy too, as she always had.

It was nice, also, spending time with my mother. We had years spent apart, and we hadn't talked like we did in the palace in… Ever.

But I was still lonely. I missed Hercules. I missed wasting hours talking to him about everything and nothing. I missed sleeping with him at night.

We kept separate bedrooms here.

I didn't like it.

"What's wrong?" my mother asked one day as we sat in the garden of the palace, where a massive play structure had been erected for Lily. She was running around, her dark hair flying behind her as she ran, her laughter filling the staid silence of the royal grounds.

I loved that.

Especially knowing what I did about Hercules's childhood.

"Nothing," I said.

"That's a lie," my mother said. "I know you well enough to know that, even if I haven't known you as well as I should have for the past few years."

"You couldn't help any of that. There's no point in regret."

"I don't say this because I am experiencing regret. At least, not so much. But I can tell that you're not happy. When you came back from your honeymoon you seemed...different."

"Well, it's nice to be on a private island without any responsibilities."

"And now you have responsibilities."

"Good ones," I said. "But it is a lot."

"I don't think hard work has ever scared you, Marissa. Somehow, I don't think that's what's bothering you."

"It's... Hercules has been very busy."

"I've never known as much about the two of you as I should. I was forbidden from speaking about you when your father was still alive. And we never got a chance to…"

"I fell in love with him," I said. "The first time I ever saw him. I was sixteen. He didn't touch me then," I said hurriedly. "But we got to know each other. Every summer. More and more. And I… I didn't have the willpower to resist him."

My mother looked thoughtful. I didn't know what to expect from her. If she would judge me for that weakness or not.

"I was envious of you in some ways," my mother said. "I was never carried away by passion of any kind. I married sensibly. I married a man that my parents approved of. There was no joy in our marriage. And we couldn't speak. I could never tell your father what I wanted from life. I let him send my daughter away because I didn't have the fortitude to stand on my own two feet and speak for myself. I let you be badly treated because I didn't stand up for you. And I have regretted it every day since."

"There is room for regret between us," I said. "Mom, I know how Dad was. I don't blame you."

"Perhaps you should. I look at the way you protect Lily, how you've given everything to her, and I should have done the same for you."

"You weren't able to. I know that. I understand it."

"I wish… I wish I would have had a different life. I wish I would have stood up and said what I wanted."

"Do you really think that he would have given it to you?"

"He might have given me a divorce, and in the end, perhaps that would have been better."

"Maybe," I said.

But I didn't really think so. I don't know what my mother would have done. I was glad that she was coming into her own strength now, but she couldn't regret who she had been all those years. She couldn't change it.

And I didn't want her to make herself sick over it.

"I guess my point in bringing any of this up is that if you want something different with Hercules, then you should speak up. Otherwise you end up with a lifetime of regret and sadness. You look back and you wonder how you spent so many great years just enduring. Brittle silence and the full absence of a loving touch. I don't know how or why I subjected myself to that. And maybe I couldn't have had a different marriage with your father, but perhaps I could have had a different life. Perhaps you could have had a different life. But you still can. Don't build castles made of regret, because they're what you'll live in in the future. Believe me."

"What if he doesn't want different?"

Because that was the thing that really scared me.

"Then you'll be angry. And hurt. But you won't have to wonder. You won't have to wonder if there was something you could have done but were too afraid. Your relationship with Hercules…it's for Lily too. If you need that, then remember that as well. But if you could do it just for yourself… Marissa, that would be a very brave thing to do." She sighed. "To do more than just endure is a brave thing." My mother's words stayed with me for the rest of the day.

I did know how to endure. I had gotten very good at it. I had accepted a life where I wouldn't have love.

Where I wouldn't have Hercules. In many ways, I had accepted my fate as a martyr to the cause of my daughter, and that was what had made it so easy to go back with Hercules and use Lily as the sole excuse.

But that hope…

That hope inside of me meant something.

It was for me. It was for him. For us and for our love. For what could be.

I had seen the possibility of all that five years ago, and I could still see it now. I wanted it. I craved it.

But I was denying myself because I had looked into my father's icy stare and been sent away before. Because my mother hadn't stood up and told me to stay. Or that she would go with me.

Because I had felt abandoned, by my parents, by Hercules.

It had been so much easier to let go, to accept the fact that I walked through life alone, except for Lily. That I lived for her, that I breathed for her.

And there was nothing wrong with that. I did. She was my daughter, and it was my great joy to sacrifice for her.

But there was more. I wanted more.

And wanting more for myself meant wanting more for Lily.

I wanted her to have a happy home. And no, it would never be conventional, because we lived in a castle. There would always be staff around; there would always be matters of state to see to. But we would never want for anything. There were incredibly wonderful, privileged things we could have as well, but why couldn't we have love on top of that?

The house that I had grown up in had been stale.

My mother had been right. It had been gray.

And I had gone to escape the gray down at the shores of the ocean, where I had found Hercules.

He had been my escape. He had been my salvation, not my ruin.

But only if I was willing to reach out a hand and ask.

Ask to be saved. For both of our sakes.

Because we could have one of two lives. The gray and the bleak, or we could have it all.

We could have paradise. A walk through the fog, or a life staring out at the bright, brilliant sea.

And I knew which one I felt we were meant to have. I knew what I wanted. But one of us was going to have to be brave enough to take it.

I knew all that Hercules had been through, and I could understand why the inside of him felt a little bit too broken for things like love.

But I also knew that he could make a decision to put it behind him.

I also knew that we could have more, that bravery might have a cost, and love might take work, but it was worth it in the end.

For what Hercules and I could have was a jewel beyond price, and I had to be willing to sell everything I owned to possess it. All of it.

I had to be willing to do more than exist in the possibility of a relationship and throw down a definitive gauntlet.

Do you always do as you're told?

He had asked me that once, so long ago. And that was when I had realized that I did, and that I didn't want to, not anymore.

It was the same now.

I didn't want to simply do as was expected. I didn't want to do as I was told.

I wanted to live bright and brilliant, with him, with our hearts twined around each other as I knew they could be.

Not two separate people living two separate lives in a massive palace, but two souls that had become one.

He might not believe in that, but I did.

And that meant that I had to be the one to fight for it.

He wanted reason, and I didn't have reason.

But I had love.

Hercules had told me once that he believed in the physical. Well, I would approach him that way. I would give him what he understood before I introduced what he felt he could not. And maybe then those two things would come together for him and create something new.

Something that was only ours.

Something that he could see and touch and feel.

I was afraid.

Like I had been afraid that first time we'd been together down on the beach.

But I was also determined. And I knew what I wanted. I knew who I was.

I could only hope that Hercules would come to understand the same way that I did.

Because if he did…

If he did, then he wouldn't want to accept less either.

But there was no way for me to know. So I had to step out in faith.

I had to be brave.

CHAPTER THIRTEEN

Hercules

I HAD DONE my very best to throw myself into the leadership of Pelion. It was difficult when I was obsessed with erotic thoughts about my wife. I knew that she was unhappy. The few times that I had seen her since we had returned from the island, she had been a bit sullen with me. At dinner she had been quiet, and the air had been filled by chatter coming from Lily, and I knew that I had been disengaged with that as well.

But I had to rule. I had to be King. There was no scope for me to be distracted by my family.

My family.

Marissa and Lily were my family.

Such a strange and foreign concept to me.

I couldn't remember having family dinners when I was growing up. No, I ate in the nursery; my mother was usually away. By the time my sister was born, I was nearly grown.

I didn't remember saying that we could have family dinners, but one evening Marissa, her mother and Lily showed up and sat at the table. The staff brought dinner to all of us, and so it had continued on every night since.

But even as we had those dinners, and Marissa would respond to the things I said with brightness, I could sense that beneath it she was unhappy.

I didn't like that, but I didn't know what else she wanted from me either.

I was the leader of a nation. I had concerns I had to put above all else. Including the two of us.

From everything I'd been told by my staff, Marissa was adapting beautifully to her role as Queen. And yet...

She was different than she had been on our honeymoon.

But then, so was I. Of necessity. I had allowed myself to be distracted by her there. I had broken there. I had shown weakness, and that could not be allowed. If my father had died, and I had not had a soft spot to land in the form of Marissa's arms, how would it have gone?

Instead, I had splintered, and I had allowed my darkness to pour out, to spill onto my wife, and that was unacceptable.

I knew that.

And so, we would continue to be separate. We would continue to have separate rooms. Until such time as I felt that I had a grip on...everything. From the running of the palace to my emotions.

My emotions. The fact that I had them at all made me feel weak.

I despised it.

Even in the form of rage I was beginning to find them unwieldy.

I disliked it.

It made me wonder if I was closer to my father than I had ever anticipated.

I liked to pretend that I was something else. Something different entirely, but I wondered.

Was there any way to fully escape being like your maker when he had fashioned you in his image? It was not something I knew the answer to, and I feared that only time would tell.

But in the meantime, I would not affect Marissa and Lily.

It was the one good thing I knew I could do. Keep my distance.

I had been spending every night in my office, staying up as late as I possibly could to ensure that I fell into bed in exhaustion that would prevent me from going down the hall and taking Marissa again and again.

She was a temptation that I was finding difficult to resist, and that was yet more reason to resist her.

I couldn't allow her to have control over me.

I couldn't allow anyone or anything to have control over me. Not my base desires, not my lust and certainly not my wife.

Those things made for a weak king, and I refused to be weak. Had I not spent my childhood trying to demonstrate my strength? I would not falter now.

My father was wrong. You did not have to be a monster to rule. I would show that until my dying day.

But in order to do that, I had to make sure that I did not falter.

When work didn't help, I went to the gym. And I exhausted myself there. Tonight, thankfully, I was exhausted without punishing my body, and when the time was past midnight, I finally went to my quarters.

The palace was quiet, dark and empty, the obsidian halls glittering bleakly in the blackness.

It felt all too close to what was going on inside of me.

I pushed the door open to my chambers, and the lights were on.

The flood of brightness was a shock after walking down the long, dark hall.

But not as much of a shock as the sight that greeted me.

Marissa, lying on the bed, completely naked.

She did not look defeated now. She did not look shy or innocent. She was bold. There was nothing on her body, and she reclined across the pillows in a way that emphasized her curves. The glorious plumpness of her breasts, the indent of her waist, the round swell of her hips.

And those nipples… Dusky berry and tight, begging for my attention. That dark thatch of curls between her thighs that I wanted to bury my face in.

I had spent days resisting this very thing, and now I wasn't certain I had it in me to resist any longer.

"What are you doing here?"

She moved her hand, and the only thing that adorned her body—our ring—glimmered there.

"I missed you," she said softly.

They were not the words of the siren, and they were not the words that I had expected. They were emotional, spoken with a sweetness that truly stunned me.

"Did you?" I asked.

"Yes," she said softly.

"You could have simply told me over dinner."

"I don't want to talk," she said.

The words were a male fantasy, and not ones I could quite credit coming out of Marissa's mouth. Because if there was one thing we had always done, it was talk. Even when passion was hot between us, we always spoke.

"You don't want to talk?"

"No," she said, shaking her head, her glossy mane shimmering in the light. "I can talk to anyone. You're the only man that I can do this with. The only man I've ever been with at all. The only man I will ever be with."

Something twisted hard and low in my stomach. "The only man you've ever been with?"

"Did you imagine that I was entertaining lovers these last few years?"

"You would have been forgiven for doing so. You are human, after all. And humans have needs."

"But you ruined me for everyone else."

"You see," I said darkly, "you ruined me for everyone else as well, but that did not stop me from…" I began to remove my shirt, and I questioned my own resolve and strength the entire time. Still, it didn't prevent me from doing it. "That made it all the worse. It was hollow. The promise of a feast, but when I reached out to take it in hand, it just turned to ash. Bitterness in my mouth. It was never what I wanted. Because I had tasted…paradise. I tasted paradise on your skin, Marissa, and then it was gone. I knew what making love could be, and it was never that, not after you."

"Well, I was just smart enough to know that I didn't want to substitute."

I felt humbled by that. Because I hadn't been. I had been angry and filled with thwarted pride, and I had tried to erase her from my body, from my skin, in the beds of other women. I didn't like the way that made me feel. I didn't like the shame. Didn't like the heavy, hot emotion that stabbed me in the chest and seemed to twist my heart into strange and unnatural shapes.

She was twisting me into strange and unnatural shapes inside, and I didn't know what the hell I was supposed to do about it. I was supposed to be supreme and sovereign ruler, or something like that, and yet… And yet.

I shoved my trousers off, left them down on the ground, and the rest of my clothes along with them.

I was past the point of pretending that I was going to resist.

It was one thing to keep separate when she was across the palace, but it was quite another when she was naked and in my bed.

I had to ask myself who this man was that he couldn't control himself around a woman. Ever.

That she had been my downfall there on the island, and I had learned nothing in the time since.

But she said she didn't want to talk, and she said she only wanted me, and why couldn't I take her like I did any other woman? She was still paradise, still Marissa, and I should be able to have whatever sort of physical relationship with her that I desired. It would feel the same.

I'd had any number of emotionless sexual experiences, and there was no reason she couldn't be the same. She would have to be. If we were going to continue, if this were going to continue, then we would have to.

And I couldn't live with her, not in the same sphere and resist her. So we would have to.

She moved, getting up on her knees and sliding her hand slowly across my chest. She was angling to kiss my mouth and I grabbed her chin, stopping her. "No."

"Why not?"

"You said you didn't want to talk," I said. "So don't talk."

A fire lit behind her eyes, but she didn't speak.

I pinched her chin between my thumb and forefinger and guided her slowly downward. She knew what I wanted.

She parted her lips, the expression in her eyes bright. And then she dragged her tongue along the head of my arousal, and I let my head fall back, luxuriating in the soft, slick pleasure as she took me deep into her mouth, making low, satisfied sounds as she did.

We hadn't had the time to play at such things when we'd been younger, desperate to couple together out in the open, and with no time for extras in case we might get caught.

I had thought about this, though. With her. So many times that I'd lost count.

She had no experience, and I could see that, but what she didn't have in experience she made up for with her very clear desire for it. For me.

She wasn't timid; she wasn't uncertain. She took me in deep, wrapping her hand around the base of me and tasting me slowly and thoroughly.

It was heaven and hell, all contained in this woman. It always had been.

She lowered her head, her dark hair falling over her

face, and I tried to force myself to pretend that she was just one of the substitutes that I'd had in the years between our coming together again.

That she didn't matter.

That she was no one.

But I couldn't, and I didn't want to. Because the minute that I tried to imagine it was anyone other than Marissa, the spark was gone. She mattered.

I gritted my teeth. I arched my hips upward, and she accepted me, took me in deeper.

I was getting close to the edge, unable to hold myself back any longer, and I guided her away. She made a soft sound of protest, but I wouldn't hear of it.

"That isn't how this is going to end," I said. "On your knees."

She looked at me. "I already am."

"Turn around," I said, and she obeyed.

I looked at her, the long line of her elegant back, moving down to the full curves of her ass. Her glossy hair was draped over her shoulder, exposing all that skin. And she was exquisite. More than beautiful.

Desire coursed through me, hot and hard as I approached her. I put my hands on her shoulders, slid them down her back, around to grip her hips hard, watching as my fingers left impressions in her skin. Then I reached between her legs and stroked her until her wetness coated my fingers, until her desire was all over my skin. She whimpered, gasping as I pushed two fingers inside of her, rocking her hips back and begging.

I had control. She might have come in here to seduce me, might have come in here to prove some kind of point, but the point would be mine in the end.

I would have her, however I wanted, whenever I wanted, and she would allow it, because she was mine.

Maybe I couldn't pretend that she was someone else. Maybe I couldn't make it carry less weight, but I could stay in control of this.

I commanded; she obeyed.

That could work.

We could work.

Because God knew I couldn't stay away.

She made a little kittenish cry, arching back, the motion pushing my fingers deeper into her body, and my arousal pulsed with need. I pulled away from her, positioning myself at the entrance to her body, teasing her, sliding my length through her folds before moving back to her opening and pushing in just slightly, before repeating the motion again.

She was panting, near to crying, when I finally gave her what we both wanted.

I gripped her hips hard and pushed in, rough and deep.

But she didn't seem to mind.

No, if her cry of pleasure was any indicator, she was more than happy with my desperation.

And that meant that I would have hers.

Because this could not be a meeting of equals. I had to make sure that she was the one who was desperate. She was the one who was reduced. Because I could not afford to be.

I pumped into her, chasing my release, chasing our end. She whimpered, and I pressed my hand between her shoulder blades, pushing her chest down flat on the bed, keeping her hips raised up. Then I grabbed hold of her arms, wrapped my hand around her wrist and pinned it to her lower back, then the other. I held her tight as I thrust into her, over and over again, the angle letting me go deep, the way I had her pinned keeping her motionless.

"Please," she whimpered, "please."

But I refused to end it. I kept it going, torturing her, torturing myself, the bright, brilliant flashes of pleasure that consumed me a torment that I didn't want to end. I knew what she needed. I knew that she needed me to touch her between her legs so that she could come. Or that she needed to touch herself, but I had her captive.

She began to shake, she began to weep, and I moved harder inside of her, until we had slid up the mattress, until I had to brace myself on the headboard, so we didn't collide into it. I freed her hands when I did, and she used the opportunity to shift, wiggling and putting her hands between her legs as I continued to pump inside of her.

"Don't," I bit out. "Not until I say."

"I need to," she said.

"You are my wife," I said. "My Queen. Your body belongs to me."

She went still. "Yes," she whispered. "But your body belongs to me."

She reached between her legs, beneath us, and stroked me at the point where our bodies met, and I shuddered, cursing as she did so.

"Witch," I said, finally agreeing to give her what she wanted.

I put my hand where I knew she needed me, and I pinched her gently, before stroking her, keeping time with my thrusts.

And then there were no games, no more fights for

control, because there was only pleasure. Wrapping around us, binding us together.

And when we both found our release, it was together, the violence of it shaking us, shaking the bed, shaking the very stone the palace was made of.

Shaking what I was made of.

And when it had ended, she curled up against my chest, and I couldn't play games any longer.

I hadn't won anything. I hadn't distanced myself.

When her fingers traced delicate shapes over my chest, I couldn't pretend she wasn't Marissa, couldn't pretend that it would ever be anything but heavy.

"Hercules," she whispered, "I love you."

Marissa

And that was when the walls fell down around us. My heart was still beating hard from my release. But more than that. From the admission that had just fallen from my lips. I wasn't afraid, though. There was no place for fear here. Inside my body. How could I fear when I was in his arms?

Hercules was my husband, the father of my daughter. He was the man that I loved. And with him I had always felt an absence of fear. With him I had always felt strong and solid in who I was. And what I knew from talking to my mother was this: what you allow will continue.

And I could allow for us to continue on in unspoken words. I could allow for us to stay in a world where I let safety mean more than truth.

But I didn't want that. And I didn't have to allow it.

"I love you," I repeated, again.

He shifted. "No," he said, simply, definitively.

"Hercules, I don't know who you think you're speaking to, but I am neither your daughter nor one of your subjects. I am your wife. And you don't get to tell me *no* as a response to *I love you*."

"I… No. I cannot accept."

"It wasn't a gift. It was a statement of fact."

On some level, I wasn't surprised at his denial. On some level, this didn't shock or wound me. Because how could it? This was who he was. A man made of rock, and for some reason he seemed to need to cling to the facade.

I knew that I would have to break the walls down. I knew that I couldn't simply walk up to the door and ask for entry. No. I had asked for entry, and now I would have to be willing to do battle.

"You don't understand. There is no room in my life for these kinds of emotions."

"Why not? What about Lily?"

"This has nothing to do with Lily."

"Do you love her?"

"But that is a foolish question. I have known her for a matter of weeks."

"She's your daughter. That's… That's not how that works. I've loved Lily from the moment she first came into the world, and I can tell you I didn't know her then. With children, it's not a matter of knowing them, is it? It's a matter of knowing that their lives are in your hands. That you must protect them, that you must care for them. That without you they won't know anything of the world. You're meant to be her conscience, her guidance. Her place of protection. And that… Let me tell you, Hercules, that produces feelings of love faster than knowing someone ever could. So do you intend to never love your daughter? Because you will be the only father that she ever has."

"I didn't need love. I didn't need love—it was weak, and it did nothing."

"Your father didn't love you. At least, not in the way that a normal person should. He didn't demonstrate love."

And then Hercules exploded. "Not my father. My mother. My father never said that he loved me. My father never lowered himself to tell such a lie. He never would. It was her. *I love you.* She would whisper that. Over my bruised body, but she would never do anything to stop it."

"Hercules…"

"She couldn't, and I understand that, but what did her love get for me? It meant nothing. She would go off, because she claimed she couldn't stand to see the way that he treated me, but she left me here with him. She had another child for the sole purpose of having one that she could…that she could love in the way that she wanted. Because she had to surrender me to him. So, you tell me what love ever did for me. You tell me how love makes a family. Because it never did in mine."

"Hercules," I said softly. "Your mother was wrong. Your father was wrong."

"That's a lot of people who were supposed to love me being wrong, Marissa. At a certain point a man must acknowledge that the problem might be with him."

"I love you. You think I would allow you to be submitted to torture? Do you think I wouldn't die for you?"

"No," he said, the admission ferocious. "Never offer such a thing to me. I don't deserve it. I am not worth that. Don't you ever say something like that to me again."

"Why must you reject it so?"

"Because I am last—do you understand me? That is how I must see myself. My father saw himself as first. Above all else, above anything, sovereign to the entire world. And look at the things he did. To me. To my mother."

"Hercules, your parents were broken. Undeniably. I am sorry if your mother had a difficult time of it, but that doesn't give her an excuse to allow her child to be abused. She had money. She could've fled with you. The UN would have taken care of you, something. There must have been a way that you could have escaped."

"It would have created a national incident. And I was not worth that. The chaos would've thrown the country into..."

"No. It would have healed your country years earlier. Your mother could have exposed him for the madman that he was, and what purpose did it serve for her to protect him? All it did was protect her position as Queen. That's what it did. Your parents loved themselves more than they loved you, and on that score you're correct. But love isn't what created the brokenness in that scenario. It was the lack of it. Surely you must see that."

"In any case," he said, "I don't know how to love."

"That isn't true. You do know how to love... You do..."

"No. I am not the right man for that. I'm a broken vessel, and if you pour into me, it's all going to leak out, and I won't hold a drop of it in the end. I'm not worth it, Marissa."

"You're worth everything."

"No. No."

And then he stood and walked away from me, walked naked out of the bedroom, as if he weren't a king and we weren't in a palace full of other people. I knew the hallways would be empty, but still.

I ran out into the hall, without bothering with clothes myself, but I didn't see which way he'd gone.

Then I returned to the bed and sank to it in misery.

He didn't love me. He didn't want to love me.

And I had the feeling that something permanent had happened just now. That he had closed the door on something with a finality that would break us both.

I had given up on Hercules once, and I had cast him as the villain before. But I could see him now. See him for what he was. The wounded boy who was afraid.

Because his mother had offered him love but not protection.

Because she had given him words and not actions.

It scared me. Because my mother had been faithful to my father, she had demonstrated love every day, and she had given him as he asked, and he had taken advantage of it, and nothing had changed.

But I would have to trust that Hercules was a different manner of man, and that our love was different. That it could be bigger, that it could be better.

And that I could change him.

I knew that it was ludicrous. I knew that there were multiple self-help books on the topic.

But if he didn't want me, I was better off leaving. Demanding everything or taking nothing.

I would have to have faith. Faith in that first moment we had ever met.

In that certainty I had felt then.

I had lost that faith over the years, but when the truth had come out, it had become clear that Hercules hadn't been the villain.

And I had to trust it would bear out again.

But, oh, that trust would take a leap. The bravery to remain open when all I wanted to do was close in on myself…

I got beneath the covers, not caring that I was in his room. And I curled into a ball and dissolved.

Because in the morning I would have to emerge whole. I would have to do it for Lily, for Pelion and for the future of my marriage—such as it was.

But for the first time in my memory, the hope wasn't there. That little bubble had burst, abandoning me when I needed it most.

I had an answer to the question of what remained when you were plunged into darkness, what remained when the last vestige of hope was extinguished inside you.

It was love.

When everything else failed, love remained.

And that was simply where I would have to place my trust.

Because love never failed.

It was a truth that I believed, and it was one that I would hold to. I had no other choice.

CHAPTER FOURTEEN

Hercules

I HAD NOT spoken to Marissa in days. And I told myself that it was for the best. I told myself that I was doing the right thing.

Love.

She loved me. What did love mean?

Do people abandon you often?

The words that she had spoken to me stuck now, stung. I couldn't get them out of my head. They were like a barb in my heart.

I love you. My mother had said that, every time she had left the palace. Every time she had left me there.

But she had never taken me with her.

She loved me, but I was the heir.

She loved me, but I was Xerxes's son, not really hers.

I had been her obligation to the Crown, and I had given her freedom with my very existence.

That was why she loved me.

But she loved her freedom more, and she had gone her own way, flitting about the world as I was tortured.

Going about her life as I was broken and reshaped into a weapon for the throne of Pelion.

For my father's own satisfaction.

What good were words of love if there was nothing behind them?

What was wrong with a child that his mother could speak those words so carelessly and then leave him to be devoured by the wolves?

I didn't know.

I didn't understand.

All I knew was that those words felt like they had fractured something between us. Because they reminded me of the ache that I had felt in my soul when she had spoken them.

No.

I would not allow emotion, words, to create that kind of pain inside of me.

What could I reason? What could I see and touch? Certainly never my mother's love.

Those words were useless.

And yet I craved them.

For Marissa.

And I thought of Lily...

Lily, my own daughter, who I was avoiding like a true coward, because...

What if I gave her the words and failed miserably in the execution of them?

I didn't even know what love was supposed to look like.

The bloodline of my family was poison. And that was all it was. A bloodline, and not a family.

It was all I knew. All I understood.

I had taken to prowling the halls at night, because I couldn't sleep. My need for Marissa was like a sickness, and I didn't trust that I wouldn't go to her in a moment of weakness. This was what she had reduced me to. A man who did not trust himself. A man who wandered the halls of his own palace, questioning his sanity and trying to breathe around fractured pieces in his heart.

It was then I heard a sound. A whimpering sound, and I stopped for a moment, trying to figure out the source of it. It was the sound of a child, and for a moment that struck me as strange. Because for a moment, I could only think of myself.

I had whimpered like that in this palace, reduced to such a thing at the hands of my father. I couldn't move. Not then.

But I was jarred back to the present, and I knew it could not be me, for I was standing on my feet, and I was a man, not a child. And I was not helpless, which meant I had to move toward the sound, whatever it was.

I stopped at the door, and her name slammed into my mind.

Lily. Of course it was Lily.

I had been pushing her away in my mind, pushing Marissa away, and there she was, crying out.

And I could not turn away from her. That much I knew.

I pushed the door open slowly and saw her lying there in the bed, turning over and over fitfully, wrapping herself up in the blankets.

Her dark hair covered her eyes, and she looked distressed.

I crossed the room, feeling like anything but a king,

feeling like the lowest of men. Because I didn't know what to do, and none of my power, none of my money and none of my status would give me insight into what the best course of action should be.

But I couldn't abandon her.

"Lily," I whispered.

I went to the bed and sat on the edge, pressing my hand against her forehead. "Lily," I repeated.

"Daddy!" She sat upright and nearly crawled up my body, wrapping her arms around my neck. "Daddy. I dreamed that we were taken away from you. From here."

I was stunned into silence by that. That Lily's worst nightmare would be to be taken from here.

"I don't want to not know you," she said. "I remember when I didn't know you. It wasn't as good."

She clung to me with trust, this child, with helplessness and sadness, and I felt undone. Because who was I to deserve this?

She was so vulnerable...so helpless...

She felt her life was better for having me in it.

She didn't know. She didn't know who I was, how broken I was inside.

And she didn't care.

She loved me with an openness that had nothing to do with knowing me and everything to do with what I represented, and I kept thinking of what Marissa had said to me.

This was the love of a child.

A love so freely given, a love that didn't even have to be earned.

No, a love like this had to be stripped away.

And my parents had done that to me.

To me, when I had been like Lily.

When I would have happily crawled into either of their laps and offered them all my small heart.

Because that was what children did, and it was how they were made.

They came into the world with innocence, and it was taken.

"I can't sleep," she said.

"You haven't tried," I said.

"I know I can't. Will you sing me a song?"

"A song?" My heart thundered in my temples. "I don't sing."

"Everyone sings," she said matter-of-factly, and I didn't know how to argue with that.

I tried to think if I knew any songs that were suitable for children. The only thing that came to mind was something my nanny used to sing to me when I was a child. Back when I'd had a nanny…when there had been one soft person in my world.

The words were in Greek, so I clumsily tried to translate them along with the tune.

"Dear child, dear child, you've no need to cry.

Dear child, dear child, count the stars in the sky.

Dear child, dear child, rest your sleepy head.

Dear child, my child, rest in my heart.

For it is I who will love you even in your dreams."

"Promise?" she asked, her voice small and tired.

"I promise," I said.

And I meant it.

I would love her. I would protect her. I would fight armies for her.

And that no one had done it for me…

It was their failure, not mine.

To see myself through the eyes of a parent was… stunning.

My father had taken me when I was as young as Lily and put his hands on me to hurt me.

I touched Lily's cheek. I could not imagine harming her, let alone ordering that others harm her.

I would kill first. Anyone who dared harm a hair on her head.

My eyes felt dry.

Marissa had looked at me with trust and love once. And it was only there as I sat on the bed holding our daughter that I realized it.

The first time she saw me. A full acceptance of what was happening between us, even though it made no sense. Just implicit love. Implicit trust.

And I had thrown it back at her. She had been alone and pregnant, thrown out on her own. She had been wounded in my absence, and what had I done when I'd found her again? I had condemned her the same way so many others had.

And then…she had married me. She hadn't punished me by withholding Lily. She had given me my daughter, given me what I needed to run my country.

And then she had given me her body.

Given me her love.

I was suddenly overwhelmed by all this love that I knew for a fact I would never be able to earn.

This love that I wasn't being asked to earn.

Love.

I had been so convinced that it wasn't real, because I couldn't reason it out.

But that, I suddenly realized, was the beauty of love.

You might not be able to reason it out, but you could see it. You could touch it. You could feel it. And anything you couldn't see, touch and feel wasn't love. It was just words.

Hollow words that lacked any action.

And I was shamed, because I had not seen what was right before me. The gift that had been Marissa for the last five years.

When I was certain Lily was asleep, I dropped a kiss on her head, and I went down the hall.

I knew it was midnight. I knew that Marissa was probably sleeping, but this couldn't wait. It couldn't.

What good was being a king if you couldn't wake people up in the middle of the night when you were having an important revelation?

I didn't knock; I opened the door to her bedroom, and I realized that it couldn't be her bedroom anymore.

We needed a bedroom, together.

Because we were one, after all.

She and I had spoken of souls, and I had rejected the notion of them, but I knew now that they were real. And mine was tied with hers. The match, the mate. All manner of mystical things that I hadn't believed in before.

But didn't they come back to faith?

I had never believed I was a man of faith, but Marissa had shown me different.

"What are you doing here?" She was not asleep; she was perched on the edge of the bed in a white nightgown, looking confused. Though I imagined she had not been looking confused before I came into the room.

"We need to talk."

"It's after midnight."

"I know, but you are not sleeping."

"No. I haven't been. Not since…"

"I know," I said, moving to where she sat on the edge of the bed. Then I dropped to my knees, debasing myself for a second time in such a short period. But it would always be for them. For Marissa and Lily, and it would never be anything less than they deserved. For they were my life, my heart, my mission. And everything good that I did in the kingdom of Pelion would be an extension of that.

Of the love that existed between us.

"Lily had a nightmare," I said.

"Oh no. Is she okay?"

"She's fine. She's… She's beautiful. She's perfect. Marissa," I said, her name broken. "Marissa, I… I didn't realize. I didn't realize how love worked. I didn't realize how a child could love a parent, because I'd forgotten. I'd forgotten what it was like. They stole it from me. They tore it away from me, stripped it right out of my body. They hurt me. Abused me, abandoned me. And I thought something had to be broken in me, but when I looked down at Lily, so vulnerable and small and crying like that… The unspeakable wickedness of someone who could harm a child, who could tell them they love them and then leave them. It was not me. And you and Lily… You showed me what love really is. You are unwavering, Marissa. You gave me more than I've ever deserved. I sure as hell didn't earn it.

"All this grace that you bestowed upon me. This unmerited, unearned, unasked-for favor… It is like salvation, and I was too afraid to admit that I needed it. But I was in the darkness without you."

"Hercules… I… I have loved you, from the moment we met, but I'm sure that you loved me since then as well. I know you have."

"I have," I said, my voice rough. "I have loved you. It took hold of me that first day, and I didn't recognize it, because I didn't know a connection with women that was about something other than lust. What we had grew into lust, after we had a friendship, and I'd never experienced anything like that. Someone who loved me after they knew me. Someone I wanted to speak to and sleep with in equal measure."

"You feel like your mother abandoned you," she said softly. "That's why it hurt you so much when you thought I'd left."

"I thought you cared about me. And I never put the two things together, because I did not think about my mother and her own fault in what had happened to me, because I could not bear to hate them both… But… Yes. That is why. Because I finally thought that someone cared for me again and then… And then that."

"I would never have left you," she said. "Believe that. And I won't now. No matter what. What we have is real. And it's worth fighting for. It's worth clinging to. Even if neither of us are perfect. Especially if neither of us are perfect. Because this was never about *perfect*. I grew up thinking that I had to be perfect. That I had to try to live up to this impossible thing. But my father left out grace. He left out joy. He left out love. And we'll fill our lives with that, surround ourselves with it."

"I never knew what it was, not really," I said, my voice rough. "But I would very much like to have a lifetime of discovering it with you."

"So would I," she said. "I knew that I found something special the first day I met you. And it scared me. Because I also knew that it would change everything. That you could ruin all of me. But I needed to be ruined. That old me, she needed to be ruined, so that I could be made whole."

"We will be whole together," I said. "I know that I told you I didn't believe in souls. That I didn't believe in things I could not see. But I see you. I see you, Marissa. And I feel that you love me. And I feel... I love you too. I have, from the beginning. I just didn't know what it was. I didn't know what to call it. I didn't know what to do with it."

"Neither did I," she said. "And I could never have known that we would end here. What a road that we walked. Separate for a while, but I'm ready to be together."

"And you know... With my father dead, we don't have to stay married. I have the throne. I have made Lily legitimate."

"You're not suggesting that we...get divorced."

"Never," I said. "But what I do want you to understand is that I'm not staying married to you for the bloodline. I'm not bound by anything. My country is not in peril. You are free to go, and I'm free to ask you to leave. But I won't ask that. I hope that you'll stay."

"You know I will," she said, scooting closer to me and grabbing hold of my face. "You know I will forever."

"I love you," I said.

And it was the first time I could ever remember saying those words to another person. "I love you," I said again. "And I love Lily." Suddenly, desperation filled my chest. "I need to go tell her."

She laughed. "No, you don't. It can wait until morning."

"It doesn't feel like it can. Everything feels desperate. So… I've never felt like this before. I love you. I love you so much."

"If it feels desperate, then perhaps we should explore that. Together."

And this time when she took me into her arms, and took me into her bed, it was not merely as lustful young people on a beach, not merely as husband and wife, but as a man and woman who were desperately in love.

And I knew that we would be that forever.

"I pledge myself to you," I said. "And I pledge to love you above all else."

"But you must love the country," she said.

"Everything good that I am comes from my love for you. My love for Lily stems from that, and what you taught me. My desire to be a good king in a richer, deeper sense than what my father was comes from loving you. I will love you above all others, above all else, for as long as I shall live."

"And I shall do the same."

EPILOGUE

Marissa

IT WAS A wonderful blessing, watching Hercules gaze at our son in the private nursing wing the day I gave birth. Lily was thrilled to have a little brother, and her excitement was difficult to contain. My mother had finally taken her home a few hours ago, exhausted. And that left Hercules and myself.

"I'm very glad that you got to see this. That you were part of it this time."

"So am I," he said, his voice rough as he gazed down at Leonidas.

Such a big name for such a tiny creature.

"You have a son."

"And a daughter," he said. "And I will protect both of them with every breath left in me. They will never question my love for them."

"No," I agreed, "they won't."

Our lives had been filled with love that no one on earth could ever question these past months. Hercules was the best King, the best husband, the best father. I was blissfully happy in a way I hadn't known it was possible to be. And it all seemed to just keep expanding.

That was the beautiful thing we were both discovering about love. It had no limits.

I looked at him, and I was cast back.

I'll never forget the first time I saw Prince Hercules, standing there on a beach.

Hercules, who was now King. Who bore a name fit for a god but who, blessedly for me, was a man. A man I loved.

And I never could have guessed that it would lead here, to a maternity ward in a hospital halfway across the world, to me being a queen, us being married, us being so blissfully in love neither of us could see straight.

I had been so certain he was my downfall. But in the end, I hadn't fallen. I had grown wings strong enough to fly. And now we flew together, my King and I.

It would be easy to call it fate, and perhaps whatever had brought us together was fate. But what kept us together was love. A love more powerful than all the pain the world had given to us.

And it was love that would sustain us.

Always.

* * * * *

JOIN US ON SOCIAL MEDIA!

Stay up to date with our latest releases, author news and gossip, special offers and discounts, and all the behind-the-scenes action from Mills & Boon...

 @millsandboon

 @millsandboonuk

 facebook.com/millsandboon

 @millsandboonuk

It might just be true love...

MILLS & BOON
MODERN
Power and Passion

Prepare to be swept off your feet by sophisticated, sexy and seductive heroes, in some of the world's most glamourous and romantic locations, where power and passion collide.

Julia James
Heiress's
PREGNANCY SCANDAL

Jennie Lucas
Chosen as the
SHEIKH'S ROYAL BRIDE

Kim Lawrence
A WEDDING *at the* **ITALIAN'S DEMAND**

Sharon Kendrick
The
SHEIKH'S SECRET BABY